Ellen Datlow has been fiction editor of OMNI since 1981. She has developed a reputation for encouraging and developing writers such as William Gibson, Pat Cadigan, Tom Maddox, Dan Simmons and K W Jeter and for publishing Clive Barker, Stephen King, William Burroughs, Ursula K Le Guin, Jonathan Carroll, Joyce Carol Oates and Jack Cady in OMNI. She has edited *Blood is Not Enough*, *A Whisper of Blood*, *Alien Sex*, *Snow White, Blood Red* and *Black Thorn, White Rose* with Terri Windling, and the World Fantasy Award winning series *The Year's Best Fantasy and Horror*, also with Terri Windling. She has also edited *Omni Science Fiction One* to *Three*.

Ellen Datlow has taught at Clarion West and the Brockport Writer's Forum and given seminars on magazine publishing, science fiction and horror.

LITTLE DEATHS

24 Tales of
Horror and Sex

Edited by Ellen Datlow

MILLENNIUM

Dedicated to Deborah Beale
who came up with the idea in the first place

I would like to thank the following people for helping in various ways to make this anthology possible: Merrilee Heifetz, Liza Landsman, Deborah Beale, Charon Wood, Keith Ferrell, Rob Killheffer, Jeanne Cavelos, Lucius Shepard, and Pat Cadigan. And of course, all the contributors.

CONTENTS

INTRODUCTION

The title, *Little Deaths*, comes from the French term 'la petite mort' a euphemism for 'orgasm' in popular use around the 17th century. Both William Shakespeare and John Donne regularly used a derivative of the expression, 'to die' as an orgasmic metaphor in their works. It was thought by many that for every climax attained, some of the male life-force was drained and therefore brought one that much closer to death. This idea can be traced to several sources including Aristotle, who believed that semen was drops of the brain and that the more a man ejaculated the smaller his brain became; Galen, the Greek physician and writer working in Rome, who thought that if Olympic athletes could be castrated in such a way that their reserves of heat would not be disrupted by the operation, they would be stronger; and Soranus of Ephesus, another Roman Greek who believed that men who remained chaste were stronger and healthier than those who did not. This idea is still popular in modern times as athletes often prefer to conserve their sexual energy before an important game or race.

But how did the connection between sex and death develop? According to Lawrence Osborne, author of *The Poisoned Embrace: A Brief History of Sexual Pessimism*, the linkage of sex and death so prevalent in Western civilization may have developed from some of the more extreme pre-Christian religious sects. Many Gnostic sects believed that everything material – that is *of* the world – distracted mankind from the spiritual, and that the human body epitomized the negative because its obvious physical needs (nourishment and sleep) defied this quest for spirituality. A few of the more extreme of these sects went even further, calling for self-castration. In 2nd century A.D., in a tract attributed to Hermes Trismegistus, the invention of sex was judged a cosmic disaster, which further stated, 'He who has loved the body, which comes from the deceit of love, remains wandering in the darkness, suffering in his senses the things of death . . .'

But it wasn't until Paul, the true founder of orthodox Christianity, copied and misinterpreted the more ascetic Gnostic sects of his time that one finds an actual gulf between male and female. Up to that time men and women could share ecclesiastic duties equally, and women had as much potential as men for spiritual enlightenment. St Paul's fear of sex and antipathy toward women and sexuality unfortunately permeated mainstream Christianity.

But historically there have been reasons other than theological extremism to explain the association of sex with death. Sex has always been a high risk activity. Before efficient birth control and modern medicine, sex could kill women – many died in childbirth or from botched abortions. Syphilis was mutilating and incurable until the discovery of penicillin. And now sex can literally kill, with 'AIDS, the pairing of love and death that has transformed our world . . . and which will continue to do so within the next century even if a cure were to be found tomorrow.' (From the Introduction to *Lovedeath* by Dan Simmons).

Originally, *Little Deaths* was meant to be an anthology of *erotic* horror, but to my surprise and disappointment, very few stories submitted were actually erotic. I received stories with a sex scene obviously thrown in in order to sell me the story and I received stories with violent sex acts that, while integral to the plot, could in no way be considered erotic. And I began to see the same disturbing pattern I'd discerned in far too many anthologies of 'erotic horror' – superficial vignettes featuring gross physical violence, more often than not, committed against women. I *did* receive some excellent horror stories in which sex was an important factor. This encouraged me to think about expanding the boundaries of the original theme. I suppose such a development shouldn't really have surprised me. Each anthology I edit transmutes during the process of reading and choosing stories, becoming something at least slightly different from the original idea. Although I may jot down ideas as I read for the book, not until the anthology is almost finished does the real focus actually become clear.

Horror fiction generally deals with man's confrontation with his own mortality and/or loss of control or loss of self. Interestingly, this characteristic dovetails nicely with Albertus Magnus's observation that experiencing intense pleasure the human heart contracts in exactly the same way as it does in a state of fear. In both sex and at death, the body loses control, so it's only natural that the two be inextricably linked in our minds.

Sex can sometimes be seen as transforming via increased awareness and self-knowledge. Yet such transformation exacts a price, and that price can be psychological and/or physical pain. The prudish protagonist of Lucy Taylor's 'Hungry Skin' gropes toward an understanding of herself and of her relationship with an absent father, but the cost is nothing she could have anticipated. The titular character of M. John Harrison's 'Isobel Avens Returns to Stepney in the Spring' seeks to make metaphor literal, with terrible consequences.

Ironically, the story that comes closest to the original theme for *Little Deaths* was the first story I bought, 'The Lady of Situations,' by Stephen Dedman. It is erotic and deeply disturbing yet has no onstage violence. This is not to say there is no physical or emotional violence in *Little Deaths*.

The stories herein range in tone from the deadpan iciness of Jack Womack's urban tale to the hot sensuousness of Nicola Griffith's tropical novella. I hope, in reading these stories you will find your own fears and desires aroused.

I'd like to thank the following for their input, suggestions, referrals, and research for this introduction:

Caroline Fireside, Terry Bisson, Justine Larbalestier, Lawrence Schimel, V. K. McCarty, the Rev Dr E. Barrett, Suzy Baker, Michael Kandel, Jennifer Ford. And special thanks to Anne Bobby, Beth Fleisher, Gregory Frost and Robert K. J. Killheffer. I'd also like to acknowledge Pat Califia's nonfictional postscript to her collection of erotic stories, *Melting Pot* (Alyson Publications) and Lawrence Osborne's *The Poisoned Embrace: A Brief History of Sexual Pessimism* (Pantheon).

THE LADY OF SITUATIONS

by

Stephen Dedman

Stephen Dedman lives in Western Australia and has worked as a video librarian, game designer, actor, experimental subject and manager of a science fiction bookshop. His short fiction has appeared in *The Magazine of Fantasy and Science Fiction* and *Pulphouse*. He has finished one novel and is working on two others.

'The Lady of Situations' was an unsolicited manuscript at *Omni*. My then assistant, Rob Killheffer, showed it to me as something more appropriate for the sexual horror anthology I was working on than for *Omni* Magazine. I agreed. It was the first story I bought for *Little Deaths*.

The lead story of an anthology can be the most important story in the book (if one assumes stories are read in order) because it gives the reader an idea of what the anthology is about – not just thematically but intent. All the stories in this book deal with relationships. 'The Lady of Situations' deals with several different ones – past and ongoing. I think the central one's horrific nature is both subtle and surprising.

THE LADY OF SITUATIONS

It was raining outside, and the hostel very sensibly lacked a television; the dishes done, we all retired to the common room. Gwen has always loved meeting new people and, travelling as we were, we met new people every night and left them behind us each day: the sort of strangers with whom you might share sex, but never your toothbrush (okay, so I'm a cynic). Tonight, there were the inevitable pair of Germans; a New Zealander, furry and clumsy as a koala bear and about as ineffectual; an amiable Australian giant named Danny; Elliot, a mathematician from Cambridge (at last, someone I *knew*, thank God) . . . and Jacqueline.

Jacqueline was the most exquisite creation I can remember seeing outside an art gallery, as fine as cut crystal, and with a voice to match – clear, hard, and without any colour that it hadn't stolen. You could not *not* watch her, and watching her, you could not help but imagine the body inside those carefully-worn sloppy clothes and the lily-gilding make-up, could not help but follow the lines and curves that converged between her thighs, could not help but be drawn deeper and deeper inside her . . . but never beyond the skin. Any deeper than that, and you would encounter the soul of a ninja. Rather than look at Gwen and risk comparing her to Jacqueline, I tried to distract myself by watching the chess game. Elliot had brought a set, of course – not his replica Lewis Chessmen, which I had murderously coveted since our first meeting, but a small board with a built-in computer. We watched him demolish the New Zealander in six moves, as though taking an hors d'oeuvre . . . well, most of us watched. Danny was lost somewhere between the headphones of his Walkman, and Jacqueline was ostentatiously reading, a paperback cover down across her thighs. Elliot accepted a challenge from Gwen; she opened with the Queen's gambit and survived for seventeen moves.

I wondered who Jacqueline was pretending to ignore, who it was she was really interested in, and decided that it had to be Elliot. He was, after all, the best-looking man in the room: slightly taller than I am, but barely half my weight, long legs and minimal hips, wavy blond hair, labyrinthine green eyes, a small mouth with generous lips, pianist's fingers . . . remember Dennis Christopher in 'Breaking Away'? Best-looking, hell; he was beautiful. I tried to remember what I knew about him. An excellent student, of course, who *should* have been a fellow Oxonian; brilliant, but also extremely serious. Single, and had been so for as long as I'd known him. Unusually for a mathematician, he had no interest in music whatsoever. He had been beating me consistently at chess, go, and (to my vast irritation) ancient and medieval wargames, every holiday for three years, and for all I knew, I might have been the best friend he had. It took me three guesses to remember his Christian name: Charles. Hell, I know more than that about Myrddin or Pelagius.

Gwen smiled, thanked Elliot for the game, and backed away from the board. Elliot glanced at the German couple, who shook their heads simultaneously. There was no way to back out gracefully, so I dropped my seventeen stone (metricize me and I will break your heathen skull) on to the chair opposite him, and tried the Danish gambit.

Elliot's king wasn't where I expected it to be: damn. Jacqueline stretched, advertising a body so perfect, I'd be scared even to dream of it, and stifled a yawn. The New Zealander, as smitten with her as I was trying not to be, hastened into the kitchen to make her a cup of coffee which I knew she wouldn't drink: he'd made the mistake, at dinner, of calling her 'Jacky' (I never did learn *his* name, but perhaps he didn't need one). She took the mug from him without thanks, or even a smile, sipped to make sure he'd remembered how she liked it (she was used to getting *exactly* what she wanted), and then put the cup on the floor.

Within a few minutes the game was all over, and I was left staring glumly at the board. Elliot switched the computer on: no one else in the room was likely to challenge him. He was doing a better job of ignoring Jacqueline than I was; perhaps he wasn't trying as hard. 'What are you playing?' I asked.

'Modern Beroni,' he replied. 'Fischer vs. Spassky, third match game.'

'How many games does it know?'

'A hundred, plus variations.'

'Wow,' murmured Gwen. 'You know, that's what I've always

wanted.'

'A chess computer?' I asked.

'No; an eidetic memory.'

'No, you haven't,' said Elliot, without looking up from the board. 'I knew a girl with an eidetic memory, once. Better than eidetic, even: a perfect memory.'

Jacqueline closed her book. 'No one has a perfect memory,' she drawled.

'She did,' replied Elliot.

'How do you know?'

'I knew her very well.'

'*How* well?'

'She was the first girl I ever fell in love with,' he said. Jacqueline looked as though she was about to comment, but didn't. Gwen glanced at me, and I shrugged; it wasn't a story I'd heard before. 'I was nineteen,' Elliot continued, leaning back in the chair and *still* not looking at Jacqueline, 'and I had a pretty good memory myself: it came in useful. I was notorious, then, for keeping a harem; I could remember all of the names and most of the faces . . . only the bodies ever became numbers. I'm not proud of it, now . . . but looking back, I don't remember that I ever lied to anyone, or broke any promises . . . but I digress.

'It started with a game of chess, a tournament, at Trinity. I was defending my title as the King of Kings. I'd only made Rook in the Intercollegiates, the year before; the defending champion of Cambridge had come second for three years running, and was stuck with the title of Queen. I believe he now works for MI5.' Gwen and I laughed; the others only looked puzzled.

'There were four males for every female in the university, back then, and any alien being taking the chess club as a representative of humanity would derive some very strange theories about our reproductive processes. Of course, he would also drastically over-estimate average human intelligence . . .' He coughed slightly. 'It was rather startling to discover a girl sitting opposite me who I didn't recognize. I thought I'd gone through them all.

'She was pretty, though not quite beautiful, but her eyes . . . Eyes don't usually show very much, whatever the poets may say,' and he stared across the room, straight into Jacqueline's; she held his gaze for a bad five seconds, then looked away. 'No,' he said, softly. 'Not quite beautiful. They were dark – not the darkest I've ever seen, but they should have been. They were like . . .' He blinked, and then brightened. 'Do you know how a pearl is created? Something sharp inside the shell hurts the oyster, and it coats it in a smooth, glossy material to hide the edges? And it grows a new layer every year . . . From the outside, it seems perfect; smooth, beautiful . . . And so were her eyes – when her guard was up. When it dropped, you saw a cross-section of the pearl; all the layers, all the years, and everything that had hurt her in the beginning.'

He smiled slightly, or as near as I'd ever seen. 'Actually, it was several minutes before I noticed her eyes, and days before I saw them that open; she didn't trust easily, and I can't blame her. The first thing I noticed was her voice; she was born in Colorado and raised in Boston, and spoke perfect English – better than mine, anyway – with an accent that was . . . unique, for all I know. Later, when I heard her speak, other languages – she knew a dozen or more – the accent disappeared; by that time, I'd become quite fond of it.'

He paused. 'After the voice, of course, I noticed the sort of things I routinely noticed in those days. She was tall, about five ten, and thin, very thin. Lovely legs – hidden by jeans and the table, alas – but no figure; a fashion model, early-adolescent sort of body. Beautiful hands; you watch the hands, and I was almost staring at hers. Her hair was as short as mine, and dark. Her face . . .' His hands came up, gently sculpting curves in the air as though he were praying – I found myself thinking of the Dürer print – and then fell back to the chessboard. He picked up the white queen, almost caressing it. 'No. I don't have the words, or a photograph, and you don't have the mathematics. Never mind. She was pretty, and female, and she could play chess. The perfect woman; what more could I ask for?' He paused again, then said, wryly, 'I *could've* asked her not to beat me.

'I didn't make any mistakes, I could swear to that . . . I didn't really mind that she'd won,' he sounded convincing, if not convinced, 'but she did it so *quickly*! She watched my moves, but she barely glanced at her own pieces. Her game was defensive, but *she* was all attack.'

He glanced at Jacqueline, impassively, then stared into the fire. 'Did she win?' asked the New Zealander. 'The tournament, I mean?'

Elliot shook his head. 'No. Bradley beat her – you remember Bradley, Geoff? He beat you, too, the next year.'

I winced. 'The maniac with the ponytail? Glasses like crystal balls?'

'Yeah, that was him. I went to console the girl, and ended up inviting her out to dinner, and she ended up accepting. She was in Cambridge alone, on holiday from the Sorbonne. She'd won a scholarship, studying French Lit — '

'Did she have a *name*?' asked Jacqueline, in her bitten-glass voice.

'Penelope,' Elliot replied, 'but she hated it. Call her Penny, and the room temperature would drop fifty degrees. I called her Sweetheart.' He smiled, or maybe it was a grimace. 'It was a trick I learnt from my sister: she was a teacher, and she had a lousy memory for names. If you can't remember someone's name, call them something flattering; it beats "Hey, you!". I'd let it become a habit.

'Dinner was okay, then we went to my room for another game of chess. She won again, then beat me at speed chess in less than seven minutes. I didn't think she was into wargames, or sex, so we played a friendly game of backgammon. That was the only win I had all night; I walked her home, and nothing but a kiss for my efforts – I *hate* walking – and a quick, superficial kiss at that. I remember thinking that she must have been the oldest virgin I'd ever met.

'I love a challenge; it was about the only type of love in my repertoire, then. I invited her out again, two nights later, and this time we talked; I mean, *really* talked. It took me nearly an hour to guess what she was trying to say; it was after midnight when she said it. Her father had been . . .' he stopped, and stared back into the fire. Then he shrugged. 'She wouldn't say it either. I guess seven years of abuse does that to you. The hell with that; call a rape a rape. He'd been raping her since she was nine. She was sixteen before she realized that other fathers didn't do that.'

Gwen gasped, very softly. Everyone else was silent, even Jacqueline. 'She told her mother,' Elliot continued, 'and her mother refused to believe her, so she applied for a scholarship that would get her the hell out of Boston . . . and here she was. One tough lady.' He shook his head, looking less like a Michelangelo, more like an Edvard Munch. 'Me? I was always ready to help myself to a damsel in distress; one of the best nights I ever had was with a girl whose parents had just broken up. Not that night. I held on to Penelope until she cried herself to sleep, put her to bed and tried to work. No good; everything kept turning back in on itself . . .' He turned to me. 'Maybe this would sound better if we put it to music. What's the saddest song you know?'

I took out my flute – I'm not the only Welshman in the world who can't sing, but I'm the only one *I* know who admits it – and played my own variation on Albinoni's Adagio. Jacqueline put her book down, next to her cold cup of coffee. Elliot took the mental equivalent of a deep breath and continued.

'She woke early, and I made breakfast – I'm quite good at it – and she left without saying anything but "Thank you".

'I gave her a few hours to sleep, and phoned her; she wasn't in. I tried again, a few minutes later; no reply. Eventually, I rushed out, grabbing a book without even looking at it, and ran over there, and sat on her doorstep, trying to read, until she came home. She arrived at ten; she could at *least* have had the grace to look surprised, but no . . .' He stared into the fire. 'No . . .

'She invited me in, shaking her head. The place was small, untidy; the only evidence that she was even passing through was a set of half-open suitcases and a travelling chess set. "What *am* I going to do with you?" she asked. I didn't even dare offer a suggestion. "I suppose you're about to tell me you're in love with me, right?"

'"How did you know?" I never knew what she was thinking.

'"I've heard it before – as I'm sure you have." I nodded. "Okay. Anything else you want to say?"

'"I *could* tell you that I've never said it before."

'She looked at me, and obviously believed me – and why the hell not? "Anything else?"

'"You're the first girl who's ever trusted me with . . . I don't know. Your secrets. Your soul, maybe."

'"My soul?" I thought, for a moment, that she was about to laugh hysterically. "Souls, now. I'll bet that a week ago, you didn't believe in love *or* souls."'

Elliot shrugged. '"I don't want to hurt you," I said.

'"I've been hurt by an expert," she replied – flatly, no hint of a boast, or of self-pity. "Do you know the worst of it? I can't forget any of it." She turned and stared at me as though I were a new species of cobra. "I'm serious. Read me a paragraph of that."

'I started, remembered that I still had a book in my hand, and read her the Crab's speech from "Crab Canon". She quoted it back to me, word-perfect. I applauded her; she only shrugged. "Party game. What would you like next? Blindfold chess? No . . ." Her voice was cold. "No, I know what you'd like next."

'"Only if . . ."

'"Only if I want it too, right?" She looked away from me and down into her lap. "Right. And I've heard that you're an expert lover – quite apart from being a Greek god."'

I saw Jacqueline's eyes widen, black pits within the jade. Elliot seemed to be blushing; maybe it was just the firelight. '"Have you ever had a virgin?" she asked.

'"One."

'"Did she enjoy it?"

'"Eventually. At least, she said she did."

'"I'm not exactly a virgin," she replied, "but I've never . . .

voluntarily . . .' The room was so quiet, it was murderous. Finally, she stood and said, "Not tonight. Go home; I'll call you." '

Elliot's voice had faded, nearly to the point of inaudibility; when I stopped playing, all I could hear was the wind under the door and a nightingale which might have been miles away. 'She rang at three thirty that morning. "Do you think you can make me happy?" she asked. I was too tired to try to lie. "Eventually," I said. "If you let me."

'I suspect she smiled. "Then you'd better come over here and get started."

' "Now?" She hung up.'

Gwen shivered, and I realized that no one had moved in nearly half an hour. I glanced at the dying fire, but Elliot shook his head, and I resumed playing. 'The rest of this story is five days long.' He closed his eyes. 'I had, in my nineteen years, tried almost everything possible between a man and a woman – between a man and *two* women, for that matter. Except for deliberately hurting each other, of course – oh, sure, sometimes we left teethmarks. And scratches.' Jacqueline quickly hid her nails, even though Elliot was facing away from her.

'Anyone insist on details? We kept the lights on – she said she wanted to see everything, remember everything – and started conventionally enough, exploring each other first with eyes, then with hands and mouths, always kissing, licking *something*, and . . . I'd expected to have to teach her, maybe play her the way you're playing that flute, but no, we played each other . . . more like a game of chess.

'Naked, she was almost beautiful, at least with her eyes closed, without her armour . . . She was wonderfully greedy for new experiences, new sensations; we tried more than a dozen positions, with whoever was least tired at the time going on top . . . We had anal sex twice, because she wanted to be *sure* she didn't like it . . . Spanish – tit-fucking, if you prefer – we couldn't manage, she wasn't built for it, but what the hell, this is a love story, not an engineering problem. She loved having her nipples sucked; apparently, no one had ever done that for her before . . .' I was glad it was becoming dark; even Danny and Jacqueline were starting to colour. 'We scarcely left the bed; even when we did, we didn't let go of each other. It once took me an hour to get to the kitchen.

'By the fifth day, I could barely feel anything below my eyebrows. We once fell asleep during foreplay, or afterplay, or whatever it was by this time. We tried playing chess, but we kept losing the pieces, so

Penelope suggested blindfold chess: she kept winning, but I was glad of the chance to shut my eyes.'

'And when you opened them, she was gone,' concluded Danny. Elliot shook his head, wearily.

'No, no . . . this was *her* room, remember? We just lay there, sometimes fantasizing aloud, playing word games, memory games . . . and in the morning, she threw me out. I was too tired to argue. When I rang her, the next day, she didn't answer; I didn't have the strength to sit on her doorstep again, and it was two days before it occurred to me that she might be gone.

'But that's not the end of the story.

'I told my tutors that I was going overseas, threatening to suffer a nervous breakdown if thwarted.' He grimaced. 'Suffer, hell: I probably would've enjoyed it.'

'Was she there?' the New Zealander asked.

'Yeah, in a grotty little closet in Saint-Germain-des-Prés. It only took me two days to find her. This time she *was* surprised to see me, but she wasn't pleased. "I suppose you'd better come in."

' "Thank you."

'She smiled at that, and shook her head. "No," she said. "No." And she started unbuttoning her blouse. "I thought you understood," she said. "How much do you know about the brain? Oh, of course, you know computers – but computers are stupid, aren't they? How do they compensate?"

' "They're fast."

' "And?"

' "They never forget."

' "Precisely. And neither do I.' She glanced at me, shook her head. "Maybe I've never learnt how. You don't have an appendectomy scar – or any scars. Ever break a bone?"

' "Yes – my left leg, when I was fifteen. Skiing."

' "Do you remember the pain?" She unzipped her jeans, dropped them. "I don't mean the accident, or the hospital; the pain. The feeling."

'I stared at the small scar just above her panties. "No".

' "No." She looked down at her abdomen, then unfastened her bra. "Luckily, I've never had a broken leg, but I can remember *that* – if I think about it. Physical pain isn't too bad; you have to concentrate, sort of. You don't wake up every morning seeing the *doctor* hovering above you."

' "Your father . . ."

' "Yeah." She grimaced. "My fucking father. No, he didn't

cause . . . this. I can remember being born, I can remember not being able to read . . . Maybe I'm some sort of mutant. It doesn't seem to have any survival value . . . Or maybe I'm wrong, maybe it *was* my father. Maybe some things, traumas, *can* take away the defence mechanisms, the ability to forget . . . shock, stress, fear, pain, hatred . . . bring back all your memories. Maybe love, too, but I wouldn't really know.' She stepped out of her panties, and lay down on the bed. "You'd better sit down." She stretched her arms out, cruciform. "Look; no hands." And she closed her eyes.'

Elliot's voice was as dry as Egyptian dust; suddenly, he stood, stalked into the kitchen. We sat there in suspense until he returned with a glass of water. 'And I sat there and watched her, damn me to hell. She didn't so much as touch herself, but I watched her fingers trace along where my spine would have been; I watched them leave deep scratches in my back; I watched her nipples swell and harden, first the left, then the right . . . watched her lubricate and open, so wide open . . . watched her arch her back . . . watched . . . watched . . . For a long time, I wasn't even sure which was the real me; the one standing in the room, or the one who was with her, touching her, inside her . . . I heard someone screaming, screaming . . .

'She came six, seven times, and finally, she opened her eyes, black basketballs . . . no. Black holes. Everything fell in and nothing left, everything was trapped at the precise moment it reached her . . .

'And then she smiled. "See? You *did* make me happy; very happy . . . Happier, I think, than you can actually imagine . . . Be happy for me, if you can." She stood, a little unsteadily, and looked straight at me. "I need a shower. Please go."

'"I . . ."

'"I know," she said, softly. "I love you, too – that *is* what you were going to say? – and I will always love you, just as much as I do now . . . but I don't need you any more, and I don't want to hurt you. If I want to see you again, all I have to do is close my eyes."'

Elliot was silent. It was at least a minute – it felt like an hour – before Danny asked, '*Did* you ever see her again?'

'No.'

The German girl might have been crying: it was dark, and I can't be sure. Then Jacqueline stood. 'At least she's never forgotten you,' she said, and went to bed; her tone made it clear that she hadn't understood. The Germans said their Guten Nachts and followed, then Danny . . . The New Zealander seemed to be on the verge of saying something, but no words came; eventually, he too drifted off towards the dorms. Gwen, sitting near me, reached out for my hand and squeezed it, but I shook my head and she disappeared. Good night ladies, good night sweet ladies, good night, good night. Elliot stared into the fire, watching it die.

'Charles?'

'Yes?' He looked up. 'Yes, it *was* a true story . . . except that her name wasn't Penelope.'

'It seemed a little too appropriate.'

'Then I'd best not tell you her *real* name. I knew a Penelope, once,' he added. 'First girl I slept with, in fact. We were faithful to each other for ten whole days.'

'Are you okay?'

'Okay?' He shrugged, then with a 'May I?' gesture, took my flute and played the Adagio – a little slowly, but otherwise perfect. 'I'm getting better,' he said.

HUNGRY SKIN

by

Lucy Taylor

———⟡———

A former resident of Florida, Lucy Taylor currently lives in Boulder, Colorado with her five cats. Her horror fiction has appeared in the anthologies *Women of Darkness, Guignoir, Hotter Blood, Hot Blood 4, Northern Frights* and *Splatterpunks 2* and in magazines such as *Pulphouse, Bizarre Bazaar,* and *Bizarre Sex and Other Crimes of Passion*. Her stories are collected in: *Unnatural Acts, Close to the Bone,* and *Unnatural Acts and Other Stories*, recently published by Masquerade Press.

In the last few years Lucy Taylor has achieved recognition as an exceptional writer of erotic horror. She demonstrates this talent in 'Hungry Skin', a story about a young woman who discovers her true nature while exploring the house bequeathed to her by her late, absentee father.

HUNGRY SKIN

'That's pornographic,' Mica said, when she first saw the statue in the downstairs hall.

'No more so than the rest of your father's work,' said Pearlstein, the trust lawyer from Templeton and McVey.

'You've been in the house before?'

'Only to draw up your father's will,' said Pearlstein, as though attempting to justify something unsavory. 'He refused to come to my office. Before he died, he was increasingly reclusive.'

Mica shuddered, envisioning her father's last days, his body host to the cancer that was eating him out of flesh and bone, alone in the sprawling, turn-of-the-century house on the outskirts of Orange, Virginia. Cattle country, home to rough-hewn farmers and small town shopkeeps, people whose idea of art was probably a black velvet Elvis or Keane urchins above a motel bed.

A life scandalized by debaucheries, real or invented, then capped by suicide. It was too much, almost an unseemly excess of melodrama.

When she first learned that he'd shot himself, Mica had been filled with regrets that she had not made more effort to get to know her father, had never even bothered to see exhibits of his work. She'd always thought there would be time. She hadn't known about the cancer until after he was dead.

'Are you all right, Ms Sjostrom? Do you want to sit down?'

Mica shook her head. 'I'm fine, Mr Pearlstein. But I'd like to be alone.'

'I thought you wanted me to walk you through the house?'

She had indeed, but that was before Mica realized how lurid was her father's work. Not for a minute did she want to view more such graphic sculptures in the company of this unctuous lawyer whose voice oozed innuendo, whose eyes relished her breasts with too obvious a gusto.

'Thank you for meeting me here, Mr Pearlstein,' she said, dismissing him.

With Pearlstein sulkily departed, she walked around the statue which occupied the centre of the foyer. An orgy, that was what it was, with an indeterminate number of human forms carnally embracing. Human, but just barely. The bodies were too smooth, too bonelessly supple, creatures soft and bendable as plants, twisted into contortions that made the positions of the Kama Sutra look like adolescent gropings.

Mica read the bronze tag at the statue's base – 'The Family Reuniting.'

She had to laugh. It was that or cry. For the first time in a long time, Mica laughed.

Mica had met her father, the famous Swedish sculptor Erasmus Sjostrom, twice in her life. The first encounter was purely chance, at the intermission of a performance of the *Nutcracker* when Mica was twelve. Mica's mother introduced her to the striking, dark-haired man with the stunning Chinese woman on his arm, then insisted that they leave. 'I hate the way he looks at you,' she hissed, pushing Mica ahead of her into a cab.

The second time, eleven years later, was an encounter of Mica's own arrangement, a stiff and awkward luncheon that ended in disaster.

Now, six years later, Mica found herself wishing that either she or her father had risked a further meeting.

She comforted herself with the thought that evidently she had meant something to Erasmus. He'd left her the huge house at Meadow Farm, including much of his work from the past decade. In addition, there was a letter, which Pearlstein had handed to her at the reading of the will. Mica told herself it would be more fitting to read it when she arrived at her father's estate, but in reality she was almost afraid to open it at all.

Despite his three marriages and uncountable affairs, Mica was Erasmus Sjostrom's only offspring. His vasectomy had been performed, in fact, soon after her conception. It was one of the reasons Mica's mother had granted the divorce – that and what she described as 'bedroom antics that became goatish, brutal, and perverse as soon as we were married.' So appalled had Mica's mother been when her husband's true character revealed itself that she had felt any contact between Mica and her father would put her daughter at grave risk.

As to why, she had not elaborated.

Mica had been afraid to ask.

But rumours, of course, circulated and inevitably found her ears. After college, teaching English in Madrid for a foreign language school, Mica encountered a Spanish duke who claimed to have known her father (the Biblical meaning of the word purred out like a befouled caress), and then there was the suit filed soon after by the mother of the thirteen-year-old girl who claimed that Sjostrom had . . . but Mica believed the child and her mother were conspiring.

Mica was sure her father's reputation for priapism was merely the kind of tabloid sewage that accompanied celebrity. She could not imagine anyone needing or desiring sex to extremes that, to her, seemed quite unnatural and indecent.

For in truth, Mica was as arid of sensuality as her famous sire had been profligate. A petite, skittish woman, she had her father's dark and sultry looks, but little in the way of charm. Her lovely features often tensed into a countenance of jittery unease, her most characteristic expression being the wary, hyper-attentiveness of one who, as a child, has been told too often and too dourly to be careful.

Abstract concepts more than objects of the senses gave her pleasure. Words and language, their structure and sound, the solidness and predictability of grammar held their own mysterious allure, the sweet trill of a Spanish 'r', the deft cadence of a finely wrought line of iambic pentameter.

Yet here she was, owner of an art collection depicting every type of fleshly pleasure and perversion, the value of which guaranteed that she need never work again.

Mica could no more imagine a life of leisure than one of unbridled concupiscence. How would she fill her days? With whom would she talk, if not to her colleagues at the foreign language institute?

As it was, she'd been hard-pressed to arrange time off from the Coral Gables Language School where she now worked (an extension of the one in Madrid, catering primarily to well-heeled South Americans with more money than time to invest in learning English). She planned to stay at Meadow Farm only long enough to inventory the sculptures on the premises and make arrangements for the bulk of them to be auctioned off at Sotheby's.

As seemed appropriate for one who barely knew the former owner, Mica chose to sleep in one of the guest rooms. There were two sculptures here – on the dresser, a pair of male hands, onyx and ivory, clasped in a veiny, knuckled grip of anguish or desire, and, by the wall, a pair of lovers on a pedestal embracing in androgynous delight. And throughout the house, other works: a woman flagellating a lover with her long hair, a young girl copulating with a goat, a Medusa's head with dreadlocks made of phalluses.

Mica couldn't help but wonder how her life might have been changed if the creator of this art had been a part of it.

'I understand why you left Mother. But why did you leave me?'

She had sat stiffly in the tall, deeply upholstered chair of the Squires' Club at the Hotel Jefferson in Richmond. It was one of the last bastions of flourishing sexism that still existed in the late '80s. As her father's guest, Mica had been allowed into the visitors' dining room, the only area of the private club where women, like exotic but potentially dangerous animals, were allowed to be displayed by their male handlers.

'Your mother wasn't inclined to give me visiting rights.'

'What about *your* rights? You could have taken her to court. You could have fought for custody. You didn't even try.'

'You're right. I let you down. I just couldn't imagine myself as a good father. I wanted to love you, but I didn't know how.'

The black waiter had brought their cocktails − white wine for Erasmus, a martini for Mica. Her first. She was trying to appear sophisticated in this stuffy place with her legendary father.

But oh, it was so difficult, because the little girl inside Mica knew only that she had been abandoned, wanted only to cry and beat her fists upon the linen tablecloth and puke up gin and bitterness on the Oriental carpet.

'I'm sorry. That answer isn't good enough.' She'd been amazed at her outspokenness with this stranger. but the fact that his eyes, his mouth were hers made it easier. How often had she spoken to the mirror, evaluating her looks, her job, her personality, and said, 'I'm sorry, but that isn't good enough.'

Her father's hands rested on the table, large and pale as the folded wings of some enormous moth. They were clenching and unclenching, straining at each other, like two lovers clasped in violent embrace.

She had sipped her martini, let its delicious fire sear her inhibitions until her self-control hung by threads.

'Do you know what it was like growing up alone with Mother? Because I looked so much like you, she hated me. She virtually imprisoned me in the house. "Mica, Mica, come out and play," the kids used to call from the front yard, and Mother'd go out on the porch and run them off. "Mica doesn't play," she told them. "Mica studies." You were a coward to leave me with that woman. You could have fought for me, but you didn't have the guts.'

'I won't be spoken to like this,' her father said. He got up and bolted from the table. She thought he'd gone to the men's room. It was some time before she realized he'd left the Club, after signing for the bill on his way out. She was yet again abandoned.

Tonight, six years later, Mica sat on the floor of the living room, drinking a Diet Coke in deference to her ulcer, as she opened the letter from her father and began to read:

'You were a beautiful baby who grew up to be a beautiful woman. But even had you been quite plain, still I wouldn't have felt safe being your father. Touching you, perhaps combing out your hair, giving you a bath – the mere thought of such things filled me with dread.

'People are not culpable for feelings, Mica, only for acting on them. I never trusted myself not to act.

'You say it was painful growing up with your mother. But how much do you know of my childhood? My own father was an alcoholic who died when I was eight. Soon after, my mother began what I suppose a romance novelist might call a descent into madness, but what, in her case, was more a solidifying into stone. She seldom spoke or answered if I spoke to her, or acknowledged my presence in any way. Yet she continued to prepare meals, to do the housework, to keep up appearances.

'For one period of over a year, she never spoke to me. I was a child ghost, haunting her life, and she tried to exorcize me in every way she could.

'Except at night. At night, she would come to my bed, silent and furtive as a ghost herself, and lie with me. She'd spoon herself around my back and nestle her face against my neck. I can still remember the feathery wisps of her hair, her dry, cool lips, her soft hands cupping and massaging me in ways that I both longed for and loathed.

'I tried to comfort her, begged her to talk to me. As I got older, sometimes I yelled at her. I even struck her once, seeking some response. I got none. She was a wraith mother, haunting my bed, my dreams, invisible in daylight.

'Occasionally, in a pique, I'd lock her out of my room and find her sleeping on the floor the next morning, curled up against the door. My heart would break – whether for her anguish or my own loneliness I never knew, and I would let her in.

'Later, when I'd grown up and my mother was living in a rest home, she grew talkative and even prone to chatter, babbling on about my carefree childhood. I asked her why she had come to my bed for all those years. She said, "Your skin was hungry. I had to feed it."

'Of course, I realize it was my mother's skin which hungered, and yet, all those years of silence and invisibility, years when my only nurturing came from her indecent touches, has created in reality what at the time existed only in her own unstable mind.

'For my skin is hungry all the time. I sometimes think that hunger is what's killing me, the cancer being only the physical manifestation of insatiable need. In a life devoted to pleasures of the flesh, I am never touched.

'I feel ashamed for running away at our last meeting. You were right. I am a coward, and I regret now making no place for you in my life. I tried, though, in the only way I knew how. Your likeness, along with my own, is part of "The Family Reuniting". I regret I didn't have the courage to show it to you while I was still alive.'

Mica put the letter down and stared across the room into the foyer, where she could see enough of the statue there to make her want to look away.

Her own face somewhere in that abomination? Was she supposed to find this flattering? Could her father have possibly imagined she shared his obsession with these so-called 'pleasures' of the flesh?

For Mica could not imagine falling victim to the kind of thralldom of which her father wrote. Sex, for her, had always seemed a mechanical, rather unwholesome chore. As a teenager, her rare efforts at self-pleasuring had seemed distasteful, an embarrassing, unnecessary bother that, in adulthood, she was happy to forego. Her few lovers had touched neither heart nor flesh in any memorable way, and while she did not especially desire men, she could not conceive of making love with women. As for more than one partner at a time, think of the sweat, the grunting weight, the sheer effort and offensiveness!

Still, she spent some time that evening, without success, examining 'The Family' for a face that bore some likeness to her father's or her own.

The next day, Mica contacted a noted art dealer who'd attended her father's furneral. He promised to make arrangements for the larger pieces to be shipped to New York for auctioning. Then she set about inventorying the house, determining which of the sculptures she'd retain for investment purposes.

With every trip upstairs or down, Mica had to pass 'The Family'. Since the sculpture occupied the centre of the foyer, it could be viewed from any direction, each time offering a slightly different perspective. Mica still could not find a recognizable face, although she paused frequently to look. The bearded man embracing the old woman, were his features those of Mica's father? The woman whose face was turned away, did she bear Mica's likeness?

It was maddening not to know, and more maddening to care.

The bodies almost did not look human. More like sleek reptiles or sheened amphibians, still moist from the sea, their mouths round and slack, remora-like as they fastened onto flesh, their hands like pale, tentacled fish.

From any one viewpoint, it was impossible to determine what act each figure was engaged in and with whom.

At the front door, for example, she could see a man with sunken, haunted eyes, collapsed atop the back of the woman (man?) beneath him, who in turn fellated the upright member of a reclining boy. From the dining room, she saw not the fellator, but a wiry husk of a woman whose breasts cascaded down to smother the upturned face of the partner underneath. From the living room the scene was worse – the man who feasted at a young boy's groin while behind him, a woman thrust her fist wrist-deep into his rectum. Upon his face was not so much arousal as bright, blinding need, the face of a new-born animal scrabbling for the teat, or the cavernous maw of a baby raptor.

Mica stared and shuddered and tore her gaze away, always vowing not to cast a glance at the sculpture when next she passed it. Always she failed – as much as she detested the images, she was determined to find her own likeness.

It took the start of her second week at Meadow Farm and a bottle of good Bordeaux (to hell with the ulcer, she'd drink milk tomorrow) to reveal a new possibility. She could look down upon the statue from the balcony of the third floor master bedroom.

Taking her glass of wine with her, Mica was surprised and irritated to find that, although she could see the heads and backs of several figures, a number of the faces were still concealed.

What Mica did see, however, and what at once seized her imagination, was more intriguing: space. From above, it was clear that, as tightly as the statues appeared to intertwine, in reality a large cavity remained at their centre, as though carved out by the sheer centrifugal force of carnal energy.

The more Mica stared down at it, the more fascinated she became. Had her father's skill failed him here? For surely the work required another body. An open mouth, a jutting phallus, a pair of parted labia – none of which were visible at eye level – all seemed to demand another set of orifices to maintain the erotic symmetry.

Mica sipped her wine, gazed down.

I wonder . . .

She leaned too far. Her own mild acrophobia caught up with her, undid her balance, and caused the balcony to tilt. Mica cried out and dug her fingers into the railing, pushing herself back. Her glass upended. Wine splattered upon the orgy. Splashed rounded buttocks and parted thighs, ran from upturned eyes like the blood Mica imagined spewing from her father's shattered head, while his mouth twisted with a cry somewhere between agony and orgasm.

Before retiring to bed, Mica inspected the sculpture once again. Between the knees of a kneeling woman and the backside of the man who thrust his haunch into her face, she found a narrow opening.

Experimentally, she ran a hand along one figure's rounded belly, let her other hand seize the knob of a knee. She could get her head and shoulders into the opening, thus discovering a heretofore unseen perspective of the work. A slight shift of her body, to avoid the elbows of an embracing pair, and she might be able to inch her way up penetrate the core of them. Trying to ease herself inside, she searched for her own face or her father's peeking out like some lurid blossom from between a pair of buttocks or squeezed lewdly between copulating loins.

When the phone rang, she shuddered as though spied upon and disengaged at once. Pearlstein, inviting her to dinner . . .

Mica remembered the lawyer's hands, tanned and manicured, their fashionable bronze doubtlessly purchased in a tanning parlour. She imagined his touch, the practiced skill with which he would exude warmth and self-confidence while leaving her depleted, chilled. He was in the middle of lauding some French restaurant in Alexandria when she pretended someone was at the door and ended the conversation.

That night, she dreamed of spider hordes that clicked and crabbed across the floor and swarmed inside her body. Spiders infesting her intestines, clinging to her heart, nesting by the hundreds in her womb. A thousand stings and deep, internal fire.

She thrashed awake to find her fingers thrusting deep inside herself, a ragged thumbnail scraping painfully at her swollen labia. She thought it was still night, the pain between her legs a dream, and was startled to see light outside and horrified to find, beneath her nails, dark gouts of blood where she had torn herself.

Light-headed, she got up, pulled down her nightgown, and went out into the hall. From where she stood, she could see 'The Family' in the entrance way below. Sunlight filtered in a bevelled window, dappled limbs and faces with shifting skeins of light. From this vantage point, she could see the opening among the figures.

She went downstairs, put water on for tea and almost started to dial Pearlstein. What harm, after all, could one dinner be? She knew she stayed too much alone, untouched and unencumbered, but empty all the same.

Then she thought of the spiders in her dream, how they had scuttled into her like avid, greedy hands, claws clicking on her bones like manicured nails. The thought of contact, even accidentally, with Pearlstein's flesh, with *any* flesh, made fruity-tasting acid sear her throat.

While waiting for the tea to steep, she wandered back into the foyer where 'The Family' piled and pretzeled. Today they looked to her like Dachau dead she'd once seen in a history book, the naked corpses stacked high and intertwining. No wonder the idea of her likeness in their ranks revolted her as much as it obsessed.

Yet why was she unable to find a face that resembled her own even remotely? She'd studied the sculpture from every angle and still had not discovered what she sought.

The answer could be one of only two possibilities, she decided. Either the faces belonged to figures only visible from within the statue itself, or her father had been lying.

She had to know.

Her nightgown, when she tried to slide inside the gap between the figures, bunched around her. Mica hesitated only briefly – who, after all, would see? – then stripped it off. Naked, she eased herself into the narrow space among the orgiasts. She slithered around a couple embracing on their knees and squirmed past a pregnant belly to encounter, level with her face, a prodigious penis. She touched it timidly, then ran her tongue across the marble shaft. What harm, she thought – no one would ever know.

To her left, there was room to wriggle sideways and penetrate more deeply, if she used the breast of the woman nearest her for leverage. The woman lapped at someone's rump. Mica was convinced she hadn't seen this figure; that, from outside the orgy, the face could not be viewed. She studied it in the sun that filtered down from the skylight, full lips and small, closed eyes, a body smooth and unformed, like an enormous foetus grown to adulthood in the womb, legs coiled beneath it in a boneless pile, albino serpents mating.

Mica levered herself onto the shelf formed by the torsos of a couple fused in soixante-neuf. She rested, put her arms out. Her right hand stroked a man's flat sternum, her left probed a gaping mouth.

How safe and cosseted she felt. Mica remembered having a playhouse in the attic as a child and how, as she grew bigger and the playhouse shrank, there came a greater sense of safety and surrender, more comforting than claustrophobic. Sometimes, too, she'd hidden there and dreamed about her rich and famous father who would come and take her away from her mother and her loneliness.

The phone.

Mica hesitated, then tried to ease her way back out. She was warm now and slightly sweaty. Her live flesh squeaked against the marble bodies.

She could not squirm free.

She relaxed, breathed deeply. Attempted it again.

Got one leg above the head of a woman kneeling, but still couldn't push herself to freedom. Her leg hurt from the unnatural position. A cramp spasmed through the arch of her foot.

The phone stopped ringing.

The bodies seemed so close now.

Mica tried to force her hips through the narrow opening. Stone gouged her ribs, her chest. She felt like something struggling to give birth, but all she managed to push out were her screams.

As night came on, she was convinced she felt them move. Oh, they were subtle, clever, they didn't let her catch them. But she could tell. That was how they'd trapped her in the first place, by closing ranks ever so slightly after she'd come in.

Oh, come and play, Mica, Mica. Come and play with us.

Only this time it was come inside and play and this time no one had stopped her from joining in the game.

Hours later, stiff and cold, she tried to shift her body to some new position. She could get her legs up on the shoulders of the foetus woman, but that position made her calves cramp unbearably, or she could sink down onto the phallus lolling at knee-level, crouch with it between her legs.

The relaxation of her weight impaled her. Mica felt the rending of membrane and tissue, an explosive blossoming of pain. The foetus woman's mouth screamed silently along with her as she doubled over, lips almost to her knees. A new face, raw with hunger, peered up at her, the mouth a starving gash, the hair and eyebrows erased by chemotherapy. In the marble visage, Mica saw the shame and sorrow and craven need. *I have my father's face*, she thought, and fainted.

With daylight, they dared not move. Mica tried again to struggle her way out. She wondered what bones she could break to make her body more compact, but had no idea how such a thing could be accomplished with her bare hands. She thought that surely, as starvation set in, her body would grow smaller, but the figures seemed to sense this, too, and embraced more tightly.

She screamed for help until her throat felt scoured with acid, then slept and dreamed of liquid kisses, rivers of saliva pouring from a lover's mouth, of food fed to her from parted lips, plucked moist from spread thighs, soft buttocks.

The phone rang again in the afternoon, but they wouldn't let her out to answer it. By this time, Mica didn't care.

With the second night, they copulated openly, took no care to fool her, but coiled their marble limbs around her, opening her up, exploring their soft new member, greedy to caress the face that had been missing from their centre. Desire flowered in Mica's emptiness, and longing overflowed her. No longer chilled, she opened herself to the throb and thrust of her family. Hands plucked and fondled, mouths devoured, but at the end, she knew it was her father's hands that drew her firmly into death, out of her hungry skin and – finally – into his.

BECKY LIVES

by

Harry Crews

Harry Crews lives in Florida and has written thirteen novels and four books of nonfiction including *The Hawk is Dying, Feast of Snakes, The Gypsy's Curse, Body, The Scar Lover, Blood and Grits,* and *A Childhood*. A reader called *Crews Classic*, which contains two novels and a book-length memoir in their entirety, plus a selection of essays, has recently been published by Poseidon Press. According to Crews he has finished the novel *Saippuakivikauppias*, which is a Finnish word meaning door-to-door soap salesman and is also the world's longest palindrome.

Crew's quirky characters range from boxers to body builders to snake handlers. 'Becky Lives' introduces two fascinating new ones in this dark and twisted tale of revenge.

BECKY LIVES

Jason Crowder walked out of 44 Wall Street, where he worked for Header, Header, and Header as a stock analyst, into the evening rush hour, and saw the girl diagonally across the street lounging against a lamp post lighting a cigarette. He had seen her there off and on for the last three weeks. She was wearing a very short black leather skirt and a ribbed pink tank top that elevated her breasts at an unnatural angle – at least the angle seemed unnatural to Jason – and she was very beautiful and appeared to be the age his daughter would have been if she had lived after being struck by a drunk driver at the age of eight, ten years ago.

Jason knew that he was going to speak to her from the first time he had seen her by the lamp post, but three weeks had passed and he had not. Today when he got out of bed he had resolved that he would approach her today or not at all. He watched now as a car pulled up to the corner where she stood. A window slid down and she leaned briefly into the car, her arms on the window for perhaps two minutes, before she stood up again and the car pulled away. Thank God she had not got in as he had seen her do on more than one occasion. Jason took it as a sign that this was the day to initiate his plan.

Not that he needed a sign, but he was superstitious and believed there was always a right time and a wrong time for everything.

And neither had he waited three weeks because he was bashful with women and felt a certain awkwardness in meeting them.

Quite the contrary. He was good with women, meeting them, talking with them and bedding them. In fact, he was excessively vain of his way with women and even more vain about his appearance. In his own mind the two – his prowess with women and the way he looked – were connected. He never passed a store window without examining himself; his carriage – chin tilted slightly upwards, his back plumbline straight – his lean, athletic body, his temples perfectly grey, which set off the smooth golden tan he kept year round by regular use of a tanning bed in his condo.

He always wore a pale pin-striped suit, white shirts, the Harvard Club tie and wing-tipped shoes. In his closet in his condo there were hanging fifteen sets of just such clothing – including the wing-tipped shoes, highly polished, each pair lined in a row under the suits. He liked to be neat and liked everything about him neat.

He had only to cross the street to meet the girl. He wished she were not chewing gum. That definitely was a bad sign. But God, she was beautiful and had not got in a car with somebody and driven away.

He knew perfectly well why it had taken him three weeks: his plan was imperfect. In spite of his best efforts, he could not bring his plan to perfect balance. And sloppiness offended his nature.

What he wanted to do was quite simple. He wanted to kill his ex-wife, had wanted to since they were divorced sixteen years ago. But of course they send people to jail, or – worse yet – execute them for that. And so he needed another plan, one that would cause him no pain and only minor inconvenience, but would destroy his ex-wife, if in no other way than emotionally. That was precisely why he was stopped now, by the lamp post looking into the gold-flecked eyes of a young girl he knew to be a whore.

The girl didn't say a word and while her expression was pleasant, the deeply layered make-up she was wearing might have been a mask.

Jason found himself suddenly nervous – something that *never* happened when he was approaching a woman – and he felt sure it was because this girl was a whore. His experience with whores was totally non-existent. He had never had to buy a woman's flesh and the mere thought of such a thing offended his sense of the natural order of things.

'Oh, young lady,' said Jason, 'I have something I want you to do for me.'

'I'm young, John, but no lady. And I just happen to be standing here waiting to do something for you.'

That she was beautiful and young and a whore all collaborated to throw Jason into a spasm of nervousness of which he would have thought himself incapable.

'Oh, no, no, no,' Jason said. 'You don't understand.'

'But I will if you'll tell me,' she said, her voice lilting and lovely, as though she had just stepped out of a finishing school. It was not what Jason had expected at all. He had assumed the voice would be gritty, street-smart and slangy and therefore cause him the most trouble.

'What?' said Jason. He had lost the subject of their conversation, if indeed there had been a subject. He had to settle down and get himself together if this was to be accomplished. It was, after all, a business deal. He understood business. Thinking of it as business would make it possible.

'I can understand anything if you'll tell me,' she said. She took a little silver gum wrapper out of her clutch purse, wrapped the gum from her mouth in it, and dropped it in the gutter. She did it all with a touch of class he would not have expected. The lashes over her gold-flecked eyes were very long and she seemed not to blink at all as she waited for him to speak, but he didn't know what to say.

'Look,' she said, smiling prettily, as though they were discussing the price of roses in a flower shop. 'You want French, Greek, a quickie – I've got a bottomless throat, if you've got a car parked nearby . . .'

He held up his palm quickly as though to ward her off. Oh, for God's sake, stop. Stop. Jesus Christ.

'I don't do dogs or any other animals. But most kinds of kinks are fine with me if the money's right.'

'I have money,' he said.

'That's good. That's very good.' She reached out and tested the quality of the fabric of his suit between her fingers. 'Nice,' she said. 'Not off the rack, either.'

'I don't buy my clothes off the rack. Haven't in years.'

'Good for you,' she said, 'but you didn't come over here to talk to me about clothes. We need to get on with this.'

Her voice had settled into no-nonsense negotiation. Jason's problem was that he did not know how to bring up what he wanted to negotiate.

She looked off down the street and then back at him. 'John, I'm missing tricks talking to you. Why don't you come back when you're ready to do business?'

'My name's not John, it's Jason Crowder.'

'That sounds like a real name. You new at this? Because I don't need your real name. John is fine. Anything real is bad for business. The less I know, the better.'

'It is my real name and you have to know it. I want you to be my daughter for a while.'

She laughed, a sweet, breathy little chuckle, and it reminded him, with something of a shock, that it sounded very much like the laugh of his child just before she was killed.

'That's cool,' she said. 'That's not even kink. You want a mother in on it? I mean, my *real* mother? She's a junkie, but she's still got a great body. Hooks over on the Deuce.' She lifted her wrist and looked at a Mickey Mouse watch. 'Unless she's turning somebody, I know right where to find her.'

'The Deuce?' he said.

She cut her eyes at him. 'You don't know the Deuce?'

'No.'

'You from the City?'

'For a long time now.'

'Jesus, what time zone you live in, man? The Deuce is 42nd Street.'

'Oh.'

'You want the both of us at once? She really is my mother. I wouldn't scam you on that.'

'You'll do nicely,' he said, 'just you.'

'You bet your balls I will. I'm young but I know what I'm doing.'

'But you mustn't talk that way.'

'You want refinement? A refined daughter? I can turn that too. I'm a sophomore at N.Y.U.'

'You're going to college and doing this too?'

She shrugged. 'It pays the bills.'

'This makes it perfect. At least you can speak the King's English . . .'

'Fuck the King's English. That's not what I do for a living. See this stretch limo headed our way? That's sure money. Good talking to you, John. Maybe another time.'

Jason took out a gold money clip and snapped off four one hundred dollar bills and put them in her palm.

'You think you could stay out of the limo and listen to me for a while longer?'

She folded the bills, put them in her clutch purse, hooked her arm through his and said: 'What limo?'

They turned and headed up the street.

'First,' he said, 'we have to shop a bit, buy you the right clothes.'

She smiled up at him and said, 'That's acceptable.'

'Then we'll go to Sardi's for an early dinner, talk a bit so you'll know what we're doing.'

With another fetching young girl smile that he relished because it reminded him so of his daughter, she said, 'I think I know what we're doing.'

'No, you don't,' he said. 'And you'll love Sardi's.'

'You're selling me short. I already know Sardi's. You couldn't believe the places I've been taken.'

'I'm sure I couldn't.' It amazed him to suddenly realize that this young girl already knew the City in a way that he – the senior stock analyst at the most prestigious brokerage house on Wall Street – would never know it.

They had not gone half a block when a silver stretch limo driven by a uniformed chauffeur pulled to a stop at the curb beside them. Jason did not know what to do. He wanted to somehow indicate that this one was already taken but he did not know how.

'This'll only take a minute,' she said, taking her hand away from Jason's arm. As she approached the heavily tinted back window, it rolled down. The man in the back seat leaned forward, giving Jason a dazzling smile full of inlaid tendrils of gold. He was very black and very handsome. Jason watched as the girl took the four one hundred dollar bills out of her clutch purse and put them into the palm of the hand that appeared briefly as the window slid silently down. The limo pulled rapidly away even as the window was going back up.

When the girl returned to Jason, he said: 'You just gave that goddam man my four hundred dollars.' Jason never cursed and his profanity shocked and revolted him.

'No, John,' she said pleasantly. 'I gave him *my* four hundred dollars.'

'All right, your four hundred dollars. But why?'

'You realize that's none of your business, John,' she said, 'but I'll tell you anyway. That was my pimp.'

'OK, it's none of my business. But what in the world does he do to earn four hundred dollars?'

She laughed quietly and in doing so managed to look extraordinarily happy. She squeezed his arm and said: 'You know, I may come to like you more than I should. You're such a baby, so naive. But never mind. I don't talk about my pimp. I don't like it much. And he doesn't like it at all. But I will tell you this to help you out with your education. A girl wouldn't last ten minutes on these streets without a pimp. Can you dig it, John?'

'I don't care – as you say – to dig it. But you've got to quit calling me John. Jason will do nicely. Or better yet, Daddy. I'll explain it to you later.'

'I don't need an explanation,' she said. 'What I need to know is how long you want me for and what you're paying.'

'I need you from now until midnight. And I'm paying what it costs.'

She stopped, her arm still hooked in his, bringing him up short. '*Midnight*. Jesus, Daddy, I don't think you know the kind of money you're talking about.'

'Give me a number.'

'A thousand dollars. And that doesn't involve the four bills you've already given me.'

'Good. There's a Chase Manhattan Bank at the other intersection. I'll pay you there, and then we really must begin shopping if we're to have dinner and get on with the job at hand.'

She squeezed herself into him more tightly and said: 'I like your style, Daddy. Sardi's I've been to, the Chase Manhattan, never. Get it in hundreds. Easier to carry.'

'If you would like hundreds, you shall have hundreds.'

'You ever thought of adopting, Daddy?' She was very nearly as tall as he and she leaned close to him to laugh the words in his ear. Her breath was sweet and slightly tinted with peppermint. And the inevitable thought occurred to him: I wonder what her cunt smells like.

At Sardi's there was a discreet hum of conversation layered over the occasional clink of silverware and the clatter of plates and saucers as busboys cleared the tables at which people had recently eaten. Jason and Dorothy, which he suspected was not her real name, sat at a table near the front of the room, a choice location. The maître d' had spoken to Jason by name when they entered, which had impressed Dorothy more than the expensive clothes he had bought for her.

They had just sat down when she said: 'Are you fucking famous or something?'

'I come here a good deal,' he said, glancing at a white gold Rolex he was wearing. 'From now until midnight, you will kindly not curse again unless I tell you to. And your name is Rebecca, but called Becky. Can you do that?'

'Bet on it,' she said, 'that's a lock.'

'And no slang. Standard English, please.'

'Standard English it is,' she said.

'Will you share a bottle of champagne with me?'

'I'd really prefer a large orange juice.'

'But of course,' he said. 'And may I say you look ravishing.'

'I ought to for what you paid for these clothes, Daddy, you really are too generous.'

'Only with those I love. And I love very nearly nobody.' He lifted his champagne glass to her. 'But I love you, Becky.'

'I just hope I get my other clothes back. That leather skirt makes me lucky.'

Jason had sent her things, including underwear and shoes with spiked heels, by messenger to the doorman, told him what was coming and to hold them until midnight when he would pick them up.

'Your clothes are safe,' he said.

She was wearing a dress made of thin white silk, pleated at the shoulders and arms, as well as below the belt line to where it fell to mid-calf. Her shoes were white flats made of the finest leather and imported from France. Her legs were covered with white stockings with a pattern of exceedingly pale roses. Her white beret sat on hair that had been cut and styled by a hairdresser whose expertise was so great that he was universally known among his wealthy clients as Mr Magic. She had turned heads at every table when they made their entrance.

Becky sighed and picked at her baked flounder.

'All dressed up and nowhere to go,' she said.

'You're going to see your mother, my dear.'

'You'd never find her at this hour of the evening.'

'Your *other* mother, my ex-wife.'

'Is that why you refused to buy me panties and a bra? I don't have to suck her off or something, do I? I'll do it if that's what you want. You paid your money. You get what you want.'

'Nothing of the sort, and I do wish you would stop talking that way.'

'Man . . . Daddy, she'll take one look at me and know I'm not her daughter.'

'She hasn't seen you since you were two years old.'

'Gee, that's kind of rotten. I guess I can assume you're divorced.'

'She left me for a bank account. A very large bank account. But how was she to know I was going to have the same kind of bank account myself someday?'

'Well, maybe I shouldn't ask but if I am the phony Becky, where's the real one?'

'Dead. She would have been your age now if she'd lived.'

'Doesn't your wife, your ex-wife, know that?'

'No.'

'Why not?'

'I didn't tell her.'

'That's cold, very cold.'

'She never came back to see the child after she left.'

'That's even colder.'

'Are you ready to go?'

'Yes, but I wish I knew what I'm supposed to do when we get there.'

'All in good time.'

'I think this might be the time.'

Jason studied her from across the table. 'My problem in telling you what I want you to do is that I don't really know myself.' He thought for a minute. 'Be the daughter she abandoned and has not seen in sixteen years. Be affectionate. Be loving. Be hurt over her sixteen-year absence. We are going to leave her with as much confused guilt as we can. In a perfect world, when we leave she will commit suicide.'

Becky frowned and pursed her lips. 'You're something of a son-of-a-bitch aren't you, Daddy?'

'You could say that. Yes, you could definitely say that.'

'How do you know she's home?'

Jason glanced at his watch. 'Forty-five minutes ago she finished her tennis lesson with the club pro. Then she fucked him. She is showering now in preparation to take a nap so she will be fresh for a night of dancing and drinking with the same tennis pro.'

'Where is her husband?'

'The Bank Account arrived in Paris two hours ago aboard the Concorde for a two-week stay, doing whatever it is he does for a living – international gun trading, I think, though I have no proof and in any event, I don't care.'

'How do you know all this?'

'It's cost me a fortune, but since my daughter was killed I've been close enough to my ex-wife's schedule that if she shits, I smell it.'

'I thought we were going to avoid that kind of talk.'

'Accidental slip on my part. Happens at times when I think of my ex-wife. I am not a man much given to hate, but when I hate, I hate hard.'

'I think I could have figured that out.'

'Good for you. You're a perceptive young lady. If you can just get your head in the right place to do this, it'll be a piece of cake. I'm hoping we can get her to pull out her picture albums of when you were a baby. I think somehow that'll do the job.'

'Why would she have pictures of me?'

'Strange woman. Very strange. When she left me and Becky for the Bank Account, the only things she took were her clothes and every single picture we had of you.'

'How do you know she's still got 'm?'

'Anything can be discovered with money. If you need anything badly enough, throw enough money at it and you'll get it. I even know where she keeps them in her apartment.'

'You've gone to a lot of trouble for this, haven't you?'

'More than you could ever imagine.' Jason made a small gesture with his hand to signal the waiter who had been hovering about the table. 'Let's get the check and get out of here.' He smiled. 'It's show time.'

'I only hope I can do the job you want done.'

'You'll be fine,' he said. 'I feel it in my bones.'

On the street, he whistled down an air-conditioned taxi. From the back seat, he said, 'Trump Towers'.

'Jesus,' said Becky, 'that's where she lives?'

'*One* of the places she lives. They have a country house in Connecticut, one that would qualify in most people's minds as a mansion.'

'She didn't run off with a bank account. She ran off with a mothering *bank*.'

He only smiled and shrugged. 'It won't be long now. I've waited sixteen years for this.'

In the lobby, Jason, holding Becky's elbow, went directly to a security guard standing beside a long table. Crossing the lobby, men and women turned and watched Becky as she passed them. Jason, holding firmly to his superstitions and signs, was beside himself with what he considered his colossal luck. He could not imagine choosing a more perfect young girl for the job at hand. And never was he more aware of his immaculate dress, his golden tan, his temples silvered to the perfect shade of grey and his youthful, lean, athletic body that he had fought so hard in the gymnasium to maintain. Perfect, it was simply perfect.

And it was all reflected in the total deference of the security guard's voice: 'May I be of some assistance, sir?'

'You may,' said Jason. 'Inform Ms Catherine Temple that Mr Jason Crowder is here for a brief visit and that he has brought her daughter, Becky.'

'Very good, sir.' He picked up a phone and punched in some numbers. 'Ms Temple, Mr Jason Crowder is in the lobby with your daughter Becky and . . . Ms Temple? Ms Temple, should I send someone?' The security guard's eyes grew round and white and his black face turned ashen.

Jason smiled. 'Did she say today was inconvenient?'

'No, sir. Not really.'

'Then what did she say?'

'She screamed. She's still screaming.' The guard's hand holding the phone visibly trembled.

Jason said: 'Perhaps I should talk . . .'

The guard held up one hand, palm out, gesturing for Jason to be quiet. He cut his eyes from Jason to Becky and back again. 'Of course. I'll be glad to. And if you need anything, just ring me here at the desk.'

The guard looked at Jason with severe disapproval. 'Ms Temple will be prepared to receive in thirty minutes.'

'Excellent,' Jason said. 'My favorite pub is just next door. I think a stiff drink'll make this all the more pleasant.'

'Whatever you say, Daddy.'

At the pub next door the bartender spoke to Jason before they ever sat down. 'The usual, Mr Crowder?'

'Yes,' said Jason. 'And a Virgin Mary for the young lady.'

'One double Jack Black up, and a Virgin Mary for the young lady.'

'Virgin Mary,' said Becky. 'That may be the best laugh of the day.'

'I hardly think so,' said Jason, knocking back his drink.

Back in the lobby of the Trump Towers, the security guard picked up the phone and started dialling as soon as he saw them. When they approached the desk, the guard put the phone back in the cradle and said: 'Ms Temple is expecting you. She's in 2701. The elevator is just behind you.'

'Thanks for your help.'

'That's what they pay me for, to be helpful.'

As they walked away, Becky said: 'He didn't much care for you.'

'I made one of his residents scream,' Jason said, smiling. 'Not liking me is only reasonable.'

'I guess.'

In the elevator, which took the twenty-seven floors absolutely smoothly and so quietly they could hear themselves breathing, Becky said: 'Jesus, can you believe it? I'm more nervous than I was when I turned my first trick.'

Jason smiled and gripped her elbow reassuringly. 'You'll do marvellously. Just remember that Catherine will be more nervous than you could possibly be. And shamed. She loved you, you know. She really did love you. But the other prize was so big that she . . .' He shrugged his shoulders. 'Who knows? Who knows anything about why people do what they do? If things had been the other way around, I probably would have done precisely what she did.'

'I just wish I knew what to do. To say. I'm really flying blind here.'

'Just follow your best instincts. And above all else, follow her. You don't have to act. Just react. To her. This is Mommy. A mommy you've loved all your life, been told about but never seen. You've carried her in your heart. There is no bitterness in you, no ill feeling of any kind. You only love her. Really love her. Do you think you can fake love?'

Becky put her palm on Jason's ass and smiled: 'Daddy, on a good night, I sometimes do it as many as twenty times, and every John zips his trousers up believing it.'

'God help us all,' said Jason.

'You take God and I'll take the money and we'll see who ends up feeling best.'

'With that kind of cynicism, you'll ruin Catherine in five minutes. And you remember, we take no prisoners here. Understood?'

'Understood.'

There was a huge, brightly polished knocker shaped like a horse on the door of 2701.

'Did I tell you your mother owns a horse farm in Kentucky, with a Derby winner standing at stud on it?'

'No,' said Becky, 'but I like horses.'

'A wedding gift from Mr Temple.'

'Man, man,' said Becky, 'what's a two-year-old bitch child compared to that?'

'Apparently her thinking exactly,' said Jason. 'Shall you knock or shall I?'

'I think I'd like to, Daddy.'

Jason stopped her hand as she was raising it to the knocker. 'Prepare yourself for a very young and very beautiful woman. A miracle of medical science: nose, eye lids, face lift, tummy tuck, ass job, implanted calves, shaped, massaged and formed by the best from around the world.'

'She's still got a heart,' said Becky. 'Even I know nobody can fix that.'

'Precisely what I'm counting on.'

On the second knock, the door swept open and a woman stood there who might have been only a year or two older than Becky. Her facial features were perfectly regular and the skin of her face was as tight as a drumhead and as golden in colour as the lighting fixtures that were tastefully placed throughout a living room that was enormous and utterly white, white, deep-pile carpet, white sofa that could have seated ten people easily. A glass, chrome and brass table sat between three deeply-cushioned chairs. The wall behind her was entirely glass, showing an enormous sweep of the New York skyline. Original art-work hung on the white walls. Jason immediately recognized a Chagall and a Miró and an early line drawing by Picasso.

'Rebecca?' said Catherine in a voice that choked and nearly broke.

'Oh, Mommy,' cried Becky and flung herself onto the slender elegant woman. 'Oh, my God, Mommy, Mommy.'

'So very good to see you, Catherine,' said Jason, holding out his hand, 'and to see you looking so well.'

But Catherine could not take Jason's hand because Becky clung to her as though she meant to never let her go.

'Please,' said Catherine, 'please.' But she could say no more than that and tears were streaming down from her blue-mascara'd eyes over the high fine bones of her cheeks. A grey pallor had overtaken her golden tan and she looked as though she might faint.

Jason took Becky's shoulders and gently pulled her away from Catherine. 'Dearest Becky, give your mother time to gather herself. Come, sit.' He led Becky to the huge sofa and set her down and then turned to take Catherine's hand in his and simply held it while he spoke. 'I knew this might be painful, Catherine, and I struggled with the decision for a very long time. But I finally thought you would want to see your daughter, today of all days.'

Catherine was pressing the tips of her fingers against her cheeks just below her eyes now that Jason had released her hand. 'Oh, Jason. Today? I . . . What?'

'Her birthday, Catherine. Your little Becky is eighteen today.'

Catherine completely broke down, her perfect mouth twisting, her eyes squinting, scalded with tears. Jason put an arm about her waist and supported her. 'There, there,' he said. 'Everything will be fine. We'll only stay a bit. I only thought it was time. Is it time, Catherine?'

Catherine raised her hands and took Jason's face in them. 'Yes. Oh, Lord, yes. I would have . . . I wanted . . . If I had just known how. Or been braver.'

'Oh, Mommy, Daddy has told me everything about you. How wonderful and loving you are. What a dear, sweet heart you have.'

'He has? Jason has told you that? My God, Jason, I owe you everything. If there's a heaven . . .'

'There is no bitterness, Catherine. What's done is done. Your daughter loves you. I love you. Please try to believe me when I say everything is fine.'

She took both his hands and pressed them to her lips. 'Thank you, oh, thank you, my dearest Jason. I only wish Peter were here, but he's in Paris on business and . . .'

'Perhaps another time,' said Jason. 'If you wish it, only if you wish it. We do not mean to intrude into your life.'

Catherine said: 'You have given me the most perfect gift I have ever had.'

'Becky will be leaving for Swarthmore at the end of the summer and . . .'

'The child is going to Swarthmore, Jason? How utterly . . .'

'I thought you'd be pleased to know that your daughter is a member of the National Honour Society, graduating at the top of her class.'

Catherine went to sit beside Becky and took her face in her hands and kissed her eyes, her mouth, her cheeks, her brow. Then she embraced her and held her to her breast and Becky said: 'My dearest Mommy, I thought you'd smell just the way you do, so warm, so lovely, I've dreamed of this very moment for such a long time.'

'Catherine, do you think you could get one of the albums and show Becky some of the pictures of herself as a child, maybe even one or two of them with the three of us in them?'

'I'll have them out here quicker than it takes the time to say it. God, the nights I've spent looking at them.' She waved toward the far end of the living room. 'There's a bar over there. An exquisite bottle of champagne on the second shelf. Open it, while I fix my face a bit and bring the albums.'

'I'll have orange juice, if I may,' said Becky.

Catherine stopped and turned to look at her a long moment. 'Swarthmore and orange juice. I didn't think such things existed any more.' Then she turned and hurried from the room.

'How am I doing, Daddy?' said Becky.

'You could not have done better if I had written the script myself. But it gets better. It gets better very soon. We'll be out of here shortly now.'

'She seems like such a good person. Are you sure you're doing the right thing?'

'I'm doing what I've waited to do for sixteen years. I want my pound of flesh and I mean to have it.'

'My poor Daddy. And you look so kind and sweet too.'

'But then so does she,' he said. 'Kind and sweet.'

'Yes, she does.'

'Even a whore with a heart of gold can be wrong.'

'Leave my trade out of this.'

'We can't entirely. But it'll be over so quickly, you'll hardly know it happened.'

'It's your money. Until midnight I belong to you.'

'So you do, my child. So you do.'

Catherine came back into the room wearing fresh make-up, her eyes dry and bright, carrying two leather photo albums, one on top of the other. She sat beside Becky on the couch and took her hand. 'If you only knew, Rebecca . . . Becky, I keep forgetting you're called Becky now . . . if you only knew how many nights I've gone through these, how I've wondered where you were, and how I've wanted to share them with you.'

'But I'm here now, Mommy. I'm here and I love you and I'll love you forever.'

'You have a wonderful and forgiving heart, child. I wish with all my heart I could explain how everything worked out the way it did. I know I must appear cruel and cold to you because of . . . because of how things worked out in the past, but I have missed you every night of my life, thought about you and wondered how you were. I'd explain but I can't. I can't even explain it to myself. It happened. It just happened.'

'Believe me, Catherine,' said Jason. 'We've brought no ill-will here, only love. All of us are flawed and failed human beings. Try not to punish yourself with needless guilt. All is forgiven. It is past and forgotten. We're together now to share these few precious moments.'

'But there'll be many more in the future,' said Catherine. 'Promise me, Jason, that there'll be more and that I'll never be permanently separated from my daughter, whom I love more than my life. There's so much I can do for her and . . .'

'Love me,' said Becky. 'Love me and be my mother, and that'll be as much as I could wish for.'

The two women embraced, pressing their cheeks together again, tears starting to course down Catherine's face.

'Please be happy, dearest Catherine. No more tears. No more separation. Show Becky the pictures.'

'Yes,' said Catherine. 'oh, yes.' She opened the first album. 'Here is the very first, a snap taken through the window at the maternity ward. Who would have thought that wrinkled little bundle of baby could grow into such gracious and marvellous womanhood?'

Becky kissed Catherine full on the mouth and said: 'I've waited for this moment for so very long.'

Jaon beamed and sipped his champagne. 'As have I, God knows.

I've waited and longed for it.'

For the next half hour the two women laughed and cried together, Catherine explaining the circumstances and situations of each picture, the three of them at the beach in Florida — Becky digging with her little shovel, her tiny pail sitting between her chubby legs — Becky on a lawn with a tiny puppy, Catherine sitting beside her on the grass. And on and on, Jason occasionally looking at his Rolex. Finally, he yawned behind his fist and said: 'That was superb champagne, Catherine. Give my congratulations to Peter.'

Catherine looked up from the album in her lap and said, 'I'm afraid I've been a bad hostess. I was so caught up in all of this. Perhaps it's time to open another bottle.'

'No,' said Jason. 'I'm afraid it's time for the truth, sweet Catherine.'

'The truth?'

'Yes, after all, that's what I really came to bring you, the truth.'

'Whatever can you be talking about, Jason?'

'This is not your daughter at all,' Jason said, the slightest smile playing over his lips.

Becky, who had had her arm about the shoulder of Catherine, took it away, and pushed herself farther away on the couch.

'Whatever are you saying?'

'Catherine, you could not believe how much blood there is in an eight-year-old child.'

'*Blood!*' The albums slid to the floor and Catherine raised both her hands to her hair. Her eyes moved frantically from Jason to Becky — growing wilder as they moved. When she spoke, her voice was already on the edge of hysteria. 'What do you mean, *blood?*'

Jason lifted a hand to Becky's breast, and Catherine watched, horror-struck, as he squeezed it. 'This is not your daughter, Catherine. Becky, tell her what you are.'

'I'm a whore,' said Becky. 'I work the street.'

'Are you a good whore, Becky? Do you suck cock and swallow come?'

'I give the best head in the city,' said Becky.

Catherine gave a long, groaning cry and slid from the couch to the floor, tearing at her hair with her hands.

'You have no daughter, Catherine. She was killed ten years ago by a drunk driver and buried where you will never, ever find her.'

Catherine, writhing on the floor, out of control and incoherent, seemed to be saying something; it was not clear what it was, but it was a single word and sounded very much like *please,* repeated over and over again.

'Please tell you more?' said Jason. 'But of course. You should have seen her in the street as I saw her, immediately after she was struck. The *blood*! You could not believe the *blood*! It covered the street from curb to curb and her arms and legs were twisted at the most unlikely angles. And this, *this*, Catherine, is best of all: she was not dead. She was screaming. And she screamed all the way to the hospital. And the only thing she ever screamed was: *Mommy! Mommy! Mommy!*'

Catherine had her face buried in the carpet and her body twisted and jerked spastically as she herself screamed incoherently. Jason reached down and took her by the hair and twisted her face to look at him as he raised the dress that Becky was wearing, raised it to the naked triangle of hair and hooked two fingers between her legs that Becky parted to accommodate.

'Now, dearest Catherine, I am going to take your darling child Becky to my apartment and fuck her. And then she will suck me off and swallow my come. Might you do that for Daddy, Becky?'

'I will do anything Daddy wants,' said Becky. But now she was crying.

'Say goodbye to Mommy, Becky.'

'Goodbye, Mommy,' said Becky, looking away, her voice breaking.

They left Catherine screaming on the floor, writhing and banging her head with her fists.

In the corridor, Becky rushed ahead of Jason toward the elevators.

'Why the great hurry?' Jason said in a pleasant voice. 'Your performance was magnificent. I congratulate you on it.'

Becky stopped abruptly and turned on Jason. 'You fucking beast! I thought I'd seen every kind of animal on the streets of the city. But what you did back there was worse than a fucking animal. I'll feel dirty for the rest of my life! I can't wait to get out of your sight.'

Jason slipped his cuff back and glanced at his watch. 'Alas, by my reckoning I still own you for the next hour and a half.'

Becky's face had gone very red and for a moment she could only sputter as she tried to speak. And then finally: 'I'll give you your fucking money back!'

Jason smiled his easy smile. 'Money I have. It is you I want, back in my apartment. After all, a deal is a deal. And the most honest people I've ever known were whores. You are not going to spoil that for me, are you?'

She stared at him hard for a full minute before her face finally relaxed. 'No,' she said. 'I'll not spoil anything for you.'

His apartment was on Central Park West and the moment he opened the door to let Becky in ahead of him, Becky felt her stomach roll and she thought she would puke. The walls, all the walls, were covered in pictures of a little girl. They were arranged by age on each wall, beginning with a baby of perhaps two and then progressing to a young girl of perhaps eight. No, eight exactly. Becky knew the last pictures were of a child of eight. And she was in no way surprised when Jason went directly to an overstuffed chair, unbuckled his belt and took off his trousers and shorts. Nor was she surprised when he sat down, spread his knees and said: 'Come here, my sweetest child, and kneel between your daddy's knees.' She said nothing but did as she was told, not even the expression on her face changing. Jason buried both his hands in her hair and felt her finely-shaped skull for a moment. 'Oh, Becky, my darling daughter, you know the game we play. Just pretend it is an ice cream cone and suck, suck it all. You will suck all of daddy's cream, won't you?'

Jason felt something hard and metallic pressing against his abdomen. 'Not hardly,' Becky said in a voice full of satisfaction. 'Not this time.'

Jason looked down and saw a snub-nosed thirty-eight revolver with an exposed hammer pressed just above his pubic hair. The hammer was cocked. 'What I want more than anything in the world is for you to give me a reason to kill you.'

Jason actually smiled. 'You'll have no reason. None at all.'

'You didn't actually think I walked around the streets of this city without protection?'

'Apparently I did.'

'Well, I don't. I never have. I knew someday I'd meet you, and now that I have, I'm prepared to kill you. You might not know how long it takes to die when you're gut-shot.'

'As a matter of fact, I do.'

'Would you like that?'

'I would distinctly dislike that.'

'Then get off the chair and lie on the floor on your back.' He did. She put one of the shoes imported from France over his face. 'Lick it,' she said. He touched the sole of her shoe with his tongue. 'Lick it all, you son-of-a-bitch. I want to hear the slobber. Just pretend it's an ice cream cone.' He did as he was told. He licked for a long time until he finally began to retch, all the while the thirty-eight pressed against his belly. 'Now turn over, Daddy. Show your little girl your ass.'

'I can pay you,' Jason said. 'I can pay you whatever you want.'

'I'm about to get what I want.'

With his face pressed into the carpet, he heard a loud metallic click.

'That, dearest Daddy, was the sound of a very long, very sharp, very dangerous switchblade knife.'

'My God, what are you going to do?'

'Unless you lie there very quietly, you'll never know because you'll be dead. This will sting a bit. Just think of it as an immunization shot, something to help you along your way in life. And for your sake, be absolutely still. This is not the sort of knife to make a slip with.'

Jason felt not a sting, but a ripping, scalding tear, a series of them in his left buttock, and then almost immediately the same searing pain in his right buttock. He turned his head and looked back in spite of himself and saw his blood pooling on the carpet.

'There,' she said, 'all done. Put your goddam face back in the carpet and keep it there until I'm gone at least ten minutes. I'll not close the door, but leave it cracked, so you'll not know if I've actually left or not. Put your watch in front of your face so you can see when ten minutes have passed. Raise your head before then and you are a dead man.' Jason heard the knife snap shut. 'One last thing, Daddy, if you ever so much as look at me, I'll have my pimp cut your balls off and leave them in your mouth.' Jason wept silently into the rug. The pain in his buttocks was unlike any he had ever felt. But he kept his eyes on his watch and when ten minutes were up, he got slowly to his feet and went into the bathroom that had one wall fully covered with a mirror. Blood was running down his legs. The cuts were deep. There was a word cut in each cheek. It took a long time to stem the flow of blood and even longer to make out the words in the mirror. The words were neatly, almost artistically drawn in his flesh, one on each cheek: BECKY LIVES.

LOVER DOLL

by

Wayne Allen Sallee

Wayne Allen Sallee is a native of Chicago. The son of a city police officer, Sallee writes extensively and unflinchingly about the city of his birth. Childermas Research in 'Lover Doll' is a thinly disguised version of a Cook County Clinic. Sallee has been writing psychological horror and police procedurals since 1984 and has published over seventy short stories during that time. His first novel, *The Holy Terror*, was nominated for the 1992 Bram Stoker Award as was his novella 'For You, the Living'. His second novel, *Cult of Freaks*, is set in the Ukrainian section of Chicago. He is currently working on his third novel, *Go Hungry*, involving a werewolf who develops Huntington's Chorea in his human form. After that, Sallee plans to write *The Skull Carpenters*, a novel involving CIA-mind control.

'Lover Doll' is one of the most viscerally disturbing of the stories in *Little Deaths*.

LOVER DOLL

She is asleep.

It is Memorial Day 1994, and perhaps it is fitting that I dwell on my past. Our past.

I stare out the window, the one facing east. Where dawn will eventually take away the night with cancerous washes of summer sun and lake breezes. The plasma-coloured digital clock blinks in three-second intervals. It is 4:57 a.m.

Celandine snuggles a little closer to me, caught up in her REM dreams. She tells me that she dreams in black and white. We rent an apartment on Wolcott Street, a common area for gangster films shot here in the forties and fifties. I dream in colour, and in my dreams, it always seems to be the hours before dawn. Like now. Streets deserted. My mind alert. I can hear my heartbeat in my nostrils, in my ears.

Celly has the sheets pulled down to her waist. She sleeps in the nude. I wear shorts and an old t-shirt. I hear soft snoring, a peaceful sound. Soft waves hitting the shores of Fullerton Beach.

I look over, recognizing the sound. More nasal than Celly's.

The vestigial twin growing out of my lover's ribcage is the one who is snoring.

The gentle sounds bring back memories.

1. 1959 Babies

The world breaks everyone and afterward many are strong at the broken places – Hemingway

Crystal Street in those days was a world removed from the gang territory it is now. There were no burned-out tenements, no need for orange signs in each window of the three-flats telling passers-by that they were treading through a Neighbourhood Crime Watch Zone. There were social clubs. But we all saw *The Blackboard Jungle* and knew things were on the verge of change.

My parents were living off Crystal and Washtenaw when I was born. It was a Polish neighbourhood, the kind where nobody ever moved. They just died, and after that, their sons and daughters stayed until they married and moved to a bigger house in Bucktown or Logan Square. Or maybe they died as well.

The summer of 1959 was sweltering. I recall hearing this much later in my life from relatives who had gone to the World Series game to see the White Sox. It was ninety-eight degrees on my birthdate, September ninth.

My mother and two of her friends from the radium watch plant she worked at – painting the dials with the luminous ink, in ten-hour shifts – had gone up and down Division and Milwaukee to the shows to get out of the heat that summer. The Banner, The Royal, the Biltmore; they were all air-conditioned.

My mother had to work into her second trimester; back then, my father was pulling in barely enough to feed a family of two working as a security guard at RB's, a now-defunct department store on Milwaukee. I fondly remember getting a Whamm-O Monster Magnet and a Rock-'em Sock-'em Robot from the store in honour of kindergarten graduation. My father let me pick out whatever I wanted, and by the time I was six, the word monster was embedded in my brain.

My umbilical cord was wrapped around my neck when I was born, and I'm certain my mother's exposure to the radium didn't help. (The factory was eventually closed, after many years of court battles; if you stand on the Ogden Avenue overpass, you can still look down and see the ghoulish lime-green glow in those windows that haven't been painted black.)

In September of 1959, my mother and her friends went to the Biltmore on Division to see the première of *Ben Hur*. I've been told that she went into labour with me then and there.

The ambulance made it to Lutheran Deaconess in time. When I made my entrance into the world, my face was blue and there were traces of blood coming from my nose and ears. To give you an idea of how limited we were medically just thirty-five years ago, all the doctors could really tell my parents was that I had a degenerative muscle disease caused by trauma to the womb.

My mother blamed herself for many years.

When I was in grade school, one of the class trips was to Ripley's Believe It Or Not Museum in Oldtown, where there was an exhibit of freaks from the Barnum & Bailey circus. Freaks was actually Phineas Barnum's get-rich-quick term. His partner later referred to people like me and Celandine as 'human curiosities'. Me with my bulging head and wrap-around eyes, Celly with the second head sticking out of her ribcage.

One of the displays was for Tom Thumb. His mother truly believed her son's diminutiveness was caused by grief she held over her puppy drowning while she carried Charlie, the boy's real name. I went home and told my mother this story, how Tom Thumb became rich and married a woman who told him he was just as beautiful as she, so that my mother needn't worry about me.

My mother smiled sadly when I told her this, and now I realize it was because she knew how my adult years would hurt me, and that my coming school years would only foreshadow this hurt. She smiled the way one does when they are recalling that the person they are talking to used to be so young and tiny. The sadness of the first recognition of mortality. My mother expected the worst. And so I would still hear her cry at night.

But the school I went to was Childermas Research, one of the Cook County clinics.

During my first year of classes, I met Celandine Tomei. Some of the other children and their parents whispered about her.

The ages of the children in class varied; some learned slower, others had inhibited body functions and needed to be taught with much patience.

Celly was a 1959 baby, just like me.

She was the first girl I ever saw naked.

Childermas Research was one weird fucking place. You entered this maze of buildings at Eighteenth and Honore, passing a little sliver of what looked like a Philadelphia rowhouse; this building that was the Burn Ward for the entire county, and the Lighthouse For The Blind. On the northeast horizon, a huge pair of red neon lips, advertising Magikist carpets, beckoned.

The classes of reading and spelling lessons weren't too difficult; our rehab sessions reflected our needs. The therapists were great. Vonnie Llewellyn and Ron Szawlus had the patience of saints, I swear. Rehab mostly consisted of coordination exercises, games to make each person use their right and left sides independently, or in tandem.

What was weird about Childermas was my classmates. Not all of us

were allowed out on class trips, like the one to Ripley's. Sometimes I
felt as if it was a prison. I was never treated badly, but I felt as if all of us
were being manipulated in some way that I could never hope to
comprehend.

Juvenile Rehab – where we were – was Room 18, big black
numerals on an orange door. Room 20 should have housed the burn
ward, but there were people of all ages in there, hooked up to various
machines. I heard several orderlies grousing about having to work the
Pain Detail, which was kat-corner to Room 20. A blank blue door.

I never saw any of what went on in that long corridor of sub-rooms.
But I heard the screams. Several times over the years, I have vomited
into my palm or my garbage can, whichever is more convenient, when
I recall those damnable, high-pitched, keening screams.

Once it had nothing to do with memories. In a medical magazine, I
came across photos of stillborn thalidomide babies like Celandine.

One of these 'stillborn' children was nothing more than a nerve
column wrapped around bone in the placenta.

*I come back into the bedroom, my hands washed fresh. I can still
smell the vomit in the faint spring air. May 31st. Chicago's first real
breakaway-from-the-throes-of-winter days. It is not a bad smell. It
will go away within a few minutes, like when me and Celly were kids
and sneaking smokes on the back porch of the Plichtas' two-flat.*

*Celandine is sleeping soundly. The sun will rise soon, the sky
already aqua. Her breasts rise and fall, rise again. The head beneath
her left breasts lolls to the side.*

*As Celandine breathes, the head looks like a buoy bobbing off
Fullerton Beach. Its eyes are open, and it is staring at me.*

Silently staring.

So many deformities in one classroom. A boy who looked like his
skull had been caved in with a lead rod, another with one bug-eye, as if
his head was a bubble being blown from a plastic pipe. Many could
barely stand. I was able to, but the weight of the excess blood in my
brain made my head slump down. My chin often touching my chest,
I'd stare up, my eyebrows framing my view, at the lovely Celandine.

There was nothing visibly wrong with her. Compared to the others,
at least. Her spine was curved to the right; I heard Ron Szawlus
mention that it might eventually realign itself. She always wore
billowy, flowered dresses. Of course, this was 1966, and all girls
dressed in clothes that covered every possible aspect of their young
sexuality, the flowers exuding innocence. These days I see the same

patterns on women wearing maternity outfits.

By the middle of 1967 the schedules of many of my classmates changed. Both Celandine and I, as well as several others, had improved enough with our mobility and coordination that we only had to come for therapy three times a month. This would continue until I was thirteen. The therapy offices – a two-flat on Aberdeen – were closer to our respective houses.

Gone were the memories of the boy in the burn ward, the one the nurses in the pain detail talked about. His mother had left him asleep on top of a coil heater. Instead of doing skin grafts, the doctors had peeled away several additional layers of skin from the boy's buttocks and performed experiments involving the injections of T-lymphocytes.

Gone, too, were the strange people kept in the psychophrenic ward, as I called it then. I now know that Jimmy Dvorak, Frankie Haid, Billy Bierce, and other infamous Chicago killers of recent past were diagnosed as schizophrenics. But this was a word my parents did not know, and I had to make do with phonetics.

I only saw Celandine during therapy classes. Celly went to Wells public school, which was a lot closer to the therapy clinic.

I learned a lot about her. The fact that she was a child of thalidomide, that wonderful sedative that pregnant women were given until 1963, when it was banned. Her mother had been prescribed the brand name Kevadon and was herself eventually diagnosed with peripheral neuritis. Being young, I thought that was really keen. A drug that back-fired. In therapy, Celandine and I both practised the FeldenKrais Method. This was something invented by a former judo instructor to help improve posture and self-image. The latter was something I certainly needed. Celly was getting more beautiful by the day. I would long for the first, second, and fourth Wednesday of every month that summer. I found out that her mother was into holistic therapy, and that she gave Celly daily injections of aconite, which was really wolfsbane, no shit, and this presumably acted as an adjuvant on her 'Vagus nerve', which was an ideal pain inhibitor. I often wondered later how much pain she had actually been in. Pretty, but still wearing frilly dresses instead of shorts and a blouse like most everybody else in Wicker Park, even the fattest of the girls.

And she liked me a whole lot.

My mother was glad that I had found a friendship in Celandine Tomei. Thinking back on it, I don't recall that they ever met during our days at Childermas. Celly and I would often walk hand in hand through Humboldt Park. She and her mother lived on Division and Hermitage, right next door to a holistic healing house that was usually tenanted by beat poets and abstract artists. Celly's father, before he died, worked as a steerer, someone who brought in potential poker players and gamers, at Mania's Lucky Stop Inn, a Polish bar on the other side of their building.

The first time I went over to Celly's house, I saw a framed quote, this being long before the cutesy arts-and-crafts-stitched logos. The bromide, in simple block letters, read:

HEALTH AND ILLNESS CAN BE
REPRESENTED BY A CONTINUUM.

Celly showed me her mother's bookshelves, Jan Smut's *Holism and Evolution*, Oliver Wendell Holmes's *Homeopathy and Its Kindred Delusions*, there were others. I remember seeing a book on EDTA. Not knowing what it meant, I thumbed through it. The letters stood for ethylene tetra-acetic acid. There were pictures in the book of dwarf-like skeletons and bodies on foetal positions. I read that EDTA chelated the calcium lost in body waste. I started to ask Mrs Tomei what this meant, as she had walked into the room with cherry Kool-Aid, but she quickly took the book away, putting it up out of reach of Celly and me.

I stayed late that evening, because my mother was putting in overtime at the radium plant. I was supposed to be home before dark, but she wasn't able to make any calls, and I knew that crazy Anna Banana, the downstairs neighbour who was supposed to check on me, was at the horse track in Cicero.

We watched Walter Cronkite on the black-and-white blond-coloured Philco, talking very seriously about the latest Mercury space flight. And *that's* the *way* it *was*, July four*teenth*, 1967. We changed channels and watched *I Dream of Jeannie* and *Batman*. Catwoman shot the Dynamic Duo with sedated darts. Robin said 'Holy D'Artagnan,' and they both collapsed. It was Julie Newmar as Catwoman. The television picture wasn't snowy like our own, the Tomeis had ordered a Channel-Master from New York state (the only place that was marketing them), the first ones in the neighbourhood to have one, I think. You see them all over now; they look like double-sided rakes up next to the chimneys.

That night, after getting a ride home from Mrs Tomei in their 1956 Olds Holiday, I had my first adult dream. It was of an older, fuller Celandine in the Catwoman outfit. My underwear was wet and it was hard to pee that morning. I felt guilty. I did not remember the dream itself until early that afternoon, then I kind of understood.

I went to see Celly that same day, the afternoon after my dream. Celly suggested that we play doctor. Her mother was out shopping at RB's, and I wondered if she would run into my father and spend extra time gossiping. We went into the back sitting room, the drapes fluttering every time the Paulina Street elevated thundered by like destiny.

Celly asked me if I was going to be afraid. I said of *what*, getting caught? She said no, and looked away.

I remember it all so clearly. The Westclox ticking a tattoo across the room, both of us bursting with fear and anticipation. We knew we'd never do anything more that day but look at each other naked. Celly's mother had left a package of Hit Parade cigarettes lying atop the bureau. I never had seen her smoke, and thought that the cigarettes were for her male visitors.

Celly was barefoot, still wearing the flowered dress. I moved forward to take the shoulder straps in my sweaty hands.

Something kicked me. It wasn't Celandine, unless she was able to lift up her leg double-jointed and plant one right in my thigh. She backed away quickly.

I was concerned that she had changed her mind. Another train went by and I started thinking about the time. I told her not to worry.

Celandine said that she would take the dress off herself.

'Close your eyes,' she said. When I had them firmly shut, I heard her whisper, 'You know I've never made fun of your head or eyes.'

I opened my eyes. I thank the lesser gods that my deformity allowed for my eyes to not bug out any more than they already did.

I looked at Celly. She stood away from me, naked, her body hairless. But.

There was a part of a body growing out of her. Like in that book I had been looking at, the one Celly's mom had moved to a higher place on the bookshelf.

I realized that her rib cage was slightly bell-shaped. To accommodate the head that protruded from below the last of the left ribs. Its eyes were closed, peaceful-like, as if in sleep.

But that wasn't all.

Celly had a tiny leg growing out from her pelvic bone; that must have been what had kicked me. From the area around her flat stomach, I could see three webbed fingers.

A thumb with no thumbnail protruded from her navel.

I was only seven and a half, but you learn fast when you don't know what the next guy on the street is going to say or do to you. I told Celly that she looked beautiful, strong not vulnerable. Now I understood the reason for the Bohemian-style dresses. She began crying.

Still dressed, I went forward, carefully kissing her face. She responded in kind. After several minutes, I felt a tugging around my waist. I thought it might have been Celly's hands, working at my pants.

I looked down from the corner of my bigger eye.

The head below Celandine's rib cage was sucking on my shirt, pulling it into its mouth. Chewing on it.

I heard a noise and panicked, thinking the front door had opened. Celandine asked me if I was afraid. I said yes I was, that her mother might catch us.

Celly looked down and said that her mother didn't care that someone might see her this way. In what had to be her own mixed-up way, Mrs Tomei was evidently proud that Celly was not afraid to show off her body.

When I backed away slightly, the head bobbed up. The eyes stared at me. The mouth did not relinquish my shirt.

Christ, I've looked up so many medical words in the time I came back to Chicago, to Celly. I tried looking up the phrase 'maternal eclampsia' and couldn't locate it anywhere. Finally called the Harold Washington Library, a girl named Colleen told me that it meant that the mother would sometimes bleed to death during childbirth.

Celandine and I remained good friends throughout the next few years. We played doctor several more times when her mother wasn't around.

More often than not, we would just walk around Wicker Park, and I would sometimes, in the steel shadows of the elevated, lift up her dress, reach under and caress the twin's head. In the books about circus freakshows, they were called 'vestigial twins'.

What Celandine's mother had was a foetal multiple cyst anomaly.

Nowadays, this is detectable by sonography. So Celly is certainly unique, especially that she lived. And the head was not stillborn.

Celly kept the leg, tiny like a chicken's, strapped around her leg with something along the lines of a Posey gait belt, the kind used to lift patients out of wheelchairs. The fingers were slowly being recalcified into her body, due to the added weight gain of her prepubescent years. Many times, I had read, a vestigial twin never formed because it had actually been recalcified into the stronger twin during the time in the womb.

Ray-Ban invented a paid of wraparound sunglasses about 1970, that fit my eyes perfectly, and Bankers Life Insurance picked up the bill. If I didn't have a full head of blond hair, I might have looked like one of the most intense punkers still visible in the old north side neighbourhoods. I think of all I know now, that I didn't know then. All the medical terms that didn't make a damn bit of difference to me. I loved Celandine Tomei.

You can find Celandine's anomaly, if you wish to call it something safe, under any book that lists Foetal Monozygous Multiple Pregnancy Dysplacentation Effects. In the Washington Library's reference book on Birth Defects, it says: SEE ALSO Michelin Baby Syndrome. Page 1433, no shit. Makes me think of John Merrick's disease and how it became known as 'elephantitis' because his mother fell in front of an elephant during a parade in the early days of her pregnancy. I wonder if she ever ran into Tom Thumb's mother and swapped bad juju stories.

The head growing out of Celly was part of a foetal cyst that had skeletal dysplasia. Larger effusions of the cyst's organs were beneath Celly's subdermal region around her lower rib cage. Most thalidomide babies born this way had general effusions in the pleural and pericardial regions, that is, the lungs, heart, and spleen, and polyhydramnios may occur. I seem to recall a child at Childerman like this, the disease itself being excess water in the organs.

April, 1968.

Our happiness was short-lived. The spring after we had first seen each other nude, James Earl Ray assassinated Martin Luther King Jr. in Memphis. The neighbourhoods around us were burning to the ground. The biggest gang in the area was the Blackstone Rangers, and they vented their frustrations on the Puerto Ricans who were moving in to the west of us. There were daily rumbles with the Latin Kings.

The Friday that Ricky's Deli, on our corner, was firebombed, my parents broke their lease on the Crystal Street apartment. I had hoped that I would continue to see Celly at rehab classes when this whole thing blew over, but it wasn't to be. My father quit his job at RB's and we moved down to Shelbyville, Kentucky to live with relatives.

Celly and I exchanged letters, and she often wrote how bitter she was at how everyone, even the therapists, looked at her. I told her not to worry. My parents said we'd be moving back to Chicago soon, maybe a nicer neighbourhood around Albany Park.

'Soon' became 1970, and when we returned to the place I was born, I found that the Tomeis had moved. Out of state and somewhere west was all I could find out. I received several letters from Celandine, postmarked Iowa City and Thermopolis, Wyoming. She sounded increasingly depressed, saying how her mother was taking her to a climate that would help her feel more healthy. They might move to Albuquerque.

I watched MASH and All In The Family, saw the Vietnam War end and Nixon resign. Around the time of the fall of Saigon, I received a letter from Celandine's mother in New Mexico. She told me that Celly had left home.

In her room she found a ticket stub for Denver. She was going after her.

2.   Zombie Tongue

The word freaks . . . sounds like a cry of pain – Anthony Burgess

'You ain't gotten anything until you had yisself some zombie tongue.' Several men on downtown Fremont Street repeated this like a litany the entire first night Norm and I were in Las Vegas.

We had taken a week off from our jobs, working at the Lion's Lair. Norm Brady was a bouncer, I was a disc jockey. Those wraparound Ray-Bans were quite the style now. It was June of 1987, and I had been living in the Denver area almost since I graduated from college six years before.

Viva Las Vegas, Elvis sang back when I was at Childermas with Celandine. Visa Las Vegas was more like it. Expensive as shit! Well, the shrimp cups were cheap. Looked like little sea monkeys, I recall David Letterman joking once.

We walked the seedier part of town, thinking our long thoughts and keeping them to ourselves. We were just damn glad to be out of Denver.

The cool neon of The Mint and the Golden Nugget that was so prominent on Crime Story were far behind us. Eighth Street was home to a bail bondsman and Ray's Beaver Bag. On Ninth, we saw The Orbit Inn, but couldn't enter because an armless fat man wearing a purple sweatshirt had passed out in the revolving door. No one inside seemed to care. We kept walking, amused at kids pitching pennies between the legs of butt-ugly whores. Looking back towards Glitter Gulch, all we saw was a tiny blob of pink and blue neon.

That, and the memory of voices whispering conspiratorially about zombie tongues.

I had a BA in English Literature from the University of Illinois. Tried my hand at Behavioral Sciences, but I couldn't cut it. I guess it was because I still thought of Celandine. I was ten when she left Chicago for points west. I think it was the Holistic Center that told Mrs Tomei that the drier air might do Celly good, by alleviating stress and 'allowing a better view of oneself'.

My actual thoughts were that the Tomeis wanted more privacy. The riots weren't just a racial thing. The blacks were hitting on the black handicapped, too. I could understand Josephine Tomei's concerns.

My family surprised me by moving back to the *south*west side of Chicago. Bridgeport, a few blocks from Mayor Daley's home on Emerald. A nice area then, the Stevenson interstate a new and wondrous thing, and most of the blocks filled with squalor had spanking new Tru-Link fences put up courtesy of da Mayor hisself. He did this several years before, because Chicago was going to be portrayed as a lovely town during the 1968 Democratic Convention, for all network television to see.

I had several mementoes of Celly; tactile things, not simply memories of her naked, and of her seeing me in the same way.

We had often exchanged books, and I still had one of her *Happy Hollisters* mysteries. They were on a ranch somewhere, is all I remember. A menu from Ricky's Deli that we had played connect-the-dots with.

I had felt comfortable on Crystal Street, where we grew up. I realized this walking past the casinos and neon signs. Even in Las Vegas, as in Denver, no one thought of me as being different. Hell, I had both my arms, for chrissakes, and wasn't blocking a revolving door. That's how it was back in the Humboldt Park neighbourhood.

The older Poles liked us – not just *tolerated* us – because they weren't too far removed from the atrocities of Dachau. The kids our age, the normal ones, well, that was an entirely different tune altogether.

To them, we were freaks. There they go, the freaks. Some offered the opinion that my mother had fucked something in the gorilla house at Lincoln Park Zoo. And though Celandine's defects weren't easily apparent, she did have a slight stoop, like the older women who cleaned office buildings in the Loop after the rush hour ended.

The other thing that made Celandine a freak in the eyes of the other kids was that she hung around with me. This was before I got the black sunglasses and I looked like those creatures from Spider County on that *Outer Limits* episode. Celly kissed me in public. Those awkward, pre-adolescent kind where it's like kissing your sister. The saddest memento I had of Celly was a photograph my mother had taken, with white borders and the date printed on the right-hand side. When everyone from St Fidelus was out on a class trip, my ma took the colour photo of Celly and me in front of the yellow brick entrance. To show off to relatives and coworkers who were never told that I was in actuality enrolled at Childermas. Ever. Always in a real world. James Trainor and Celandine Tomei, February 1967. Here in the real world.

In the real world, I graduated from college and left town. Found a job in a bookstore in Streator, then moved on to Navaoo, near the Mississippi. I was going west, too, you see. One night in the latter town, I came home from my job at the International House of Pancakes to find my place ransacked.

The memories of Celandine gone. Everything else didn't matter. I left the state that night. Carthage, Missouri. Colcord, Oklahoma. Whoever would have me. Not many places would. And the ones that did eventually found excuses. I was The fucking Fugitive, all through the early eighties. Just like in the tv show, I'd have some menial job, be there a few weeks, and then some self-righteous person or group would make up a rumour to get the funny looking bug-eye out of their safe little hamlet.

Until Denver. It was pure luck that I heard about the ADAPT program for handicapped people while I was passing through Sedalia, Colorado. I don't know why I shucked it for the dj gig; guess I liked the nights better. Denver's compact skyline, the Flatiron Mountains invisible until the grey of false dawn.

Best yet, I found a friend in Norm Brady. I was at the Wax Traxx on Twelfth Avenue in Capitol Hill, hunting down a copy of Robert Mitchum singing 'Thunder Road' for one of the bar's theme nights. Norm had retrieved the last 45, seconds before I walked down the aisle. We struck up a conversation about Elvis and actors who should have never recorded albums, all the while walking down Colfax On The Hill. Norm lived in a studio apartment above the Metropolis Cafe on Logan; I was three blocks over on Galapago. Norm tended bar at a place on Wazee, over near the viaduct, in addition to bouncing at The Lion's Lair.

Living there was the best time of my life. Waking up to those beautiful and hypnotic blue mountains to the west, always covered with snow, even in July. Until we went to Vegas on a whim and I saw what the city and the real world had done to Celandine Tomei.

Our curiosity had gotten the better of us. We had gambled; breaking even, more or less. Neither one of us drank much. Alcohol has adverse effects on my health and I get massive headaches. So our decision was a sober one. A man dressed in lilac, a bargain basement Prince impersonator of the wrong race, told us where to find this . . . zombie tongue.

I was feeling natty; dressed in non-touristy black with an olive green jacket. Thin lapels, flowered tie, but mellowed out with a button of Elvis Presley playing the ukulele in *Blue Hawaii*. Norm was dressed in jeans and a Road Kill Press t-shirt he picked up back in Arvada, at The Little Bookshop of Horrors, topped off with a St Louis Cardinals baseball cap.

The directions were not that difficult. Maryland Parkway connected with Rue H Street past Eleventh. In the middle of the three-way intersection, cross-hatched in shadows, there was a white building, railroad flat-styled. The logo was a woman in teal wearing a low-brimmed hat.

The name of the place, also in teal script, was BELLADONNA.

Celandine says she doesn't remember much about those days in Vegas. Hell, she doesn't remember much now, with the drugs she's still taking, trying to forget. A staff sergeant at Nellis Air Force Base tipped Celly to a way to make money, the kind of shuck you read in any of the Chicago classifieds. Celly knew that she'd never be working as a waitress in some greasy spoon off Flamingo Road.

The bar catered to those who really wanted a thrill, something different. Something obscene.

Amputees, burn victims. Parading on a stage. I wondered if the armless man propped in that doorway all those months ago ever visited Belladonna's.

Zombie Tongue.

Vegas is like the Miss America pageant. It uses you, and you use it right back.

The building vibrated with the passing of trucks on the parkway overhead. Overhead gels of red and blue, beaded doorways. Flashing squares of soft light on the floor, alternating in chequerboard patterns. Maybe a discotheque in a different time. The décor reminded me of the Go-Go bars in Calumet City, back in Illinois.

The woman on stage was a burn victim; in the lights and nicotine haze you couldn't tell unless you were looking up at her. She was devoting most of her time to a gaggle of skeletons at the other end of the bar.

Where we were sitting, a dwarfish woman with hair growing out of a mole in her cheek passed by with an empty potato chip can. Money for the jukebox. The current song was some oldie but goodie from the seventies. 'Fool For The City' by Foghat, maybe. Or 'Toys In The Attic'. Aerosmith always drew their biggest crowds at strip bars. The mole was the size of a .38's exit-wound. The woman blew away the long strands of hair from her mouth before trying to seduce us with a bloated, grey tongue.

It made me think about Celandine. And of myself. Time changes nothing but the contours of our bodies. (The burn victim on stage had no contours at all – we saw that when she moved our way; she was eternally young. A survivor of Vietnam, in fact. Her crotch smooth, like a Barbie doll.)

The hours passed and the drinks took their toll.

I had thought that the term 'zombie tongue' was some street phrase for whores, like meth-moxie was anywhere else for drugs. But I couldn't leave. In the middle of a Widows of Whitechapel song – the burn victim grinding her smooth, gashless pelvis against the far wall – I tried loping over to the john. Green shag carpeting covered the walls and ceiling of the rooms down the hall. I was reminded of Elvis's Jungle Room at Graceland, the plushness acting as sound-proofing. I saw the sign marked ME off to the right.

Near the opposite door, painted black, a tall guy with a shirt that read I LOVE YUMA, ARIZONA came out of the room, nodding his head in a 'your turn' gesture. I noticed blood on his lip, purple in the thin track of lighting imbedded in the overhead carpeting. I was ready to go into the bathroom when my eye caught a glimpse of something beyond the still open black door.

A bookcase, and in the wedge of light, the unmistakable – to me, at least – yellow and red binding of a *Happy Hollisters* book. I thought, fuck, no. Squeezing every bit of emotion out of me, I pushed the door open. I saw Celandine.

She was naked and tied down spread-eagled on the bed. Her body was thinner than I might have expected. But I knew it was her, you see, because of the head. Celly's bush had grown up in a thin straight line, like a fuzzy black worm. Her nipples were small and pink. Sure enough, with age, the fingers that had protruded from her stomach had decalcified back into her. Where the small leg had been was a pale nub above the pelvic bone. Maybe it had been sanded smooth.

Celandine looked drugged or weary from crying. I could not look at her. But I found the courage to walk into the room. I looked around the sparse rectangle of living area. Hell, it was a mansion compared to the Cal City titty bars where you fucked the women on the stairwell landings, against the walls like it was Victorian England. If you fucked them in the ass, they spent the few moments reading the new graffiti.

Tubes of salve and Ben-Gay were crafted into strange stick figures. Pill containers littered the vanity unit like perfume bottles. Tricyclic anti-depressants like Elavil, stronger shit like Denzatropline. All labelled with a post office box in Groom Lake, Nevada. The doctor's name was unpronounceable. Blank postcards, her own mementoes. Deer feeding near Backbone State Park, Iowa. Thornton's Truckstop Diner (Con Mucho Gusto!) Beaumont, Texas. The Big Chief Hotel in Gila Bend, Arizona. The sun setting over Roswell, New Mexico.

Other, more 'grown-up' books: Nelson Algren's *The Man With The Golden Arm*, and Frank Norris's *The Pit*. Theodore Dreiser's *Sister Carrie*, the collected Sherwood Anderson reader. All Chicago authors; Celly never forgot her roots. I saw a small cassette recorder on a table and flipped through the tapes. Came across Elvis's *Jailhouse Rock* soundtrack. Imagined him singing the title song, 'You're So Young And Beautiful'.

I heard a moan.

It was the head. Mouth open, like a dog begging for a biscuit. The tip of the tongue was bitten off. It *recognized* me. It was *showing* me.

Jailhouse Rock

I ran out the door and into the john, vomit already nearing my teeth. Sweating, numb. And there he was in the doorless stall nearest the entrance, my new friend. The man who had been in Celandine's room before me.

The man with blood on his lip. He smiled then, said how the head felt no pain. He *knew* I knew what he was talking about. Said it was like raping a girl and then killing her after because she knows who you are.

Do the crime without doing the time.

When he smiled a bloody thin-lipped grin and compared it to having your cake and eating it too, hiking up his belt like a *real* man, I hit him. Caught him by surprise. I pummelled him until my knuckles were bloody. Left him face over the chipped porcelain bowl, hair hanging into the water like he had got a swirly.

I walked past the condom machines to the mirror. Took my Ray-Bans off and stared at my bulging face. Beat holy hell out of the mirror, out of my reflection.

But had the common sense to wash my hands and calm down.

Went back to the stage with my hands in my jacket pockets, told Norm I wanted to head back to the Plaza.

The girl dancing on stage as we walked out the door had two mastectomy scars.

That night, I dreamt horrible things, like a guy forced to sleep the night before he is to be strapped down into the electric chair.

I was back at Belladonna's, sitting front centre stage. Celly was dancing, glassy-eyed. Cradling the head as Patsy Cline belted out 'I'm Back In Baby's Arms'. The crowd going nuts.

Celly snake-dancing to 'The Stroll', winnowing across the stage, the head dangling over the edge. Men stuffing dollar bills into its mouth. Celly standing and swinging her head back and forth, the cystic head below flopping like a colostomy bag. Celly oblivious to me, the head the only one recognizing me in the whole place, the whole city, the whole world.

Down on her hands and knees, shoving her ass in someone else's face. Inching down the stage, flashing red, blue, red, orange. Her nipples tiny points. Celandine's pussy seemingly enormous in the shadow of her body. The stage covered with wadded bills, spat out of the head's mouth.

The head with a mind of its own, making Celly move towards me.

So that the zombie tongue could lick the dried blood from my knuckles.

I woke up to find it was almost two in the afternoon. Norm was watching CNN. He told me that it was about time I got up, he'd been awake when I got back.

I asked him what the hell he was talking about.

He told me that halfway back to the Plaza, I got out of the cab and said I wanted to go back to Belladonna's. Then he told me to go do something about my breath.

*

We got back to Denver okay. Part of me wanted to go back to Vegas, to Celly. But I was embarrassed, shocked, even sickened at the depths I had lowered myself to. I took some spare Tegretol for my headaches. I tried for months to forget what I had seen at Belladonna's.

I watched the WGN superstation for Chicago news after the Cubs and Bulls games. Read about The Painkiller, killing wheelchair victims in the Loop back in Chicago in late '88, and of Richard Speck (still unrepentant) dying a day before his fiftieth birthday, bloated from a distended bowel, although the cause of death was listed as emphysema, in December 1991. Everyone felt cheated that the drifter who had mutilated eight nurses in 1966 – around the time Celly and I were getting to know each other better – got off so easily.

Norm Brady and I hung around The Lion's Lair in the evenings and I spent my days rereading old medical textbooks from the Denver Library on Seventeenth. I also read the *Rocky Mountain News*, my native city showing up increasingly as the civil war in the former nation of Yugoslavia continued unabated. My home town was indeed a melting pot, much of the coverage came from the Chicago wire services. Items about the Midwest in general, the Mississippi flooding from the Quad Cities to St Louis, a crazed gunman killing patrons at a Kenosha, Wisconsin restaurant. A skinhead shooting a plastic surgeon who 'dared' change someone's Aryan features; what would the neo-Nazi think of myself or Celly?

I dreamt about hot neon the colour of clotted blood, of deformed faces that looked as if they had been squeezed between unrelenting elevator doors. Sometimes I would realize that I had been awake and staring into a mirror.

Occasionally, I would come across copies of *The Chicago Tribune* at the library. Usually they only carried West Coast papers like the *Seattle Intelligencer* or the *Vallejo Vestry*.

One day six months ago, I read of a scandal involving a prominent Chicago network newswoman. Rumours circulated of a lesbian affair with a woman with an acardiac twin. This particular shit was slung because the woman was up for a national news desk spot. But, still. I flew back on United to see if the Tomeis were back in town.

Josephine and Celandine had been back in Chicago since the summer of 1991. Someone besides me had seen her in Vegas and knew an even better way to use her. A local writer exploited her for shock value in one of his novels, saying that she had become one of the highest paid call girls in the city, and that the head under the ribcage was dead and often mutilated.

The guy in Vegas was right. The head feels no pain.
But that doesn't mean you don't have to fix it.

She is asleep.

I stare out the window, the one facing east. Josephine Tomei died this past Christmas. It is just me and Celandine. I called Norm and told him I had family matters to take care of here.

I left things open.

She is asleep because she still is taking the drugs that she started on in Vegas. The only reason she hasn't lost all of her self-esteem. I swear I will get her straight. It is 5:30 and the sun is coming up.

I play the Elvis soundtrack to Jailhouse Rock. 'I Wanna Be Free'; the title song. Finally, 'Lover Doll'.

I listen to the younger, pre-bloat King of Rock 'n Roll, singing about how he loves his lover doll madly.

I pull the sheets gently away from Celandine's drugged form. The head is still watching me. Dawn's light slashes a diagonal across Celly's black pubic hair. I pull off my shorts.

I reach forward, kissing Celly's closed mouth. It doesn't open. I lick her breasts, the left one, then the right.

I reach into her cunt with my hand, one finger at a time. I can put three fingers in comfortably. She does not respond. My dick is still limp.

'. . . let me be your lover boy . . .'

I take my fingers out of Celandine and stroke the head's hair. Its mouth opens. The eyes have a certain curiosity.

I swear I will get Celly off the drugs, get our lives together. Take her back to Denver with me.

I move towards the head, my dick growing to half-mast. There is early morning traffic outside. In the real world. Our real world.

Straddling Celly's sleeping body in a half-assed way, one foot on the ground, the other leg's knee near her armpit. Positioning myself over the head. Guiding my dick into its mouth.

It is not hard to believe that it begins sucking.

(For Denise Szostak)

THE SWING

by

Nicholas Royle

———◦※◦———

Nicholas Royle lives in London, England and has published over sixty-five short stories in such anthologies as *Book of the Dead*, *Dark Voices 4 & 5*, *Narrow Houses*, *Obsessions*, *Dark Fantasies*, Karl Edward Wagner's *The Year's Best Horror* and Ellen Datlow and Terri Windling's *The Year's Best Fantasy and Horror* and magazines such as *Interzone*, *New Socialist*, *Fantasy Tales*, and *The Fred*. He is also the editor of the original anthologies *Darklands* and *Darklands 2*, the first of which won the British Fantasy Society's Best Anthology Award. His first novel, *Counterparts*, was recently published by Barrington Books and he is working on his second, *In the City*.

Relationships are a balance of power. In good relationships that balance shifts regularly between the two participants. In his story 'The Swing', Royle takes this idea and gives it a tangible demonstration.

THE SWING

I'd just cleared the ball off my line and kicked it back up the park when I noticed this beautiful girl standing near to the goal. She was applauding my save and didn't look away immediately when I grinned at her. While she was looking down I had a good look. She didn't seem to have any holes as far as I could see. Her ears weren't pierced and I couldn't see any scars on her face or hands. Still, I thought, no harm in looking.

As the first half was quiet I stayed on the goal-line and talked to her. Even if there was no future in it, I was flattered by her attention. I talked about the game and the lads on the team, my job, how to avoid arrest for burglary if you're carrying heavy bags stuffed with books and records; rubbish, in fact. I talked rubbish because I was scared of drying up. Also because it didn't look like anything could happen between us and so it was hard to justify the desire to talk.

It was the middle of winter and although the sky was almost all grey, the sun shone for a short time and struck her face like it would a statue's. She was wearing glasses with an attractive black frame and the lenses were coated with something that made them reflect strange colours. Her skin appeared perfect in the sideways light and she wore her hair casually flicked over the right side of her head. She had jeans on that looked warm and comfortable. I wanted to tell her how stunning she looked, but it might have confused her. I wished I had a camera with me, despite the obvious handicap of my goalkeeper's gloves.

I asked the girl her name and she said it was Georgie. Her hair was long and dark. I told her my name. She said, 'That's a lovely name.' I didn't have any holes either so I couldn't work out why she was being so nice to me.

There was an attack on my goal which came out of the blue and I fumbled the ball. It fell to an attacker but I blocked his shot. Georgie was clapping again, her breath freezing in front of her face like big white roses bursting into flower. Our midfield must have fallen asleep because suddenly the opposition were coming at me again. Their winger put in a cross and I jumped for the ball, along with three other men — two of their forwards and one of our defenders. Normally I would have been more cautious but, in spite of myself, I was showing off in front of Georgie. I got hit in the face. Someone's elbow caught me in the cheek. It was a mighty blow and I felt instantly sick, as if I'd walked into a tree. I fell to the ground, too badly hurt to clutch my face, too shocked to know how to react. The pain was startling and I was terrified in case the damage was . . . what? . . . worse than I expected? A footballing injury. Surely it couldn't be that bad, could it?

With players crowding round me I tried to feel with my tongue inside my mouth. The rich taste of blood was in my throat. My tongue found the point of impact, where the inside of my cheek had been pressed against my teeth. There was a hole. My tongue seemed to go on for ever as it felt for the end of the hole. What if it goes right through? I thought anxiously. What if I've got a hole through my cheek?

And when I looked up and saw the expressions on the faces of my teammates I realized that was exactly what I did have.

Gingerly I fingered my cheek. I felt the edge of the hole and drew back, like a tourist on the lip of a volcano. The only person who came forward instead of backing away was Georgie and she came so quickly I didn't have time to react. Deftly she threaded a large silver ring through the hole, attached a strong-looking chain and snapped the ring shut. 'I love you,' she whispered unnecessarily.

The rest of the lads were watching, some exchanging knowing glances and nudges and winks. They didn't seem to mind that they'd lost their keeper. A game's a game but some things are more important, they would have been thinking. Even if they hadn't scored, I had. Things like that. They would have all seen similar things before. I knew for a fact that Jon, the left-back, had seen a girl he fancied in a pub the week before and had slipped a thin wire through the hole in her pierced ear while she was waiting to be served. Since he'd wanted to go to the pub anyway they stayed for a while before going back to his flat on the outskirts of the city.

With Georgie it was love at first sight. So she said later, after she'd led me away from the field. We didn't bother to go via the changing rooms and pick up my clothes. She made no concessions like that, and there was no reason why she should, obviously. My life had changed and I had to accept it. It wasn't as if it had never happened before; just not on a football pitch in front of 21 blokes. It was a bit embarrassing.

We spent the next 36 hours at her flat, moving from the bed only to run a bath – which we let go cold – or to get more orange juice from the fridge. We got to know each other's bodies to the most intimate degree and talked when there was an opportunity. She didn't take the ring out of my mouth once. It was far too early for that degree of trust.

During those first few days I submitted myself to everything without question. It felt good to be with someone again, but I knew that before long I'd have to start looking for weaknesses. Realistically, the balance couldn't stay the same for long.

Georgie took me to see her friends. In the car she took no chances, securing me to the door handle with a stout chain. I liked watching her drive. She didn't wear a seatbelt and her lips never stopped moving as she mouthed abuse at any driver who either cut her up or proceeded too slowly. I liked to see them get out of her way fearfully, especially because if they didn't, it tended to mean a violent jolt which jarred the ring in my mouth, reopening the wound and causing blood to flow. I put my hand on her leg at one point and she covered it tenderly with hers before taking hold of my little finger and applying a twist that threatened to break it. We both laughed at this.

On arrival at her friends' house she led me into a chatter and appraisal and endless questions rattled at Georgie. Where did you find him? What does he do? Is it good? Better than the last one? 'He looks good to me,' one woman in a gold dress said as she ran her hand flirtatiously up my chain, stopping just before the ring so that I could feel her trembling with suppressed excitement.

The host emerged from the kitchen with a flourish and a black woman whom he kept in tow by means of a length of gold rope, the type you see in theatre foyers and outside posh hotels, which was plaited into her bleached hair. The black woman was carrying a tray of cocktails in outrageously tall glasses. I could only imagine the punishment she might receive for dropping one. In fact, as she passed me I noticed several barely healed welts on her cheek and up the back of her neck.

In the main living room everyone reached for a glass. I thought I'd try to get one for myself, just to test Georgie's reaction. She was on the ball, all right, whipping out a short riding crop – much to my surprise – with which she beat me twice on the arm. I was surprised because the only other couple I knew who kept a riding crop were my parents. To my knowledge they never used it because their relationship seemed as close to perfect as you could get. They had matching holes pierced through the nasal septum and both wore rings. Whoever had the benefit of the swing led the other with a thin chain. When the swing changed, they seemed to accept the fact mutually and switch the favour of the chain. Of course, their relationship was the exception rather than the rule.

Georgie's second stroke with the crop raised a thin red stripe. That's what I don't like about love affairs – the blood. My own or anybody else's. But in most cases it's inevitable.

'Don't touch, darling,' Georgie said gently. 'We're not at home now. These are my friends.' Then she kissed me slowly and deeply, probing the hole in my cheek, much to everyone's enjoyment.

Out of the twenty or so people in the room, the host and his black partner were obviously very much in love. Probably, like Georgie and myself, they had only recently met. There were several single people and a few other couples at various stages of getting to know each other. One woman wore a hood and had been hobbled with nylon fishing line, but she kept a respectful two paces behind her partner, a tall, thin man with silver hair and four fingers missing on his left hand. At regular intervals he would turn and run his good hand under the folds of her tunic and she would appear to shiver. It was hard to tell if her reaction was one of pleasure or disgust. Another couple stood at opposite sides of the room, each partner flirting wildly with other people. Every so often one would tug the long thin flex that snaked across the wooden floor between them. They looked as if they were hungry for new experiences but reluctant to throw away what they'd got.

I felt my head being pulled round. Georgie was unclasping the chain from the ring. She smiled at me indulgently as she held on to the ring itself and said, 'Go on, have a run about.'

She was taking a chance. The other women gathered round me, hands reaching out to pet me and stroke my head. One or two touched the ring and threaded it round through the hole. It hurt but I tried to put a brave face on it for Georgie's sake. There were at least a dozen women touching me. It only needed one to take a fancy to me and snap some kind of lead or chain on to my ring and Georgie would have lost me. I imagine that the risk gave her some pleasure because she seemed to be enjoying herself as she watched the frenzy of hands and bared teeth.

There was something about the episode which struck me as less than tasteful and I felt it reflected badly on Georgie. This was probably the moment – when she snapped the chain back on the ring, all but smirking with self-congratulation – that I began to love her slightly less and the swing began. In the car on the way back to her place I think we were probably about level, but I was the one who was chained up. The thing about relationships, of course, is that when you're in one, all the normal rules by which you live change. Georgie had had to wait for something to happen to me in the first place before she could put the ring on me. Had she just marched up and pierced a hole in my cheek, it would have been rape – an act upon which society still frowns. But when you love somebody, the gloves are off. Georgie should perhaps have taken my docility less for granted.

I watched her at the wheel as she negotiated the ill-lit rainy streets north of the city, her dry lips constantly fluttering. At one point she turned her head and looked at me and gave me a smile. Sickly in the orange glimmer of street lighting and the green display of the car's dash, her face seemed years older than the one I'd seen on the football field, awash in early sunlight.

With a sudden movement I reached for the handbrake and jerked it up.

The rear of the car pitched up in the air and the front wheels swivelled. the steering wheel spun out of control and Georgie's head punched into the windscreen, which shattered like a huge chandelier crashing to a wooden floor. I had braced myself adequately and was still sitting in my seat unharmed when the car stopped moving. I unclipped my chain from the door handle and looked at Georgie. She was bent in half, her face on the bonnet, her legs stuck under the wrenched steering column.

I walked to the nearest phone and called for an ambulance.

When Georgie came home from hospital she was in a wheelchair. Because I had sold her flat while she was in intensive care, she stayed at my place. The swing had happened and I started leaving things out of reach on high shelves and on top of cupboards. We were still sleeping together but the relationship – like Georgie – wasn't really going anywhere. I didn't need to chain her. Her legs were useless and I lived on the fourth floor. There was no lift. The hole in my cheek healed up nicely, leaving a neat scar. I went out to work as normal and thought about her sometimes as I sat at my desk looking for pierced ears among the secretaries and personal assistants.

She took to ringing me at work to tell me she couldn't wait for me to come home, so one night when I got home I ripped out the phone

and bound her wrists behind the back of the wheelchair. I should
have been enjoying myself both at home – where I should have been
grateful for Georgie's attention – and at work, and in the pubs and
clubs, sitting waiting for someone to fall on a smashed glass. But I
felt increasingly numb, unable to appreciate what I'd got. I began to
have serious doubts about the swing and only realized what was
really going on one day when I stayed late to finish sorting some
papers at work.

A very attractive woman whom I'd noticed looking at me several
times over the past couple of weeks came into my office and leaned
against the desk facing me. She made much of the short skirt she was
wearing. 'Your wife loves you very much, doesn't she?' she said.

'She's not my wife but yes,' I answered.

'That's what makes you so attractive.'

Then she took the long thin letter opener from my stationery
holder and, laying her left hand flat on my desk, plunged the blade of
the letter opener into the middle of it. Although clearly close to
fainting, she managed to pull the blade out of the desktop in which it
had become embedded and show me the palm of her hand. Blood
dripped from the fresh hole.

Clearly the swing was in Georgie's favour again, because I felt no
desire for this other woman. I just watched her bleed for a few
moments before picking up the phone to dial Georgie. The number
was unobtainable and I remembered why. 'I love you,' I whispered
desperately into the receiver.

SAHIB

by

J. Calvin Pierce

After trying to make a living as a musician, J. Calvin Pierce claims that he took refuge in more practical occupations for a number of years before deciding to write fiction. He is the author of the *Ambermere* series of fantasy novels and a couple of short stories. He is currently working on a realistic contemporary novel.

'Sahib' differs in both form (journal entries) and era (nineteenth century) from most of the other stories in this book.

Here, a young doctor is consulted by a cruel and self-righteous man about a mysterious and embarrassing ailment.

SAHIB

The hour is late, the weather vile, the shops long since shut. I am, for the time, a captive in my own rooms. The rain beats against the window; the street below is awash and deserted. I am prevented even from walking to my office, a mere block away. At any rate I am safe from interruption. It would be a serious illness or injury indeed that would send any Londoner abroad in search of a physician on a night like this.

Isolated thus, and yet unwilling to defer this task for even a few hours longer, I find that, for lack of other paper, I must press into use my devotional book, which has heretofore served for the recording of prayers, bits of scripture and points of interest from sermons, to write of matters that it would not be seemly to commit to the pages of my professional journal. I hope the religious content of the leaves that precede this private medical diary will be an omen of good, presaging the relief of the sufferer in my care, and serve to ameliorate the evils, hysterical imaginings though they must be, that will be written of here.

I was called a fortnight ago to the town house of a Colonel Peter Burgess, late of the tropics, who has urgently returned to England for medical treatment. How I came to be chosen, I understood to some degree before the revelations of this afternoon. Now I understand still more. How to say such things to any man, any stranger? I suspect Colonel Burgess thought that to confide in one younger than himself would be less damaging to his pride than to lay his fancies bare to the judgment of a physician of established reputation.

This I am not, but I flatter myself I have some skill, and I must pray God to aid me in the relief of this poor man's anguish and suffering, which I fear come as much from the disorder of his mind as his body.

Here I mean to repeat what I have heard from Colonel Burgess, but his words I shall not always transcribe. His own ills leave him little patience for niceties. That, combined with a certain native direct-ness, if not coarseness, persuades him at times to relate what he has experienced in language that is, for me, if merely burdensome to hear, impossible to write. I must paraphrase, and in doing that must yet say more than I should wish.

On that first day I was conducted by his military servant to his sitting room. There I was greeted by a sight for which I had not prepared myself. I had thought to visit a man debilitated, wasted by some tropical pestilence, perhaps dying and beyond the help of my skills. Instead I found a hugely fat man, certainly twenty-five stone, seated in an oversize chair and staring from a window. He acknowledged me with a curt nod and dismissed his corporal.

He told me that, six months before, he had been fit and lean, weighing no more than eleven stone, which meant that since then his weight had increased by approximately one pound per day. This was scarcely to be believed, but the corporal later confirmed it, as did Mrs Burgess when I spoke with her.

In that first interview with my patient, I at once confessed myself to be confronted with a complaint for which I was acquainted with no precedent. I began to speak of the eminent physicians we must have recourse to. His reaction was almost violent in its intensity. He seized my hands as he might have those of some dear friend or family member.

'No,' he cried. 'I will have no parade of bearded doctors come here to judge me – to look solemn and shake their heads.' He stared at me fixedly, whether to implore or intimidate I could not tell. 'You must treat me by yourself, and leave me yet some little shred of dignity.' He released my hands and turned away as though finding his own display of emotion distasteful.

Seeing his state, I agreed to his terms, hoping in due course to influence him to another, wiser path. I began to discuss with him the history of his complaint. The only other symptom he could – or would then – report was the irresistible daytime slumber that overtook him at unexpected moments.

'It is perhaps just as well,' I offered. 'The body must have rest to make its repairs, marshal its defences.'

'It is not a restful sleep,' was all that he would say then. How much those few words concealed I learned today.

It was necessary that I visit him daily, as my plan of action was to begin him at once on a strict fast, and I dared not set him such a course without monitoring his health. As to exercise, he would not go out by day. He and the corporal walked in a nearby public garden late at night when there would be no one abroad to see him.

It was at such an hour, and such an hour only, that he would consent to visit my office, though visit it he must, for he would not hear of having a scale in his home. Late that night I recorded his weight as nearly one hundred and sixty kilograms. Over twenty-five stone; over three hundred and fifty pounds.

'Some wretched tropical humour,' was the colonel's diagnosis, adding his opinion that he had been 'poisoned by unwholesome air'. He insisted that his diet had never altered, that his gain in weight had not been brought on by any change in habits. His wife, whom I saw on my second visit, confirmed this to me in a private talk we had as she accompanied me to the door.

Cynthia Burgess herself showed signs of the trials of the recent months. If one was struck first with her remarkable beauty, one soon after noticed the traces of fatigue that had begun to engrave themselves around her eyes, her mouth.

But what beauty! I have seen her a number of times now in the past two weeks, and yet I am never prepared for the effect her presence has on me. A striking figure, clear complexion, a fetching eye – these things are not uncommon. But the beauty of Cynthia Burgess is not the sum of a catalogue of perfections; she has rather a force of attraction than a list of excellences that one can enumerate. Her beauty cannot so much be seen as felt, almost breathed. An emanation.

I cannot say I take much pleasure in her talk; it is confined to answering questions about her husband. It is not her conversation, but her speech or, more exactly, her voice that captivates one so. It is low in pitch, dark in timbre, and seems to inhabit the ear like the murmurings of some exotic musical instrument. One does not care what she may say, if only she will speak.

I make no apology for being susceptible to charms that few men who retain breath and blood could resist. And in this journal I further make no apology for delineating them, for they may shed light on, or even in some strange way be at the root of the torment that was only today revealed to me.

Sadly, Peter Burgess can now take no pleasure in the company of his wife. If she enters his room, he becomes silent. I can see it is at the cost of considerable effort that he brings himself to look at her. She stays away, therefore, though I must suppose it gives her pain. But she is brave, and hides it well. I believe her sole concern is that her husband has as much comfort as he can achieve. No doubt she feels that it tortures this proud man for his wife to see him brought to such a state.

That is a belief I shared with her until today.

In the first week of treatment the colonel was gloomy and dispirited. I made no progress in my efforts to draw him out, but I continued in those efforts all the same. I was convinced even before the second time I weighed him that the problem was not entirely a somatic one. The physical aspect, dealing with my patient's obesity, I expected to be a simple matter. Though the body resists, a fast can have dramatic results, or so I have read, and so the records of many wars and famines tell us.

Nonetheless, when he came to be weighed the second time, seven days having intervened, he had gained nearly half a stone, some seven pounds. The next day I interrogated the corporal closely. I was determined not to have my patient eat himself to death while I fancied he was fasting.

The patient himself claims to suffer no inconvenience from the strict regimen, I suppose because his general misery serves to mask any particular pain. In recent days, though, he has begun to feel that effect that the close attendance of a physician often brings. He has begun to give over the superintendence and some of the worry of his disease to me. There are those who say this is the chief good a medical man can do, and that if only we would leave off doing harm, we should be worth our fees.

In any event, I welcome it, for it makes this stiff man more easy with me. I first noticed it the day after he was disappointed by the scale. I began then to hope he might eventually speak of more than his physical symptoms, for I had formed the notion of treating the whole man.

And now today he has at once gratified and shocked me. I am gratified that I have so far advanced in his trust that he begins to tell me his secrets. I am shocked – perhaps I am *naïve* – at their nature.

He had begun, this second week, to tell me of the horrors that infested his dreams. In sleep he found himself pursued by a pack of voracious gnomes with pincer claws and tiny pointed teeth. He left his bed each morning more weary than he had entered it. Today I determined to see if I could not probe this wound. Might not a psychical injury be cleansed and healed like a physical one?

This afternoon I asked him if he didn't think the slumbers he sometimes fell into during the day did not stem from the restlessness of his nights. I mentioned this simply to broach the subject of his nightmares, but it was not of those we were to speak.

He laughed. As always, his laughter was without mirth. Had anything the power to cheer this troubled man, I wonder how he might express the unaccustomed emotion.

'You think,' he said, 'that these fits of sleep might be sent as relief?' Again he laughed, turning his eyes heavenward. 'I wish you could prescribe a powder that would relieve me of such relief.' For a moment he said nothing. I had grown used to the silences that often punctuated his speech, but on this occasion he went on.

'Shall I tell you something of these intervals of repose?' He spoke without looking directly at me, as though addressing a person in another part of the room.

I encouraged him with a nod and a few words, fearing to do something to make him change his mind. I did not seek his eye, but studied my hands folded in my lap. There ensued a silence which I was resolved not to break. At length he spoke.

'To see my wife is to know what there is to know of her. She is a fresh, plain English girl. No beauty, to be sure, but presentable enough.'

To hear Mrs Burgess so inaccurately described nearly brought a protest to my lips unbidden. Had I not known better, I should have thought I had been talking to the wrong woman, some dark beauty that shared their house, or some voluptuous phantom that haunted it. It was as though Colonel Burgess held in his hands a rare orchid and described it to me as a daisy.

'As to carnality – don't start, sir; you are to hear much worse – I have long since resigned myself to the fact that in that respect she will remain forever the innocent . . .

'And that is what makes these dreams so vile!' He turned from the window to face me.

'When you dream, doctor, do you ever see images that could not be distinguished from reality? That even when you wake and recall them, still might have been events that actually took place, with nothing of the dream-image about them?'

I was determined not to interrupt my patient. I shook my head and maintained my silence. He turned again to the window.

'Well, for six months – more now – I have had this . . . gift.' He lowered his voice, not in the manner of one who whispers a secret, but as though he spoke unwillingly.

'The first vision came on one of those devilish hot mornings one must endure in the tropics. I grew suddenly and unaccountably tired at my desk. I cursed the heat and let my eyes fall shut, then found I could not open them.

'It was no sleep that gripped me. I felt as though I had swallowed some drug that blinds and paralyses. Then came the dream. But as the sleep was not sleep, so the dream resembled no dream I had ever had. My disembodied consciousness seemed to rise from my drowsing form in the chair and was drawn through rooms and corridors like some wandering ghost or phantom. I had acutely the senses of sight and hearing, but no others. I saw servants, heard distinctly each syllable of their babbling, but felt no heat, or touch, or breath of air.

'I came to the small private garden behind the house. There was my prim wife, alone with her dying roses. Cynthia was obstinately convinced that she could make an English garden in that hellish climate. She would let no one help her. She said it took English hands to make an English garden.

'Something odd happened. A boy of fifteen or sixteen, a native, was there. He hadn't entered, nor had he materialized like some apparition. He was simply there. He stood among the roses as though he had been present all along, unnoticed. He was of the labouring class, barefoot and dressed in nothing but a cloth at his waist. Cynthia looked up from her hopeless pruning.

'She should have ordered him out. Instead she watched him without saying a word. Finally I noticed what he was about. He was lifting sickly blooms from where they drooped on the bush. But when he released a flower it didn't fall back. It was like a fakir's trickery. He appeared to be reviving them with his touch.

'Cynthia said nothing – only watched. From time to time he would look up from a flower to glance at her. His appearance was unusual. His eyes were not dark, but some indefinable pale colour, and were framed with long, womanly lashes. His hair was deep black, but instead of being straight, and cropped in the local manner, it was curly and fell in profusion over his forehead and ears. His skin was darker than one saw in our neighbourhood, and he was taller than was usual, particularly considering his youth.

'As I said, my hearing in this dream was acute. I noticed the sound of Cynthia's breathing, which had quickened, as though she had just run uphill.

'The boy left the flowers and came to her. He didn't make the slightest pretence of bowing. Had I been there in the flesh I should have whipped him myself on the spot. He leaned forward on his tiptoes like a French dancer and whispered in her ear. I was, to my perception, twenty paces away and yet I heard all that he said.'

(Here the colonel repeated the appalling words, a graphically explicit invitation – more a threat, really – to engage with Mrs Burgess in a number of carnal acts and perversions.)

'Cynthia was holding a trowel. It might have made a good weapon, but I had no expectation of seeing her draw blood. I hoped she might scream, but feared she would fall into a weeping collapse. Her face, and even her forearms, were flushed, a deep pink almost like her favorite China roses.

'She dropped the trowel on the pebble walkway. I hoped she might raise an alarm. The boy reached out his hand and stroked her cheek. She was silent. His hand dropped to her breast. He stepped closer. Her breathing became shallow and dry. With his other hand he raised her skirts and reached beneath them . . . '

(I will not here repeat the colonel's description of the intimate liberties he saw the boy take with his wife.)

'At this she made, indeed, a little noise, but hardly any. Not enough. Her mouth was open, her eyes glazed. I thought surely that someone would come to rescue her. I myself, I thought, would rise up from my sleep in the chair and fly to the garden. But I found myself powerless to move even my incorporeal self, much less my body.

'Finally she twisted away from the little beggar. She stepped back from him with a wild look in her eye. Were it possible for a shade to sigh with relief, I should have done so. Run, I thought. Fly! The boy made no move to detain her. Still she did nothing to escape, but only looked around with a frantic expression as if unable to decide in which direction to flee.

'The boy began to turn from her. With a sudden movement she reached out and seized his arm with both hands and began to pull him along the path.

'They were soon out of sight among the hedges. I strained to follow them but was becalmed there above the garden. I heard the door of the potting shed open. Then, though it immediately closed again, I could hear them inside, every word they said, every sound they made.'

(In his dream Peter Burgess heard his wife produce every wanton noise of uninhibited coupling that his tortured imagination could counterfeit, and use the language of a drover to say things that would make a harlot blush.)

'All the while they were in there, and it was an impossibly long time, I was trapped in that hell of a garden, listening. The boy seemed inexhaustible, my wife insatiable. He had whispered to her that he

was the god of love, and it was with the capacity of a god of love that
he performed. Finally there was a long period of silence. After a time
I could see Cynthia walking back on the path alone. She drifted
through the garden, dishevelled, smiling. She noticed the trowel on
the path and stooped to pick it up. A moment later she entered the
house by the garden porch.

'Still I hung there like a dead grouse ripening on a hook. I know not
how much time passed. Then, in an instant, I was awake in my chair.
I was ready to dash to the garden – odd now to think of leaping from a
chair and dashing anywhere – when I heard a rapping at the door and
Cynthia put her head in.

'I'm sure I stared at her wildly, but she didn't notice. "Peter,
remember it's Mr Phipps and his committee for dinner tonight, so
please make up your mind now not to be grumpy or I shall be quite
put out." She was gone before I could say a word. But gone also was
the foul dream, for there was my wife – so very, very far from being
the wanton – in the flesh and zealous that I should behave myself at
dinner with the impossible missionary and his squadron of
meddlers.

'How foolish I was that afternoon. How quickly I banished the
pain of that dream. It was as soon as that night that I had further
intimations of troubles. As I prepared for bed, I thought it appropriate somehow that if the phantom of my wife had been so eager that
afternoon, I should visit Cynthia's *boudoir*. I amused myself by
imagining that I had been the recipient of a message from Cupid
announcing a change in my too well-mannered, too decorous
partner. A message of hitherto absent ardour.'

Once again the colonel turned his eye on me, then addressed the
window in a voice ever more distant.

'But it was in myself that the ardour was lacking. This was a thing
that had never happened to me. I had been ever a man of . . . ready
passion. But there I found myself as unready as any failing dotard
who ever disgraced himself by pretending to the capacities of a bull,
only to display the virility of a calf. Cynthia's bedclothes were not
disordered that night, unless by some restlessness of her own.'

He paused as though he had lost his train of thought.

'Nor have I disordered hers, or any other woman's, since that day.'
He hesitated, then went on in a voice not much above a whisper.

'I have lacked both the desire . . . and the ability.'

With this confession the poor man desired that day's visit to
conclude. I think he felt a certain relief at having so unburdened
himself, but was not prepared to, as he must have thought it, shame

himself further.

I must look into these matters — read further in the Viennese *doktors*. How can Peter Burgess look at his wife, who could serve as a painter's model for a sultry *odalisque*, and see a 'presentable girl' of no particular distinction? In these private pages, and only to emphasize how odd I find his perception, I shall be so bold as to say that even his distorted dream-vision of Cynthia Burgess as a shameless wanton fits, in caricature, his air and appearance better than his waking one. It may be that *Herr* what's-his-name is after all correct about sex.

And as to the gain in weight, can it be that the mind can find a way to create flesh without fuel? If so, then how has anyone starved? Or can my patient be so madly resolute to make himself physically into what he feels his inner self to be (if this speculation of mine be correct) that he is indulging in secret feasts that no one has detected? I must put it to the corporal that we shall entirely satisfy ourselves on this matter. I wish not to engage with demons if my adversary is the pastry baker.

September 23rd, 1911

Still it rains. It seems the music of my nights is ever the rain against the window and the scratch of the pen. But this is London, and I a Londoner, formed by Nature to endure fogs and rain.

This morning before I saw the colonel, I sought out Cynthia Burgess. To see the colonel's 'plain English girl' dressed for the bedroom! Perhaps I must look to his eyesight. I think myself a chaste and sober man, but Cynthia Burgess seems to radiate a sensuality that is all but suffocating. I enter her chamber with the innocent intention of discussing her husband's diet and my eye is drawn to the lace of her gown, my thoughts to the rising bosom beneath it. I say — confess — this to emphasize once more that she is a woman of potent charms, not at all the *lassie* her husband sees.

I cannot help but muse: what if a man — one who prized his virility, his manliness — brought to his bed a chaste and virginal bride who, within the sanctified bounds of marriage, proved an adept, and an athlete, of lovemaking? What if he found himself overpowered — a Phaëthon at the reins, thinking to drive, and pulled headlong? And if he denied this to himself, recast reality into a form radically altered, but more to his liking, might reality not, banished from his waking hours, find its way into his dreams, to torture him with symbolic representations of the thing that he denies?

But if I am to make such diagnoses, I must move to Vienna. And if I can thus account for dreams, how shall I account for twenty-five stones?

Today I was told of further dreams. Their erotic nature seems lost on the colonel; he narrates them with no passion save that of a man being robbed, as though his goods were being carried off before his eyes. I, however, am not indifferent to the pictures his words paint. How am I to look upon this lady again, now I have these images in my mind?

'By the time the second dream came,' he began, 'I had noticed my increase in girth. I altered my diet, meaning to wear my clothes tight until I returned to my normal size. From time to time in the afternoons I would go to the window above the rose garden and observe my wife there at her solitary labours. Then one day I found myself in the garden as before, present there as a wandering spirit while my body slept upstairs.

'The boy appeared. Cynthia noticed him at once and ran to him eagerly.'

(The colonel described in embarrassing detail the shameless fondlings and eager importunings with which his wife greeted her lover. They left his sight and conducted themselves as they had on the first occasion.)

'The visits became more frequent, and soon were daily. Every day my spirit was trapped in the garden and my body in whatever place the sleep overtook me. All my duties I had delegated. I stayed entirely at home. I had gained over two stone, and changed my wardrobe twice. I had begun to make plans for our return to England.

'Then one day he came to her in the house. In my disembodied state I saw him walking through the upper hallways. His eye fell on the spot that I seemed to, but did not occupy. He made a careless gesture in my direction and I was drawn irresistibly in his wake until we both, wraith and lover, stood in Cynthia's bedroom. From that day forth I had to watch as well as listen. And my wife did things willingly, eagerly, that no woman, not even my little heathen of a housegirl, had ever done for me.'

(If the postures and practices described by the colonel were startling in their ingenious wickedness, more shocking still was the matter of Savi, a village girl employed in his house. He had forced her to be his paid concubine, which he explained with no sense of shame or contrition. After telling me of his sinful behaviour with her, he mentioned almost casually that he had had her whipped and turned out of the house for the crime of daring to protest her situation. How am I to listen to him with sympathy?)

'This then went on week after week until we finally left. I was growing ever fatter, the wife I spied on ever more depraved. I even began to see the dream-Cynthia in her when I was awake. It was as though she were being remade in the image of the wanton I had so intimately observed. It became painful for me to look at her.

'On the day before we sailed he came to her one last time, this potent boy. I watched them, as always without the power to look away. She, my Cynthia in form, in actions a rutting beast, was belly-down on the bed, clutching wildly at the counterpane in a transport of lust. Her lover, in contrast, was a study in calm. In the past he had been indefatigable but also active and enthusiastic. Now his expression was one of detachment, as if he were performing some routine chore. His eyes were on her body, her helpless contortions, but showed no more passion than might be raised by a view of the frenzied copulation of a pair of insects.

As I watched, his form slowly began to change. His pretty, boyish features were marred by alterations that at first were only slight. He seemed to grow larger. The change accelerated. He became horrid, a devil or monster like the creatures of my dreams at night. His teeth now were fangs, his fingers claws. And yet in this demonic form, swollen and grotesque, could still be traced the likeness of the boy. As my wife writhed and pressed herself back against him, crying out from pleasure, he laid a clawed hand on her twisting buttocks and drew it downward to where her thighs strained and quivered, cutting into the white flesh and leaving four thin trails of blood. She screamed, and thrashed convulsively, more caught in passion than ever before in these couplings, then finally fell unconscious, sprawled naked on the bed. She lay as though dead. The boy, no more a monster, withdrew himself from her, and then was gone. I have never seen him again.'

Colonel Burgess turned to face me, to address me directly.

'And you, doctor, I see are shocked at my talk of the housegirl.' He shook his head indignantly. 'The natives!' he spat. 'They're dirty, these people, and they have no moral sense at all. My gifts of money to that girl were keeping her family from starvation, as she told me repeatedly. She was shameless in her efforts to play upon my sympathy. I can tell you, sir, I was good to her – better than she deserved. I treated her well until she broke faith.'

Although my policy was to say as little as possible, I could not forbear to ask precisely in what manner she had transgressed. The colonel sputtered and swore, became very nearly incoherent. The

burden of his angry narrative was that the girl – one can only imagine
a helpless and frightened maid – had gone to the leader of a local
religious cult with the unhappy story of her situation.

'But that disloyal and ungrateful wench paid for her faithlessness.
She stumbled from our gates naked, clutching her rags, with welts
down her back that won't quickly fade. And the fakir – the little
brown beggar had the gall to confront me – he sits in a cell to this day
unless some meddling government man has set him loose.'

Colonel Burgess sat in his oversize chair with his jaw set, an
expression of stubborn implacability on his bloated features. To his
mind he had described a scandalous wrong, not against the villagers
he oppressed, but against himself. It is impossible to imagine an
attitude more obtusely self-righteous. Equally, it is perhaps not
impossible, but difficult, to imagine that his ills stem in any way
from a deeply hidden sense of guilt.

But though my patient be contemptible, his history despicable, as
his physician, my principal concern is with his recovery.
Accordingly, I refrained from taxing him with his infamous behaviour. I kept my expression neutral and waited for him to
continue. When he had regained his composure, he went on with his
narrative.

'For the first week of our voyage I was seized by no afternoon
dreams. I began to have hope that they had been left behind in that
tropical hell.

'My optimism was unjustified. One day as I dozed in a deck chair, I
found myself once more a disembodied observer. I watched Cynthia
in the passageway outside our cabin discussing the day's menu with
the black man that brought us our meals. As she spoke, she stared
into his eyes. Her voice was most unlike the one I know. It fondled
the ear. When she moved closer to the servant, he closed his eyes as
though overcome by dizziness. At her command he followed her
into her cabin. Unbidden and unwilling, I followed as well.

'With irresistible caresses she aroused him, though he was at the
same time fearful and reticent. She undressed herself and then him.
They lay together and practised every lascivious excess that
depravity could encourage, ceasing, she most unwillingly, only
when the man was spent.'

(As was his usual practice, the colonel was explicit in his
descriptions. I am glad today has seen the end of these disturbing
recitals.)

'Every day thereafter she had her eager nigger, I my unwelcome
visions. Yet at meals this same man served us. I have wondered

sometimes if I might be watching, not visions, but reality, but his demeanour convinced me, as my wife's has from that first day, that these dreams are counterfeits. He could not be her daily partner in these lewd tumblings and then humbly pour my wine at dinner with never a glance to betray him. An ignorant darky could never be so subtle. He could lie, of course; all the lower races can, but they lack the intellect for sustained duplicity.'

He turned to me. 'Since I have been under your care, I have had no more of this torture. Now my dreams torment me only at night. And they are but frights and phantoms, menacing images, demonic visages.' He closed his eyes. 'The little ones are the worst – hiding, waiting in the mist. They whisper gruesome promises through their small sharp teeth. They taunt me.' He sneered down at his bulging flesh. 'I am being fattened, they say, for a horrid feast.'

When Colonel Burgess had finished, I left him. He finds these narratives taxing. From that he can recover, but how shall I regain my sympathy for him, now he is revealed a brutal tyrant? It is well that tomorrow I visit friends in the country, and see him not at all.

October 1st, 1911

For this past week there are no entries for this private journal. The colonel has gained less weight, but such fluctuations are to be expected. Two days from now he visits the scale again.

Cynthia Burgess has this week shown an unprecedented interest in my treatment of her husband. A number of times I have found her waiting for me in the hallway outside the colonel's room. I think she has begun to lose hope. In her face sometimes I can, if she is standing near me, read a look of agitation, almost desperation. How I wish there were something I might do to bring comfort to this unhappy lady!

October 3rd, 1911

Through no skill or efforts of my own, Colonel Burgess has ceased, for the moment, to gain weight. He credits my care, and the exercise he gets each night in walking. Two things I wish: that I knew less of this man, so that I could more unreservedly wish him well, and that I did not fear the scale will disappoint him next week. I tried to caution him against hoping too much.

But when I left the office a few minutes behind the colonel and the corporal, I saw he had dismissed his waiting cab. Down the deserted street I could see them, a man and a rotund parody of a man, strolling as two gentlemen might on a sunny day, except that it was after midnight.

Had I been going their way I might have caught them easily, but I followed them just to the first crossing. For a few minutes I stood there, looking after them in the lonely night. The only other souls abroad were a band of children wrapped in hooded cloaks – Gypsies, they must have been, doubtless bent on thievery or other mischief. Before turning toward home, I watched them as they seemed almost to evaporate into the shadows of a foggy lane.

October 4th, 1911

Today I hoped to find Cynthia Burgess cheered. My cautions to the contrary, the scale last night had yielded a hopeful sign.

She shook her head, I cannot say if sadly – her slight smile was impossible to read.

'The curse has not been lifted,' she said.

'Really, Madam,' I said, somewhat startled. 'Your metaphor is too gloomy. Your husband's illness . . .'

'I was not speaking metaphorically, Doctor. I refer to the curse the fakir warned him of.'

I said nothing. Evidently my expression was eloquent.

'Of course,' she said with the same unreadable smile on her lips. 'My husband has said nothing of this, then?'

'Yes, yes,' said the colonel when I pressed him. 'That imbecile Phipps brought me the fakir's impudent message. He had been to the prison to "bring the message of Christ to those poor wretches", as he put it. "Inhuman conditions," he said to me, speaking, mind you, of a gaol – a place of punishment. He was a most unthinking man, even for a missionary.

'The fakir told him that a curse had been laid on me. Phipps hemmed and hawed but finally found a way to put it that didn't compromise his clerical dignity. My "dealings" with the housegirl, as well as my harshness with the fakir, had attracted the attention of the local gods – some damnable hair-and-wicker deities in a stinking hut, you see – and they had marked me for revenge. They would infect my life with torment, then set their harpies on me. And Phipps, a man of God, gave every evidence of being taken in. He began to maunder on about "mysteries" and "unusual occurrences".'

The colonel fixed me with an outraged stare, as though he suspected I might be as foolishly credulous as the Reverend Mr Phipps.

'It is utter rubbish!' he cried with great vehemence, turning crimson with emotion. 'The fakir is just an insignificant little wog. I swatted him as I might a fly. He has no power over me. I was the law in that filthy place. I was a curse to him, yes! He is nothing to me. Nor are his gods.' He gritted his teeth and trembled visibly with anger. 'I am not one of his ignorant heathen villagers. I am a Christian,' he spat, 'and a civilized man!'

As soon as I had assured myself that my patient was not going to die, just then, of apoplexy, I left him, unable to bear his company any longer.

What am I now to think? I have known the colonel is unbalanced, I know now that he is cruel and has been vicious, but can he be so stupid? This curse that he despises is as efficacious in him as it would be in the fakir's most credulous parishioner. I resist the idea, but hiding somewhere deep inside that corrupt man must be a conscience. And that conscience is visiting on him a punishment that would satisfy the fakir's gods and move an enemy to pity.

October 5th, 1911

My patient is intransigent. In his view – and it is not too much to say he cherishes it – he is ill, suffering from a physical complaint, which has begun to respond to the ministrations of a proper English physician.

I did not lay before him the theory I have developed in my midnight ponderings. I merely alluded, most obliquely, to the subject of non-physical causes for seemingly physical ailments.

I need not have been so subtle. The colonel has a talent, if not a genius, for not recognizing views that oppose his own. It is as though they have no existence. And since that which lies unexamined lacks the occasion to be found inexplicable, he is not puzzled by his impossible gain of weight, his preternatural dreams. In his view they are no more a mystery than a fever and the delirium that accompanies it.

I did not trouble him long today, and was not pressed to stay. He is satisfied I have cured him. I even fancied I saw some change in his demeanour. It is as if looks forward to a day soon when he will be again as he was and have no need of an unknown physician of unfashionable address.

I should upbraid myself for entertaining such a cynical and uncharitable view, if I did not know so much to the man's discredit.

Tomorrow I shall see him not at all. We have arranged that I shall attend his wife, who has asked me to examine her for some unspecified complaint, I should suppose fatigue and perhaps a hint of melancholia. So now I am to have some degree of intimacy with the *femme fatale* of whom I have written in such extravagant terms. I shall stand closer to her than a dancing partner and look into her eyes. I shall touch her, put my ear to her bosom, and hear at length the voice that, as the colonel put it, fondles the ear — but he was speaking of the phantom Mrs Burgess.

And all this will mean no more to me than if I were having a similar *rendez-vous* with the lady's grandmother. My professional detachment will assert itself. Unless she is suffering from something of which I am unaware, she will be fully clothed. But were it necessary for her to remove every stitch of clothing, I should see before me, not an undraped beauty, but a patient.

October 9th, 1911

A hundred times in the past days I have restrained the impulse to throw this accursed journal into the fire. But I am determined I shall complete this painful record, if only to prove to myself that I have not entirely lost the capacity for responsible action.

I have brought my treatment of Colonel Peter Burgess to a conclusion. He is dead.

His physician did not kill him. It would be melodramatic to put it so. But I cannot disguise from myself the fact that his torment was increased and his end hastened by my sinful weakness.

It is four days since my last fatuous and *naïve* entry in these pages. It seems four years — it seems yesterday. Yet what has happened . . . No. I delay.

I arrived at the appointed hour for my examination of Cynthia Burgess. Though it was mid-afternoon, she wore a nightgown. I know not at all what she spoke of in those first minutes. I am certain I uttered no word. My memory is filled with the intoxication of her presence. Her sexuality enveloped me. My ardent imagination was beneath the silk of her gown before she had closed her bedroom door behind us. As for my 'professional detachment', it manifested itself as a suffocating shortness of breath, a generalized trembling, and an inability to pull my eyes from my patient. In those moments before my powers of rational thought deserted me, I was frantically wondering how I might disguise my condition from Mrs Burgess and conduct my medical errand, and what my reaction might be if that errand entailed opening her gown.

Her voice was a caress. For all the sense I took from them, her words could have been Turkish, or Formosan. She stepped close to me, then closer still. I remember her moist, parted lips, her half-closed eyes. When she raised her arms to embrace me, her gown fell open. From then my memory is of sensation – sight, smell, touch, taste and flooding ecstasy.

Our strivings, at times almost combative, lengthened finally beyond my endurance. I slept, only to be awakened with my lover astride me. Her intensity was punishing – frightening – as was the fervour of my spontaneous and unwilled response. Later, frenzy abated, we touched and kissed luxuriously. My hand caressed the back of her thigh, then rose. It must have lain a dozen times before on the spot that now caught my attention. Alone of all her silk-smooth skin this was rough. She squirmed against me at my touch. I pulled her unresisting body over until she lay sprawled face down on the bed. With my fingers I traced across the mesmerizing curve of her *derriére* the path of four thin scars that descended to meet her thigh.

It was late when I stumbled into the hallway from her room. I glanced at the colonel's door at the end of the hall, then quietly descended the stairs and stole from the house like a bishop leaving a brothel. My capacity for sensation had been exhausted. A man emerging from an opium cellar could not have been more numbed and stupid. I walked to the corner and crossed the small square. My coat was open and hung on my shoulders but I did not feel the cold; a tropical heat surrounded my body. A cabby cursed me as I nearly stepped into the path of his horse. Safely on the far pavement, I leaned against the cold granite of the corner house and stared back across the distance I had crossed as though it were a desert in lonely Araby.

I must have stood so for a long time. I recall a series of distinct images: a noisy, swaying hansom with the pale elfin face of a child framed in the window; a trudging workman shorter than I by a head, with a dirty, lumpy cap that precisely matched his dirty, lumpy face; a brilliant moon bisected by a spire; a patch of fog incongruous on a dry October night.

My reverie, or stupor, was broken when the colonel stepped from his house. He was alone. He did not bother to close the door behind him. As he descended the few stairs to the street it gaped behind him like an open mouth. When he reached the corner he looked across the square and saw me. We stared at one another like two souls across the Styx. He stood motionless, his eye fixed on me, then abruptly turned and walked away in haste, diminishing into the narrowing distance. I looked back to the open door, then to the other end of the street. A band of Gypsy children – judging by their dress, the same I had seen near my office a week before – were slinking through the shreds of thinning fog.

In my rooms I sipped whisky slowly and without conscious thought until I fell into a dreamless sleep that held me until nearly noon. I awoke sore and stiff. My back was striped like a flagellant's from the scrapes and cuts of my lover's nails.

In those first minutes my thoughts were two. I was ravenously hungry and I burned for my lover's body, her whispers, her bites, her frantic embraces. I was half dressed before a thought of her husband, my patient, entered my consciousness. I saw the image of haunted eyes across the square. He knew! He had seen us. I was convinced at once that in some way he had been an observer to all those long hours of lust. I thought of the four thin scars that I had first heard of from him, and that yesterday I had seen for myself. A devil had made them, or a god. This was beyond the limits of my credulity. But if I were willing to grant that Peter Burgess could see things that occurred not in his presence, what might I not come to believe?

'First, do no harm.' What harm had I done? And what good could I hope now to do? I finished dressing with great carelessness and left my rooms. What course to take? I dared not enter the Burgess house. Not for fear of the colonel, but of his wife. I had sinned, indeed, but in ignorance and weakness. If I went there now, and if I fell again, I should be guilty not of being overcome by sin, but of pursuing it.

I stopped in the street and steadied myself against a lamppost. It seemed that the reality before my eyes was being replaced by the image of Cynthia Burgess. I could taste her lips, feel the heat of her. After a moment I proceeded down the street. At the inn at the corner I had a half-pint of ale, followed by the most substantial feast they could offer. It was while I lingered over coffee, still trying to formulate some plan of action, that I learned of the fate of my patient.

According to the newspaper his body, what remained of it, had been found in a deserted lane. It was supposed that he must have been attacked by a large and starving pack of feral dogs. No other explanation could account for his condition. The only mystery was that while most of the flesh had been torn from his body, none of his bones had been broken. On some there were marks of teeth, but as they were too small to have been left by dogs, they were presumed to be evidence of the rats that must have followed.

The rest of the day I wandered the streets, ostensibly on my way to the Burgess residence. I never arrived. I drank as many pints as I could, distributing such money as I had by me to the publicans whose establishments were located on streets that might have led me to my putative destination. I was forced, late in the day, to return to my rooms by cab. I was too intoxicated to be a respectable pedestrian, but not so intoxicated that I didn't care. The cabman was kind enough to make a purchase of whisky for me and deliver it to my door. It wouldn't do, I thought, to find myself with an empty bottle.

It was not until the next afternoon that I finally made my way to the dreaded house. A carriage loaded with trunks waited at the door, which was open, as it had been when I last saw it. I was at the bottom of the steps when Cynthia Burgess emerged. She nodded to me as she handed a parcel to the driver.

I was speechless. This was the Cynthia Burgess I had been acquainted with for these past weeks, of whose charms and beauty I had written, and with whom I had shared those hours of unholy passion. This was she, and yet it was not, for it was also the colonel's ordinary English girl, not unattractive, but not the *houri* that had ensorcelled me.

I thought she would leave without noticing me more, but she turned after talking to the driver. Her manner was of one whose composure is bought with some effort. She thanked me for my services to her late husband. I am afraid I made no reply. Her flat Sussex voice rattled in my ear. She raised her eyes to mine; they matched her voice. I looked her up and down and saw — a presentable young woman of no particular distinction. My stare was discourteous, I am sure, but beyond my control. A bit of colour rose to her cheek and did not transform her. I managed a few words of condolence and helped her into the carriage without fear that her touch would inflame me.

Since then I have attempted to sort out in my mind what really occurred in that house. That colonel Burgess was unbalanced cannot be doubted. But what of his wife, and his physician? Was it she who was mad, or I — or both of us? Was I her victim, or she mine? Did she project the bewitching image I have described, or did some hysterical madness of mine imbue her with it?

One thing only is certain: the fakir's curse could not have been more deadly if the gods he served were real. Colonel Burgess has met an end as horrible as any band of devils could bring him. His widow has been encumbered with a lurid and shameful memory – perhaps many. As for me, both my self-respect and my confidence in my reason have been undermined. When, if ever, will my lover cease to inhabit my thoughts? I can feel her touch, hear her urgent cries. If passion can so seize us and shake us, of what use then is intellect, piety, philosophy? I have met my animal nature as never before, and cannot think myself its master. To what excesses may I next be led? With what force of will or shield of faith shall I resist?

What need for demons when we have ourselves?

From my window I see that again the night is cloaked in mist. But damp and chill notwithstanding, I shall walk awhile in the quiet lanes. To hope for sleep is to hope for too much. And even if sleep would come, I might choose rather to walk and think, than to sleep and dream. I mean to worry out the night, and hope that morning will bring a better day.

THE CAREFUL GEOMETRY
OF LOVE

by

Kathe Koja and Barry N. Malzberg

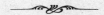

Kathe Koja and Barry N. Malzberg have been collaborating since 1992; their work includes a novel and twenty-five to thirty short stories which have been or will be published in *Omni* Magazine, *Alternate Outlaws*, *Dinosaur Fantastic*, *Off Limits: Alien Sex 2*, and other anthologies.

A story about the artistic process enabling the artist to let go, 'The Careful Geometry of Love' perfectly melds Koja's and Malzberg's individual writing styles into a new entity.

THE CAREFUL GEOMETRY OF LOVE

She paid him well; this was not the most important thing, but it mattered a hell of a lot. She paid up front and with a cashier's cheque and a smile. She had a beautiful smile; she was a beautiful woman but that in the end mattered less than he would have expected if he had met her, say, on the street, in a bar, at someone else's party at which he would have taken her hand, not to shake it but to hold it, squeeze it maybe lightly between his own considering fingers, smell that smell she seemed not to wear so much as exude. Exude: was that the word? Put out, yes, a smell warm and faintly fruity or perhaps not fruity so much as purely fecund, the smell of something growing, moist and flavoured in the soft recesses, the folds and peaks and gullies of her flesh and of her skin.

He did not want particularly to fuck her which was also a surprise but not as big a surprise as it would have been ten years ago, fifteen; he did however want to see her naked, wanted that very much indeed, but without the simple hunger of prurience, that old and easy, cavalier lust with which he lusted for others: women he knew, women he saw on the street, women he would never know; that beautiful girl he saw sometimes at the fruit market, always hoping she would be squeezing mangoes, pouting at the bananas on the scale, murmuring to herself. Her he would never see naked either, but with her it seemed more of a loss than with Elaine; that was her name, Elaine, in her suits and with her smells, sliding out the cashier's cheque and saying, with that faint smile, *Now this is what I want, David, this is what I want you to do.*

It was not easy, exactly, but neither was it difficult; she had her wishes and her wants, she knew exactly what she expected to receive and he tried, always, to give it to her: he was a professional, after all, and she was a client, a demanding client but a good one, a valued one; you wouldn't believe, he had told her once, some of the things I have to do, you wouldn't believe me if I told you.

I'm a realtor, she said, smiling. I know what it is, working with people. People are shits.

It isn't just that, he said (although it was in some cases): it's what they *want*. Make me look beautiful, make me look young. For God's sake, this is a woman sixty-eight years old with thirteen grandchildren and tits down to the floor, make me look young she says. Who am I, Merlin the Magician?

So what do you do? she had said then, amused, her purse snapping closed with a muffled, velvet sound, the applause of gloved hands. What did you do for her?

His shrug, the cashier's cheque already disappeared; he knew how to handle the money, knew how to minimize its importance in the larger dance of transaction; it was all transaction from the minute they made the appointment, it was the selling and the buying of pictures, images, not even dreams but the *idea* of dreams; make me look young. I did what she wanted, he said to Elaine. I gave her what she asked for.

You're good at that, she said, her smile transmuting into something warmer. You're very very good.

Thanks, he said and the toilet flushed, running water and out of the bathroom his subject, her object, her boy: nineteen years old, too dumb to run loose, zipping up his pants like he expected to be praised and she linked long fingers with him smiled; smiled. Thank you, she said, already gone, thanks very much.

We'll be talking, he said, but she was not paying full attention; full price was all he was going to get and it was certainly enough, she never haggled, she never bitched or complained even if they had to reshoot, even if they had to do two or three sessions. It's worth it to me, she had told him at their first meeting, I know what I want and I don't mind paying for it.

Tell me what you want. Tell me exactly what you expect so I can —

I want pictures of them, she said. Naked. As beautiful as you can make them but don't retouch, don't use an airbrush; I want to see everything, see them exactly as they are.

Warts and all, he said, smiling, right?

Warts and all, she said. Although most of them won't have any, most of them are too beautiful even to be models; you'll see, she told him, and he had.

And she was right: they were beautiful, a long string of beautiful boys, men, women: mostly men but she had what she called with some humour her Oestrogen Period, four women very different but all so lovely that he had been able to make exceptional pictures, incredible photographs so heartbreaking and so lush that even he had been astonished; he knew he was good, very good and he charged accordingly, but these pictures were something else; you're going to like these, he had told her, and she had. The cashier's cheque, the smile; and a month, six weeks later another appointment, another shoot; another cheque.

Where she found them, he found he was not interested, in fact it might have ruined it for him, make her something less in his eyes, less of a collector, more of a – what? If she were a man he would have known what to call her, but as it was he found it better to admire it all impersonally, the beautiful women, the beautiful men and boys: like that last one, another nineteen year old with a big dreamy smile and hair cut short as a child's, a child fresh from his first trip to the barber's: standing less coy than truly modest, it had been somewhat of a struggle to get him to take off his clothes, all of his clothes, but in the end Elaine had prevailed: with a smile of her own, not gentle but soft, soft; soft as the tip of a finger, or a nipple, of the first brush of alien skin, and the boy had given in, abashed, more beautiful than ever: and Elaine had smiled and smiled, truly pleased as if he had given her a gift impossible from anyone else, the one gift she wanted more than anything in the world.

Some of them would not take off their clothes, no matter how she smiled; but for those it did not seem truly to matter to her, she even warned him about it beforehand: 'He won't do it,' she would say, or 'Forget it, don't even ask. Just use jeans or whatever he shows up in, I told him something casual, wear something you would wear to the park.' It was not, he knew, the nudity that was important to her; although she obviously preferred it, in the end it was not what she was after.

He did not know what she was after; he had no trouble admitting it, to himself, to her when he got to know her better: after a year he knew her very well indeed, she was making the payments on his studio with those regular cashier's cheques. They would talk, sometimes, after the appointment was set, he would fix her coffee, espresso, wine in thin exquisite glasses, the best he had; for her it would have to be the best he had. Drink wine and talk, her fingers on the dark stem of the glass, her long legs crossed at the knee, her head lightly to one side as if tilted by the pleasing weight of her opinions.

Subtle, she was very subtle and he was too, with her; he did not ask flat out; he did not ask at all. Subtle and sipping wine, talking about her job – she liked to talk about her job, she loved selling real estate, she said it was the best game she had ever played and the money she made, oh the money; she never discussed figures or gave amounts but if she could afford to pay him what she was paying, if those amounts were expendable at the rate that they arrived (and they were), why then she was making a very great deal of money, more money probably than he would ever see, but it was not, she said, the money that mattered.

I'm serious, she said; and she was. I would do it for half that, one-tenth that. The money's just a counter, like chips when you play cards, like when you played when you were kids. What matters to me is the game.

I know what you mean, he said, and he did; the money, the cashier's cheques did not in the end matter to him either (except as solid bricks in the bottom line, of course, where it all mattered more than anything else). What was important was the light, the way it touched a face, an arm, the curve of a breast, the pensive droop of a scrotum, the motion of light and the varieties of situations, postures, and uses to which it could be subjected; the subjects to which it could be put and he tried to explain that, all that, got tangled up in metaphor and theory and shrugged, finally, palms up and said I don't know how to say what I mean, I can't tell you what I mean but I think you know, already; I think you already know.

I know, she said. It's the same for me. It's partially why I want the pictures; partially. Some of it is (and a smile that included him, drew him in, wrapped him up) that they're just so *beautiful*, you know.

I know, he said; because they were.

And part of it . . . well. Naked pictures, and she smiled, they both smiled at the way she said it, the faint face she pulled to summon the spectre of ugly slutty polaroids, transitory snapshots that by their very nature (not to say existence) proclaimed both proclivity and taste for the one-night stand, the anonymous, the cheap; when all of this was none of that, this was on another level entirely and having said that she had somehow said everything, defining what it was by saying what it was not.

And: wine drunk in one last amber swallow, rising up with that grace (how he would have liked to photograph her; but he knew better than ever to ask) and that smile, a dark blue suit today and very high heels, she loved to wear high heels, she had the legs for it. And saying, I'll see you soon, then, and Yes, he said, next Tuesday. At one.

See you then, she said.

And she did.

This one was not so beautiful; surprising, but exhilarating somehow to find that it was so. A young man, maybe twenty-five or six, thick muscles, long equine face with a big fat prizefighter's nose and hair that could have used a washing, maybe a couple of washings; but there was great interest in that face, it was wonderful in certain kinds of light and he made the most of it, he went through four extra rolls of film, all those exposures just to get that face in that light. Afterwards he was pleased, deeply pleased and so was she when she came to see him, turning the contact sheet to the light: and smiling in the motion, in the turning of her head.

These are wonderful, she said.

Yeah; smiling, he knew what he had there, that handsome ugly face with the bricklayer's body, that big nose and all that light: he could have been a Rodin there, some crude rich stone beaten by sweat and genius into shape; into posture; into pose, in all that light. Yeah, he said, they are.

It was a longer wait till the next time, almost three months; but there had been fallow times before, he was not worried. She always came back. And did, this time with an older man, greying and somewhat soft in black T-shirt and tailored black pants, but when he took off his clothes something happened, he got bigger somehow, more muscular: uglier: meaner with a pure aggressive meanness captured like a beast in a clever cage by the camera, silver print, black and white and – Oh he's something else, she said, smiling, touching the contact sheet with the tips of her fingers, long fingers, long nails polished to a pallor more interesting than mere colour could have been; he's a real minotaur, that one.

Where'd you find him? he wanted to say but of course did not, it was none of his business anyway and anyway he was getting some amazing work done, very possibly his best ever; beside the cheques and he ought to be grateful, who cared where she found him, them, any of them. She had her tastes and her methods; let her choose. It was none of his business anyway.

Another wait, even longer this time and then she brought to his studio a man in a long coat, long blond hair to the middle of his back and past the shoal of the hair something small and peculiar: a tiny little knob of flesh growing directly from the back of his spine: like a tail, or part of a fin. Vestigial, the word swam beneath him, his directions, his requests: turn towards me, he said, that's right. Look a little to the left; a little more; too much, turn back. Okay, good.

Okay and the sound of the camera, the artificial burn of the lights and the little tail, hump, stump was present in every picture, she had stipulated that, she wanted it that way: and in the end asked for prints that showed the tail most closely, with the most pale and excruciating detail; he imagined he saw a faint corruption in her smile, a kind of sly excitement as she handed back the contact sheet, a voluptuousity in the way she left the room that excited him in some manner that he wished neither to understand nor explore; so she's into freaks now, he told himself, meticulous as always to mark the date, time, number of prints to be made from the shoot. So what, what does it matter. She doesn't put a gun to anybody's head, including mine.

Two weeks, four, six; six months and he was getting worried, really worried now: she had not called, she had left no message, nothing. He was busy, it was not as if he missed the money (although he did); wondering, anxious above the moving hands in the dark-room, competent hands, competently making appointments, taking orders for prints from other, less idiosyncratic clients, straight boudoir photography; make me look young. Get the breasts up, show the black against pink, make the deadly and half-exposed ridges of bone decay into my desire. But where is she? standing staring through the camera at a man and woman, both in their late forties, glossed and primped and nearly naked, dressed like cherubim with scarves across their loins as they grinned at the camera in the sheer exhilaration of their audacity and mutual lust, as they grappled and clamped one another, as they sweated and squirmed the way they would giggle and joke when they arrived, in a day or two, to look at the contact sheet, to select the prints; where is she? with the cable release in hand, finger on its tiny trigger, its minute metal proboscis. Where is she, what is she doing; who is she seeing now? At length he used the telephone, the number she had given him, helplessly addressed the metallic tone of the answering machine, the call he had said he would never make. I'm concerned, he said, and gave his name, I haven't heard in so long, I wanted to know that you were all right. Are you all right? he said and had no time because of all his pauses to leave his number at the beep and so had to call again to get it in and this time she picked it up.

Why? she said. Why are you calling? Her voice was different on the telephone, just as flesh refracted through the lens was not the common flesh beheld; over the phone she sounded older and remote in ways he could not have defined. If I had wanted to come over there, she said, I would have come over. What do you want?

I want to see you, he said. She knew perfectly well what he wanted, always had, no lies between them. And then what? she said. Do you think that this will make any difference? Do you think that the seeing is any different from the not seeing? What is there in your mind? There is nothing between us, she said, nothing at all, it was only business. I hadn't thought you were a fool but I should have known better. Shouldn't I? she said, or am I making the usual misjudgments? He did not know what to say to that. There was really nothing to say, that dreamy, hallucinate desire which he had felt with the camera afflicted him over the phone, would afflict him in bed with her, he knew, would leave him crouched and stupefied before her, an unmanned ape grinning crazily at mirrors and the pink scatter of her trivial bedclothing. All right, she said into the silence, perhaps gloating over his inarticulacy, perhaps embarrassed for it, trapped like him in the circumstantial moment she could not apprehend. I was about ready to call anyway, perhaps, she said. It's been a long time for a reason, but I want you to take more pictures if you can. These pictures will be different. I don't know if I can trust you, she said. That's why I didn't come to you; I am considering this and that and many things. What do you say? Are you ready to take the pictures and ask no questions? Because otherwise it is impossible. I will ask no questions, he said, I'm a professional. I run a studio, I'm a businessman. He heard the sound of her laughter, strident and focused in a way he could not fathom, pouring into his ear. Oh yes, she said, all of you are professionals. You are so serious. You are possessed by your roles. You ask no questions even when questions should be asked. I'll be there tomorrow, she said and he could not ask when because the connection was dead. He put down the telephone and wandered back into his studio looking at the photographs hanging on the walls, the dazzle of Hasselblad and Mamiya, the breasts and eyes and lips like lush fruit glimpsed through damp foliage glinting at him. He was at that moment absolutely devoid of thought, as wiped free of a stream-of-consciousness as if he had been one of those dismembered breasts gleaming in closeup from the high wall, he was as senseless as if he had been axed by some brutal visitor with an extra key and special plans. He wandered around the studio, trying to work out some agenda and realized only that he had none, that in some practical sense he had had no agenda all his life, it was all stimulus response, the reflex of the dead frog's leg twitching against the current. The current was his life, the dead twitch was himself and in that moment of insight he wanted to turn on the studio and sack it, begin to systematically wreck and dismember his studio as if it had been an enemy installation. He had fucked two hundred and fifty-five women over these last thirty-nine years (he had kept count and once a diary), he had accumulated a minor reputation and a gallery and a few showings and a bank account, but he realized in some essential sense he had gathered nothing to himself; it was the dead twitches of the dead leg which had carried him this far. Sleeping with no one, his life retracted to a perfect constancy of work and self-annihilation, he minimally cleaned the studio, ordered his equipment, ate dinner in a restaurant down the street, stayed in the studio until it was so late that it was almost the next day. Then he returned to his furnished apartment. He realized, not for the first time, but in a way which had never been more shocking, that he had no inner life, none whatsoever; he lived only on the screen of his reflectivity. The underground man had at least an underground; the invisible man had the clear and undefinable fact of his invisibility but the photographer had not even the stain of his own negatives, his own received and calculated image. He had constructed a life for himself composed of responses, composed of the vacant posturing of the camera toward received angles but there had been no sensibility in it, none whatsoever.

Perhaps she had recognized this. Perhaps this was part of the reason why she had chosen him and why she had brought her increasingly strange companions to his place, knowing that he would without comment submit to her desire and never afterward think about any of it. He did not know if it was the force of her contempt or perhaps the inference of her admiration which had so seized him, he only knew after hearing her on the telephone in her refractory guise that he had to see her again or die. Perhaps he was dead already and this was the slow unravelling of his life by other means.

The man with her was squat, short, more bestial, he thought, than Caliban, more of a primate than many species of monkeys, and the posture of the man, his motions as he had come in beside her, had not been human. Trustingly, this man held her hand, posed for her, posed for the photographer showing off the suit in which he was encased as if he were an animal model in some grotesque but sophisticated European production. She looked the same to him when she came in, but as he looked at her more intently her own posture seemed to shift, he could see levels of pain or perhaps it was vulnerability in her that he had never seen before and her hands were trembling. The short ape-like man seemed to have used her in ways which he could barely assess but inference seemed to come from the

stain of exhaustion which rose from her. Take his picture, she said to
him and then gestured toward the ape-like man, said something in a
language he could not understand and the man began to undress,
exposing his body to the harsh, stricken light of the exposed strobe.
Look at him, she said, I want you to see what I see. I want you to
know. Do you know? Staring at the ape-man he could see the
curvature of the arms, something not quite human, then the exposed
chest, the nipples sunk very deep, so small as to be nearly invisible
but with a hint of erection, then the collapsed wrinkled stomach, the
hair curling the navel. The penis was enormous and in the shadow it
cast over the scrotum he thought he could see three, perhaps four
testicles, then clawed feet as the shoes came off. Monsters. She was
escorting monsters, he thought, and for the first time it came clear to
him what she had been bringing here, what this studio might have
represented, what her true nature might be. The ape-man said
something in a slow, chittering language and she spoke back to him
in that same tongue, then gestured and the ape-man revolved
beneath the light. There were four testicles, he could see that clearly
now and as the ape-man slowly turned, the cleft of the buttocks,
revealed, seemed to be springing flowers. Slowly he brought the
tripod to position, the camera to his eye, focused and peered through
the aperture. In the glass the ape-man was enormous, solemn,
stricken with an attitude of reverence which he might never have
perceived other than in this taut focus. He began to take the pictures.
The ape-man froze into position, moved at her command, he took all
of one roll and then another, the strobe one socketing centre of felt
intensity. He knew that he had an erection but would not
acknowledge it. Nor would she, standing away from him, her
expression clean and light and bright, a cast reverence to match that
of her companion. Do you like it? she said to him, do you like what
you see? Do you like what he's doing? He did not know if she was
talking of the ape-man or his erection or her own posture and
commands; he did not know either if any of this mattered against the
spattering, received sounds of induction. Her breath was briefly
harsh and short, a squawk, then it was even again and the ape-man
was fondling his four hairy testicles in the intense light. That's
enough, she said, that's quite enough for now and he came from his
posturing and quite casually put on the coloured squares of clothing
which had been discarded. She watched the ape-man dressing and
then turned her gaze toward him and in those eyes it was as if he
could see not only himself but his coiled and damaged history, hers
too, all of their intimations and disasters conjoined in this one

specious and pointless moment. I'll come back, she said, I'll be back tomorrow. You understand now, don't you? You understand what I ask of you and what you must give?

Yes, he said, not understanding, but possessed of her urgency and feeling himself as well on the precipice of some insight which might come in time and which would, when at last infused, release him from his tormented and impractical history. Yes, I know what you want now, and she said something in that foreign language again and seized the ape-man by the arm and left the studio, saying nothing else at all. He supposed in the blaze of her exit that he might indeed have understood what she meant, not that he could put it into any language, foreign or not.

He printed the photographs, mounted them, placed them within the individual frames the way he knew she liked them and when that was done closed up the studio, but not to return to his furnished apartment but rather to walk the promenade all night, staring toward the ruined bathhouses and the greater mysteries of Brooklyn to his north, to the East the terrible grey waters of the Bay which Hudson had patrolled, his face against the water flat and stricken in ways which were ineluctably private. Not having an inner life was not an excuse for a lack of introspection just as not wanting children was no reason to abstain from sex. He did not know if he understood her but he did not think that he misunderstood her either; it was in some abyss between comprehension and brute stupidity that he thought of her now, her own ape-man converted by circumstance. He knew that she would be back the next day and soon again after that and so on; if there had been a cleavage in their relationship it had now been sutured and the price had been that of his utter submission. That was fair enough. He had submitted, he was past consideration.

The next day she was back with a thin, thin woman, not so much a woman as a female: no breasts, no softness or shallowness of skin and only the barest suggestion of a pudendum when quickly the creature had been stripped of its clothing. Six and a half feet tall with nipples which appeared painted rather than genuinely attached, the mouth, when parted by the straining hands of the female, enormous, a Munch scream exacerbated to a canyon screaming from the centre of that face. Methodically, calmly he took the pictures. She retrieved from him the photographs of the ape-man and gave him the largest cheque he had ever received from her, three times the amount he would have asked and then taking the female by the bony wrist left without a word. The next morning she brought in a dwarf without a penis and with feet shaped like palm leaves; in the afternoon she brought in a bearish female, so small that she had to be carried, who turned out to have three breasts between her legs and an open thing like a vagina in the place where the heart must have been. He took pictures of all of these methodically, without comment or suggestion of any kind. He was inured to his work now; he had come to understand what he was and in that knowledge knew then what she was as well. In the late evening he was still in the studio and she brought in something in the shape of a bird that seemed to be in terrible pain, which wept through feathered eyes through all of the pictures and cried and clawed at the woman in later embrace. He took care of that as well. Then, toward the dawn, she came back yet again with two midgets, leaking stigmata and coughing through the two mouths each of them had. I want you to get all of this, she said, and put them under the lights, I want you to understand to what I have been driven. She did something then which a year ago would have made him insane, but which now seemed invested only with a unique and quivering pathos, she undressed and placed herself in pietà with the midgets. Her breasts had once been very beautiful, but now seemed to have been subtly damaged by small and dense cross-hatchings and her nipples leaked, just as the feathered eyes of the weeping bird creature had bled tears. In the pietà she looked up at him. You understand now, she said. You understand everything. It had to be you, she said. It could only have been you. He peered through the lens, found her in frieze, in pietà and the blaze of the lights might have lit the darkness within but only for a moment and to no real purpose. You know now, she said. You know everything. No he did not. He knew nothing, but that was all right too, that was the human condition and if anyone had showed him that commonality it was her. He froze them in the light, then as the three creatures convulsed before him he methodically removed his own clothing and stepped into that strange and intense stricture of light. All of his life he had been waiting for this; he had become a photographer as a means of resisting. No need to resist. He crouched before them. They came against him easily, their mouths warm and seeking. In pietà, in mordancy, in his sudden and invested knowledge, the ceremony of alien souls began.

YAGUARA

by

Nicola Griffith

Nicola Griffith is the author of the novel *Ammonite*, which won a
Lambda Literary Award and the James Tiptree, Jr. Award. Her short
fiction has appeared in *Interzone* and several anthologies. Originally
from Yorkshire, England, she now lives in Atlanta with her partner,
Kelley Eskridge. Griffith has just finished her second novel, pro-
visionally titled *In My Eyes*, and is working on a third.

   'Yaguara' takes place in the jungles of Belize. It is a languid and
sensuous novella about self-discovery and letting go.

YAGUARA

Jane Holford did not travel directly from England to Belize. She packed her cameras and flew to the Yucatan, and from there took a boat to Ambergris Cay. She wished to acclimatize in private. *Your father is a duke and I'm seen on the screens of a dozen countries*, her mother used to say. *Never forget that; the paparazzi never will. Show them only what you would like to see on the front page tomorrow.* And so, even on Ambergris where Katherine, the ex-governor's niece, was drunk by ten o'clock in the morning and forgot, most of the time, that she had a guest, Jane maintained a perfect control. Even when the sun was licking at her shoulders and the Caribbean wove about her its scents of wide open space and hot driftwood, she did not throw back her head and laugh; she did not take off her sandals and squeeze the seaweed between her toes. When a beautiful woman in the market smiled at her, she did not smile back, did not allow herself to blush, to feel the heat building in her belly.

Alone in her room, which she had made sure was not overlooked by any tree or bush that could provide cover to the cold, unwinking eye of a camera or the snout-like boom of a sound deflection microphone, it was another matter.

After three weeks she no longer felt vulnerable: she could walk outside in the sun without fainting; she knew how much water she needed to drink every day to remain hydrated, and her skin was dark enough to protect her from sunburn. Armour in place, she left for the Maya Mountains in the far south and west of Belize. Dr Cleis Fernandez and the ruins of Kuchil Balum were waiting.

'Why do you want to take pictures of me?' the epigrapher had asked when Jane had phoned the University of New Mexico a month earlier, at the beginning of March.

'Because I'm putting together a book on women at the top of their professions.' *Because you made it, against the odds. Because you're an outsider, like me.* 'You're — '

'Get someone else.' And the phone had gone dead in Jane's hand.

Jane re-dialed. 'Dr Fernandez, it's Jane Holford again — '

'Holford? Holford who did that series last year on the Lascaux paintings? The ones in *Life*?'

'Yes.' At last. 'And I might excerpt a similar photo-essay from the book in one of the glossies — '

'I'm not interested in that.' Her voice was hot and rough, like black glass. 'But I do have one condition.'

'Go on.'

'I want you to photograph the glyphs at Kuchil Balum.'

'Tell me about them.'

'It's classified as a minor ceremonial site in Belize but it's anything but minor. As for the rest . . . well, you'll come or you won't.'

'I'll call you back.'

She had checked. Kuchil Balum was in the Maya Mountains, first excavated two years before. Nothing there that could not be found in dozens of other, more accessible ruins in Belize or Guatemala. And yet . . . Apparently Fernandez had been applying for grants all over the place, for money and time to go study these ruins and their glyphs. She had been turned down. Jane read and re-read Fernandez's articles in the journals, and *The Long Count*, her single book. The passion and dedication, the need to know, came across loud and clear. Why was Kuchil Balum so important?

She called back four days after their original conversation. 'I'll do it.'

'You will?' Fernandez sounded challenging. 'The jungle isn't a good place just before the rainy season.'

'I understand that. Now, about schedules — '

'I'm going there next week and won't be coming out again until the rainy season, May or June. Take it or leave it.'

The road was a track torn through the tropical forest by logging skidders, deteriorating to dust and potholes and broken bridges. Leaves brushed the jeep on both sides and smeared the dusty paintwork with sap, leaving Jane with the feeling that the greenery was closing in behind her and she would be encysted in the forest forever.

Not long after noon, she stopped to drink water from her canteen and eat a banana. It was hot; mosquitoes and bottlas flies whined about her head. Wind, sly as a great cat's breath, stole from banak to ironwood to Santa Maria pine, stirring hot perfumes and the iridescent wings of a blue morpho butterfly. When she turned the key in the ignition, the jeep's roar seemed too loud and it seemed to Jane that when she moved, the breath of the forest followed.

Over an hour later, the jungle ahead of her thinned abruptly, melting from dense emerald to sunlit mint. The breeze stiffened and expelled her into a green-sided bowl floored with dirt-brown: a clearing. Adobe huts roofed with thatch stood in an irregular west-east line; a macaw hung in a cage outside the nearest. Chickens scratched in the dirt and a pig rooted in the undergrowth at the edge of the clearing. She turned off the engine and found herself staring into the solemn eyes of a group of thin-armed children.

Stranger, those unblinking camera eyes said, *you cannot hide.*

One child wiped his nose with the back of his hand, another tilted her head at Jane like a bird. Then at some unseen signal they ran like a pack of startled deer back towards the forest and melted into the trees.

Jane climbed down from the jeep and began to lift an aluminium case from the back.

'Don't do that.'

She whirled, found herself facing a lean woman wearing shorts and boots and vest, muscles showing long and tight over knobby bones; neck tendons flat and hard; face planed by heat and hard work; hair in rough curls as black as volcanic rock.

'I'm Cleis Fernandez.' When they shook hands, Cleis's long fingers reached past Jane's wrist. 'It would be best to leave your things in the jeep. It's another half mile or so to our shack. We can drive if we go very, very slowly.'

Our shack. She had prepared for everything but sharing a room. Jane climbed numbly back into the jeep.

Jane knew she drove well: poised, unhurried, competent. She glanced in the side mirror, caught the flash of brown eyes studying her in turn. She imagined the grainy telephoto picture, the copy underneath: *The Ice Maiden, Lady Jane Holford, was yesterday spied driving through the jungle as cool and unconcerned as though going for a spin up the Strand.*

'This is it.' It was a square building of breeze block and corrugated aluminium. They climbed down. 'It was built by the logging company. Never got used – they went bust. It's more comfortable inside than it looks.'

A wooden step led into a single room, low and dark, about eighteen feet square, with plasterboard walls and a dirt floor. There were bunks with sturdy wooden legs rising to small posts.

Two bunks, each with a blue blanket. No room into which she could retreat and close the door.

'There's a toilet over here,' Cleis pointed, 'though I, we, have to fill the cistern from a bucket. The well's in the village; Ixbalum lets me, us, use that at least. The stove uses propane.' She lit a match, turned a knob, demonstrated. 'I cleared some of the shelf space for your things.'

Jane looked at the clothes already on the shelf. They looked new. Aggressively good quality. She had seen clothes like that before, when she had shared a room at Cambridge with a scholarship girl.

The windows were holes cut in the wall and screened, the door a flimsy affair. Jane looked for a lock.

'No one will steal anything. Ixbalum won't even let anyone near this place.' Jane nodded, wondering who Ixbalum was. 'We've got three Coleman lamps . . .'

Jane closed her eyes. Sharing. The hut smelled of heat and mildew and sweat, and faintly of gas and matches, but behind that lay the musk of forest animals and the heavy green scent of ceaseless growth. She felt trapped.

'. . . last as long as possible, because I hate the drive to Benque Viejo for more supplies, though if you're willing, we can take turns on that chore. Jane?'

She opened her eyes, smiled her warm, practised smile. 'Thank you for going to so much trouble.' *How am I going to survive this?*

The well was at the western edge of the village. Jane wound up the bucket. 'Where is everyone?'

'Tending their milpas. Hunting. Some are hiding in their houses. The children are running wild, or maybe watching us right now.'

Jane could see only trees, and the inevitable chickens.

The bucket creaked to the lip of the well. Jane concentrated on pouring from the wooden bucket into the galvanized steel pail. She was fascinated by the cool clear flow, the fact that water could stay cold in one hundred degree heat. She dipped her hand in it.

Someone behind her spoke in a throaty voice. Jane turned, saw a short, muscular woman with squat powerful limbs and a large jaw.

'Jane, this is Ixbalum.'

'What did she say?'

'That rivers are for playing with, well water for drinking.'

Ixbalum lifted Jane's left arm, laid it next to her own, pointed to the mahogany brown then the honey, dropped the arm, lifted Cleis's arm, compared the mahogany to teak, spoke for a while, then padded away into the trees.

Jane realized she was wiping her hands on her shorts, stopped. 'What did she say?'

'She said you're not made for the mountains.'

It was just over a mile from the village to the ruins. The trail was a twisty tunnel through the green. Sweat ran down the underside of Jane's arm, and she felt as though she were breathing sap. Ahead of her, Cleis's shorts whif-whiffed as she walked. Their boots were silent on the thick leaf mould. Insects hummed and whined. Jane slapped at something that landed on her neck.

'Got to be careful of the insects,' Cleis said over her shoulder without slowing down. 'Especially mosquitoes. They carry botfly eggs and things out of your worst nightmares.' Cleis had no idea about her nightmares, Jane thought.

They walked on in silence. The heat pushed its strong fingers under Jane's skin, slicked muscle and bone until she felt slippery inside, like a well-oiled machine. The jungle eased down her throat, sighed in her ears, whispered *You could let go here and no one would know.*

Jane realized she was stroking her belly, walking with a loose open-hip sway. *Only what you want to see on the front page the next day . . .* She jerked her hand away from her stomach and laid it on the hard black case hanging down by her hip. She was the only one with a camera here. She was in control.

Cleis stopped abruptly, turned. 'We're almost there. You have to remember that this is classified as a minor site, not to be confused with the great centres like Tikal.' Cleis's hands moved as she talked, emphasizing phrases with precise gestures like movements distilled from tai chi or wing chun. 'There's only one pyramid, and that hasn't been fully excavated. Nothing has. It may not look like much, but Kuchil Balum is more important than anyone knows.' Her hands stopped, fell back to her sides. 'I just wanted you to know that.'

They climbed the last few yards up a steep rise and looked down at Kuchil Balum.

Grassy hummocks and walls choked with vines lay scattered around an area the size of a small urban park, perhaps two acres, level, but slightly sunken. It reminded Jane of the huge ruined amphitheatres of Greece, only here it was wood, not stone, that formed the sides of the bowl; great vertigo-producing trunks that spun themselves up and up to bridge earth and heaven.

Over the faint susurrus of leaves a hundred feet from the ground, Jane thought she heard something else, something that she felt as a faint vibration under her feet. 'What's that noise?'

Cleis smiled. 'We'll save that for last.'

Jane clambered over a pile of tumbled stone to the top of a small mound. It was not hard to envisage this place as it had once been: people coming and going, sun flashing on jade and gold; children playing with a ball. Why had they left?

The north western corner of the site was hemmed in by grey rock. In front of that lay a whole complex of ruins. Something just inside the trees caught her attention, something golden that slunk from light to shadow, lifting heavy paws, turning its massive head from side to side. Slowly, heart hammering under her ribs, Jane lifted her camera.

'What is it?'

The golden animal was gone. Perhaps she had imagined it. Jane lowered her camera. 'Nothing.'

'Over here is the mat house.' They walked back down the slope to a small green mound with one side exposed: a few grey stones, beautifully fitted, a doorway and lintel. 'I'm particularly interested in the glyphs on the western wall.' They squeezed through. Inside it was dim and smelled of animal fur and musk, like a woman's hair after the rain. Cleis ran her hand along the wall. 'This section here is vital.' She tapped a relief carving, a seated jaguar-headed figure. 'The throne indicates temporal power, but other indicators point to the human figure being female. That's very unusual.' She looked at Jane. 'About as usual as a Latina professor in your Anglo world.'

Jane said nothing, refusing to be baited. Cleis smiled slightly, then continued. 'Over here,' she traced her way across the name glyphs and dates, 'another jaguar-human, but this time not in the regalia of the royal house. See the scythe? A peasant. I've seen jaguars as thrones, jaguars as symbols of shamanic and from there royal power, but this is the first time I've seen jaguars as ordinary citizens, or vice versa. I don't know what it means.' Frustration deepened the grooves on either side of her mouth for a moment, then she shook her head. 'It's dark in here. I hope photographing them won't be a problem.'

'No.' Jane touched the glyphs lightly with her fingertips.

The strange, bulbous carvings were everywhere she and Cleis went. Cleis's hands were never still as she pointed out the date glyphs and name glyphs, explained the long count and the calendar round. She saved the north west corner for last.

They climbed up the remains of four huge terraced steps and then through all that remained of what had once been a corridor. The vibration became a thrumming hiss. 'See these hinges here? This corridor was once gated on both ends. Very unusual.'

They stepped out into sunlight. Cold spray brushed Jane's cheek.

'A waterfall . . .' But Cleis did not give Jane long to admire the fall, or the pool bobbing with lilies. 'This way.' They went down steps cut into the stone, underground for five yards, then up again into what had once been a vast courtyard.

Cleis pointed to the wall that ran across the courtyard in six separate sections. It was covered in glyphs. 'This is the heart of Kuchil Balum. This is why I'm here.'

Jane posed Cleis at the well, at the ruins, outside the shack, trying to catch the intensity that seemed to burn at the woman's centre. They stopped when the light faded.

At dusk the air tasted like hot metal. Jane sat on the step outside their shack and sipped at a battered tin cup: rum, lime juice and well water. Night light, Cleis called it. From inside, the galvanized pail clanked as the epigrapher flushed the toilet. Jane heard the laughter of children float up from the village.

'Not one child in that village has ever seen the inside of a school.' Cleis filled her cup, sat next to Jane. 'If only Ixbalum were willing to talk, the lack of education could be invaluable to me . . .'

Jane was glad to keep the conversation impersonal. 'In what way?'

'Virtually all the schooling in Belize is done by missionaries: Catholics, Methodists, Seventh Day Adventists, the Assembly of God – you name it, they're here.' She sipped meditatively. 'There are probably three million people around today who still speak various Mayan tongues, but none of them can read these glyphs. The rituals that gave meaning to all these things were destroyed and discredited by the missionaries.'

'But not here?'

'Not here. They probably still tell each other bedtime stories about Queen Jaguar Claw and how she ruled over Mommy and Daddy's great-great-great-to-the-nth-degree grandparents, and how she gave their children jade beads for . . . I don't know . . . maize productivity or something. But they won't talk to me. Ixbalum won't let them.'

'I wonder what Ixbalum's afraid of.'

Cleis was quiet for a long time. Plum-purple shadows gathered under her cheekbones and in the hollows of her neck. 'That I'll make them famous.'

Jane nodded slowly in the gathering dark. They had evaded notice for a long time. 'How was Kuchil Balum discovered?'

'Three years ago a logger was tracking a jaguar. Came across some funny looking stones. He didn't think much of them at the time. Apparently he never did find the jaguar, but on the way back, he was bitten by a fer-de-lance. By the time his friends got him to the clinic at Benque Viejo, he was bleeding from the eyes and babbling about a city of stone. He died a few hours later. But one of the nurses remembered what he'd said and told her friend. The friend knew someone who worked for the State Archaeology Department. They sent someone down, some idiot who took a cursory look, labelled it "Minor Ceremonial Centre", and forgot about it. It was listed, of course, but these sites turn up all the time. Still, I was curious, I'm always curious, so when one of my grad students told me he was planning to spend the summer at Caracol, I asked him to check out this place. He brought back a polaroid of those jaguar figures I showed you this afternoon. And I knew someone had made a big mistake.'

Jane was still thinking about the logger. 'It was lucky, for the villagers I mean, that the logging operation went bust when it did, just a mile from the site.'

'Luck? I'm not sure I believe in luck.' Cleis's long hands hung loosely between her knees. 'Look into Ixbalum's face and tell me you still believe it was just bad luck that the skidders kept breaking down, that the bridges collapsed, that the workers who didn't get bitten by a fer-de-lance ran off in ones and twos babbling about the jungle cat that was out to get them.'

Jane remembered driving along the logging track, her feeling that the jungle was breathing on the back of her neck, stalking her like a big cat.

Jane listened to the steady, still-awake breathing of Cleis in the other bunk. She could see the next few weeks unrolling before her like sticky fly paper, the jungle whispering to her *Let go, let go, there's no one here to care*, but if she let go now, if she let her armour slip just once, the damage would be permanent: she would have been seen, known. Cleis was always there.

Jane turned on her side, careful not to make any noise or disturb the sheet that was pulled up to her shoulders. She thought about Cleis's toffee-coloured eyes, the way they watched her all the time. What did they see?

*

At mid-afternoon the sun was still strong and heat wrapped around Jane like a thick tongue. A hundred yards away, the waterfall roared, tossing spray into the already humid air. The light was perfect: green-gold and viscous as honey, seeping into every crevice and old chisel cut, easing out details ordinarily invisible. With luck, she would be able to photograph this whole section while the light lasted. She set up her specially adapted tripod and tilted the camera up to the next section of curtain wall. More jaguars, more pictures of the plant that Cleis did not recognize.

'I just don't know what it is,' Cleis had said the night before, and pulled out four polaroids she had taken days before. 'And it's depicted exactly the same in each glyph, always bent with these six fronds facing outward to show the spider web veins. That's significant. It suggests ritual function. And it's always in conjunction with these glyphs here.' She tilted the pictures towards the feeble light of the Coleman lamp streaming through their doorway, so that Jane could see.

'Jaguars and women?'

'Jaguars, yes, but they're not portrayed symbolically. It's almost as if they're . . . pets or something.' She sighed and rubbed her eyes. 'And these women are all young. You can tell by their clothes.' Jane took Cleis's word for it. 'If I didn't know better, I'd say these glyphs represented some kind of purdah, spent behind the curtain walls. Though what that has to do with the jaguars I don't know. It's so frustrating! If only these people would talk to me!'

Jane looked at the photos again, tapped two glyphs of women covered in what looked like blood. 'What does this mean? Some kind of execution?'

'No. Look at them carefully. Both are wounds to the left shoulder, on the muscle: ritual again.'

'Scarification?'

'I don't know what the hell it is. I feel as though I should understand what all this means, but it's just out of my reach.'

Jane touched the limestone carvings, weathered now, and tried to imagine the glyphs fresh and new. The carver had squatted out here in the ninety degree heat with only soft bronze tools and pieces of dirty string to make sure everything was straight. A labour of months. Years. It was terrible to think that all that effort – the sweat and bruised palms, the pads of fingers callused and permanently white with limestone dust – now meant nothing because no one knew what these enigmatic, bulbous figures represented.

The camera whirred, clicked, whirred again. Jane, stiff after squatting so long, stood and stretched. Froze. Behind her, arms folded, face dappled with tree shadow, stood Ixbalum.

They looked at each other. Jane could not speak Mopan Maya. She lifted a hand in greeting. Ixbalum stared back impassively. Jane cleared her throat. It sounded impossibly loud. She wondered how long Ixbalum had been watching her. 'I have to take these pictures,' she said, pointing at her camera. 'The light won't last forever.'

Ixbalum did not move.

She cleared her throat again. She hesitated, then wiped the sweat from her face and doggedly tilted the camera to a different angle. She had a job to do.

Ixbalum's gaze settled on the back of her neck, as hot as the sun. She bent to the viewfinder, focused carefully on a jaguar figure. *All that work . . .*

She straightened abruptly, turned to Ixbalum.

'Tell me what it means,' she said, pointing at the glyphs. 'They're your people, Ixbalum. Don't you want the world to hear what they had to say?'

Ixbalum might as well have been carved from the same stone as the glyphs, but the breeze in the trees stirred and the leaf shadow on the Mayan woman's face shifted. Her eyes were yellow, like hammered gold.

Jane stepped back, bumped into her tripod, had to turn quickly to catch it. When she turned back, Ixbalum was gone.

Later, when the sun was slipping behind the trees and the light was more green than gold, when Jane was treading carefully along the trail, camera slung over one shoulder, tripod on the other, she felt that same heat on the back of her neck, as though she was being watched. She stopped, turned slowly. Nothing.

Ten yards further down, she felt it again. This time she put down her camera, dropped her tripod into her other hand to hold it like a club, and turned.

Six feet away, inside her own bootprint, was a jaguar track so fresh that a piece of dirt tottering on the edge of one of the toe marks fell into the depression as she watched.

'Jaguar? You're sure?' Cleis was sitting cross-legged on her bunk, surrounded by notes.

'It looked like cat to me.' Jane leaned her tripod in the corner, began to sort automatically through her film stock. 'And the print must have been four or five inches across.'

'Ocelot, margay?'

'I didn't think they got that big.'

'You heard nothing?'

'Not a thing.' Fear made her sound angry. If she had not remembered so clearly touching the spoor with her fingertip, then retrieving her camera, taking a picture, she might be tempted to assume she had imagined the incident. But it was real. A jaguar, a predator, had been a few feet behind her and she had not known it.

Cleis set aside her notes, rubbed her eyes. 'The light's terrible in here.' Jane remembered the hot gold of Ixbalum's eyes, and shivered. Cleis studied her. 'Did you know that "jaguar" comes from a South American word, yaguara, that means "wild beast that kills its prey in one bound"? They have very short, powerful limbs and the strength of their jaws is incredible. Pound for pound, they have the most powerful bite of any land-based predator. When I was in the Xingu Basin two or three years ago, I saw a tapir that had been killed by a jaguar: the back of its skull was sheared clean off.'

All Jane could think of was Ixbalum's short, squat legs, the muscles along her jaw.

'As far as I know, there has only ever been one reported case of a jaguar attacking people and that was thirty years ago in Guatemala.' Cleis, Jane realized, knew she was scared, and was giving her information to deal with because it would help. She was being humoured. 'Apparently, four men were killed at a convent.'

Despite herself, Jane was intrigued. 'A convent?'

Cleis grinned. 'They probably did something very unchristian to one of the novices and the other nuns banded together and hacked the men to death with machetes, scythes, garden shears. No local doctor is going to argue cause of death with good sisters, especially when the church probably controls the medical supplies and the hospital.' She glanced at her notes, then back to Jane. 'Anyway, my point is that jaguars simply don't attack people. Why should they? There's too much to eat around here as it is. Maybe it was following you because you smelled interesting. Maybe it was an adolescent, practising.'

Maybe it was trying to intimidate me. But that was ridiculous.

The humidity was thick enough to stand on and the sky was low and grey. Cleis threw her knapsack into the jeep, climbed behind the wheel. 'I'll stay overnight in Benque Viejo,' she said. 'I've a few things to do.'

Jane glanced at the sky. 'Think it'll rain?'

Cleis shook her head. 'It can't. I can't afford it to.'

Jane's clothes were already stuck to her. 'Don't forget the beer.'

'I won't.'

Later, alone on the trail to Kuchil Balum, Jane felt as though she were walking through another world: there was no breeze, and every sound, every smell was singular and intense.

The air under the trees grew hotter and more damp.

Jane stumbled over a hidden tree limb. She fell to one knee, her nose seven inches from the log over which Azteca ants marched in an endless, silent line. And it was as if she had been looking at the world through a camera and had only just found the right focus. Everywhere she looked life leapt out at her: huge black carpenter bees buzzing around red melastoma flowers the size of roses; a leaf-frog, gaudy and red-eyed, peering from the depths of a sapodilla; the flicker of a gecko's tail. And there were millipedes and rove beetles, silverfish and woodlice, and spiders spinning their silent webs to catch them. The air was luxuriant with rot, like the breath of a carnivore.

She stood up feeling hot and hunted and hemmed in. A snake slithered in the undergrowth. Her heart began to thump like a kettle drum. She licked salt from her lips, wondered how many different eyes were watching her from behind tree trunks or under leaves. A twig snapped under a heavy paw. Something big was coming towards her. . . . *yaguara, a South American word meaning 'predator that kills its prey in one bound'.* She ran.

Night seeped through the trees like tea and gathered under her bunk. She sat on the rough blanket fully clothed, facing the door. A shelf bracket pressed into her shoulder blade but she stayed where she was. The jungle was full of eyes.

She dozed and dreamed she was walking to the ruins in thin moonlight. Sliding earth and metal sounds came from the direction of the purdah house. Cleis was digging feverishly, lips skinned back with the effort, teeth glinting like old bone. 'It's here somewhere,' she was muttering to herself, 'I just have to keep digging.' Jane wanted her to stop, just for a moment, but she could not seem to get close enough to touch Cleis. She would walk towards her and stretch out her hand only to find that she had gone the wrong way and Cleis was behind her. Then suddenly Cleis was laughing. 'Yes!' she shouted, and threw away the shovel, and she was digging with her hands, throwing the dirt back between her legs like a cat. 'I've found it!' She looked up at Jane, and her eyes were golden, and the dirt was piling up around Jane, burying her, and she could not breathe —

Jane surged off the bunk, swallowing, and staggered outside. The night was silent; the four in the the morning lull before dawn.

The jeep bumped into the clearing a little after midday. Jane ran to greet Cleis.

'Well, hello to you too,' Cleis said. 'What have I done to deserve this honour?'

Jane stopped abruptly. 'Did you bring the beer?'

Cleis nodded. 'I would have driven faster if I'd known you were so desperate. Give me a hand unloading this stuff.'

They lugged the new gas bottles inside. Cleis pulled the cardboard off a six-pack and submerged the bottles in the galvanized pail. 'Should cool off quickly.' She trundled an empty gas bottle out of the way for Jane. 'You get some good pictures yesterday?'

'Yes.'

'Any rain?'

'No.'

They unloaded foodstuff for a while in silence. 'According to Radio Belize, the rains will be late this year.'

'That's good.'

'I see you've lost none of your talent for conversation.' Cleis sighed. 'Sorry. That was uncalled for. It's just that I've got things on my mind and I wanted . . .' She shook her head. 'Doesn't matter.'

Jane watched Cleis slide the orange tubing into place on the gas bottle, turn the knob on the stove, listen for the hiss. She looked different. Something had happened in Benque Viejo.

Cleis opened a beer. 'Let's go up to the site. It's cool by the water.'

They took the pail and an extra six-pack up the trail and sat on the grassy bank together. Cleis threw stones, opened her second beer, sucked half down without pausing. They listened to the waterfall.

Cleis popped open her third bottle, seemed to come back from wherever she had been. 'So, how was your night alone in the jungle?'

Jane wondered if Cleis knew she had been terrified. 'I was . . . Well, I felt skittish, had bad dreams.'

Cleis nodded. The sun glinted on tiny beads of sweat on her upper lip. 'It was like that for me the time I spent four months in the Xingu basin in Brazil. Years ago. Strange place, the jungle. Feels alive sometimes, and then other times . . . you wonder what the hell you were worried about.'

Jane started in on the second six-pack about mid-afternoon. Despite the weight of the heat, she felt lighter than she had done in a long time.

'How come your first name's Cleis?' she asked. She was sitting next to Cleis who was sprawled out on the turf, hair almost touching Jane's thigh. Jane wondered idly what that hair would feel like wrapped around her fingers.

'My mother was fond of poetry. Read lots of the classics in Colombia, when she was young. Don't look so surprised.'

'I'm not surprised.'

Cleis did not seem to hear her. 'She may have ended up in poverty in East LA, and I might have had to do everything on scholarship, be twice as good as the Anglos to get what I wanted, but we have a history, a past. America isn't the only place where people know things.'

'Cleis was Sappho's daughter.' *Now why did I say that!*

'I know.'

A kingfisher flashed blue and green and black across the pool. 'Get kingfishers in England,' Jane said.

'I know that too.' Cleis climbed to her feet. 'Time for a swim.' She pulled off her shirt, unzipped her shorts. 'Aren't you coming in?'

Fear squeezed Jane's throat. 'I'm not sure it's wise to swim after so much to drink.'

'Wise? Look at this place!'

The pool was green and quiet. Damsel flies hummed over the surface at the edge away from the fall where water cabbage floated, leaves like huge furry clams. Along the northern bank heliconias with leaves as big as canoe paddles made a dense wall between the forest and water on one side. No one would see.

Jane shook her head. 'No. I can't swim.'

'Well you could just paddle a bit.' Cleis's body gleamed like polished hardwood. 'The floor slopes gently. No danger of falling into a pit. And I'm here.'

I know. 'I'd rather not.'

'The water's cool.'

Jane was aware of sweat running over her stomach, trickling down the small of her back, itching at the back of her knees. Swimming would be lovely. She almost moved. Almost stood up and took off her shirt, but years of habit and training brought her up short just as effectively as a chain around her neck. 'No.' It came out flat and hard.

Cleis's eyes narrowed. 'What is it? You don't think a bare-assed Latina is good enough to swim with?'

'It's not that.'

Cleis stood with her hands on her hips. 'What then?'

Jane unscrewed the top of the rum, took a warm mouthful. *I am not the Ice Maiden. I am not.* 'You wouldn't understand.' Immediately, she knew she had said the wrong thing.

'So now I'm stupid as well as inferior. What is your problem, Lady Jane? You drive in here, cool as cut glass, and act like you're queen of the fucking world. You smile at me so politely and ask me questions for your damn article. You take my picture, you listen to me rambling on, but you give me nothing. Not one thing. Why? Because deep down you think you're better than me. Better than everyone.'

'No. That's not it. It's just that . . .'

Cleis lifted her eyebrows, waiting, and Jane realized that she was being goaded. For once, Jane allowed it.

'All my life I've been on display. Do you know what that feels like? Cameras, tapes, telephoto lenses, parabolic reflectors. They even have a picture of my mother giving birth to me. The paparazzi paid off one of the obstetrical nurses and fitted a fibre-optic cable into the theatre lights. That was on the front page. The only way to stay me is to not let them have anything.'

'What exactly are you afraid of?'

Jane blinked. 'What do you mean, what am I afraid of? I'm terrified, every day, that they'll take a picture of me doing something I'm ashamed of. Something that will embarrass me and my family.'

'Why does that scare you so much?' Jane stared at her. 'Look, suppose they wired up your bathroom and made a tape of you taking a dump, complete with groanings and strainings, so what? So fucking what. It's something every person on this earth does.'

'Not everyone has a duke for a father. I have to be more careful than most . . .'

'Because dukes and their daughters are better than the rest of humanity, right?'

'No!'

'Then why?'

And all of a sudden, horrifyingly, Jane did not know. She was twenty-nine years old and had spent her whole life hiding behind a mask and she did not know why. She had denied herself so much: never had a lover, never been naked in public, never been drunk or screamed out loud with pleasure except in the privacy of her own apartments. She had never had a friend, never had a real argument, never wept over a dead pet.

She looked blindly out over the water. Normal people swam naked and did not care. She was not normal. She did not know what she was, or who. She wanted to lay her head down on the turf and cry:

grieve for all those lost years. But even now the habit of privacy was too strong.

'It's never too late to change,' Cleis said. And she waded out into the pool and dived underwater.

Jane watched the ripples. She knew she could not swim naked in that pool. Not today. But she could, at least, get drunk.

The sun was sinking when she woke. She sat up, and her head thumped. There were mosquito bites on her legs and one already swelling on her left breast. She looked around. Cleis's clothes were gone.

She knelt down and splashed her face with water, trying to think. Beer bottles clinked. She gathered them up, then felt foolish and put them down; counted them. Twelve, and one empty rum bottle. She swayed and realized that she was still drunk. But she never got drunk.

'Cleis!' She climbed carefully up the western slope to the purdah house. 'Cleis!' She listened, walked south towards the glyph-covered walls, stopped. She heard something, a vague scrabbling coming from the tumbled remains of a masonry wall.

Cleis was half lying, half sitting against a stack of newly fallen stone. Her left arm hung useless and bloody. She was swearing, very quietly, and trying to push herself upright.

'Cleis?'

Cleis smiled lopsidedly. 'Fucking thing.' She sounded cheerful. Shock, Jane decided.

Jane peered at her eyes. They were glassy. 'Do you hurt anywhere except your shoulder?'

'Shoulder?' Cleis looked at it. 'Oh.'

'Yes. Do you hurt anywhere else? Did you fall, bang your head?' Cleis's left arm was broken by the looks of it, and the gashes on her shoulder would need stitches. There was no sign of a head injury, but you could not be too careful.

'. . . fucking thing knocked the wall down on purpose. Kill that fucking thing . . .'

It was getting dark. She needed to get Cleis to a safe place. First she needed to make a sling.

She touched the buttons of her shirt, hesitated. *Does it matter?* Oh yes, it still mattered. But there was no real choice. She wrenched it off and shivered, even though it was still hot. *If they got a picture of this* . . . She draped it around Cleis's neck, tied the sleeves together. 'Help me, damn it.' But Cleis was lost in a world of shock and pain.

Jane thrust the arm into the support.

Later, Jane never really knew how she managed to get them both back down the trail safely. She womanhandled Cleis out of the rubble and laid her on the smooth grass. Cleis was too heavy to carry far, Jane could not drag her by the arms . . . She took off her belt, slid the leather tongue under the small of Cleis's back, under and around Cleis's belt, then threaded it through the buckle. Tugged. It should hold.

The forest was hot and close. The light was going rapidly. Jane plodded along, dragging Cleis behind her like a sled.

Two thirds of the way down the trail, Ixbalum was there, standing in the leaf shadow, eyes invisible. *Eyes. Cameras. Don't think about it.* 'Help me.' She did not know if Ixbalum understood or, if she did, whether she cared. 'Please.'

Ixbalum turned and said something over her shoulder. Two men with the same sloping foreheads and closeset eyes of figures depicted in thousand-year-old glyphs stepped from behind her.

'Be careful,' Jane said, half to Ixbalum, half to the men. 'Her arm's broken.'

Ixbalum gestured for Jane to move aside. Jane stayed where she was. If she could just keep hold of the belt that connected her to Cleis she would not feel naked. 'She might have hurt her head, too.' The men stepped around her. One gently pried the belt from Jane's hand.

'It was a jaguar,' Cleis suddenly said, very clearly.

'What — ' But they were picking Cleis up and Jane had to scramble to follow them down the trail.

The tallow candle flickered and sent shadows dancing over Cleis's sleeping face. On her chair by the bed, Jane huddled deeper into the coarse cotton wrap that Ixbalum had held out to her without comment, and tried to stay awake. She felt feverish with too much sun and alcohol and fatigue, and she wondered when Ixbalum would be back.

Cleis opened her eyes. 'This isn't our shack.'

'You're in Ixbalum's house. How do you feel?'

'I don't know yet. Confused. What happened?'

'A wall fell on you. About eight hours ago. Don't move your arm. It's splinted.'

'Broken?' Jane nodded. Cleis closed her eyes. Opened them. 'Help me sit up.' She hissed with pain when Jane lifted her. 'Feel like I've been run over by a truck.' She wrinkled her nose. 'What's that terrible smell?'

'Some salve or other Ixbalum put on your shoulder. You have some bad cuts.'

'On my left shoulder?' She seemed tense. Jane nodded. That answer did not seem to please her. 'Anything else?'

'Just bruises.'

'Where?'

'Legs, mainly.'

'No . . . blood?'

'Except from your arm, no.'

'You're sure?'

'I'm sure.'

Tears ran, sudden and silent, down Cleis's cheeks. Jane looked around; there was nothing in Ixbalum's hut that might do as a tissue.

'You're all right.' Jane realized she had never had to reassure anyone before; there had always been someone else, someone closer to do the comforting. 'Really. No head injury. And your arm should be fine in a few — '

'I'm pregnant.'

Jane did not have the faintest idea how to respond.

'I found out for certain in Benque Viejo. Just over three months gone.' Jane got up, dipped her a bowl of water from the barrel by the door. 'Thank you.' She looked up, met Jane's eyes. 'Aren't you going to ask me if it's good news?'

Cleis seemed thin and vulnerable, her eyes big, and Jane wished she knew how to comfort her. 'Is it?'

Cleis nodded. 'I'm forty-one. I've never loved anyone enough to have a child with them. Last year I realized I probably never would. So I decided to have one on my own. It took me ten months of trying. I thought that wall coming down . . .' She was crying again. This time Jane wiped away the tears with her hands.

'You're all right. You're all right.'

'I'm sorry.' And Jane thought she might be apologizing for more than the tears.

After a while, Cleis looked around at the smooth adobe walls, the herbs hanging from the roof. 'Where's Ixbalum?'

'She went out about two hours ago.' They had not exchanged a single word. Jane had just watched while the Mayan woman washed Cleis's wounds, slathered them with an already-prepared salve, bound them. When Ixbalum had gestured for her to help with the split-branch splints, she had.

'I want to get out of here.'

So did Jane. She never wanted to see Ixbalum and those golden eyes that had seen her naked again.

Cleis pushed aside the glass of water and the pills that Jane was holding out. 'I don't want them. Not yet. I don't know what's going on, but I don't like it.' She was flushed, sweaty. Jane wondered if she had made a mistake encouraging Cleis to walk back to their shack so soon. At least she was lying down now.

'Take the pills. You have a fever, and your arm must hurt.'

'Of course it hurts. Christ knows what crap she put on it. How do I know my arms's not rotting off?'

They had already been through this. 'I watched her wash it. She seemed to know what she was doing.' She should have come here and got the first aid kit, proper antiseptics, antibiotic creams, but she had been too drunk, too shaken up from the conversation by the pool. And Ixbalum had been so . . . competent. She said, again, 'I don't know what the salve was but it was fresh – moist, green-smelling – and the bowl looked clean.'

'But why was it fresh? How did she know I'd need it?' Cleis was getting more and more fretful.

'Just take these pills. Everything will seem better when you've had some sleep.'

Cleis plucked for a moment at the blanket. 'Oh, give me the god damn things then.' She swallowed them. 'Now will you listen to me?'

Jane sighed. 'Go ahead.'

'I was looking at the glyph wall, wondering what was under all those vines, thinking maybe I should start clearing them away the next day, when it suddenly struck me how, I don't know, how orderly the vines seemed. So I squatted down and had a closer look: they were growing from the dirt an even eight inches apart. They'd been cultivated. To hide the glyphs. I stood up, thinking maybe I'd tug on them a bit, see how — '

'No wonder the wall came down!' Jane's voice was loud with relief, and it was then that she realized how scared she was.

'But I didn't actually pull on them. I was just thinking about it.'

'You'd been drinking a lot. We both had. All that beer, rum . . .' *Go to sleep*, she was thinking. *I don't want to hear this.*

'I didn't touch that damn wall. The jaguar did it.'

Jane closed her eyes. Those dreams of danger and golden eyes.

'Did my face look like that when you were telling me about the jaguar that followed you home from the ruins?' Cleis reached out, grasped Jane's wrist. Her hands felt thinner, dry. 'Listen to me, Jane.

Just listen. Don't think, not yet. A jaguar knocked down that wall, wounding my shoulder, my left shoulder, like those young women in the glyphs. Ixbalum knew we were coming and that I was hurt. She had to know, there's no other explanation for the salve and her appearance on the trail. How much do you bet that some of those herbs hanging upside down from her roof are the same as the plants pictured on the glyph wall?'

No, Jane thought, and felt the same fear as that day when she had turned around and seen a jaguar print crumbling inside her own footprint. 'You're feverish,' she said firmly. 'Maybe there was a jaguar, yes. Maybe the ruins have become the stamping grounds of some solitary cat. But that doesn't alter the fact that you need to get to sleep. Now. You need to get some rest and get well.'

Cleis was pale now, her lids drooping. 'You believe me, I know you do. Because you're scared. I'm scared.' Her chin was sinking onto her chest now, eyes barely open. 'Ritual wounding . . . How did she know?' Her eyes closed. 'Fucking thing. You'll see . . .'

Jane sat where she was for more than half an hour, watching Cleis sleep, telling herself that Cleis was wrong.

Jane half woke in the middle of the night. Her muscles were relaxed, soft; she felt content. Across the room moonlight showed a tangle of blankets pushed back from an empty bed. There was some reason why she should be disturbed by that, but she was already falling back to sleep.

The next time she woke, moonlight and shadow patterns had moved further along the wall, and Cleis's bed was no longer empty. She crept out of bed, padded over to the other bunk. She must have dreamed that Cleis was gone, earlier. Cleis was sleeping soundly, naked as usual. Jane checked to make sure no blood was seeping through the bandages, then simply watched her for a while.

Cleis woke late the next morning. Jane brought her water and fruit, checked her fever. 'Not as bad as yesterday, but still too high for you to be out of bed.'

Cleis twisted restlessly under her blanket. 'You should be out working. Just because I have to spend the damn day in bed wasting precious time doesn't mean the rains are going to come later than planned.'

'Your colour's better,' Jane said.

'Well I hurt. My legs, my shoulders . . . strange places. All my tendons feel pulled.'

'You'd better take some more painkillers.'

'I don't want any more drugs.' She touched her stomach. 'Anyway, they give me strange dreams. I feel exhausted from running around the jungle in my dreams.' She looked up at Jane crossly. '*Now* what's the matter? I'm fine. I'll take the damn pills. Go do some work.'

Work, at least, would mean she would not have to think.

'And before you go, hand me those notes. I can be of *some* use.' Jane picked up the nearest camera case, opened the door. 'And Jane, I think I was a bit delirious last night. Said some wild things. Just forget it, okay?'

Jane nodded mutely.

Cleis's fever lasted three days. She was up and about before then. 'Don't tell me I should rest. I'm fine. Never better. I don't need two good arms to study the glyphs. And the rains won't wait.'

The first couple of days at the site, Jane kept a surreptitious eye on Cleis, but gave up when Cleis caught her at it and glared. They worked in silence, Jane moving crabwise with camera and tripod along walls, changing filters, checking light levels; Cleis making notes, taking measurements, staring blankly at the trees and muttering to herself.

On the fourth day, Jane got back to the shack to find Cleis sitting on the bed with her notes, and the remains of the splint piled in a heap on the table. 'I took it off,' Cleis said. 'My arm feels fine. It was probably just a sprain.'

There was nothing Jane could say. She cleared away the mess.

Something had changed since Cleis's accident: children now ran past their shack, playing games, and more than once Jane had seen villagers walking through the trees to their milpas, mattocks on their shoulders. They had greeted her with a smile and a wave.

Sometimes, too, she would look up from her camera to see Cleis and Ixbalum together, out of earshot, talking. Jane wondered why Ixbalum was now willing to speak to Cleis; wondered what she was saying, what craziness she was spilling into Cleis's eager ears. But she did not ask. Instead, she tried to push Cleis from her mind by working from first light until last. At night she would lie down, exhausted, and fall into troubled sleep. Her dreams were vivid and fractured. More than once she woke to find Cleis gone from her bed. *Where do you go?* Jane wanted to ask, *and how?* But she never did. She imagined Cleis and Ixbalum gliding through the jungle, looking into the dark with their golden eyes . . .

One night her dreams were jumbled images: time running

backwards while she watched the ruins reform into a city; vast storms overhead; Cleis talking to her earnestly, explaining. 'Ixbalum doesn't care what I know anymore. It doesn't matter what the children tell me. I'm hers now.' Jane woke drenched in sweat. She looked over at Cleis's bed: she was sleeping like a baby.

Am I going mad?

She needed to get away. She got out of bed, pulled on her clothes.

She waited until just after dawn to wake Cleis. 'The photography is ahead of schedule, and we need supplies. I'm driving to Benque Viejo. I'll be gone two or three days.'

Jane had expected to reach Benque Viejo, walk through its streets, loud with traffic and thick with the stink of leaded gasoline, and come slowly out of her nightmare. All the time she was pulling Belize dollars from her wallet for bottled gas and beer and canned food she wondered when it would stop feeling strange and dangerous to be back in the world.

She booked herself into a hotel and took a bath, but the water was only lukewarm and she found herself longing for the lake with its water cabbage and kingfisher.

After weeks of eating fish and fruit and corn, the steak dinner was alien and almost inedible. She left a tip on the table and walked from the restaurant into the street. The sky was dusky pink, streaked with pearl grey clouds. She wished Cleis could be there to see it. And then she knew she did not want to spend three days here in Benque Viejo when she could be at Kuchil Balum. The rains would be coming soon. There was no time. Because when the rains came, Cleis would go back to New Mexico, and she . . .

What is happening to me? She did not know. All she knew was that she had to get back.

It was mid-afternoon of the next day when she parked in front of their shack. Cleis was not there. *Probably at the site. No matter.* Jane took her time unloading the supplies, nervous about seeing Cleis again.

Then there was nothing left to do; she had even washed the enamel plates that had been lying on the table – the same plates she and Cleis had eaten from the night before she had left for Benque Viejo. She tried not to worry. Cleis had probably been eating straight from a can, too busy to take the time to prepare anything. She checked the shack one last time, then set off for the ruins.

The waterfall fell peacefully, a flock of black and orange orioles wheeled about the crown of a tree at the edge of the clearing, but there was no Cleis.

'Cleis!' The call echoed back, and Jane remembered the last time she had called to Cleis here. Had something else happened, something worse?

She ran through the ruins, calling, ducking in and out of half-excavated buildings. Nothing. Maybe she was at the village, talking to Ixbalum.

Two women stood at the well, a man plucked a chicken on his doorstep. They looked up when Jane ran into the clearing. 'Cleis?' she asked. They frowned. 'Cleis?' she asked again, pantomiming curls falling from her head. 'Ah,' they said, and shook their heads.

Jane ran to Ixbalum's hut. The door was closed. She banged on it with her fist. No reply. She banged again, then pushed her way in.

Without the candles, the hut was cool and dark. There was no one there. Jane brushed aside bunches of herbs on her way back to the door, then turned around again and plucked a leaf from each bundle. She could look at them later, see if any matched the ritual leaf on the glyphs.

She was just putting them in her pocket when Ixbalum came in.

The Mayan woman stood there with her arms folded, looking at Jane, looking at the floor where one leaf lay in the dirt. Jane picked it up and put it in her pocket with the others. This woman had already seen her naked, and drunk, and she was too concerned for Cleis to feel any shame at being found in Ixbalum's hut. 'I want to know where Cleis is.'

Ixbalum said nothing. Jane could feel herself being studied. This time she did not cringe.

'If you know where she is, I want to know. She's pregnant, and I think that fall was more of a shock than she knows. I want to take her away from here.' *Do I*? 'I'm asking for your help.'

Ixbalum moved so suddenly that Jane thought she was going to strike her, but Ixbalum reached up past Jane's left ear and drew a leaf from one of the bunches. She held it out to Jane.

'I don't understand.' But she did.

Ixbalum shook the leaf in front of Jane's face. The message was unmistakable: Take it. Jane did. Ixbalum nodded, very slightly, then made a *Go now* gesture and turned her back.

Not knowing what else to do, knowing only that it was pointless shouting when neither understood the other, Jane went back out into the sunshine. The leaf was a big one, dull grey-green now, but it would have been bright when fresh, the colour of the paste Ixbalum had smeared on Cleis's shoulder. It had six points, and a tracery of veins like a spider's web.

Night came as a rising cloud of living sound. The creaky chorus of thousands of insects rubbing together chitinous legs and wing combs echoed and reverberated through the trees. Fireflies streaked the dark with yellow.

Jane lay on her back on her bunk. Her arms were grazed and scratched from pushing aside branches, being caught by unexpected thorns. She had cut her palm on a frond of razor grass. Her throat was sore from calling. For the first time she was unclothed and not covered with a sheet. She lay naked to the world, as an offering. *Please come back. Just come back safe.*

Cleis returned at dusk the next day. She pushed the door open and walked in slowly. Her hair was filthy, her face drawn. She stopped when she saw Jane. 'You're back early.' Her voice was flat with exhaustion.

Jane wanted to touch her face, hold her, make sure she was all right. 'I got back yesterday. I've been waiting, and worrying. I went out looking.' Cleis swayed a little. 'It's dangerous to get too tired out there.'

Cleis sat down on her bunk, sighed and closed her eyes as she leaned back against the wall. 'I didn't know you'd be here to worry.'

'I just . . .' Jane did not know how to explain why she had come back early. 'I just wanted to know where you've been.'

Cleis's eyes flicked open. Underneath, her skin was dark with fatigue, but the eyes themselves were bright, intense. 'Do you? Do you really?'

Jane took a deep breath; she felt very vulnerable. 'Yes.'

'The simple answer,' Cleis said, over a cup of hot tea, 'is that I don't know where I've been.' They were sitting at the table, a Coleman lamp drawing moths that fluttered against the screen. Jane had insisted that Cleis eat something, rest a little, before talking. 'The complex answer . . . What do you know about dreaming?'

Jane was momentarily thrown off balance. 'Not much.'

'Dreams are something I researched in my twenties, a long time before becoming interested in Mayan civilization. Simply stated, the human brain exists in three parts, one cobbled onto the other, comunicating uneasily, each with different . . . behaviours. There's the first evolutionary stage, the reptile or R-complex, the crocodile brain whose realm is sexual, hierarchical, aggressive, and ritual behaviour. Then when mammals evolved from reptiles, they developed the limbic system, which meant they perceived the world differently – in terms of signs, and vivid sensory and emotional images. To do this, they had to bypass the crocodile brain, suppress it. They couldn't ignore it altogether, though, because it controlled a lot of the body's physical functions: the urge to fuck and fight and eat.'

'What does all this have to do with where you were last night?'

'I'm getting there. Anyway, mammals found a way to turn the R-complex, the crocodile brain back on, harmlessly, during sleep. Which means, of course, that our dreams are the crocodile's dreams: sex and food and fighting.' Her eyes were bright. 'Haven't you ever wondered why we get clitoral erections during dreams?'

'No.'

'Then some mammals developed the neocortex. We became self conscious. Ever wondered why you can't read or do math in your dreams?'

Jane opened her mouth to say she had never noticed whether or not she could, then remembered countless dreams of opening books only to be frustrated by meaningless squiggles.

Cleis noticed and nodded. 'The neocortex handles analytic recollections. It's usually turned off when we dream. That's why dreams are so hard to remember. When I change, I become a mammal with no neocortex. My waking state is like a dream state. When I change back, when I "wake", I remember very little. So, in answer to your question: I don't know where I've been.'

There was a bubble of unreality around Jane's head, around the whole room. She concentrated on her hands, neatly folded together before her on the table. *My hands are real.* 'What are you trying to tell me?'

Cleis reached out and touched those neatly folded hands. 'I think you already know.'

Jane felt very calm. She pulled the six-fronded leaf from her pocket. 'You believe in this.'

Cleis said nothing.

'You think . . . You think that those glyphs on the purdah wall are true. That the ritual wounding has purpose.' She remembered Ixbalum shaking the leaf in her face. 'You think your accident wasn't an accident. That Ixbalum infected you with some kind of, I don't know, changing agent, a catalyst. That you can become . . . that you change into a jaguar.'

Now laugh. Tell me it isn't true. But Cleis just nodded. 'Yes.'

'Do you know how that sounds?' Her voice was very even, but her heart felt as though it was swelling: so big it was pushing at her stomach, making her feel ill.

'You've seen the evidence with your own eyes — '

'I've seen nothing! A wall, some pictures, some leaves. You got drunk, pulled the wall on top of you, broke your arm and probably took a bang on the head. Ixbalum fixed you up. You disappear at night and come back looking like hell, with a pseudo-scientific explanation that basically boils down to this: you can't remember and you're not responsible. All the evidence points not to that fact that you've discovered some mystical Mayan rite, but that something is wrong in your head, and getting worse.' She put the leaf down carefully on the table. 'Look at it. Look at it hard. It's just a leaf.'

'I've read the dates on the stelae, Jane. Kuchil Balum, Place of the Jaguar, was occupied up until the sixteenth century.'

'What has that got to do with — '

'Think!' Cleis's voice was thin and hard, bright as wire. 'The lowland Mayan culture began to die more than a millennium ago: population pressure, some say, and crop failures, but I'm fairly sure it was more to do with a loss of faith. But not here. Here the power of the gods was tangible. Young girls from every family were sent to the purdah house at puberty. They were ritually wounded, infected. Some changed, most did not.' She searched Jane's face. 'Every family had the opportunity, the chance to join the elite. That welded the community together in ways we can't even begin to comprehend.'

A moth fluttered frantically against the window screen.

'But even jaguar gods can't stand against guns and missionaries,' Cleis continued. 'So they pulled down their beautiful stone buildings and built themselves a village that appears unremarkable. They hid, but they've kept their culture, the only Mayans who have, because they have people like Ixbalum.'

They sat for a moment in silence. Jane stood up. 'I'll make some more tea.'

She busied herself with the kettle and teapot. There had to be a way to get Cleis to see past this delusion; some way she could persuade Cleis to pack her bags and leave with her and have her head X-rayed. She did not know what to say, but she knew it was important to keep the dialogue open, to keep Cleis anchored as much as possible in the real world.

The kettle boiled. Jane brought the pot to the table. 'It's not the same without milk,' she said.

Cleis smiled faintly. 'Being an ignorant American, I don't think it's the same without ice.'

She seemed so normal . . . Jane asked sharply. 'When you change, how do you think it affects your child?'

Cleis looked thoughtful. 'I don't know.' She leaned forward. Jane could feel Cleis's breath on her face. She wanted to strain across the table, feel that breath hot on her throat, her neck. 'You haven't asked me how it feels to change. Don't you want to know?'

Jane realized she wanted to know everything about Cleis. She nodded.

'It's like walking through a dream, but you're never scared, never being chased, because you're the one who's dangerous. I'm not me, I'm . . . other.'

'Other?'

'Here, now, I have a sense of self, I know who I am. I can use symbols. It's . . .' She frowned. 'It's hard to describe. Look at it this way.' She patted the table. 'I know this table is made of wood, that wood comes from trees, and that this wood is pine. Underlying all that knowledge is the ability to work in symbols – tree, furniture, wood – the ability to see beyond specifics. When I'm changed, symbols, words . . . they become meaningless. Everything is specific. A barba jalote is a barba jalote, and a chechem is a chechem. They're distinct and different things. There's no way to group them together as 'tree'. The world becomes a place of mystery: unknowable, unclassifiable, and understanding is intuitive, not rational.'

She toyed absently with the leaf.

'I'm guided by signs: the feel of running water, the smell of brocket deer. The world is unpredictable.' She paused, sighed, laid her hands on the table. 'I just am,' she said simply.

The rainy season was not far off. The days were hotter, more humid, and Jane worked harder than before, because when she was busy she did not have to deal with Cleis, did not have to look at her, think about how her skin might feel, and her hair. She did not have to worry about getting Cleis to a hospital.

The nights were different.

They would sit outside under the silky violet sky, sipping rum, talking about the jungle.

'The jungle is a siren,' Cleis said. 'It sings to me.' Sweat trickled down the underside of her arm. Jane could smell the rich, complex woman smells. 'Especially at night. I've started to wonder how it would be during the rains. To pad through the undergrowth and nose at dripping fronds, to smell the muddy fur of a paca running for home and know its little heart is beat beat beating, to almost hear the trees pushing their roots further into the rich mud. And above, the monkey troops will swing from branch to branch, and maybe the fingers of a youngster, not strong enough or quick enough, will slip, and it'll come crashing down, snapping twigs, clutching at leaves, landing on outflung roots, breaking its back. And it'll be frightened. It'll lie there eyes round, nose wet, fur spattered with dirt and moss, maybe bleeding a little, knowing a killer is coming through the forest.' Cleis's nostrils flared.

Jane sipped her rum. She could imagine the jaguar snuffing at the night air, great golden eyes half closed, panting slightly; could taste the thin scent molecules of blood and fear spreading over her own tongue, the anticipation of the crunch of bone and the sucking of sweet flesh . . . She shivered and sipped more rum, always more rum. When the sun was up and she looked at the world through a viewfinder she did not need the numbing no-think of rum, but when there were just her and Cleis and the forest's nightbreath, there was nowhere to hide.

And so every night she staggered inside and fell across her bed in a daze; she tried not to smell the salty sunshiny musk of Cleis's skin, the sharp scents of unwashed hair, tried not to lean towards the soft suck and sigh of rum fumes across the room. Tried, oh tried so hard, to fall asleep, to hear nothing, see nothing, feel nothing.

But there would be nights when she heard Cleis sit up, when she could almost feel the weight of Cleis's gaze heavy on the sheet Jane kept carefully pulled up to her chin, no matter how hot she was. On those nights she kept her eyes shut and her mind closed, and if she woke in the middle of the night and felt the lack of heat, the missing cellular hum of another human being, she did not look at Cleis's bed, in case it was empty.

But one night, Jane woke sitting up in bed with her eyes open after a dream of sliding oh so gently over another woman, sliding in their mutual sweat, and she saw that Cleis was gone.

I'm alone, she thought, and was suddenly aware of every muscle in her body, plump and hot, of her thighs sliding together, wet and slippery, of her skin wanting to be bare. *There are no cameras here.* She lay her hand on her stomach, felt tendons tighten from instep to groin. And before she could really wake up and realize what she was doing – tell herself that this was not the same as being alone in her own room, one she could lock – she was standing naked before

Cleis's empty bed, before the wooden corner post. It came to mid-thigh, a four-by-four rounded off at the top and polished. She stroked it with one hand, her belly with the other. Her pubic hair was a foot away from the post; a foot, then eight inches, six. She sank to her knees, rubbed her face on the post, held one breast, then the other. One thick drop of milky juice ran down the inside of her thigh. She pressed her belly to the wood, stood up slowly, feeling the top of the post run down between her breasts, down her stomach, her abdomen, then moved away very slightly, oh so very slowly, so the post skipped a beat then skimmed the tops of her thighs.

'Oh yes,' she said, imagining Cleis lying face down in front of her, moonlight on her buttocks. 'Oh yes.'

She crouched down, crooning, leaning over the post, palms resting on the bunk, feet braced on the cool dirt floor. She began to lower herself.

The door creaked open. Jane froze. Something behind her coughed the tight throaty cough of a jaguar; another drop of milky juice ran down her thigh. The animal behind her rumbled deep in its chest. Jane did not dare turn around. It rumbled again: *Don't stop*. Her vulva was hot and slick and her heart thundered. The cough behind her was closer, tighter, threatening: *Do it now*.

Jane licked her lips, felt the golden eyes travelling up her achilles, her calves, the back of her knees, the tendons in her thighs, the cheeks of her bottom. She dare not turn, and she dare not disobey, nor did she want to.

'Ah,' she said softly and laid her cheek on the sheet. *Between Cleis's shoulder blades*. Touched the rumpled blanket above her head. *Cleis's rough curls*. And lowered herself onto the beautifully smooth oh so lovely rounded and rich wood. *The swell and heat of Cleis*. She moved gently. 'Oh, I love you.' And she felt breath on her own clenching bottom, the close attention of whatever was behind her, and suddenly she knew who, what, was behind her and loved her, it. 'Yes, I love you,' she said, but it was a gasp as she felt the wood round and slick between her legs slide up and down and her breath caught and 'Ah,' she said, 'ah,' and she was grunting, and then she felt a sharp cool pressure against her shoulder where claws unsheathed and rested, possessive, dimpling the skin, and she was pulling herself up and over that wooden corner, *Cleis's soft plump slippery-now cheek*, her face tight with effort, and her breasts flattened on the bed as she thrust and her chin strained forward and the muscles under her skin pumped and relaxed and sweat ran down her legs and the room was full of a rumbling purr. Fur brushed her back and she was pressed into the bed by an enormous weight, a weight with careful claws, and the heat between her and the wood was bubbling up in her bones and 'Ah!' she shouted, 'ah!' hardly able to breathe, and could not stop, not now not now, and she humped and rocked and grunted until she shuddered and screamed and opened and pushed and came, curling around the bunk, *around Cleis*, like a fist. Sweat ran from her in rivers; a pulse in her temple thumped.

Claws slid back into their sheaths, the heat and weight withdrew. A throaty rumble: *Don't move*. And then it was gone.

Jane buried her face in the damp sheets that smelled of Cleis, that smelled of her and Cleis, and cried. *I don't know where I've been*, Cleis had said, *when I change back, I remember very little*.

When Jane woke up, Cleis was fast asleep in her bunk.

The mid-morning sun poured like buttermilk over Jane where she knelt on the turf before the glyph wall.

What is happening to me?

She rested her fingertips on the glyphs. 'What do you really say?' she whispered.

She was alone. Cleis had gone into the forest that morning, saying she wanted to examine the area for evidence of fruit tree cultivation.

She found herself standing by the fall, staring into the sheeting water, mind empty.

Wake up! she told herself fiercely. *Think. Don't let this just happen to you* . . . She jumped fully clothed into the water.

She bobbed back to the surface, gasping. It was cold. *Good*. She swam back to the bank, climbed out just long enough to strip off her sodden clothes.

She did not even think about whether or not anyone might be watching.

She dived back in and swam in a fast crawl to the waterfall, let it thunder on her head for a moment; swam again.

This is real, she told herself. *This: sun, water, air. Not dreams, not Cleis's delusions.*

She swam until she was exhausted, then climbed out onto the bank and lay in the sun. She fell asleep.

When she woke, the memory of the dream, the soreness between her legs, was still vivid. She sighed. Her rational mind told her one thing, *all my needs*, all the evidence, told her another. Which did she want to be real? She did not know.

Her clothes had dried in a wrinkled pile. Jane shook them out one by one and put them back on.

The inside of the shack was hotter than the outside. Cleis had been cooking.

'Here,' she said, and handed Jane a tin plate. 'Beans and tortillas and fresh corn. Let's eat outside.'

Jane wondered where the food had come from, but obeyed silently. Cleis seemed different. Cheerful. Jane wondered if it was anything to do with last night, felt the world spin a little. A dream. It had been a dream.

They sat very close together on the step, arms brushing against each other as they ate. Jane watched the small muscles along Cleis's forearm ripple as she chased beans with her fork, wiped at the juice with her tortilla. Her arms seemed thicker, the muscles more solid than they had been. Jane wondered if that was a result of pregnancy. Women plumped out a little, didn't they? She studied Cleis. Not long ago her muscles had been long and flat, face hollow as though the intensity of her concentration burned away all subcutaneous fat. Her eyes had peered bright from dark hollows. Now she seemed squarer, stronger, more lithe.

'I'd like to take more pictures of you.'

'You already have all the pictures you'll need for that article.'

Jane had almost forgotten the reason she had come to Belize. She felt as though she had always been here, always eaten from tin plates and drunk rum with Cleis. 'I didn't mean that. I mean of you, as you . . . as your pregnancy develops. I want to document your changes.'

Changes. The word hung in the air between them.

'Ow!' A sharp pain shot through Jane's left breast. 'Christ!' Another shooting pain jerked her arm, sending the tin plate flying, beans spattering on Cleis's shorts. Cleis jumped to her feet. Jane clapped a hand to the fire in her breast.

'Move your hand.' All Jane could do was gasp. 'Move your hand, Jane. I need to see.'

But Jane was scared. She did not know what was happening, was afraid to see. 'It hurts!'

'Move your hand.' This time Jane let Cleis move her hand away, did not protest as she unbuttoned her shirt. She turned her head away as Cleis sucked in her breath.

'What is it?'

'Botfly. It's eating its way out of your breast.'

'Get it out! Get it out!' Jane wanted to rip at her breast, at the thing that was eating her flesh, but Cleis was holding her hands.

'Listen to me. Fasten up your shirt again. It's not big. There won't be any permanent damage, but I have to go get something. Can you do that?'

Jane nodded, thinking Cleis meant to get something from the shack. But Cleis set off down the track that led to the village. 'Wait!'

'I won't be long. Be brave, bonita.'

Jane sat with her breast cupped in her hand. *Bonita.*

It must have been from that mosquito bite she got the day Cleis had broken her arm. The egg of a botfly had hatched on her skin and burrowed its way down into her breast. Now it was big enough to need food. It would stay in her breast, feeding on her flesh, breathing through the hole it would chew through her skin, until it was large enough to hatch into the botfly. Unless they could get it out. The pain was excruciating.

Bonita.

Cleis returned, slightly out of breath and slick with sweat.

'Chew this.' She held out a large dried leaf.

'Where did you get it?' Cleis just looked at her. Ixbalum, of course. 'What is it?'

'Tobacco.'

'Tobacco? What good will that do? That won't take away the pain!'

'It's not for the pain. Just chew it.' Cleis tore off a piece, held it out. Jane took it, reluctantly, put it in her mouth, chewed gingerly.

'Tastes terrible.'

'Just chew. Don't swallow. No, chew some more.' Cleis put down the rest of the leaf and started to unbutton Jane's shirt again. Jane watched her, saw the way the skin around her eyes was wrinkled in concentration, saw the faint sparkle of perspiration on her lip. Jane wondered how those long brown hands would feel wrapped around her breasts. She could feel her colour rising. She was afraid that her nipples would harden. She cleared her throat. 'How does it look?'

'See for yourself.'

Jane, still chewing, looked. There was a hole, no bigger than the knob on her watch, about three inches right of her nipple. So small for so much pain.

Cleis held out her hand. 'Spit it out.' Jane did, feeling a little self-conscious. Cleis pinched off a tiny clump of soggy pulp and rolled it between the strong fingers of her right hand. 'This might hurt.' She put her left hand on Jane's breast, one finger on each side of the hole, then spread them slightly, so that the pink under her nails turned white and the larva's breathing hole stretched open. Her fingers were very gentle, very precise. Very human. Cleis plugged the hole neatly with the tobacco. 'Very brave, bonita. The nicotine will kill it. Then we'll pull it out with a pin.' They watched each other's faces as Cleis began to fasten Jane's shirt again, then hesitated. Cleis's eyes were very dark, and a vein in her throat pulsed.

Jane panicked. 'The food was nice. Thank you.'

Cleis studied her a moment, then half turned away. 'Don't thank me, thank our mysterious benefactor. When I got back this afternoon, I found a little pile of stuff, tortillas, corn, fresh fruit for later, on the doorstep.'

Jane closed her eyes against sudden nausea as the real world threatened to come unglued.

Cleis, still not looking at her, did not notice. 'They've probably finally figured out we're not burning-eyed fanatics clutching bowdlerized Bibles in one hand and McDonald's franchises in the other.'

Jane nodded, as though she agreed, but she knew the food was a gift, to their new god.

Every afternoon when they got back from the site there was something: sometimes fruit, or a plucked chicken; eggs; once a clay pot full of some sticky alcoholic beverage. They drank that on the night Cleis used a pin to pull the plug of tobacco, black now, from Jane's breast, and then teased out the botfly larva. Jane held the pin with the skewered larva over the gas ring until it was ashes. She had bad dreams that night, dreams of being eaten alive by wriggling maggots, but when she woke up, Cleis was there. 'You killed it Jane. It's dead.'

Most nights, Jane woke up to find Cleis gone. She did not speak of it. *Don't reinforce the madness*, she told herself, but sometimes she wondered whose madness. She felt as though she were being sucked into an increasingly angled world, where the beliefs of Cleis and Ixbalum and the villagers, the evidence of forest and ruin, all made sense, if only she would let go of everything that made her sane. Everything that made her human.

The forest is a siren, Cleis had said, and Jane could hear it singing, day and night.

Cleis was changing, spending more and more time in her own world, content to drowse on the warm, sunlit terraces, or stare off into the distance while Jane worked.

Perhaps it was her pregnancy. Jane did not know much about the process, but Cleis grew visibly more pregnant every day, which she did not think was normal.

'We should take you to Benque Viejo for a check-up,' she said one afternoon when Cleis was waking from a nap. 'You're too big for four months.'

Cleis shrugged. 'The process is being accelerated. Jaguar gestation is only three months.'

For the first time in her life, Jane deliberately broke an expensive piece of equipment: she threw the camera she was using against a rock and did not bother to pick up the pieces.

Now when Jane woke up in the mornings she could taste the damp in the air, a different damp, cold, spelling the end of their time here.

Cleis seemed to smell it too. She became restless, always moving about, standing up two minutes after she sat down. She was eating less and less, and barely bothered to listen when Jane told her she should eat, for her own health and her child's. Sometimes Jane would come back from the site and find Cleis staring at something – a pen, the stove – as though it were utterly alien.

Cleis began to stay away for longer stretches: all night, then twenty-four hours.

'Why?' Jane wanted to know. 'Why are you doing this?'

'I can't help it. It . . . Everything is so simple out there. I don't need to worry about always having to be better than everyone else just to stay in place. I smell the green and it's like opium. It makes me forget.'

And Jane knew she was losing her.

Four days later, Cleis disappeared.

She did not come home one night, or the next day. One night stretched to two, then a week. Jane thought she would go mad. She searched the jungle by day, left messages on rocks and carved words on trees with a knife. She cooked every night, hoping the smell of food would draw Cleis back.

She still went to the site to take pictures. There were probably a hundred thousand glyphs, some of which would not survive another rainy season. And there was always wildlife to photograph. If she just kept taking pictures, Cleis would come back. She would. They would go back to New Mexico together, and Jane would alternately help Cleis put together her notes and visual evidence, and work on a book of photographs of Belize. Everything would turn out all right. She just had to make sure she had everything done for when Cleis returned, before the rains.

One day, walking through the trees with her camera in search of a purple-throated hummingbird, Jane heard a strange noise. A pattering. Something cold hit her face, then her leg, her shoulder. All around her leaves started to bounce, and the stem of a bromeliad trembled as it filled. The patter became a rush.

Rain.

Rivulets of the stuff began to run down the trunk at her back and the rush became a hiss. There was too much water for the forest to absorb and within seconds there was a muddy brown stream running past her feet. A leaf floated past, with a spider balanced on it, as though it were a life raft.

One week became two, then three. Jane wandered in the rain, imagining Cleis as a jaguar, drinking from the new pools, licking rain drops from her whiskers. Jane no longer left written messages, only her scent, and still Cleis did not come.

One night, something woke Jane. She sat up, listened: the rain had stopped. She got up, went outside. All around the shack there were jaguar tracks pressed into the mud.

'Cleis?' But she whispered, afraid. The windows of her shack were screen, and the door flimsy. There were many jaguars in the forest.

When she woke again in the morning, the rain was thrumming steadily on the tin roof. She sighed, pulled on a long shirt and opened the door to take a look at the world.

There, curled in the mud, naked and still, was Cleis. Jane stood in the open doorway, unable to move, throat tight. Then she ran down the steps and knelt beside her. Cleis's hair was reddish brown with mud and a large scratch stretched over her ribs. She looked nine months pregnant.

'Cleis?' Jane touched her, hesitantly, then jerked back when she felt cold flesh. But Cleis opened her eyes.

Getting her up the steps and into the shack was harder than dragging her down the trail, but Jane managed, eventually. She stripped the covers from Cleis's bunk so they would not get wet, sat her down. 'Now you keep still while I put a kettle on.'

Cleis sat like a cold soapstone carving while Jane rubbed her down with a towel and talked about the rain, the hot tea she would make, the photographs she had been taking. After a few minutes, Cleis began to tremble. Jane kept rubbing.

'That's right. You're home now. You're safe with me.' The trembling became great rolling shudders. Jane wrapped a clean dry towel around her. 'You don't have to worry about anything. I'll take care of you.' She stroked Cleis's hair. 'While you've been gone I've been at the site every day, taking pictures. It's changed with the

rains, got more lush.' Cleis's eyes were still blank, uncomprehend-
ing. 'The waterfall used to be so clear but now it's muddy. The other
day I saw a turtle sunning itself on the bank . . .' She talked on and
on, about everything and nothing, until she felt a hot tear on her
shoulder. Then she made the tea, guided Cleis's hand to the cup.
Watched until she was sure Cleis would hold the tea without
burning herself.

'Good. Now you drink that all up while I put a fresh sheet on this
bunk, and then we'll get you tucked in nice and cosy and you can
sleep for a while.' Cleis watched her while she made the bed. Her
eyes were deep sunk, surrounded by grainy brown circles the colour
of tannin. 'There. Everything will look better after some sleep.'

In sleep, Cleis looked fragile. Her eyelids were delicate with purples:
lavender, indigo, violet. Her face was drawn, leached of colour; a
kind of dirty tan. She had kicked the sheet down to her waist and
Jane could see that her breasts were a different shape.

She would give birth soon.
But that's impossible.

Jane sighed. She no longer knew what was possible and what was
not. All that mattered was that Cleis had come back. She stroked the
lean hand lying on top of the sheet. The fingernails were filthy now,
and ragged, but Jane saw only the way that hand had opened her
shirt, weeks ago, had gently moved away her own hand, had made
her feel better.

She lifted the hand and kissed it. 'Oh, I have missed you.' Cleis
slept on. 'As soon as you're well enough, we'll leave this place.'

She got up and started packing.

Cleis slept for nearly ten hours, then woke up long enough to be fed
some soup. When the soup was gone, she went back to sleep.

When it got dark, Jane lit all three Coleman lamps, even though
the heat was overwhelming. If Cleis woke up in the middle of the
night, the first thing she wanted her to see was light. Bright, artificial
light. She stood by Cleis's bed, hesitating: the other bunk was
covered in open suitcases and piles of clothes. Moving them would
wake her. Jane drew back the sheet and fitted herself carefully
around the strange mix of bone and muscle and pregnancy that was
Cleis, and fell asleep almost instantly.

When she woke up it was still the middle of the night. Cleis was
whimpering, burrowing into her neck. 'Sshh, sshh. I'm here. What is
it?' But then Cleis was clinging to her and crying and Jane was

stroking her side, shoulders arms side of breast ribs belly-bulge hip
and back, up and down, telling her it was all right, it was all right, and
then the heat Jane felt was more than the hiss and spit of Coleman
lamps, more than the warmth of a humid Belize night. And Cleis was
no longer sobbing on her neck but kissing it, and the arms wrapped
so tightly around her were pulling her in, until their mouths were
almost close enough to touch, and Jane's arm was under Cleis's
neck, supporting her head, and her leg was wrapped over Cleis's and
her other hand stroking her breast, her hips, her thighs.

'Kiss me,' Cleis said.

Jane expected her lips to be dry and rough, but they were soft as
plums.

At first they made love as though they were underwater: coming
together too fast, bumping, drifting apart, but then they were
moving together, rising towards the surface, a roaring in their ears,
and the muscles in arms and thighs and belly were clenched tight as
each breathed the other's breath as though it were the only oxygen
available.

'Show me I'm real,' said Cleis, and slid her palm up to the hot slick
between Jane's thighs. 'Come in my hand.' And Jane did.

They lay in each other's arms, slippery as newborns, while Jane
kissed Cleis's forehead, again and again.

'I've packed almost everything,' Jane said as they ate breakfast. Cleis
was wearing a long shirt. Nothing else would fit her. 'We need to get
you to a clinic as soon as possible. You look like you're ready to give
birth any minute.'

Cleis rested a hand on her belly. She nodded but did not say
anything.

'I'll check the jeep as soon as we've had breakfast.' Jane decided not
to mention her worries about the passability of the trail in this wet
weather. 'Will you be all right for the journey?'

Cleis moved her eyes sideways, lifted her shoulders slightly in a
who knows? gesture.

'Well . . . do you feel well enough at the moment?'

Cleis nodded, then seemed to realize she would have to give more
than that. 'Everything is very strange for me. Different. Sitting here,
talking to you, is like looking through a kaleidoscope. Someone
keeps twisting it out of shape, and then I don't know who you are, or
who I am, or what we're doing here. Talking is sometimes . . .
difficult.'

Jane did not want to ask the next question, because she was scared of the answer. But she had to know. 'Do you . . . Is leaving what you want to do?'

Cleis hesitated, then laid a hand on her belly and nodded. Jane knew she would get no more from her for a while.

They set off at midday. It was cold and pouring with rain. Jane helped Cleis to the passenger seat, more because of Cleis's mental state than any physical disability. Cleis moved easily, muscles plainly visible beneath her skin. Once she was in the jeep Jane wrapped several shirts around her bare legs.

It was slow going. Twice, Jane had to climb out of the jeep and tuck canvas under rear wheels that could find no traction in mud. But she did not mind the rain or the mud or the cold: she was getting Cleis to safety.

All this time, Cleis sat in her bundle of clothes, silent and distant.

Eight miles down the trail they came across a tree that had fallen across their path. Jane turned off the engine. 'Stay here. I'll go take a look.'

The trunk was too big to drive over and the undergrowth on either side of the trail was too thick to drive through. Jane walked back to the jeep. 'I'm going to try to hack us a path around this thing.' She reached under the driver's seat and pulled out the machete. 'Just stay here and keep the windows and doors locked.' Cleis did not seem to hear her. Jane rolled up both windows and locked the doors, hesitated, then took the car keys. 'It might take a while.'

Jane hurried, swinging the machete heedlessly through vines and flowers. Her arms were aching and her face itched with spattered sap by the time she had a path cleared.

She hurried back to the jeep. 'That should — '

Cleis was gone. A pile of empty clothes lay on the passenger seat.

'No,' Jane said quietly, 'not now.' She would not let the forest have her. 'Do you hear me?' she bellowed. 'I won't let you have her!'

She crashed through the undergrowth, smashing past branches, pushing through tangles, the machete forgotten. She had no idea how long she trampled through the forest, blinded by grief and rage, but eventually she found herself by a stream, sobbing. She wiped the tears from her eyes. Maybe Cleis was already back at the jeep. Maybe she had just wandered off for a moment then remembered who she was. Yes. She should get back to the jeep.

But the jeep was still empty. Jane sat behind the wheel, staring into the trees until it was dark. Then she switched on the lights and drove back to the shack.

*

She did not unpack the jeep. For the next five nights she left a Coleman lamp burning on the step, just in case. She barely slept any more, but wandered through the trees, calling. On the sixth night she did not go back to the shack. Perhaps if she stayed out here, lived as Cleis lived, she could understand. Her back itched: her shirt was filthy. She took it off, left it hanging on a branch.

That night she slept curled up on a tree bough, like a jaguar. Like Cleis. She woke hours later, heart kicking under her ribs. Did jaguars dream of falling?

The next day she wandered aimlessly through the forest, eating fruit where she found it. She ran her hand across the surface of a puddle, wondered what it would be like to have paws heavy enough to break a paca's back, how it would feel to lean down to lap with a great pink tongue, to see the reflection of round golden eyes and white whiskers. She wandered. Time ceased to mean anything much.

Maybe it would not be so bad to walk through the forest on four feet. The world would look very different, but things would become very simple. And she would be with Cleis.

She found herself back at the shack, taking a large knife from the table. It did not take long to get back to the ruins. She knelt by the glyph wall. She would cut open her own shoulder and ask Ixbalum to give her the change salve. Then she could join Cleis. They could be together. She laid the knife against the muscle of her left shoulder, and cut. Her blood was shockingly red, the pain incredible.

She blinked at the knife. 'What am I doing?'

She had to find a way to get Cleis out, not to lose herself. She threw the knife away from her, and stood up, holding her arm. The cut was deep. It needed cleaning up. She had to get back to the shack.

That night, as she lay on her bunk, bandaged shoulder aching, the endless chorus of frogs and insects fell silent. Jane was suddenly full of hope. She pulled on her boots, and went to the door. Then she heard it, a low moaning yowl, like a cat on heat. A big cat. The yowl leapt to a scream, then another. The scream turned into a tight cough. She heard harsh panting, hissing, and then that terrible scream.

'Cleis!' Cats sometimes fought over territory. Jane snatched up the lantern and ran out into the dark, following the noise. Fifty yards into the trees the screaming stopped and there was a thrashing in the undergrowth, then silence. Jane ran harder.

There was no sign of the cat, but it had flattened an area of undergrowth with a diameter of about ten feet, and the grass was covered in blood. She cast about for tracks, or a trail of blood, anything. There was nothing. Exhausted, she headed back to the shack and lay down, refusing to imagine what might have happened to Cleis.

Someone was shaking her shoulder. Jane opened her eyes. Cleis stood before her naked, thin as a rail, holding something. Must be a dream. Cleis was pregnant.

The shaking did not stop.

Thin. Jane sat bolt upright. Cleis was holding a baby. 'Take her. She can't stay with me.' Cleis thrust the child at Jane, then opened the door.

'Wait!'

'I can't. She's been fed. Take her away from here.'

'No. I'm not going anywhere without you.' Jane climbed out of bed, scrunched the blanket into a nest, and laid the child down. 'I'll follow you, leave the baby here.'

'You can't.'

'I can. I will. You're not well, Cleis. You need to leave with me. I want you to. Please.' Cleis stood, uncertain. 'Don't you want to?'

'Yes!'

'Then why don't you?'

'I can't!' Cleis backed up against the wall.

Jane sat down. She did not want Cleis to bolt. 'Come and sit. Just for a moment. We'll have some tea.'

'No. I can't, Jane. I really can't. I have to stay here. Under the trees. It's where I belong now. I need to stay.'

'You need to look after your child.'

'No. Don't you see? It's stronger even than that. I need to be out there, to live. I need it, like I need water, or air.'

'I'll follow you. I'll leave the child here and I'll follow you.'

'Then she'll die,' Cleis said, sadly. And it was that sadness, that resignation that finally told Jane that Cleis would not change her mind. Could not. That Cleis would rather run through the trees than stay here, or anywhere, with Jane. If it was not for the tiny life on the bed . . .

'What if she . . . what if she grows up to be like you?'

'She won't. If you take her away. She'll never miss what she's never had.'

'I love you.'

'I know. I'm sorry.' She moved to the bed, picked up the baby, put her in Jane's arms. 'Love my child for me.'

They did not say goodbye.

She wrapped the child carefully in a clean shirt and walked down to the village. Two women took a look at her face and went back inside their huts. Ixbalum's hut was empty. A bunch of children gathered at the edge of the trees. Jane stood in the middle of the clearing and addressed the air. 'Where is Ixbalum?'

A chicken clucked.

'Where is Ixbalum?'

A woman put her head out a hut and called to one of the children, shouting instructions. The girl listened, looked sideways at Jane, then darted into the forest. Jane waited patiently. The baby in her arms yawned and opened its eyes. They were the colour of brand new copper pennies.

The girl came back with Ixbalum.

'You did this,' Jane said finally. She thought she saw pity on Ixbalum's face, but perhaps she imagined it. 'I need your help. I'll need milk.' She pointed to her breasts, then the child. Ixbalum walked over to her hut and disappeared inside. Jane waited. She did not know what else to do.

Ixbalum came back out holding a pile of soft rags and a gourd. She held them out. The gourd was full of milk. Some spilled on Jane's thumb as she took it. She sucked at it: rich, not cow's milk.

'You knew, didn't you? You knew.'

But Ixbalum shook her head wearily and pointed to Jane, to the baby, and made a flicking motion with her hand. It was unmistakable: *Go away.*

'I'll go for now, because that's what she wanted. But you better . . . You keep her safe for me. Just keep her safe.'

The journey to Benque Viejo was not difficult. No more trees had fallen across the skidder trail and the baby, whom she called Penny, because of her eyes, slept soundly in the cardboard box Jane had strapped into the passenger seat. She stayed in Benque Viejo only long enough to buy diapers and baby formula and a feeding bottle, fill tanks with enough gas to get her to the capital city, Belmopan, and to make a phone call to the niece of the ex-governor, on Ambergris.

'Katherine, I want someone who will fill out a birth certificate, no questions asked.'

'Who on earth for?'

'My adopted child.'

Silence. 'Well that's a turn-up for the books. Are you sure? Think of the scandal if you get back to England with a baby in tow . . .'

'I don't care about that anymore.' And she did not. She really did not.

She climbed back in the jeep. Penny opened those startling eyes, stretched. Jane wondered if she would look like Cleis when she was older.

ON AMEN'S SHORE

by

Clive Barker

Clive Barker sprang into the horror field's consciousness with his brilliant six volumes of short stories, *Books of Blood*. Since then he has shown that he is equally adept at writing novels, screenplays, and at directing and producing movies. In addition, his art has graced some of his books and has been collected in *Clive Barker Illustrator*.

Unfortunately for readers of his short fiction, Barker rarely writes short stories these days; but the rare one will occasionally appear in such venues as *The Time Out Book of London Short Stories*, *The New York Times* op ed page, and in the case of 'On Amen's Shore', in a limited edition Phantom Press/Fantaco Enterprises four-author anthology called *Demons and Deviants*. 'On Amen's Shore' takes off from the world of Barker's novel *The Great and Secret Show*.

ON AMEN'S SHORE

Foreword

It was in the novel called *The Great and Secret Show*, published in 1989, that I first journeyed to Quiddity, the so-called dream-sea.

I lingered there for only a few chapters, but the volume, which was sub-titled *The First Book of the Art*, clearly promised further explorations of that region.

The short tale which follows is not – let me be plain – that promised sequel. But it does mark my first tentative investigation of the other territories that look on to Quiddity. One of those continents is occupied by the Iad Ouroboros, who are briefly glimpsed in the closing chapters of *Show*, and seem to pose a considerable threat to our species. But theirs is just one of many civilizations that, like ours, stand on the shores of Quiddity. The fragment that follows is set in another of those realms, and concerns itself with two wanderers who encounter the powers of the dream-sea.

One or two pieces of information may aid the reader's understanding the tale. First, that we humans are granted only three glimpses of Quiddity during our natural span: at birth, at death, and on the night we sleep beside the love of our lives; and second, that the waters of the dream-sea are not passive. Our presence there excites them to all manner of behaviour, and our dream-selves may well end up transformed by our immersion.

Let me leave it at that, and invite you to wander with two travellers of my acquaintance, as they descend into the fishing town of Joom, on an afternoon that promises only hunger and exhaustion, but may yet astonish them.

Clive Barker
Los Angeles, October 1992

'My pagan soul is greatly comforted by this place,' Beisho Fie announced to Rutaluka as they descended the steep, winding thoroughfares of Joom to the harbour. 'It may not be *entirely* godless – I'm sure there's some dupe on his knees somewhere in the vicinity – but I don't see a steeple and I don't hear a call to prayer, so maybe the gods are illegal here.'

'That's ridiculous.' Rutaluka – universally called Ruty (as in beauty) – remarked.

'It's no more ridiculous than wishing there were gods watching over us every moment of our lives,' Beisho replied, slipping his spectacles off his lumpen nose and squinting down the hill at the purple-black lake. 'There's talk between the two of us I wouldn't want heard by anyone, least of all some gossiping god.'

'What kind of talk?' Ruty wanted to know. He was much the squatter of the two wanderers – the mule to Fie's thoroughbred; the parrot to his stork – and had developed a way of walking backwards a step ahead of his comrade, so as to watch Beisho's face without putting his neck out of joint. 'What have we talked about?'

'You tell me,' Beisho replied.

'Well . . . food, of course,' Ruty said. He wore his taste for candies and pig flesh on his hip and backside. 'And the state of our shoes,' he went on. 'And *lust*.'

'Ah . . .'

Ruty smiled, a vale of dimples appearing on his round face. So that was the subject Beisho the Laureate felt so tender about. 'You'd rather nobody knew that your equipment leans to the left,' he said, 'is that it?'

Beisho glowered down at his comrade. '*Rutaluka . . .*' he said.

'How many times have I asked you not to call me that?'

'Then never again mention the angle of my erection,' Beisho countered. 'I shared that with you in a very private moment.'

The moment had indeed been private. They had been locked together in the water closet of the Margravine of Cataglia, who, in order to pay off her gambling debts, had invited the pair into her château to filch – for a price – her husband's collection of erotic vases. Unfortunately her spouse had returned from his dog-racing early, and the Margravine, her legendary taste for farce never more evident, had shut Beisho and Ruty in the toilet and had proceeded to distract her husband from his suspicions (the scent of Beisho's cologne hung in the air like laughter at a wake) by making her body available to him from every possible direction. As the sound of coupling had drifted under the door, Beisho's prong had swelled in his pantaloons, and in reply to Ruty's confounded stare Beisho had confessed, in a whisper, that it had always leaned to the left.

The escapade had ended better than this sweaty interlude might suggest. With her husband coupled comatose, the lady had smuggled the thieves and their booty out of the château, and they had subsequently parlayed the five vases (one of which depicted acts even the Margravine, in her desperation, had not stooped to) for a considerable profit. But all profit dwindles, unless invested or saved, and the pair had too little patience for the former and too much appetite for the latter. The money was spent on bread, beer and bosom in a matter of days, leaving them near as dammit penniless.

'What I need to find is an *author*,' Beisho announced. 'Someone who needs his works translating.'

'I doubt you'll find much in the way of writers here,' Ruty replied. 'This is a fisherman's town.'

'Fishermen tell tales,' Beisho observed.

'Yes,' said Ruty, 'but how often do they write them down?'

Beisho never had a chance to reply to this, because the sound of sobbing drew the attention of both he and Ruty down a trash-strewn alley off to their left.

'A woman weeps!' Beisho said.

'So?'

'So it's the first sign of finer feelings we've encountered in this damn town. We should seek out its source.'

Ruty shrugged. 'Whatever,' he said. 'You go. I'll wait here.'

Beisho was already off down the alleyway, leaving his companion to idle at the corner to watch the good people of Joom climbing and descending the hill. It would be a poor place to look for loveliness, Ruty mused. Maybe it was the effort of struggling up the slope that left the citizens looking so vacant. Or – more likely – the fact that every dish served in Joom was scaly, finny and glassy-eyed.

He glanced back along the alleyway, to see that Beisho had discovered one of the town's better-looking women sobbing on a doorstep.

'What's the problem?' he asked her.

She looked up from her grief, her eyes large and silvery.

'Do we *know* each other?' she asked him.

'I am Beisho Fie. Poet, whittler and seducer of wild dogs.'

'Well, you're not much use to me,' the woman replied, 'I don't need poems—'

'What *do* you need?'

'—unless it was a dirge,' the woman sent on, tears coming again. 'Yes, maybe a dirge, for my beloved brother.'

'Is he dead?'

She shook her head.

'Dying?'

Now a nod, and she pointed towards the lake.

'Drowning?' Beisho said.

'Eaten!' the woman replied. 'He's in the belly of some fish.'

'And yet you know he's alive?'

'We're twins,' the woman explained. 'And our minds are . . . *intertwined*. I would know if he were dead.'

'Terrible,' Beisho said. 'Terrible.'

'What is?' Ruty enquired. Bored with watching Joom's piscine parade, he had come to find out what all the sobbing was about.

'This lady—'

'My name is Leauqueau,' she put in.

'Leauqueau's brother has been devoured by a fish.'

'That's unfortunate,' Ruty replied. 'Was he a midget, or was it a very big fish?'

'There are all manner of beasts out there,' Leauqueau replied, staring off towards the lake's obsidian waters. 'And not all of them are fish.'

'Oh?' said Ruty, interested now. He had for many years been creating a bestiary; a catalogue of every species of fauna in the Colonies. Perhaps there was an unknown creature out there in the lake's cold waters, awaiting both a discoverer and a name to be known by. 'We should find this man-eater,' he said. 'And save the lady's brother.'

'We would of course,' Beisho swiftly replied. 'But regrettably we have no boat.'

'Then we'll hire one.'

'We have no money.'

'I have money,' Leauqueau promptly interjected.

'But how will we *find* the beast?' Beisho protested. 'In such vast waters?'

'Maybe we won't,' Ruty said, 'but I'd rather spend the day fishing than trying to find a scribe—'.

'You want a scribe?' said Leauqueau. 'Then we are indeed well-met. My brother is a poet.'

'Indeed?' Beisho replied, feigning indifference.

'Are his works translated?' Ruty asked. 'Only Laureate Fie can perform that function, for a *very* modest consideration.'

Leauqueau turned her silver gaze on Beisho. 'I think the gods intended our paths to cross,' she said.

'Are there gods in Joom?' Ruty enquired.

'I didn't believe there were, until now,' Leauqueau replied.

Ruty laughed. 'There!' he said to Beisho. 'She thinks you're proof of the very thing you denied.'

'Sophistry,' Beisho snapped back.

'Then let's turn our attention to more practical matters,' Ruty said. 'Lady, if you will supply the wherewithal, I will hie down to the harbour and hire a vessel forthwith.'

'Don't tell anyone what we're about,' she warned, passing a few coins over. 'The mariners are superstitious.'

'Then they're fools,' Beisho said. 'We'll find your brother for you, without the aid of gods. And then I'll turn his rhymes to quicksilver in a dozen tongues, and we'll all be happy.'

'How do you know your brother is in the lake?' Beisho asked Leauqueau as he escorted her down to the harbour. 'Perhaps he was eaten by a Steliamak. I've seen several circling.'

'I know it was the lake,' she said. 'It obsessed him.'

'Why?'

'Because of Quiddity.'

'Quiddity?' Here was a word not often breathed in daylight.

'You have heard of it?'

'Of course. What man of culture has not heard of the great dream-sea? Why, we met a fellow just a few months ago, Ruty and me, who claimed to have been a beacon-keeper on its shores. But it's a thousand miles from here.'

'More. Much more.'

'So how—?'

'There's a legend in Joom. A legend my brother believed to his very soul.' That said, she fell silent.

'Are you going to tell me what it is?' Fie asked.

She dropped her voice to a whisper. 'It's said that in certain seasons the waters of the dream-sea find their way through channels far below the earth into the lake,' she replied.

Beisho made a low whistle. 'That *is* a tale,' he said.

'There's more,' she told him. 'The legend says that we're all descended from dreamers cast up by those tides. Dreamers from another realm of being.'

'The *Sapas Humana*.'

'That's right.'

'It's certainly better than believing we're descended from gods,' Beisho observed. 'Do you believe all of this?'

'I believe it for my brother's sake.'

'That's reason enough, I suppose.'

Ruty was climbing the slope towards them, looking somewhat mournful. 'Well, I found us something,' he said, 'and it floats. That's about the best I can say for it.'

They followed him back down to the quay, and while they walked he explained that all the fishermen had either refused to hire out their boats or demanded absurd sums of money for their services. Only one captain had been willing to take them out onto the lake for such a piffling sum.

'His name is Flimchen,' Ruty said, 'and I think he's half crazy.'

'What makes you say that?' Beisho asked.

'Judge for yourself,' Ruty said, standing aside to let Beisho and Leauqueau have sight of the vessel and its master.

It was impossible to say which was in a sorrier state. Both had seen too many storms, too many crackings and patchings; both were sodden to their core: one with water, the other, to judge by his stare, with something stronger.

'Don't expect your money back,' the grizzled sailor announced from the slimy boards of his boat. 'Whether you come or not it's no matter to me, but I'm keeping the fee.' He tapped his pocket. 'So fuck you all.'

'Do you still want to go?' Ruty asked Beisho.

'Of course,' Fie replied, making no effort to approach the boat.

'You two may come,' Flimchen replied. 'But not your . . . passenger.' He jabbed a hang-nailed finger in Leauqueau's direction.

'Is this mariner's lore?' Beisho wanted to know.

'No,' said the fisherman, 'I have a fear of that sex, since all my six brothers died in the arms of a woman.'

'The same woman?' Ruty said, amazed.

'I'm not telling,' came the reply. 'And neither are they.'

'I'm afraid we can't go without her,' Beisho said.

'Yes you can,' Leauqueau replied. 'You must. I'll wait here for you.'

'Make up your minds,' Flimchen demanded. 'We only have two hours before night fall. The lake's a deal more lethal under the twelve moons.'

'We're going, for sure,' Ruty said, seizing hold of Beisho's arm and ushering him to the puddled steps that led down to the boat. 'Do you have nets and knives aboard?'

'Of course,' said Flimchen. 'What manner of fish are you after?'

'Something large enough to have devoured this woman's brother.'

'I daresay we can find you such a beast,' Flimchen said, with a sideways glance at Beisho. 'As long as you're ready to haul it in and brain it.'

'Never readier,' Beisho replied, as he gingerly set foot on the rocking vessel. 'As long as you can find the fish, we'll brain it with one *thwack*!'

His show of courage brought a sly smile from the fisherman. 'A *thwack*, eh?'

'I have no fear,' Beisho replied.

The mariner's smile disappeared. 'Then take a little of mine,' he said, 'for I've got plenty. I've never turned my bow towards those waters without fearing what I would find. Or what would find me.'

And so saying, he loosed the rope that secured the boat against the quay and returning to the stern, turned on the motor and guided his chugging vessel out of the little harbour towards the deeps.

More to keep his mind off the sickening motion of the boat than because he genuinely valued the mariner's opinion, Beisho related what Leauqueau had told him about the legends of the lake and asked Flimchen if he believed the stories.

'Some people say we come from *fish*,' he replied, 'but I've been handling fish all my life and I never saw one – not *one* – with a shadow of a soul in its eyes.'

'So you believe we're descended from human castaways?' Ruty said.

'More than likely.'

Ruty made a sour face. 'Does that trouble you?' Beisho required of him.

'To be descended from a dreaming species?' Ruty said. 'Yes . . . that troubles me.'

'Why?'

'Because it means we're *accidents*, Fie. Bastard children. Without purpose. Without meaning.'

'Then we must make our meaning,' Beisho said.

The mariner seemed to approve of this, to judge by the little grunt he gave.

'And when we die?' Ruty said. 'What then? When we can no longer make meaning for ourselves? Do we just fade away, like dreams?'

'That will not be so bad,' Flimchen said, 'if that's the way of it.'

'Will it not?' Ruty said, his voice lowered to a melancholy

whisper. 'I wonder . . .'

There was a long silence then, while the boat moved out over the dark waters. It was Flimchen who broke the hush.

'There,' he said, and pointed across the water.

A large form was breaking surface, turning as it did so, showing its mottled flesh.

'What is it?' Beisho breathed.

'At a guess . . .' came the reply, '. . . your man-eater.'

As if it knew it was being debated, the creature raised its ungainly head from the water. It was a wretched thing, no doubt of that, lacking both grace and symmetry, its head eyeless and encrusted, its flanks gouged and raw.

'I don't see its mouth,' Ruty said.

'Perhaps it doesn't have one.'

'Then how does it eat men?'

'Maybe it doesn't,' Beisho said, still studying the creature. 'Maybe it's the wrong animal.'

'It hears us,' Flimchen said, and as he spoke the beast came at the boat head-on.

'Knives! Knives!' Beisho yelled.

Flimchen was already scrabbling in the bottom of the boat for weaponry, but before he could lay his hands on a blade the beast struck the boat. The vessel lurched, and Ruty lost his footing on the rot-slickened boards. Flailing, he was pitched over the gunwales and into the water. Despite his fat he sank in an instant, and for a moment Beisho thought he'd had his last sight of his comrade. A sob of grief and rage escaped him, but it was drowned out by a great commotion at the bow, and in a roar of frenzied water Ruty was borne up out of the lake on the snout of the beast. He reached for Beisho's arm, caught hold of it and was hauled back into the vessel, gasping for breath.

'*It comes again!*' the mariner cried. This time he was armed with a short harpoon, and as the beast ploughed towards the tossing boat he threw the weapon, striking his target in the centre of its misshapen head.

A din escaped the beast that would have better come from a woman's throat: a shriek of agony that stopped so abruptly Beisho thought the creature had been dealt a mortal wound, and had perished then and there. But no; no sooner had the shriek ceased that the beast began to thrash with such vehemence it threatened to capsize the boat entirely.

Flimchen had lashed the harpoon rope to a rusted ring set in the gunwale, and then returned to the stern.

'What are we going to do?' Beisho demanded, his eyes wild.

'We're going to drag its foul carcass back to shore.'

'We still don't know that this is the right beast,' Ruty reminded them.

'I've not seen a thing the like of this in forty years of fishing,' the mariner replied. 'If there's another man-eater out there then let somebody else catch the fucker.'

He gunned the motor, and turned his vessel around, pointing its bow towards Joom. 'Hold on!' he said. 'I'm going to drive the boat up onto the shingle, and beach the beast at the same time!'

If the wounded creature understood what plans were being laid against it, then it made no attempt to resist, even though its bulk suggested it might well have succeeded.

'It's surely dying,' Beisho said as he watched the creature turning belly up in the bloodied spume.

'Perhaps,' said Ruty.

'You doubt it?'

'This thing has neither eyes nor mouth,' Ruty observed. 'Doesn't that strike you as odd?'

Beisho stared at his comrade. 'What's your point, Rutaluka?'

'There's more mystery here than we comprehend,' Ruty replied. 'Remember what the beacon-keeper told us about Quiddity's waters? How they *grew* on those that floated there?'

Beisho's gaze returned to the beast.

'Perhaps we're looking at some kind of encrustation around living flesh,' Ruty said.

'The flesh of *Humana*? Our ancestors?' Beisho murmured.'

'Perhaps.'

A tiny smile crossed Beisho's face. 'Now I wish the gods *were* in their cloudy courts, Ruty, to see how we discover ourselves.'

The beast's scream had carried across the lake's clear air and a small crowd had come down to the harbour to watch the spectacle. Seeing that the boat was headed for the shore, the throng made its way from the quay to the shingle, its numbers swelling as word of what had taken place spread. Leauqueau was more impatient than the rest. She was standing knee-deep in the water, her arms outstretched as if to will her sibling into her embrace.

'Be ready!' Flimchen said. 'As soon as we strike the shore haul on the rope.'

Seconds later the boat grated on the shingle, its momentum

carrying it up the shallow beach until its stern had cleared the water entirely. Ruty was first out, ploughing into the surf to haul the beast in. Beisho followed, but not before he announced to Leauqueau:

'We have it? See? *We have it!*'

Flimchen called for some help from the crowd, and four of the witnesses came to their aid, bending to the task of dragging the beast out of its native element and up onto the shingle. There were several cries of disgust as it cleared the waves, and several more of astonishment: the lake had never given up anything that resembled this monstrosity.

Beached, the creature was even uglier than it had been when half-submerged: an ill-made, wretched thing, the like of which even Ruty – who had catalogued fauna glimpsed by only a handful of souls – had never laid eyes on.

'What now?' Beisho hissed to him when the creature was so far out of the water it had no hope of struggling back.

'We take a blade to it,' Ruty said. 'If her brother's inside, we have to cut him out.'

Beisho looked decidedly discomfited by this prospect, but with Leauqueau's eyes – and the eyes of perhaps fifty onlookers – upon him, this was no time for squeamishness. Reaching into the boat, he snatched up a sizeable knife and with a smile that he trusted was impressively casual he drove the blade into the beast's flank. The creature convulsed, but not to escape the blade. Rather it seemed to *present* its body to the cutting edge, as if eager to be gutted.

The hide of the thing was tough (it didn't bleed; nor was there sign of bone or sinew beneath) and had Ruty not also snatched up a knife and stooped to help, the night might well have fallen before Beisho made an impression. But together they unknitted the carcass from one end to the other, gobs of encrusted flesh coming away with every slice. And suddenly, as they worked, a sob of anguish rose from the interior of the thing, answered a moment later by a cry from Leauqueau.

'It's him!' she said. 'It's my brother!'

Beisho and Ruty worked with fresh fervour now, abandoning the blades for fear of doing harm to the living flesh inside. They plunged their arms into the wound they'd opened, and like midwives at some monstrous birth, dug to deliver the prisoner from his cell. Blood began to seep from the opening, though it was not, they both knew, the blood of the beast. It was the victim who was bleeding, not the devourer.

Unable to stand by any longer, Leauqueau lent her sinew to the struggle, and Flimchen, who had until now watched with bemusement, bent to labour beside them. Under the assault of eight hands the flank of the creature gaped, and they finally had sight of the victim.

There was not one body inside, but two. Both naked, and embracing. One was Leauqueau's brother, his flesh white and wasted, his gaze crazed. The other was a woman. She had been pierced by the harpoon, and was still bleeding copiously. The point had entered the top of her skull and emerged at her chin.

Leauqueau unleashed a deafening shriek, and retreated from the carcass into the surf.

'*Gods! Gods!*' she shrieked. 'See what he has done!'

Her imprecation shook her brother from his stupor. He let the dead woman – with whom he had surely been in congress – slip from his arms, and started to crawl out into the open air, careless of his nakedness.

'She was nothing to me!' he said to Leauqueau, 'I saw her in the water, and I went to rescue her!'

Beisho shook his head. 'I'm not following any of this,' he complained.

'I am,' Ruty replied, directing Beisho's gaze back to the body of the woman. 'That's our human dreamer,' he said. 'She was carried up into the lake from Quiddity.'

'And he swam out to save her?'

'Or make love to her.'

'And the beast took them both.'

'There *is* no beast,' Ruty said, 'it's as the beacon-keeper told us. The waters take human flesh and *fantasticate* it . . .' He tore at the innards of the beast. 'This thing has no heart. No lungs. No entrails. It's a veil, built around dreaming tissue.' He looked at the dead woman. 'This is her subtle body. The real thing is dead on a bed somewhere, far, far from here.'

'Pitiful,' said Beisho.

'At least we saved the lad,' Ruty replied.

He turned as he spoke, in time to catch sight of Leauqueau stooping to lift a rock from beneath the waves. Seeing murder in her eyes, he started towards her with a shout. But she ignored him. She raised the stone high above her head and brought it down on her brother's skull, striking once, twice, three times, and opening a grievous wound with each blow. Blood gushed from his head, and he fell backwards into the surf. He was dead by the time Ruty reached him; one of his eyes struck from its socket, the other gaping, as if in astonishment that salvation and death had come in such close succession.

Leauqueau put up no defence against arrest. She waited tearlessly on the shore while officers were called, and was in due course taken away, without uttering another word. By the time Beisho and Ruty had told their part of the tale, then watched the bodies of the lovers removed, and finally bade their farewells to Flimchen, night had long since fallen. Their limbs ached for want of rest, and their bellies for want of nourishment.

'We have no money,' Ruty said as they wandered back up the steep street.

'No, but we may yet prosper,' Beisho said.

'How?'

'Will this story not become legendary?'

'Perhaps.'

'And will people not ask: *What did the dead lad do before the dream-sea took him?* And hearing that his profession was that of *poet*, will they not ache to have a copy of his sonnets?'

'Ah . . .' said Ruty.

'I shall be his sole translator, my friend. And we shall make a little fortune from his works.'

'But where *are* his poems?'

'We'll find them,' Beisho replied confidently, and led them back to the step where he had first discovered Leauqueau weeping.

The door was sealed, but no lock or bolt had ever bested Ruty's fingers. The two adventurers were inside the humble house in thirty seconds, and duly separated to look for the works of the deceased poet. It was a melancholy search, turning over the belongings of the doomed siblings, but after several minutes it bore fruit. In the drawer of a dresser in one of the upper rooms Ruty found a book bound in scaly ochre skin, and brought it down to Beisho with a triumphant whoop.

'This binding comes from a species that's not in my bestiary,' he said, handing the volume over. 'It's probably out there in the lake somewhere. I want to hire another boat when you've made your fortune . . .'

'You can go fishing alone,' Beisho replied. 'I'm going to buy myself a pavilion on the hill-top, and watch you from the comfort of my pillows.'

He started to flick through the pages of the book, while Ruty mused on this zoological mystery.

'It looks to be the skin of a serpent,' he said.

'That's fitting,' Beisho remarked dryly, 'given the subject of the works it encloses.'

'He writes of serpents?'

'He writes of *one* serpent,' Beisho replied. 'The beast between his legs. 'He kept flicking and scanning, his face a portrait of disgust. 'I've never ready anything so obscene in my life. This isn't poetry. It's instructions on how to violate your sister, orifice by orifice.' He passed the book to Ruty. 'Nobody's going to publish filth like this.'

Ruty glanced through the book. The dead man's masterworks were barely doggerel, the vellum on which they were scrawled suspiciously stained here and there. Ruty pocketed the book, for perusal at a later date.

'For the binding . . .' he explained, as Beisho cast him a baleful glance.

Their business in the house done, they wandered out into the night. On the step Beisho stared up at the twelve moons admiringly.

'Do you think the same heavens gaze down on *Sapas Humana*?' Ruty wondered.

'Of course not,' Beisho replied. 'They live in cells, my friend. And they dream because they long to escape them.'

'I'd like to meet one . . . a *living* one, I mean . . . and send him back to tell the human world about us. Wouldn't that be something?'

'And where would they find the words to capture our charm?' Beisho asked him. 'We're beyond description.'

'Then maybe *we* should go to *them*,' Ruty said. 'Steal a vessel and set sail upon the dream-sea until we reach their island.'

'Why bother?' Beisho replied as he started up the hill.

'Because we're *nothing* here. Less than nothing. But there, we'd be like gods, wouldn't we?'

Beisho gave his companion a curious look; two parts contempt to one of stupefaction.

'I never know with you, Rutaluka—' he said.

'You never know what?'

'Whether you're a genius or an imbecile.'

'Oh that,' Ruty said, with a sly grin. 'Well I know the truth of it, but I'm not telling.'

Beisho opened his mouth to voice some pithy reply, but thought better of it. Instead he headed on up the street, towards the fish-market where they would be obliged to find food and lodging in yesterday's sawdust.

Ruty lingered a moment, to cast a glance down the slope to the harbour and the lake beyond. The dozen moons gleamed in its waters, but their mellow radiance did not pierce the depths. Whatever sleeping souls the lake concealed, they were safe in their slumbers tonight, and would not be woken until their dreams were done.

ISOBEL AVENS RETURNS TO STEPNEY IN THE SPRING

by

M. John Harrison

M. John Harrison's writing career began in 1966 during his seven-year stint as Literary Editor on *New Worlds* magazine, when he published his first novel *The Committed Men*. Since then he has published six novels, three collections, and a graphic novel, the latter in collaboration with artist Ian Miller. In 1989 he won Great Britain's Boardman Tasker Memorial award for his novel *Climbers*, the first work of fiction ever to do so. His most recent novel is *The Course of the Heart*.

This was a story I could not turn down, despite my initial doubts that it fit the parameters I had in mind for *Little Deaths*. But as the story went through the editing process and I reread it a few more times, I thought about Isobel and her odd yearnings and my doubts vanished.

ISOBEL AVENS RETURNS TO STEPNEY IN THE SPRING

The third of September this year I spent the evening watching TV in an upstairs flat in North London. Some story of love and transfiguration, cropped into all the wrong proportions for the small screen. The flat wasn't mine. It belonged to a friend I was staying with. There were French posters on the walls, dusty CDs stacked on the old-fashioned sideboard, piles of newspapers subsiding day by day into yellowing fans on the carpet. Outside, Tottenham stretched away, Greek driving schools, Turkish social clubs. Turn the TV off and you could hear nothing. Turn it back on and the film unrolled, passages of guilt with lost edges, photographed in white and blue light. At about half past eleven the phone rang.

I picked it up. 'Hello?'

It was Isobel Avens.

'Oh China,' she said. She burst into tears.

I said: 'Can you drive?'

'No,' she said.

I looked at my watch. 'I'll come and fetch you.'

'You can't,' she said. 'I'm here. You can't come here.'

I said: 'Be outside, love. Just try and get yourself downstairs. Be outside and I'll pick you up on the pavement there.'

There was a silence.

'Can you do that?'

'Yes,' she said.

Oh China. The first two days she wouldn't get much further than that.

'Don't try to talk,' I advised.

London was as quiet as a nursing home corridor. I turned up the car stereo. Tom Waits, 'Downtown Train'. Music stuffed with sentiments you recognize but daren't admit to yourself. I let the BMW slip down Green Lanes, through Camden into the centre; then west. I was pushing the odd traffic light at orange, clipping the apex off a safe bend here and there. I told myself I wasn't going to get killed for her. What I meant was that if I did she would have no one left. I took the Embankment at eight thousand revs, nosing down heavily on the brakes at Chelsea Wharf to get round into Gunter Grove. No one was there to see. By half past twelve I was on Queensborough Road, where I found her standing very straight in the mercury light outside Alexander's building, the jacket of a Karl Lagerfeld suit thrown across her shoulders and one piece of expensive leather luggage at her feet. She bent into the car. Her face was white and exhausted and her breath stank. The way Alexander had dumped her was as cruel as everything else he did. She had flown back steerage from the Miami clinic reeling from jet lag, expecting to fall into his arms and be loved and comforted. He told her, 'As a doctor I don't think I can do any more for you.' The ground hadn't just shifted on her: it was out from under her feet. Suddenly she was only his patient again. In the metallic glare of the street lamps, I noticed a stipple of ulceration across her collar bones. I switched on the courtesy light to look closer. Tiny hectic sores, closely spaced.

I said: 'Christ, Isobel.'

'It's just a virus,' she said. 'Just a side-effect.'

'Is anything worth this?'

She put her arms around me and sobbed.

'Oh China, China.'

It isn't that she wants me; only that she has no one else. Yet every time I smell her body my heart lurches. The years I lived with her I *slept* so soundly. Then Alexander did this irreversible thing to her, the thing she had always wanted, and now everything is fucked up and eerie and it will be that way forever.

I said: 'I'll take you home.'

'Will you stay?'

'What else?'

My name is Mick Rose, which is why people have always called me 'China'. From the moment we met, Isobel Avens was fascinated by that. Later, she would hold my face between her hands in the night and whisper dreamily over and over – 'Oh, China, China, China. China.' But it was something else that attracted her to me. The year we met, she lived in Stratford-on-Avon. I walked into the cafe at the little toy aerodrome they have there and it was she who served me.

She was twenty-five years old: slow, heavy-bodied, easily delighted by the world. Her hair was red. She wore a rusty pink blouse, a black ankle-length skirt with lace at the hem. Her feet were like boats in great brown Dr Marten's shoes. When she saw me looking down at them in amusement, she said: 'Oh, these aren't my real Docs, these are my cheap imitation ones.' She showed me how the left one was coming apart at the seams. 'Brilliant, eh?' She smelled of vanilla and sex. She radiated heat. I could always feel the heat of her a yard away.

'I'd love to be able to fly,' she told me.

She laughed and hugged herself.

'You must feel so free.'

She thought I was the pilot of the little private Cessna she could see out of the cafe window. In fact I had only come to deliver its cargo – an unadmitted load for an unadmitted destination – some commercial research centre in Zürich or Budapest. At the time I called myself *Rose Medical Services, Plc*. My fleet comprised a single Vauxhall Astra van into which I had dropped the engine, brakes and suspension of a two litre GTE insurance write-off. I specialized. If it was small I guaranteed to move it anywhere in Britain within twelve hours; occasionally, if the price was right, to selected points in Europe. Recombinant DNA: viruses at controlled temperatures, sometimes in live hosts: cell cultures in heavily armoured flasks. What they were used for I had no idea. I didn't really want an idea until much later; and that turned out to be much too late.

I said: 'It can't be so hard to learn.'

'Flying?'

'It can't be so hard.'

Before a week was out we were inventing one another hand over fist. It was an extraordinary summer. You have to imagine this—

Saturday afternoon. Stratford Waterside. The river has a lively look despite the breathless air and heated sky above it. Waterside is full of jugglers and fire-eaters, entertaining thick crowds of Americans and Japanese. There is hardly room to move. Despite this, on a patch of grass by the water, two lovers, trapped in the great circular argument, are making that futile attempt all lovers make to get inside one another and stay there for good. He can't stop touching her because she wants him so. She wants him so because he can't stop touching her. A feeding swan surfaces, caught up with some strands of very pale green weed. Rippling in the sudden warm breeze which blows across the river from the direction of the theatre, these seem for a moment like ribbons tied with a delicate knot – the gentle, deliberate artifice of a conscious world.

'Oh look! Look!' she says.

He says: 'Would you like to be a swan?'

'I'd have to leave the aerodrome.'

He says: 'Come and live with me and be a swan.'

Neither of them have the slightest idea what they are talking about.

Business was good. Within three months I had bought a second van. I persuaded Isobel Avens to leave Stratford and throw in with me. On the morning of her last day at the aerodrome, she woke up early and shook me until I was awake too.

'China!' she said.

'What?'

'China!'

I said: 'What?'

'I flew!'

It was a dream of praxis. It was a hint of what she might have. It was her first step on the escalator up to Alexander's clinic.

'I was in a huge computer room. Everyone's work was displayed on one screen like a wall. I couldn't find my A-prompt!' People laughed at her, but nicely. 'It was all good fun, and they were very helpful.' Suddenly she had learned what she had to know, and she was floating up and flying into the screen, and through it, 'out of the room, into the air above the world.' The sky was crowded with other people, she said. 'But I just went swooping past and around and between them.' She let herself fall just for the fun of it: she soared, her whole body taut and trembling like the fabric of a kite. Her breath went out with a great laugh. Whenever she was tired she could perch like a bird. 'I loved it!' she told me. 'Oh, I loved it!'

How can you be so jealous of a dream?

I said: 'It sounds as if you won't need me soon.'

She clutched at me.

'You help me to fly,' she said. 'Don't dare go away, China! Don't dare!'

She pulled my face close to hers and gave me little dabbing kisses on the mouth and eyes. I looked at my watch. Half past six. The bed was already damp and hot: I could see that we were going to make it worse. She pulled me on top of her, and at the height of things, sweating and inturned and breathless and on the edge, she whispered, 'Oh lovely, lovely, lovely,' as if she had seen something I couldn't. 'So lovely, so beautiful!' Her eyes moved as if she was watching something pass. I could only watch her, moving under me, marvellous and wet, solid and real, everything I ever wanted.

The worst thing you can do at the beginning of something fragile is to say what it is. The night I drove her back from Queensborough Road to her little house in the gentrified East End, things were very simple. For forty-eight hours all she would do was wail and sob and throw up on me. She refused to eat, she couldn't bear to sleep. If she dropped off for ten minutes, she would wake silent for the instant it took her to remember what had happened. Then this appalling dull asthmatic noise would come out of her – 'zhhh, zhhh, zhhh', somewhere between retching and whining – as she tried to suppress the memory, and wake me up, and sob, all at the same time.

I was always awake anyway.

'Hush now, it will get better. I know.'

I knew because she had done the same thing to me.

'China, I'm so sorry.'

'Hush. Don't be sorry. Get better.'

'I'm so sorry to have made you feel like this.'

I wiped her nose.

'Hush.'

That part was easy. I could dress her ulcers and take care of what was coming out of them, relieve the other effects of what they had done to her in Miami, and watch for whatever else might happen. I could hold her in my arms all night and tell lies and believe I was only there for her. But soon she asked me,

'Will you live here again, China?'

'You know it's all I want,' I said.

She warned: 'I'm not promising anything.'

'I don't want you to,' I said.

I said: 'I just want you to need me for something.'

That whole September we were as awkward as children. We didn't quite know what to say. We didn't quite know what to do with one another. We could see it would take time and patience. We shared the bed rather shyly, and showed one another quite ordinary things as gifts.

'Look!'

Sunshine fell across the breakfast table, onto lilies and pink napery. (I am not making this up.)

'Look!'

A grey cat nosed out of a doorway in London E3.

'Did you have a nice weekend?'

'It was a lovely weekend. Lovely.'

'Look.'

Canary Wharf, shining in the oblique evening light!

In our earliest days together, while she was still working at the aerodrome, I had watched with almost uncontainable delight as she moved about a room. I had stayed awake while she slept, so that I could prop myself up on one elbow and look at her and shiver with happiness. Now when I watched, it was with fear. For her. For both of us. She had come down off the tightrope for a while. But things were still so precariously balanced. Her new body was all soft new colours in the bedside lamplight. She was thin now, and shaped quite differently: but as hot as ever, hot as a child with fever. When I fucked her she was like a bundle of hot wires. I was like a boy. I trembled and caught my breath when I felt with my fingertips the damp feathery lips of her cunt, but I was too aware of the dangers to be carried away. I didn't dare let her see how much this meant to me. Neither of us knew what to want of the other any more. We had forgotten one another's rhythms. In addition, she was remembering someone else's: it was Alexander who had constructed for me this bundle of hot, thin, hollow bones, wrapped round me in the night by desires and demands I didn't yet know how to fulfil. Before the Miami treatments she had loved me to watch her as she became aroused. Now she needed to hide, at least for a time. She would pull at my arms and shoulders, shy and desperate at the same time; then, as soon as I understood that she wanted to be fucked, push her face into the side of mine so I couldn't look at her. After a while she would turn on to her side; encourage me to enter from behind; stare away into some distance implied by us, our failures, the dark room. I told myself I didn't care if she was thinking of him. Just so long as she had got this far, which was far enough to begin to be cured in her sex where he had wounded her as badly as anywhere else. I told myself I couldn't heal her there, only allow her to use me to heal herself.

At the start of something so fragile the worst mistake you can make is to say what you hope. But inside your heart you can't help speaking, and by that speech you have already blown it.

After Isobel and I moved down to London from Stratford, business began to take up most of my time. Out of an instinctive caution, I dropped the word 'medical' from the company description and called myself simply *Rose Services*. *Rose Services* soon became twenty quick vans, some low-cost storage space, and a licence to carry the products of new genetic research to and from Eastern Europe. If I was to take advantage of the expanding markets there, I decided, I would need an office.

'Let's go to Budapest,' I said to Isobel.

She hugged my arm.

'Will there be ice on the Danube?' she said.

'There will.'

There was.

'China, we came all the way to Hungary!'

She had never been out of Britain. She had never flown in an aeroplane. She was delighted even by the hotel. I had booked us into a place called the Palace, on Rakoczi Street. Like the city itself, the Palace had once been something: now it was a dump. Bare flex hung out of the light switches on the fourth-floor corridors. The wallpaper had charred in elegant spirals above the corners of the radiators. Every morning in the famous Jugendstil restaurant, they served us watery orange squash. The rooms were too hot. Everything else – coffee, food, water from the cold tap – was lukewarm. It was never quiet, even very late at night. Ambulances and police cars warbled past. Drunks screamed suddenly or made noises like animals. But our room had French windows opening on to a balcony with wrought iron railings. From there in the freezing air, we could look across a sort of high courtyard with one or two flakes of snow falling into it, at the other balconies and their lighted windows. That first evening, Isobel loved it.

'China, isn't it fantastic? Isn't it?'

Then something happened to her in her sleep. I wouldn't have known, but I woke up unbearably hot at three a.m., sweating and dry-mouthed beneath the peculiar fawn fur blanket they give you to sleep under at the Palace. The bathroom was even hotter than the bedroom and smelled faintly of very old piss. When I turned the tap on to splash my face, nothing came out of it. I stood there in the dark for a moment, swaying, while I waited for it to run. I heard Isobel say reasonably: 'It's a system fault.'

After a moment she said, 'Oh no. Oh no,' in such a quiet, sad voice that I went back to the bed and touched her gently.

'Isobel. Wake up.'

She began to whimper and throw herself about.

'The system's down,' she tried to explain to someone.

'Isobel. Isobel.'

'The system!'

'Isobel.'

She woke up and clutched at me. She pushed her face blindly into my chest. She trembled.

'China!'

It was February, a year or two after we had met. I didn't know it, but things were already going wrong for her. Her dreams had begun to waste her from the inside.

She said indistinctly: 'I want to go back home.'

'Isobel, it was only a dream.'

'I couldn't fly,' she said.

She stared up at me in astonishment.

'China, I couldn't *fly*.'

At breakfast she hardly spoke. All morning she was thoughtful and withdrawn. But when I suggested that we walk down to the Danube via the Basilica at St Stephen's, cross over to Buda and eat lunch, she seemed delighted. The air was cold and clear. The trees were distinct and photographic in the bright pale February light. We stared out across the New City from the Disney-white battlements of Fisherman's Bastion. 'Those bridges!' Isobel said. 'Look at them in the sun!' She had bought a new camera for the trip, a Pentax with a motor-wind and zoom. 'I'm going to take a panorama.' She eyed the distorted reflection of the Bastion in the mirror-glass windows of the Hilton hotel. 'Stand over there, China, I want one of you, too. No, *there*, you idiot!' Snow began to fall, in flakes the size of five-forint pieces.

'China!'

For the rest of the day – for the rest of the holiday – she was as delighted by things as ever. We visited the Zoo. ('Look! Owls!') We caught a train to Szentendre. We photographed one another beneath the huge winged woman at the top of the Gellert Hill. We translated the titles of the news-stand paperbacks.

'What does this mean, "Nagy Secz"?'

'You know very well what it means, Isobel.'

I looked at my watch.

I said: 'It's time to eat.'

'Oh no. Must we?'

Isobel hated Hungarian food.

'China,' she would complain, 'why has *everything* got *cream* on it?'

But she loved the red and grey buses. She loved the street signs, TOTO LOTTO, HIRLAP, TRAFIK. She loved Old Buda, re-deemed by the snow: white, clean, properly picturesque.

And she couldn't get enough of the Danube.

'Look. China, it's fucking huge! Isn't it fucking huge?'

I said: 'Look at the speed of it.'

At midnight on our last day we stood in the exact centre of the Erzsebet bridge, gazing north. Szentendre and Danube Bend were out there somewhere, locked in a Middle European night stretching all the way to Czechoslovakia. Ice floes like huge lily pads raced towards us in the dark. You could hear them turning and dipping under one another, piling up briefly round the huge piers, jostling across the whole vast breadth of the river as they rushed south. No river is ugly after dark. But the Danube doesn't care for anyone: without warning the Medieval cold came up off the water and reached on to the bridge for us. It was as if we had seen something move. We stepped back, straight into the traffic which grinds all night across the bridge from Buda into Pest.

'China!'

'Be careful!'

You have to imagine this—

Two naive and happy middleclass people embracing on a bridge. Caught between the river and the road, they grin and shiver at one another, unable to distinguish between identity and geography, love and the need to keep warm.

'Look at the *speed* of it.'

'Oh China, the Danube!'

Suddenly she turned away.

She said: 'I'm cold now.'

She thought for a moment.

'I don't want to go on the aeroplane,' she said. 'They're not the real thing after all.'

I took her hands between mine.

'It will be OK when you get home,' I promised.

But London didn't seem to help. For months I woke in the night to find she was awake too, staring emptily up at the ceiling in the darkness. Unable to comprehend her despair, I would consult my watch and ask her, 'Do you want anything?' She would shake her head and advise patiently, 'Go to sleep now love,' as if she was being kept awake by a bad period.

I bought the house in Stepney at about that time. It was in a prettily-renovated terrace with reproduction Victorian street lamps. There were wrought iron security grids over every other front door, and someone had planted the extensive shared gardens at the back with ilex, ornamental rowan, even a fig. Isobel loved it. She decorated the rooms herself, then filled them with the sound of her favourite music— The Blue Aeroplanes' 'Yr Own World'; Tom Petty,

'Learning to Fly'. For our bedroom she bought two big blanket chests and polished them to a deep buttery colour. 'Come and look, China! Aren't they beautiful?' Inside, they smelled of new wood. The whole house smelled of new wood for days after we moved in: beeswax, new wood, dried roses.

I said: 'I want it to be yours.'

It had to be in her name anyway, I admitted: for accounting purposes.

'But also in case anything happens.'

She laughed.

'China, what could happen?'

What happened was that one of my local drivers went sick, and I asked her to deliver something for me.

I said: 'It's not far. Just across to Brook Green. Some clinic.'

I passed her the details.

'A Dr Alexander. You could make it in an hour, there and back.'

She stared at me.

'*You* could make it in an hour,' she said.

She read the job sheet.

'What do they do there?' she asked.

I said irritably: 'How would I know? Cosmetic medicine. Fantasy factory stuff. Does it matter?'

She put her arms round me.

'China, I was only trying to be interested.'

'Never ask them what they do with the stuff,' I warned her. 'Will you do it?'

She said: 'If you kiss me properly.'

'How was it?' I asked when she got back.

She laughed.

'At first they thought I was a patient!'

Running upstairs to change, she called down:

'I quite like West London.'

Isobel's new body delighted her. But she seemed bemused too, as if it had been given to someone else. How much had Alexander promised her? How much had she expected from the Miami treatments? All I knew was that she had flown out obsessed and returned ill. When she talked, she would talk only about the flight home. 'I could see a sunrise over the wing of the airliner, red and gold. I was trying hard to read a book, but I couldn't stop looking out at this cold wintery sunrise above the clouds. It seemed to last for hours.' She stared at me as if she had just thought of something. 'How could I see a sunrise, China? It was dark when we landed!'

Her dreams had always drawn her from ordinary things. All that gentle, warm September she was trying to get back.

'Do you like me again?' she would ask shyly.

It was hard for her to say what she meant. Standing in front of the mirror in the morning in the soft grey slanting light from the bedroom window, dazed and sidetracked by her own narcissism, she could only repeat:

'Do you like me this way?'

Or at night in bed: 'Is it good this way? Is it good? What does it feel like?'

'Isobel—'

In the end it was always easier to let her evade the issue.

'I never stopped liking you,' I would lie and she would reply absently, as if I hadn't spoken:

'Because I want us to like each other again.'

And then add, presenting her back to the mirror and looking at herself over one shoulder:

'I wish I'd had more done. My legs are still too fat.'

If part of her was still trying to fly back from Miami and all Miami entailed, much of the rest was in Brook Green with Alexander. As September died into October, and then the first few cold days of November, I found that increasingly hard to bear. She cried in the night, but no longer woke me up for comfort. Her gaze would come unfocussed in the afternoons. Unable to be near her while, thinking of him, she pretended to leaf through *Vogue* and *Harper's*, I walked out into the rainy unredeemed Whitechapel streets. Suddenly it was an hour later and I was watching the lights come on in a hardware shop window on Roman Road.

Other times, when it seemed to be going well, I couldn't contain my delight. I got up in the night and thrashed the BMW to Sheffield and back; parked outside the house and slept an hour in the rear seat; crossed the river in the morning to queue for croissants at Ayre's Bakery in Peckham, playing 'Empire Burlesque' so loud that if I touched the windscreen gently I could feel it tremble, much as she used to do, beneath my fingertips.

I was trying to get back, too.

'I'll take you to the theatre,' I said: 'Waiting for Godot'. Do you want to see the fireworks?'

I said: 'I brought you a present—'

A Monsoon dress. Two small stone birds for the garden; anemones; and a cheap Boots nail brush shaped like a pig.

'Don't try to get so close, China,' she said. 'Please.'

I said: 'I just want to be something to you.'

She touched my arm. She said:

'China, it's too soon. We're here together, after all: isn't that enough for now?'

She said:

'And anyway, how could you ever be anything else?'

She said: 'I love you.'

'But you're not in love with me.'

'I told you I couldn't promise you that.'

By Christmas we were shouting at one another again, late into the night, every night. I slept on the futon in the spare room. There I dreamed of Isobel and woke sweating.

You have to imagine this—

'The Pavilion', quite a good Thai restaurant on Wardour Street. Isobel has just given me the most beautiful jacket, wrapped in birthday paper. She leans across the table. 'French Connection, China. Very smart.' The waitresses, who believe we are lovers, laugh delightedly as I try it on. But later, when I buy a red rose and offer it to Isobel, she says, 'What use would I have for that?' in a voice of such contempt I begin to cry. In the dream, I am fifty years old that day. I wake thinking everything is finished.

Or this—

Budapest. Summer. Rakoczi Street. Each night Isobel waits for me to fall asleep before she leaves the hotel. Once outside, she walks restlessly up and down Rakoczi with all the other women. Beneath her beige linen suit she has on grey silk underwear. She cannot explain what is missing from her life, but will later write in a letter: 'When sex fails for you – when it ceases to be central in your life – you enter middle age, a zone of the most unclear exits from which some of us never escape.' I wake and follow her. All night it feels like dawn. Next morning, in the half-abandoned Jugendstil dining room, a paper doily drifts to the floor like a leaf, while Isobel whispers urgently in someone else's voice:

'It was never what you thought it was.'

Appalled by their directness, astonished to find myself so passive, I would struggle awake from dreams like this thinking: 'What am I going to do? What am I going to do?' It was always early. It was always cold. Grey light silhouetted a vase of dried flowers on the dresser in front of the uncurtained window, but the room itself was still dark. I would look at my watch, turn over, and go back to sleep. One morning in the week before Christmas I got up and packed a bag instead. I made myself some coffee and drank it by the kitchen window, listening to the inbound City traffic build up half a mile away. When I switched the radio on it was playing Billy Joel's 'She's Always a Woman'. I turned it off quickly, and at eight o'clock woke Isobel. She smiled up at me.

'Hello,' she said. 'I'm sorry about last night.'

I said: 'I'm sick of it all. I can't do it. I thought I could but I can't.'

'China, what is this?'

I said: 'You were so fucking sure he'd have you. Three months later it was you crying, not me.'

'China—'

'It's time you helped,' I said.

I said: 'I helped *you*. And when you bought me things out of gratitude I never once said "What use would I have for that?"'

She rubbed her hands over her eyes.

'China, what are you talking about?'

I shouted: 'What a fool you made of yourself!' Then I said: 'I only want to be something to you again.'

'I won't stand for this,' Isobel whispered. 'I can't stand this.'

I said: 'Neither can I. That's why I'm going.'

'I still love him, China.'

I was on my way to the door. I said:

'You can have him then.'

'China, I don't *want* you to go.'

'Make up your mind.'

'I won't say what you want me to.'

'Fuck off, then.'

'It's you who's fucking off, China.'

It's easy to see now that when we stood on the Erzsebet Bridge the dream had already failed her. But at the time – and for some time afterwards – I was still too close to her to see anything. It was still one long arc of delight for me, Stratford through Budapest, all the way to Stepney. So I could only watch puzzledly as she began to do pointless, increasingly spoiled things to herself. She caught the tube to Camden Lock and had her hair cut into the shape of a pigeon's wing. She had her ankles tattooed with feathers. She starved herself, as if her own body were holding her down. She was going to revenge herself on it. She lost twenty pounds in a month. Out went everything she owned, to be replaced by size nine jeans, little black lycra skirts, expensively tailored jackets which hung from their own ludicrous shoulder pads like washing.

'You don't look like you any more,' I said.

'Good. I always hated myself anyway.'

'I loved your bottom the way it was,' I said.

She laughed.

'You'll look haggard if you lose any more,' I said.

'Piss off, China. I won't be a cow just so you can fuck a fat bottom.'

I was hurt by that, so I said:

'You'll look old. Anyway, I didn't think we fucked. I thought we made love.' Something caused me to add, 'I'm losing you.' And then, even less reasonably: 'Or you're losing me.'

'China, don't be such a baby.'

Then one afternoon in August she walked into the lounge and said, 'China, I want to talk to you.' The second I heard this, I knew exactly what she was going to say. I looked away from her quickly and down into the book I was pretending to read, but it was too late. There was a kind of soft thud inside me. It was something broken. It was something not there any more. I felt it. It was a door closing, and I wanted to be safely on the other side of it before she spoke.

'What?' I said.

She looked at me uncertainly.

'China, I—'

'What?'

'China, I haven't been happy. Not for some time. You must have realized. I've got a chance at an affair with someone and I want to take it.'

I stared at her.

'Christ,' I said. 'Who?'

'Just someone I know.'

'Who?' I said. And then, bitterly, 'Who do you know, Isobel?' I meant: 'Who do you know that isn't me?'

'It's only an affair,' she said. And:

'You must have realized I wasn't happy.'

I said dully: 'Who is this fucker?'

'It's David Alexander.'

'Who?'

'David Alexander. For God's sake, China, you make everything so hard! At the clinic. David Alexander.'

I had no idea who she was talking about. Then I remembered.

'Christ,' I said. 'He's just some fucking *customer*.'

She went out. I heard the bedroom door slam. I stared at the books on the bookshelves, the pictures on the walls, the carpet dusty gold in the pale afternoon light. I couldn't understand why it was all still there. I couldn't understand anything. Twenty minutes later, when Isobel came back in again carrying a soft leather overnight bag, I was standing in the same place, in the middle of the floor. She said:

'Do you know what your trouble is, China?'

'What?' I said.

'People are always just some fucking this or that to you.'

'Don't go.'

She said: 'He's going to help me to fly, China.'

'You always said *I* helped you to fly.'

She looked away.

'It's not your fault it stopped working,' she said. 'It's me.'

'Christ, you selfish bitch.'

'He wants to help me to fly,' she repeated dully.

And then:

'China, I *am* selfish.'

She tried to touch my hand but I moved it away.

'I can't fucking believe this,' I said. 'You want me to forgive you just because you can admit it?'

'I don't want to lose you, China.'

I said: 'You already have.'

'We don't know what we might want,' she said. 'Later on. Either of us.'

I remembered how we had been at the beginning: Stratford Waterside, whispers and moans, *You help me to fly, China*. 'If you could hear yourself,' I said. 'If you could just fucking hear yourself, Isobel.' She shrugged miserably and picked up her bag. I didn't see her after that. I did have one letter from her. It was sad without being conciliatory, and ended: 'You were the most amazing person I ever knew, China, and the fastest driver.'

I tore it up.

'"Were"!' I said. 'Fucking "*were*"!'

By that time she had moved in with him, somewhere along the Network South East line from Waterloo: Chiswick, Kew, one of those old-fashioned suburbs on a bladder of land inflated into the picturesque curve of the river, with genteel deteriorating houseboats, an arts centre, and a wine bar on every corner. West London is full of places like that – 'shabby', 'comfortable', until you smell the money. Isobel kept the Stepney house. I would visit it once a month to collect my things, cry in the lounge, and take away some single pointless item – a compact disc I had bought her, a picture she had bought me. Every time I went back, the bedroom, with its wooden chests and paper birds, seemed to have filled up further with dust.

Despite that, I could never quite tell if anything had changed. Had they been in there, the two of them? I stayed in the doorway, so as not to know. I had sold *Rose Services* and was living out in Tottenham, drinking Michelob beer and watching Channel 4 movies while I waited for my capital to run out. Some movies I liked better than others. I cried all the way through *Alice in the Cities*. I wasn't sure why. But I knew why I was cheering Anthony Hopkins as *The Good Father*.

'You were the most amazing person I ever knew, China, and the fastest driver. I'll always remember you.'

What did I care? Two days after I got the letter I drove over to Queensborough Road at about seven in the evening. I had just bought the BMW. I parked it at the kerb outside Alexander's clinic, which was in a large postmodern block not far down from Hammersmith Gyratory. Some light rain was falling. I sat there watching the front entrance. After about twenty minutes Alexander's receptionist came out, put her umbrella up, and went off towards the tube station. A bit later Alexander himself appeared at the security gate. I was disappointed by him. He turned out to be a tall, thin man, middle-aged, grey-haired, dressed in a light wool suit. He looked less like a doctor than a poet. He had that kind of fragile elegance some people maintain on the edge of panic, the energy of tensions unresolved, glassy, never very far from the surface. He would always seem worried. He looked along the street towards Shepherd's Bush, then down at his watch.

I opened the nearside passenger window.

'David Alexander?' I called.

I called: 'Waiting for someone?'

He bent down puzzledly and looked into the BMW.

'Need a lift?' I offered.

'Do I know you?' he asked.

I thought: Say the wrong thing, you fucker. You're that close.

I said: 'Not exactly.'

'Then—'

'Forget it.'

He stood back from the car suddenly, and I drove off.

Christmas. Central London. Traffic locked solid every late after-noon. Light in the shop windows in the rain. Light in the puddles. Light splashing up round your feet. I couldn't keep still. Once I'd walked away from Isobel, I couldn't stop walking. Everywhere I went, 'She's Always a Woman' was on the radio. Harrods, Habitat,

Hamleys: Billy Joel drove me out on to the wet pavement with another armful of children's toys. I even wrapped some of them – a wooden penguin with rubber feet, two packs of cards, a miniature jigsaw puzzle in the shape of her name. Every time I saw something I liked, it went home with me.

'I bought you a present,' I imagined myself saying, 'this fucking little spider that really jumps—

'Look!'

Quite suddenly I was exhausted. Christmas Day I spent with the things I'd bought. Boxing Day, and the day after that, I lay in a chair staring at the television. Between shows I picked up the phone and put it down again, picked it up and put it down. I was going to call Isobel, then I wasn't. I was going to call her, but I closed the connection carefully every time the phone began to ring at her end. Then I decided to go back to Stepney for my clothes.

Imagine this—

Two a.m. The house was quiet.

Or this—

I stood on the pavement. When I looked in through the uncurtained ground floor window I could see the little display of lights on the front of Isobel's CD player.

Or this—

For a moment my key didn't seem to fit the door.

Imagine this—

Late at night you enter a house in which you've been as happy as anywhere in your life: probably happier. You go into the front room, where streetlight falls unevenly across the rugs, the furniture, the mantelpiece and mirrors. On the sofa are strewn a dozen colourful, expensive shirts, blue and red and gold like macaws and money. Two or three of them have been slipped out of their cellophane, carefully refolded and partly wrapped in Christmas paper. 'Dear China –' say the tags. 'Dearest China.' There are signs of a struggle but not necessarily with someone else. A curious stale smell fills the room, and a chair has been knocked over. It's really too dark to see.

Switch on the lights. Glasses and bottles. Food trodden into the best kilim. Half-empty plates, two days old.

'Isobel? Isobel!'

The bathroom was damp with condensation, the bath itself full of cold water smelling strongly of rose oil. Wet towels were underfoot, there and in the draughty bedroom, where the light was already on and Isobel's pink velvet curtains, half-drawn, let a faint yellow triangle of light into the garden below. The lower sash was open.

When I pulled it down, a cat looked up from the empty flowerbed: ran off. I shivered. Isobel had pulled all her favourite underclothes out on to the floor and trodden mascara into them. She had written in lipstick on the dressing table mirror, in perfect mirror writing: 'Leave me alone.'

I found her in one of the big blanket boxes.

When I opened the lid a strange smell – beeswax, dried roses, vomit, whiskey – filled the room. In there with her she had an empty bottle of Jameson's: an old safety razor of mine and two or three blades. She had slit her wrists. But first she had tried to shave all the downy, half-grown feathers from her upper arms and breasts. When I reached into the box they whirled up round us both, soft blue and grey, the palest rose pink. Miami! In some confused attempt to placate me, she had tried to get out of the dream the way you get out of a coat.

She was still alive.

'China,' she said. Sleepily, she held her arms up to me.

She whispered: 'China.'

Alexander had made her look like a bird. But underneath the cosmetic trick she was still Isobel Avens. Whatever he had promised her, she could never have flown. I picked her up and carried her carefully down the stairs. Then I was crossing the pavement towards the BMW, throwing the nearside front door open and trying to get her into the passenger seat. Her arms and legs were everywhere, pivoting loose and awkward from the hips and elbows. 'Christ, Isobel, you'll have to help!' I didn't panic until then.

'China,' whispered Isobel.

Blood ran into my shirt where she had put her arms round my neck.

I slammed the door.

'China.'

'What, love? What?'

'China.'

She could talk but she couldn't hear.

'Hold on,' I said. I switched on the radio. Some station I didn't know was playing the first ten bars of a Joe Satriani track, 'Always with You, Always with Me'. I felt as if I was outside myself. I thought: 'Now's the time to drive, China, you fucker.' The BMW seemed to fishtail out of the parking space of its own accord, into the empty arcade-game of Whitechapel. The City loomed up then fell back from us at odd angles, as if it had achieved the topological values of a Vorticist painting. I could hear the engine distantly, making that curious harsh whine as I held the revs up against the red line. Revs and brakes, revs and brakes: if you want to go fast in the city you hold it all the time between the engine and the brakes. Taxis, hoardings, white faces of pedestrians on traffic islands splashed with halogen pink, rushed up and were snatched away.

'Isobel?'

I had too much to do to look directly at her. I kept catching glimpses of her in weird neon shop-light from Wallis or Next or What She Wants, lolling against the seatbelt with her mouth half open. She knew how bad she was. She kept trying to smile across at me. Then she would drift off, or cornering forces would roll her head to one side as if she had no control of the muscles in her neck and she would end up staring and smiling out of the side window whispering:

'China. China China China.'

'Isobel.'

She passed out again and didn't wake up.

'Shit, Isobel,' I said.

We were on Hammersmith Gyratory, deep in the shadow of the flyover. It was twenty minutes since I had found her. We were nearly there. I could almost see the clinic.

I said: 'Shit, Isobel, I've lost it.'

The piers of the flyover loomed above us, stained grey concrete plastered with Anarchist graffiti and torn posters. Free and ballistic, the car waltzed sideways towards them, glad to be out of China Rose's hands at last.

'Fuck,' I said. 'Fuck fuck fuck.'

We touched the kerb, tripped over our own feet, and began a long slow roll, like an airliner banking to starboard. We hit a postbox. The BMW jumped in a startled way and righted itself. Its offside rear suspension had collapsed. Uncomfortable with the new layout, still trying to get away from me, it spun twice and banged itself repeatedly into the opposite kerb with a sound exactly like some housewife's Metro running over the cats-eyes on a cold Friday morning. Something snapped the window post on that side and broken glass blew in all over Isobel Avens' peaceful face. She opened her mouth. Thin vomit came out, the colour of tea: but I don't think she was conscious. Hammersmith Broadway, ninety-five miles an hour. I dropped a gear, picked the car up between steering and accelerator, shot out into Queensborough Road on the wrong side of the road. The boot lid popped open and fell off. It was dragged along behind us for a moment, then it went backwards quickly and disappeared.

*

'China.'

Draped across my arms, Isobel was nothing but a lot of bones and heat. I carried her up the steps to Alexander's building and pressed for entry. The entryphone crackled but no one spoke. 'Hello?' I said. After a moment the locks went back.

Look into the atrium of a West London building at night and everything is the same as it is in the day. Only the reception staff are missing, and that makes less difference than you would think. The contract furniture keeps working. The PX keeps working. The fax comes alive suddenly as you watch, with a query from Zürich, Singapore, LA. The air conditioning keeps on working. Someone has watered the plants, and they keep working too, making chlorophyll from the overhead lights. Paper curls out of the fax and stops. You can watch for as long as you like: nothing else will happen and no one will come. The air will be cool and warm at the same time, and you will be able to see your own reflection, very faintly in the treated glass.

'China.'

Upstairs it was a floor of open plan offices – health finance – and then a floor of consulting rooms. Up here the lights were off, and you could no longer hear the light traffic on Queensborough Road. It was two-fifty in the morning. I got into the consulting rooms and then Alexander's office, and walked up and down with Isobel in my arms, calling:

'Alexander?'

No one came.

'Alexander?'

Someone had let us in.

'Alexander!'

Among the stuff on his desk was a brochure for the clinic. '. . . modern "magic wand",' I read. 'Brand new proteins.' I swept everything off on to the floor and tried to make Isobel comfortable by folding my coat under her head. 'I'm sorry,' she said quietly, but not to me. It was part of some conversation I couldn't hear. She kept rolling on to her side and retching over the edge of the desk, then laughing. I had picked up the phone and was working on an outside line when Alexander came in from the corridor. He had lost weight. He looked vague and empty, as if we had woken him out of a deep sleep. You can tear people like him apart like a piece of paper, but it doesn't change anything.

'Press 9,' he advised me. 'Then call an ambulance.'

He glanced down at Isobel. He said:

'It would have been better to take her straight to a hospital.'

I put the phone down.

'I fucked up a perfectly good car to get here,' I said.

He kept looking puzzledly at me and then out of the window at the BMW, half up on the pavement with smoke coming out of it.

I said: 'That's a Hartge H27–24.'

I said: 'I could have afforded something in better taste, but I just haven't got any.'

'I know you,' he said. 'You've done work for me.'

I stared at him. He was right.

I had been moving things about for him since the old Astravan days; since before Stratford. And if I was just a contract to him, he was just some writing on a job sheet to me. He was the price of a Hartge BMW with racing suspension and seventeen inch wheels.

'But you did this,' I reminded him.

I got him by the back of the neck and made him look closely at Isobel. Then I pushed him against the wall and stood away from him. I told him evenly: 'I'm fucking glad I didn't kill you when I wanted to.' I said: 'Put her back together.'

He lifted his hands.

'I can't,' he said.

'Put her back together.'

'This is only an office,' he said. 'She would have to go to Miami.'

I pointed to the telephone.

I said: 'Arrange it. Get her there.'

He examined her briefly.

'She was dying anyway,' he said. 'The immune system work alone would have killed her. We did far more than we would normally do on a client. Most of it was illegal. *It would be illegal to do most of it to a laboratory rat.* Didn't she tell you that?'

I said: 'Get her there and put her back together again.'

'I can make her human again,' he offered. 'I can cure her.'

I said: 'She didn't fucking want to be human.'

'I know,' he said.

He looked down at his desk; his hands.

He whispered: 'Help me to fly. Help me to fly!'

'Fuck off,' I said.

'I loved her too, you know. But I couldn't make her understand that she could *never* have what she wanted. In the end she was just too demanding: effectively, she asked us to kill her.'

I didn't want to know why he had let me have her back. I didn't want to compare inadequacies with him.

I said: 'I don't want to hear this.'

He shrugged.

'She'll die if we try it again,' he said emptily. 'You've got no idea how these things work.'

'Put her back together.'

You tell me what else I could have said.

'Here at the Alexander Clinic, we use the modern "magic wand" of molecular biology to insert avian chromosomes into human skin-cells. Nurtured in the clinic's vats, the follicles of this new skin produce feathers instead of hair. It grafts beautifully. Brand new proteins speed acceptance. But in case of difficulties, we remake the immune system: aim it at infections of opportunity: fire it like a laser.

'Our client chooses any kind of feather, from pinion to down, in any combination. She is as free to look at the sparrow as the bower bird or macaw. Feathers of any size or colour! But the real triumph is elsewhere—

'Designer hormones trigger the "brown fat" mechanism. Our client becomes as light and as hot to the touch as a female hawk. Then metabolically-induced calcium shortages hollow the bones. She can be handled only with great care. And the dreams of flight! Engineered endorphins released during sexual arousal simulate the sidesweep, swoop and mad fall of mating flight, the frantically beating heart, long sight. Sometimes the touch of her own feathers will be enough.'

I lived in a hotel on the beach while it was done. Miami! TV prophecy, humidity like a wet sheet, an airport where they won't rent you a baggage trolley. You wouldn't think this listening to Bob Seger. Unless you are constantly approaching it from the sea, Miami is less a dream – less even a nightmare – than a place. All I remember is what British people always remember about Florida: the light in the afternoon storm, the extraordinary size and perfec-tion of the food in the supermarkets. I never went near the clinic, though I telephoned Alexander's team every morning and evening. I was too scared. One day they were optimistic, the next they weren't. In the end I knew they had got involved again, they were excited by the possibilities. She was going to have what she wanted. They were going to do the best they could for her, if only because of the technical challenge.

She slipped in and out of the world until the next spring. But she didn't die, and in the end I was able to bring her home to the blackened, gentle East End in May, driving all the way from Heathrow down the inside lane of the motorway, as slowly and carefully as I knew how. I had adjusted the driving mirror so I could look into the back of the car. Isobel lay awkwardly across one corner of the rear seat. Her hands and face seemed tiny. In the soft wet English light, their adjusted bone structures looked more rather than less human. Lapped in her singular successes and failures, the sum of her life to that point, she was more rested than I had ever seen her.

About a mile away from the house, outside Whitechapel tube station, I let the BMW drift up to the kerb and stop. I switched the engine off and got out of the driving seat.

'It isn't far from here.' I said.

I put the keys in her hand.

'I know you're tired,' I said, 'but I want you to drive yourself the rest of the way.'

She said: 'China, don't go. Get back in the car.'

'It's not far from here,' I said.

'China, please don't go.'

'Drive yourself from now on.'

If you're so clever, you tell me what else I could have done. All that time in Miami she had never let go, never once vacated the dream. The moment she closed her eyes, feathers were floating down past them. She knew what she wanted. Don't mistake me: I wanted her to have it. But imagining myself stretched out next to her on the bed night after night, I could hear the sound those feathers made, and I knew I would never sleep again for the touch of them on my face.

THE PAIN BARRIER

by

Joel Lane

Joel Lane was born in 1963 and lives in Birmingham, England where he works in educational publishing. His stories have appeared in various magazines and anthologies, including *Ambit*, *Critical Quarterly*, *Skeleton Crew*, *Darklands*, *Darklands 2*, *The Sun Rises Red*, *Sugar Sleep*, *Best New Horror* and four volumes of *The Year's Best Horror Stories*. A selection of his poems appeared in *Private Cities*, a three-author anthology from Stride Publications.

'The Pain Barrier' is a brief but powerful piece about the darker side of sexuality.

THE PAIN BARRIER

After midnight, the city centre was an island of light and activity amidst the blank vacancy of the industrial and commercial districts. The ring road that surrounded the centre was flanked by building sites and wire fences. Aston, on the north side of town, was a mist-clogged blur of walls and road signs; Lee still had trouble finding his way around. He was drinking in a night club when he saw the face. At once, it took him back. He remembered sitting in a little private cinema, or alone in a dark room with a video. It was the same face, but no longer in pain. Except, in a way, it was. He was standing against the mirrored wall at the back of the dance floor. As the overhead lighting shifted, red and white lamps blinking off and on, his face disappeared and then came back. Lee finished his drink quickly, trying to remember the name; but he had never known it.

The lounge was a quieter, less crowded room to one side of the dance floor. When the youth moved through there to the bar, Lee followed him; they exchanged glances. He was less sure now, seeing a real face (and an uneasy one) rather than an image. The actor, if it was him, bought a measure of something and drank it almost at once. He appeared to be on his own. Lee hung back, where a red curtain covered the fire exit in the side wall, and looked around. A few small groups were clustered around the tables, talking; solitary figures passed between the doors and sometimes back again. Five couples were sitting on the imitation-leather sofas lining the far wall. Lee counted them, and saw how the shadows welded each couple together. An old torch song was playing from the speaker on the near wall; beneath it, he could hear and feel the thudding beat from the disco. His blood felt thin again. Was that just the effect of fear? The friction in his muscles was like particles of ash. When he looked back at the bar, the youth was watching him. Lee crossed the room and asked if he wanted a drink.

They were both drinking gin and lemon. Tony was his name. He looked about twenty, three or four years younger than Lee. 'I haven't been here in a while,' Tony said. 'Nobody I know is here tonight. I don't think people like to go out now. Unless they're too lonely to stay in.' He smiled; Lee didn't recognize the smile. It was something else he hadn't seen. Tony said he worked for a glass manufacturer, packing and delivering windows in reinforced glass for new Government buildings, prisons and the like. Lee had done jobs like that in the past, chiefly undeclared. The black economy had been steadily growing for years, as more services were deregulated and real jobs evaporated like so many verbal contracts. You learned how to improvise. Perhaps it was surprising that Tony wasn't working in films any more. But perhaps it wasn't. Lee didn't say anything. They danced together in the circular pit of the disco, where the figures jerked like anxious puppets in the strobe light. The music, heard like this from the inside, was hard and metallic; it gave nothing away. A cold smell of amyl cut through the dense air.

Afterwards, they sat in the front bar and had another drink. Lee could feel cramps building up in his thigh and calf muscles. He felt undermined by his own body. More exercise might improve the circulation. He held his glass in both hands to keep it steady. 'You recognized me, didn't you?' Tony said. Lee nodded, with some reluctance. 'That was why I looked back at you. But from?'

'*Mercury. Scar Tissue. Never Cry.*' They were the names of films; short films without dialogue, or at least without words. Films that located pleasure in suffering. Or the other way round. All made by Carl Austin, and circulated privately and illegally. 'I've seen others . . . of his, but those are the only ones I remember you from.'

'Surprised you want to remember them. To most people, they're just bad pornography. Or did they turn you on?'

It was an unexpectedly direct question. Lee didn't know how to answer it. He looked away. 'They bothered me. I don't know . . . something I couldn't understand. They're not sex films. They hurt.'

Tony laughed slightly. 'Tell me about it.' The night club would close in half an hour, but people were still coming in. 'So what's your interest? Carl?'

God, he was sharp. Lee shook his head. 'Not even the films. Just you.' He hoped that was the right answer. It probably wasn't the truth.

Tony looked at him, then seemed to reach an inner decision. 'Where shall we go?' They couldn't go back to Lee's room: the hostel staff wouldn't let Tony in. Lee explained that his freedom was limited. He was on parole now. Tony didn't ask from what; though the answer would hardly have shocked him – possession of drugs and illegal films. 'I'm homeless,' Tony said in reply. 'But I've found a house to stay in. We can walk, it's not far.'

Outside the club, the first thing they saw was a fight. Five or six men had stopped a car in the road and one was trying to pull the driver out from behind the wheel. There were two men in the car; the passenger had blood on his face, so the attack must have started on the pavement. One of the attackers was holding an empty bottle. Lee and Tony walked away quickly. As they turned the corner, Lee heard glass break; he couldn't tell if it was the bottle or the car window.

They walked in silence for some time, unable to look at each other. Lee thought of a joke he'd heard in school, eight years before: the city council were building a special graveyard for witnesses. It hadn't been funny then. They passed the barracks on what used to be the university site, and crossed the canal bridge at a strange junction of new roadways and old buildings; the streets had names like Lister Street and Oxygen Street. Further out of town, the lights thinned out and fibres of mist clung to the upper walls. Three cooling towers stood like chesspieces above a factory complex, walled in on all sides. The narrow streets were lined with parked vans and lorries; a continuous stream of traffic passed down the expressway, supported on concrete pillars above ground level.

A lot of these factories and offices had closed down. Every viable property was surrounded by a wire fence: warehouses, scrap yards, car parks. And building sites, which were everywhere in the inner city. Not because much was being rebuilt; the best way for Government to save face, where a district had been mutilated by successive riots and continuing neglect, was to fence off the damaged areas and place an array of signs in front of the view. Here and there the rubble had been levelled, and the ground marked out with trenches and wooden posts.

Nobody stayed here except vagrants. Lee felt as though the wire fences were built to shut in the streets. He thought of the hostel at Five Ways, where he'd been transferred a couple of months before: the naked rooms, dim corridors, policemen waiting in the reception hall. There seemed to be no nameplates here to identify the roads; only signs to direct traffic. 'You sure you know where we're going?' Lee said.

'Don't worry, I was brought up round here. I'm a walking map.' Tony caught hold of Lee's arm and squeezed it for a moment. 'We're

nearly there.' In the next road, a café was open; a few people, either
vagrants or patrollers, sat inside. You couldn't tell the street gangs
from the militia a lot of the time. That was the point: authority was
everywhere. A few drunks were kneeling or sitting on the pavement
outside the café, like performers on stage just before the lights came
on. One was singing to himself, a love song. The February night
made everything chilly and stark. There was a crisp moon that
shivered as clouds blew across it.

Further on, the buildings were largely ruined though that didn't
mean they were unoccupied. New doors and padlocks showed where
ground floors were being used for trading or storage. They were
somewhere between the industrial estate and the jewellery quarter.
Tony stopped outside a three-storey house on a street corner. It could
be a workshop or a patrol HQ or a tenement building. You never
knew around here. Windows were either boarded up or protected by
wire grids. 'Here we are,' Tony said. Lee stared at the front door; two
planks of wood were nailed across the doorframe. 'This way.' Tony
stepped into a narrow side passage between one house and the next;
Lee followed him. It was utterly dark, smelling of damp and split
stone. At the far end, Tony fumbled with a latch and stepped through
into a back yard. There was gravel and mud underfoot. A light shone
in the distance; Lee focused on it by reflex. He could see a railway
line, on the other side of a wire fence. 'Are you all right?' Tony said.

'Sure.' Their hands joined for a moment. Tony pointed to the fire
escape at the back of the house. It was quite easy to climb, though
being painted black, the steps were hard to see in the moonlight.
Flakes of paint came off on Lee's hands and elbows. On the second
floor, two windows were close together; the left-hand one was
boarded. Tony removed the board from the frame, like someone
taking a patch off an eye. There was no glass behind it.

Inside were two chairs, a small table, a mattress. You could see all
there was to see by moonlight and the distant railway lamp. Lee felt
an uneasy sense of recognition. The iron-framed mirror above the
table showed him only a negative image, like a shadow, of his own
body. This was where they had made at least one of Austin's short
films. '*Never Cry*?' he said.

Tony nodded. 'And *The Pain Threshold*. They used the fire escape,
too. Remember?' There was an awkward silence. Lee rubbed his
hands on his coat, trying to wipe off the fragments of black paint.
Surely there couldn't still be blood, after all this time. Fake blood, he
reminded himself angrily. It all seemed more disturbing than at the
club. A film was a film, wherever it was shot. But how had it really

been? He remembered seeing a youth (Tony) chained to the fire escape, against the background of the city at night: streetlamps, tower blocks, distant fires, stars overhead. Austin's technique of cross-cutting had made this landscape appear to be projected on to the wall of a prison cell. The youth was being beaten by two faceless attackers. Burned with strips of magnesium. In isolated frames, semen drying on his neck. It had excited Lee, but he didn't know why. He didn't know what it meant. But then, Tony was exactly his type: short black hair, pale skin, dark eyes, the narrow features of someone starved of comfort.

Lee sat down at the table, staring past Tony at the empty window-frame. Tony moved towards him, stopped. His eyes were black pits, devoid of expression, in the weak light. He gripped Lee's hand, leant across the table, and spoke. Lee saw his mouth form the words before he registered their sound. 'When you see a film, you don't ask yourself what's real and what's acted. Let alone what's been created by editing and dubbing in. It's all just there. Even the effects of how the film's been copied and botched up – illegal films go through nine or ten generations on video. Chinese whispers. Even the place you see it in, and what's in your mind at the time. You get me?' Lee nodded. 'For actors, it's just the same.' Tony sat down, his hand on Lee's arm.

'I worked with Carl for three years. Even when I knew how little he cared about what we were doing. He never actually had me, you know. Or if he did it was by proxy. What is he to you? A sexual rebel? A subversive artist? To me, he wasn't anything *in particular*. He was everything we had. Whatever he did, whatever we did for him. A complete world. Do you understand?' Lee said nothing. He tried to form an image of Carl Austin from the photographs, articles and fragmentary interviews he'd come across over the last few years. Blond hair, a determined face, a constant half-smile. He was an underground figure, a man perpetually on the run; but, Lee thought suddenly, one who had never been jailed. Nobody was sure what (if anything) he stood for. Lee had learned a lot about the porn trade during his six months in prison. It was like the drug trade: the police used it as a network, a chain of connections that they could tap into at various points. By applying pressure in one place they could affect things from a distance, assert control, gain information. It was one of their maps.

Lee thought of a remark Austin had made in a magazine interview: 'Pain is a universal drug. My films show you how it feels to cross the pain threshold. They take you to the edge of identity – the point beyond which death comes to life, darkness becomes light, pain becomes the most intense pleasure.' At the time, Lee had thought he understood what Austin was saying; but now, the words seemed empty of meaning. I don't know about reaching *nirvana* through pain, he thought. But I know about punishment. And I know about police surveillance. Is Carl the same? Or is he a visionary? I'm not. I'm just a voyeur.

When he spoke, it was to ask something he could never have imagined asking. 'Was it real? The torture?'

'Yes,' Tony said. 'And no. There was more to it, there always is . . .' He leaned over and kissed the side of Lee's neck. 'The pain was real. Even if the rest was fake. That's why I went on with it.' He put his hand on Lee's shoulder, pushing himself back. 'Have you wondered why I'm here? I'm trying to break away from the group. Carl's people. I want to go where nobody knows me. Even in this city, shithole that it is, I've got too many connections now. But I'm an exile, you understand? If I register for work or accommodation, they'll trace my records. I'll go to prison. Because I used to work for Carl. And I don't have any protection now, because I've gone.' Lee stared at him, feeling cold. His hands were numb. 'I want to live for myself. When I got to Birmingham I couldn't find anywhere to sleep. I knew about this place, so I came here. Not much good at escaping, am I? You can never escape. Do you know who Walter Benjamin was?'

'Sorry?' Lee was totally confused. 'Who? Did he work with Carl?'

Tony shook his head. 'He was a writer in the last century. A Jewish socialist who was captured by the Nazis, panicked and committed suicide. I read somewhere something he said about the Holocaust. He said *The real death is the death of the witness*.'

The moon had crossed the window, and it was near to complete darkness. There was no lightbulb, and probably no electricity supply; Tony lit a candle and stood it in a mug on the table. He lit a cigarette from it; the smoke was metallic, a mixture of tobacco and some narcotic, probably manufactured. In between drags, he took pills from his shirt pocket and chewed them. He crossed to the window and fitted the board back in the right-hand frame. There was an ancient oil heater in the corner of the room; Tony, with some difficulty, got it to light. A blue and orange flame jittered in the heater's oval mouth.

Lee felt the cramps returning to his legs and making his fists close up. A brief sense of helplessness passed through him. He took three capsules of plasma from his coat, along with the pen-sized injector.

The only clear light was at the table, so he rolled back his sleeve and injected there. It made him angry – having to depend on drugs from other people's bodies. The anger was an image on the screen of fear.

Slowly, his muscles returned to their normal tension. His vision cleared slightly, the focus moving outward. He got up to go to the toilet. The bathroom, at the end of the hallway, seemed too bright; the light made a silver web in the frosted glass. Then he realized the moon was still visible from this side of the house. There were crystals of ice on the walls, glinting; when he touched the plaster surface, they crumbled. The powder stuck to his fingers. It was cold enough to hurt. He rubbed his hand on some tissue paper, staring at the wall as though it held a secret pattern that would reveal itself, given time.

When he walked back into the room where Tony was still smoking, Lee could see the tiny ice fibres encrusted on the ceiling and upper walls. They made vague geometrical patterns in the candlelight. Perhaps he was hallucinating. It was like one of Austin's visual effects. Or like the effect of repeated copying. Tony looked at him. 'You're thin-blooded,' he said. Lee nodded. He supposed it was widespread now; people were less afraid of it than when he had developed the condition. The first cases were less than a decade ago. It was known to be an effect of contamination, though whether the cause was radiation or some chemical agent was still not clear.

'How long have you been like that?'

'Three years.' It limited his power to live alone.

'You're lucky. It killed my mother. Five years ago, before they could treat it. Her muscles just seized up. She became like wood. My father panicked and left. He was afraid it might infect him. I watched her die. It should have been my father. He used to hit her. I remember. He called her a lunatic. When he beat me, he'd shout *You're like her, you're wrong in the head, you'll be put away*. I was fourteen when my mother died. A couple of years later I started working with Carl. I was doing porn films already. Made some contacts, got in touch.

'The death of the witness, you see. I thought being a victim would save me. And more . . . it was something to belong to. An extended family. People who'd look after me.' He laughed. 'That was my trouble. I didn't just want a lover. I wanted a community. Outside all this shit. But they . . . well, they were either in it for Carl or for themselves. They think they own me. Now I want nothing. Except this.' He stubbed out the cigarette on the table, went across to Lee and embraced him. Lee felt at a loss. He wanted to talk, but the script was missing. It had been years since he'd seen any film that didn't separate people into attackers and victims. He took it for granted, even when he wasn't sure which he was himself. Tony stepped back and took off his coat. They'd be cold, despite the flickering heater.

There were blankets on the mattress. Lee had been in worse places; he sat down to unlace his shoes. He felt more sure of himself watching Tony undress than he had holding him. There was too much about this situation that felt unreal, as though these were parts that Carl Austin had written for both of them. In the light from the table, Tony's shadow was a blurred giant. Lee could just make out the narrow white scars running down and across his back. It was like a chessboard. When Tony turned round, Lee saw the same criss-cross pattern on his chest and stomach. Somehow, the cuts seemed too deep and regular to be the work of human hands. They had the look of something industrial.

Tony's fingers moved over Lee's body, slowly, finding its shape. They knelt on the bed, facing each other. Lee tried not to look at the scars. There it was again: the starved look on Tony's face. Like someone who needed to be whole, but couldn't be. Tony gripped Lee's shoulders and pulled him close. Their mouths clasped together like open hands. He seemed so hungry; they both did. And then they were lying side by side, kissing each other's bodies, biting, hardly able to breathe. There were no roles. Lee felt terrified at being close to this man he had wanted so badly; though he still didn't know *what* he wanted. Was this really the same one? He was shaking with tension. However tightly they held each other, it seemed there was no security, no peace.

They came into each other's mouths, almost at the same moment. Lee swallowed the chalky fluid with a compulsion he'd never felt before. Then he sat up and looked at Tony's face. Very briefly, the other man smiled. Leaning over him, Lee kissed the sweat from the rough hollow of his cheek. Pain echoed in his head, harsh as a guitar note. Not a pain that could be filmed. He was trapped in himself again. They hadn't spoken.

Minutes later they were curled together on the bed, trying to sleep. They both faced the window, Tony in front; Lee's right arm was folded across Tony's chest. For a few moments, his left hand traced the lines in Tony's back. He closed his eyes and tried to imagine meeting Tony a long time before, perhaps in early summer; a close friendship that had flowered into romance. That eased the stress in his head. His own body felt still and unfamiliar. The scars kept him at a distance; a fence that wouldn't let him through. They seemed to link the sleeping body to the city outside. *An extended family. Too many connections. A walking map.* The cold in the walls and the outside world wrapped itself around their little shell of warmth.

Not long before daybreak, Lee dreamed of a wire fence, too high to climb and sharp enough to cut your hands if you tried. The fence stood between him and a mass of people who were trying to reach him. It was night; there was mud and gravel underfoot. Distant trees were narrow cuts in the view. What he had at first taken for the moon was some kind of white lamp positioned high overhead. By its light, he could see some of the people moving behind the wire. They looked thin and distorted, as though they were suffering from malnutrition. Though they pressed their faces and hands against the wire mesh, they didn't seem to be aware of him in particular. Their faces were like pictures from newspapers, the features stubbled in with carbon. The eyes were gaps; the mouths were scars, healed shut.

Lee turned and began to pace along the wire, wondering what was on the far side of the enclosure. He turned a corner and found the desperate figures still just beyond the mesh. It caught the light here, made a grid of silver lines that mapped out all of the panic and loss filling his view. He was unable to turn his back to the wire. But he walked on until he had made a complete circuit, several times over; without once finding a way out. And without meeting anyone else on the inside.

When Lee woke up, it was daylight. Tony was still asleep beside him, half-curled and facing the window. Lee couldn't move his own arms or legs; at first, he thought the cramp had come back. Then he realized that his limbs were joined to the other man's. Their bodies were half merged, around the edges of the barrier. There were faint traces of blood on Tony's back now, darker at the nodes where the scars crossed. Lee stared for a long time. Then he started to pull himself free. It felt strange, as though he were becoming divided. But it didn't hurt at all. He raised his arms, crouched and then stood up, leaving the shapes of his night tangled inside the still figure on the bed. He needed to inject some plasma; he'd have to go back to the hostel for that. He dressed, as so many times before, and left by the fire escape.

It took him an hour to reach his hostel on the other side of town. The sky was white; rays of sunlight glinted through the torn clouds like crystals, reflecting from steel crash barriers and broken glass. Such a waste of light, he thought, when there was so little to be revealed. But perhaps what you saw wasn't as important as how you saw it. Traffic shot past him on the expressway, feeding substance to the patches of faintly glowing mist that hung over the office buildings. Lee wished he had a cigarette; it would make his breath more solid.

When he got back to his room, he would close the curtains and listen to some tapes and find something to eat. Beyond the city centre, a few naked trees lined the roadway. Three tower blocks stood on a hilltop, their upper windows glittering in sunlight, as though nothing lay behind them but the sky. The building where he lived was one of them.

SINFONIA EXPANSIVA

by

Barry N. Malzberg

Barry N. Malzberg is the author of over seventy novels, among them *Herovit's World*, *Beyond Apollo* (winner of the John W. Campbell Award), *Underlay*, *The Men Inside*, *The Remaking of Sigmund Freud*; the essential essay collection *Engines of the Night* and two short fiction collections, *The Man Who Loved the Midnight Lady*, and *The Many Worlds of Barry N. Malzberg*. He lives in New Jersey with his wife and daughter.

'Sinfonia Expansiva' is in Malzberg's trademark terse, elliptical style, in which maximum content fills the minimum space. It deals, as do many of the stories in this volume, with sexual politics in a dangerous age.

SINFONIA EXPANSIVA

This is Samuel's song:

> *I know the erotic. And I know horror. But I am not sure that I know that point of synthesis, that hot intersection at which horror and the erotic at last conjoin, mesh in the darkness. I have searched for that intersection all of my life, scrambled for it, sought blood and the steaming purity of deadly congress but I cannot delude myself that I have found it yet. Perhaps it is not to be found. Perhaps the goal is not the orgasm after all but that peering death, that hole of death, that lasting death toward which we strain in the hump and bump of our necessity. Mild and necessary death, thy sting our own faint jab in the pubis. And then again, perhaps that conjoinment exists and it is all they say and more.*

That's sick, she said, that's really sick. Are you out of your head? She stared at him with an intentness only she could have managed, a blurred attention. I mean you have to be really some case, you want to do that, she said. No. Absolutely not. She leaned against the sheets. Forget it, she said. Let's just call it quits this very minute. Let's put on our clothes and get out of here. Jeez, she said. You are really something, Sam, you know that? Something and a half.

Samuel said nothing. Now, in the abyss of his shame, there was nothing that could be said, his small and wistful secrets exposed before her and laughed away, the shadows of the room themselves winking at him. Oh, he said, you shouldn't have said that. You really shouldn't have said that, Marie. You don't shame a man when he shows you his soul.

His soul! she said. Her breasts which he had thought so soft and loving were, Samuel could now see, deadly ordnance, metallic turrets facing him, ready to cast him in deadly fire. Oh, Marie said, I've heard a lot but that's a new one on me. Come on, she said, what are you going to do, then? You going to go all crazy and violent on me, turn into one of those rapist lunatics, some guy that I met at an

Ethical Culture social? You try any moves on me, I'll cut your balls off with a knife, she said. I'm just the one to do it, too. Come on, start talking crazy, start acting crazy and see what happens, what do you say?

What *do* you say? There was nothing to say. Samuel rolled on the open canvas of the bed, reached for her, his need sudden and enormous in the bleeding space of the room and as he reached toward her, as he gathered himself against her he felt a moment of yielding more splendid and terrible than any he had ever known, Marie opening against him as he had once fantasied was possible with some stranger met two hours earlier, suddenly declothed and humping violently in her private boudoir – but then it stopped, she receded from him in small and then larger pieces, the ordnance of her breasts retracting, gone from him. So now you've turned out straight after all, she said. But where's the protection? You don't think you're just going to do me, do you, some guy I've never seen in my life and may never see again? You better put on something right now. This is no better than the other stuff, she said. You better pull yourself together, these are new times.

He looked at her, feeling the heat, the shifting warmth moving through the panels of his body, but even as he stared at her yapping little face, her features screwed into a kind of certainty which he understood represented the death of all feeling, he could sense the slipping away and then the slow, helpless relaxing of his limbs. Oh, you've got me, he said, you've got me two ways now and all within the same five minutes. You are an expert on this stuff, aren't you? And watched the disgust pour into her once more, knowing then that he had fouled this up big-time. *Big-time* and where did you go now? When they shut out the lights and then shut out the lights, with whom did you boogie? Where was Miss Molly when the preacher came through the door? Doggerel assaulted him, old rhymes and snatches like prayer. He could have been fucking Marie at this moment, so retracted was he into himself. I'm through with this, he thought. I'm through with it big-time just like I screwed up big-time. There were other possibilities he would explore. Do not, he thought, tell them your secrets. And if you do, get new secrets. Obtain new secrets at the door in this era of lies and constant exchange.

That's really sick, he said, you know that? I've been around uptown and downtown but that's a new one on me. You have to be really something. He shook his head, feeling the heat of his surprise cooling to revulsion as he stared at the woman backed naked against the wall, the instruments grasped hesitantly in her little hands. Speak for yourself, you want to talk about sick, she said. Maybe what goes down for me doesn't go up for you but you don't talk to a stranger like that. What's your name, Sam? Sam I am, the necessary man? Get out of here, she said. Her body had dimpled, the skin gathering into little bumps which seemed to cleave toward, then away from her pubis. Really something, she said again.

Listen, Sam said. Everybody has secrets. Some are one way and some are the other and there is no shame in revealing them. Everyone must let them out some way. But I just can't do that. I never heard of anything like that. But that doesn't make it a *bad* secret, it's just something I cannot handle. He was babbling, as he found to be more and more the case under pressure. All right, he said, I reacted a little badly. It's a strange night, a strange time here. What do you say we forget the whole thing, just do it straight? He reached for her. Come on, he said, I'll show you that the ordinary can still be wonderful if you let it take over. I even have protection, he said. Here, you have nothing to worry about.

She shook her head, seemed to retract. Her breasts were not ordnance but convex craters, pitted and scarred with the impact of forgotten stones. Not after what you said. I just can't do anything with you. I want you to go, she said, I want to forget this ever happened, you hear? Samuel could hear but only as if from some far distance. All right, he said, I'm sorry. I'm sorry I said what I did. I'll try. I'll try that if you want. But as she continued to back from him, as the convex glare of her breasts seemed to claw at his vision, he could see that it was too late, that he had once again found a way to mismatch and that there was no way that it could possibly work. Goodbye, she said, please go. Go now or I'll scream. My neighbours are caring people, this is a caring place. We all watch and listen for one another and I can tell you—

This was disaster. Once again Samuel could feel its casual embrace, the swaddling folds of humiliation. All right, he said, all right then and comforted himself, scrambling for his clothing, with what was an important notion: in this era of burgeoning secrets and deadly intersection he had secrets of his own, secrets which were, he would insist, at the heart of his certainty. Oh, the hell with secrets. Fuck the secrets.

In what he thought of as the sacristy of his empty bed, Samuel thought about the secrets, the precious and deadly confidences, the exchange of bodily fluids in the heat and hustle of the dark which would leave their stain and implication forever. Looking through the haze of his sudden tears at the ceiling, Samuel thought about those transactions he had made, some of them emboldening, others shameful, many unspeakable and as he tried to trace some line of connection amongst them he understood then that he could not, that there was no pattern after all. This one found him sick, he found another one even sicker, practices and standards were appalling at this time and seemed to work at utterly divergent purposes. Lying there in the shame of his isolation, Samuel tried to push past the pall of memory, tried to see some way in which it could be put together, the shameful and the shameless alike, one grand and unadorned fuck emerging past all compromise, past all negotiations, lies or transfers which would save him. But knew then as he had known so many times before that this was impossible, that what he dreamed in these plague years, this time of locusts and bleeding wounds was something more disastrous, less connected to true possibility than any of the sly confessions made to the women, which the women had made to him. Within and without he could feel the heavy, thunderous portent of his own death and all of this reaching and scrambling only a means of stripping away the skin so that the death could emerge. Oh my, Samuel thought, oh my, oh my, and it was as if there was someone else in the bed, perhaps there *was* someone else in this bed, what he had thought was private was only a stupefied dream at the centre of some tangle of limbs and he would awaken in just a moment, in a moment he would rise from this stupor to see the woman — perhaps, even, it was the man — to whom he had blurted out his most sacred and terrible revelations. I will not awaken, Samuel thought, I will not open my eyes, I will hold the sheets against my head against the possibility of breath sounding in the room. I will not turn, I will not open, I will not assess, and knew then, clinging to this tormented passage, that he would have to hold until, the last exhalation, he could hold out no longer and then what? Then what would become of him? And waited, then, waited.

Fucking up big-time.

Samuel, free of these doubts and terrors, blown free of his history and diagnosis, the mad-dog rapist at his ease and loose in the city of dreams and desire. Samuel, trotting the streets with an umbrella as decoy, a point-thirty-eight calibre Smith & Wesson deep in a pocket as insurance, Samuel, the insistent mad-dog rapist at last torn from regret, hesitancy or accusation to run on the streets of the city.

Hither and yon he goes, here and there, seeking his quarry, dreaming of the terrible confessions he will wring from them as again and again he pockets his insistence. In his embrace the woman is hurt, devastated, pained past reckoning, struggling to breathe in the expanse of his grinding, the dimensions of his desire. Who's sick now? Samuel says but very quietly, a monotone here, not wanting her to know what he has said. Essentially it is a private act in a public and terrible time. Who's sick now? he says and mad dog that he is turns over the woman, cornholes her, has her this way and that way, listening to the thin screaming line of her voice carrying him home.

Take it, he says in that quiet chamber of his head, his breath ragged but without the words, take it and take it, you bitch, know the judgement of the plague years and his orgasm, thunderous, strips him to an astonished weakness. Astonished, he collapses over her, lies there steaming. She is crying. Is it possible that she is crying for him? No, it is not possible. No one ever has. Never, *nyet*.

A goner, two goners in the bed, he sings to her of never and nyet time in the golden spasms of his spent desire.

Not nyet but yes.
  Yes.
  HIV-positive. For two years now and sinking in the world of secrets.

FEVER BLISTERS

by

Joyce Carol Oates

In addition to being a respected novelist, short story writer, playwright, poet and essayist, Joyce Carol Oates is the Roger S. Berlind Distinguished Professor in the Humanities at Princeton University. She is the author of over twenty novels, winning the National Book Award for *Them*. Her most recent novels are *Black Water* and *Foxfire: Confessions of a Girl Gang* and her newest collection, *Haunted: Tales of the Grotesque* (Dutton) was published in the United States in February 1994. While she is best-known for her work in the literary mainstream at least two of her collections, *Night-Side* and *Haunted* are firmly entrenched in the fantastique and the grotesque.

'Fever Blisters' shows a side of Oates not usually associated with her fiction – a touch of humour.

FEVER BLISTERS

'Why am I here?' — on foot, in absurdly high-heeled sandals, in a tight-fitting red polka dot halter-top dress that showed the tops of her breasts, in Miami. In waves of blinding, brilliant, suffocating heat. Not Miami Beach, which, to a degree, though she had not visited it in years, she knew, but Miami, the city, the inner city, which she did not know at all. And she had no car, she must have parked her car somewhere and forgotten the location, or had someone stolen it? — there were so many scruffy-looking people on the street here, and the majority of them black, Hispanic, Asian; strangers who glanced at her with contemptuous curiosity, or looked through her as if she did not exist. She could not remember where she'd come from, or how she'd got here, dazed with the terrifying tropical heat which was like no heat she had ever experienced in North America. Carless, in Miami! — she, who had not been without a car at her disposal since girlhood, and, in the affluent residential suburb of the northerly city in which she lived, a young widow whose children were grown and gone, famous among her friends for driving distances no longer than a block, and often shorter.

It was a nightmare, yet so fiery was the air, so swollen the sun in the sky, like a red-flushed goitre, she understood that she was not asleep but hideously awake — 'For the first time in my life.' On all sides people were passing her, pointedly making their way around her as she walked nearly staggering in the high-heeled sandals, forced frequently to stop and lean against a building, to catch her breath. The mere touch of the buildings burnt her fingers — the sidewalks, glittering with mica, must have been blisteringly hot. The wide avenue was clotted with slow-moving traffic and flashes of blinding light shot at her from glaring windshields and strips of chrome; she had to shield her eyes with her fingers. How was it possible she'd come to Miami without her dark glasses?

Had the sun become unmoored? — the temperature was surely above 120°F. The air was thick and stagnant, she had to propel herself through it like a clumsy swimmer. Overhead, a flying pigeon, stricken with the heat, suddenly fell dead to the pavement; she saw, horrified, in the gutter and on the littered sidewalks, the bodies of other birds shovelled in casual heaps. In doorways of buildings derelicts lay unmoving as death, ignored by pedestrians. Everywhere there was a stench as of garbage, raw sewage, an open grave.

Hazy in the distance, luminous with blue, was Miami Beach — causeways, high-rise buildings silhouetted against the fiery sky. She knew the ocean was beyond those buildings, but she could not see it. She sobbed with frustration — 'So far!' The beautiful city unreachable by her, separated from her by miles of heat, as if the very molecules of the air were ablaze.

The shabby hotel across the littered, sun-blazing square was her destination: *The Paradisio*. This was the hotel, or a derelict version of it, that had once been on the ocean, on Arthur Godfrey Boulevard. Its stucco façade, painted a garish flamingo-pink, with mildewed white awnings, and a foreshortened, stubby look; a limp American flag hung motionless over the portico. How changed *The Paradisio* was, yet unmistakable! — she could have wept, seeing it. For she was to meet her lover there, as they'd done, years ago, in secret.

And she seemed to know, with a thrill of despair, that *The Paradisio* would have no air conditioning.

'And if he doesn't come? — what will happen to me, then?'

The lobby of *The Paradisio* was so dim-lit, after the dazzling sunshine, she could barely see at first.

Except to note, nervously, lifting her arms so as to hide her over-exposed bosom, that several men, all strangers, were staring at *her*.

She looked away, shivering. The lobby was hot, humid, its air impacted as the interior of a greenhouse, yet she felt chill. Was her lover supposed to meet her here in the lobby, or in the cocktail lounge: or was he waiting for her up in the room? And which name, of the numerous names they'd used over the years, would he have used?

She could not recall clearly that first assignation, here in *The Paradisio*. That is *The Paradisio* that was.

How shabbily romantic the lobby was now, and how much smaller than she would have imagined! Frayed crimson velvet draperies, absurdly ornate gilt-framed mirrors, enormous drooping

rubber plants with dying leaves; underfoot a grimy fake-marble
floor. Her nostrils pinched with the co-mingled odours of disin-
fectant, insecticide and a lilac-scented air freshener. A uniformed
bell boy – hardly a boy: an aged black man with a face creased as a
prune and rheumy eyes – walked past her very slowly, carrying
luggage in both hands, but taking no notice of her. As if she did not
exist. Yet the men elsewhere in the lobby continued to stare rudely
at her: one of them was a red-faced white-haired Texan-looking man
in a dinner jacket, another was a portly fellow with an embarrassed
face, in a wilted sports shirt and Bermuda shorts; another was a
stocky silvery-blond gentleman of late middle age in a candy-striped
seersucker suit, white shoes with tassels. This man, obviously
suffering from the heat, wiped his flushed face with a tissue, yet
peered at her shyly, even hopefully – 'But I don't know *him*.'

The shame of it washed over her, that she, who had prided herself
upon the exclusivity of her taste in men, she, who in even the worst
years of her marriage had never been so much as mildly promiscuous, should have to have her assignation with a stranger: how sordid,
how demeaning!

'Unless that is my punishment, in itself?'

After some awkward minutes, during which time she tried
unsuccessfully to examine her reflection in one of the lobby mirrors,
but found her reflection cloudy, like something dissolving in water
or radiant waves of heat, the gentleman in the candy-striped
seersucker suit disengaged himself from the others at the rear of the
lobby, and made his way to her. When their eyes met, he took a quick
step forward, smiling – 'Ginny, is it *you*?'

She stared in amazement, trying not to show her surprise. She too
smiled, shyly – 'Douglas, is it *you*?'

They clasped hands. But for the heat, and the envious stares of the
others, they would have embraced. She wiped tears from her eyes
and saw that her lover was wiping tears from his eyes, too.

On the fifth floor of the hotel they wandered looking for their room,
still clasping hands, and whispering together; the hotel was one of
those old-fashioned hotels in which corridors lead off in all directions and numerals run both forward and backward. Several maids
pushing carts heaped with soiled linen, damp towels, aerosol spray
cans of insecticide and room freshener and supplies of miniature
soaps and other toiletries, regarded them with barely disguised
smiles of contempt. The maids were Puerto Rican, Jamaican,
Cuban–Haitian? The youngest was an attractive, busty Hispanic

woman who laughed openly at the lovers, took pity on them, and led them to their room at the far end of a corridor rippling with heat. In her torrent of amused Spanish they could recognize only the words, 'Señor, Señora! this way, eh?' For it seemed that she too was headed for room 555 with her cleaning implements.

The maid's boisterous presence in the room was a distraction and an embarrassment to the lovers, but there was nothing to be done. Out of consideration for their predicament, she began in the bathroom.

Virginia and Douglas clutched hands, whispered.

'*Can* we? Here?'

'We *must*.'

But how unromantic, their room – meagrely furnished, with a sagging double bed covered in a stained, scorch-marked bronze satin spread; an imitation-mahogany bureau with a cloudy mirror; a squat, old-fashioned television set which the maid had switched on mechanically to an afternoon game show. The room's single window had no blind and looked out upon a glaring, smoggy, featureless sky; the ceiling was strangely high, as if set precariously in place, dissolving in an ambiguity of hazy light. And pervading all was the odour of stale cigarette smoke, human perspiration, insecticide and room freshener. Ginny wanted to cry – 'It's so cruel, after so many years!'

She scanned her lover's face anxiously, even as he scanned hers.

Of course, she recognized him now: Douglas' younger, handsome face was clearly visible in this face, only lined, flushed, a bit jowly, creases beneath the eyes. His hair had gone silver, and thinned, but it was his hair, with its singular wave, and there were his grey-blue eyes, crinkled at the corners, unmistakable.

'Ginny, darling, you *did* love me? Didn't you? Those years—'

'Douglas, of course. Yes—'

Virginia's voice faltered as, in the bathroom, the maid rapped sharply on the partly opened door, and called out to them in Spanish.

Douglas whispered, 'I think she wants us to hurry.'

'Oh yes. My God.'

They embraced, and kissed, tentatively; but their lips were so hot and parched, Virginia flinched away, 'Oh!' A tiny fever blister began to form instantaneously on her upper lip.

Douglas stared at her, appalled. 'Ginny, I'm *sorry*.'

'It wasn't your fault.'

It was the heat, and the dazzling light. And no shelter from it.

Yet there was the need to continue, so, stricken with self-

consciousness the lovers turned aside to undress, with a hope that
the maid would not interrupt further. The game show ended amid
rowdy applause and a sequence of gaily animated commercials
followed.

How much longer it took to undress than ever in the past! Arms
bent up awkwardly behind her, Virginia fumbled with the zipper of
her tight-fitting dress. She had not worn so low-cut and uncomfortable a dress for a decade, what had possessed her to wear it today?
The ribbed bodice, supported from inside, had cut into her tender
flesh – 'Damn it!' At least, in this heat, she was not wearing a slip;
only a pair of scarlet silk panties, tight too, which she kicked off in
relief, along with the high-heeled shoes. Her hair, which she'd
thought she had had cut recently, was in fact glamorously long, a
thick glossy pageboy that fell heavily to her shoulders; the nape of
her neck was slick with sweat. She did not dare sniff at her armpits
for fear of what she might detect. And no deodorant! And no
makeup! She dreaded to think what the heat had already done to her
carefully applied makeup: the pitiless overhead light would expose
every flaw in her face.

Fortunately, the bureau mirror was too cloudy to show anything
more precise than wavering fleshy forms, like molluscs out of their
shells, where she and her lover stood.

She could hear the man murmuring to himself, half a sigh, half a
sob – 'Hurry, hurry!'

At last, they turned shyly to each other. Virginia saw, with an
intake of breath, that her lover had gained perhaps thirty pounds
since she'd last seen him in such intimacy: the flesh bracketing his
waist was flaccid and raddled, and he had a distinct pot belly. He, of
all men, so vain of his body! 'It doesn't seem possible.' Among their
circle of friends, Douglas had been the most competitive tennis
player, the most energetic yachtsman; the most generally admired of
the men. (Virginia's husband, years older, had been the richest.)
Now, though she was making a womanly effort to smile
encouragingly, she could not keep a look of dismay out of her face:
Douglas' chest and pubic hair were so silvery as to resemble
Christmas tinsel, and his legs, even his thighs, once so solid with
muscle, were now strangely lank and thin. There was an eerie
disconnectedness to the parts of his body she had never seen before.

Nor was his penis erect, yet. This too was an anomaly.

In turn, Douglas was staring at her in – amazement? apprehension? dread? *desire*? Self-conscious as a girl, Virginia made a vague
effort to hide her breasts, which were still rather full, beautifully

shaped, and her belly, where a faint incision showed, curving gently
upward like an unbent question mark.

'*You* – you're beautiful!' – the exclamation, passionate as if it were
the truth, seemed snatched from him, like a sob.

On the television, an evangelist named Reverend Steel was
shouting a sermon about Jesus Christ and alms.

Slowly, Virginia drew the bronze bedspread back, dreading what
she might see; and, yes, she saw it. So humiliating! demeaning! 'The
sheets haven't been changed since God knows when.' Douglas,
close beside her, looking, winced. Murmuring, in husbandly fashion,
'Well. I don't think, Ginny, we have any choice.'

Yes. She knew.

Yet, 'If only we could draw a shade!' The room was as bright, she
couldn't help thinking, as an operating room. But the window was
raw, open, perhaps it did not even have any glass, a great gaping hole
in the wall; and outside, a smoggy haze. Where was the city of
Miami? Had it been forgotten, or erased? And if Miami was gone,
how would she return to her life? – *to where would she return*?

Her lover, reading her thoughts, asked, in a low, worried voice,
'*Why* are we here, Ginny, do you know?'

'I don't! I don't know!'

At this, the Hispanic maid leaned out of the bathroom to call out
something to them, part Spanish, part English; her tone was
admonitory and jeering. Douglas winced again, urging Ginny to lie
down on the bed. 'She says, "To do it right, this time."'

'What?'

'"To do it right, this time."'

Where in the past lying in bed with Douglas had been the
extinguishing of consciousness, ecstatic and voluptuous as slipping
into warm dark water of sleep, or of oblivion, this afternoon the
experience was one of full, hideous wakefulness. Shutting her eyes
tight did no good, for the harsh sunshine was empowered to
penetrate her eyelids; burying her face with erotic abandon in
Douglas' neck did no good, for his skin was so slick with sweat it felt
clammy. Virginia could have wept – 'How are we to make love, in
such circumstances!' The fever blister on her lip throbbed like a bee
sting.

Douglas, gamely stroking her hair, did not seem to hear. He was
speaking with the eager hopefulness of a man intent upon explaining
the inexplicable; as a successful corporation attorney, it was his
habit to fall back upon words as a means of defence. 'I think when we
– that time – that first time, in Miami Beach? When we first became

lovers, Ginny?' pausing as if the memory in fact eluded him, so that Virginia nudged him to continue, gravely, 'We set so much in motion we could not have anticipated. My wife, and my daughter Janey; *your* husband and children. We were selfish, unthinking—'

At this, before Virginia could reply, or even to collect her thoughts sufficiently to know whether she agreed, or disagreed, there came a loud rapping from the bathroom doorway: the Hispanic maid interrupted again, to shout a vehement corrective. Virginia, cringing in Douglas' arms, the two of them pathetically naked, exposed, could comprehend only a cluster of words here and there.

Fortunately, Douglas knew a little Spanish. Humbled, he whispered in Virginia's ear, '*She* was the maid for the room, she says. And we forgot to leave her a tip.'

Virginia's eyes flew open, astonished. 'What? Is that it? Is that all?'

In her fever state, she began to laugh. Douglas joined her, in a helpless spasm. Peals of laughter mingling with ecstatic shrieks and groans from the television set where Reverend Steel was exhorting the faithful in his studio audience to surrender themselves to Our Saviour.

'Is that all? A *tip*?'

How hot, how prickly-hot, their skin! Their skins! In dread fascination, determined not to wince, or to cry out in pain or distaste, Virginia helped her lover lower himself upon her, and try to insert his only partly erect member into her; she wished he would not keep muttering, *Sorry! sorry!* – 'It isn't romantic at all.' Where they pressed together, the length of her spreadeagled body, her flesh felt as if it were being assailed by hundreds of tiny stinging ants.

Now too the maid was running water loudly in the bathroom, flushing the toilet repeatedly. How inconsiderate!

Virginia could have wept – 'It isn't romantic at *all*.'

Yet she and Douglas gamely persevered. For, in *The Paradisio*, there is no turning back.

Lovemaking after so many years is inevitably awkward. Calculation has replaced blind passion. This had an air of the clinical, for Douglas had gained that weight in the torso and stomach, and Virginia, dehydrated from fever, was thinner than she'd been during the five years of their affair. She shut her eyes, trying to recall her fever in that other life. That life out of which she had stepped, into *The Paradisio*. Or had she died? Stricken in the Yucatán, collapsing in a seething pool of sunshine. Luscious bougainvillaea flowers reeling overhead. Or was it in the hospital? the glaring lights, and the infection that followed? But, no, for God's sake stop — 'It isn't romantic at all.'

And poor Douglas needed her help, he was whispering to her in desperate appeal, so, sighing, Virginia reached down to caress his poor damply-limp organ, recalling how, once, she'd been so in awe of it, and of him; of how, when *The Paradisio* had been a sumptuous luxury hotel overlooking the Atlantic Ocean, they'd made love passionately, blindly, unthinkingly . . . not once, but several times. And afterwards, dazed with love, and with the violence of their erotic experience, they had been reluctant to leave the privacy of the hotel room and return to their spouses: Douglas had gripped Virginia's shoulders hard, declaring, 'I will never want anything again!' and Virginia had laughed, it was such an extravagant statement. Yet, hadn't she felt the same way?

'My God.'

Virginia opened her eyes, and saw what Douglas meant — several boil-sized blisters had formed on their chests! Virginia pinched one just above Douglas' left nipple, and a watery warm liquid ran out.

'Oh, sorry! Did it hurt?'

Douglas grimaced stoically. His face was a shimmering mask of sweat. 'No. Not much.'

Impatient with the lovers, the Hispanic maid had begun vacuuming the room, and the roaring pelted them from all sides. 'So rude!' In other circumstances, Virginia would have complained angrily to the front desk; here, at least, the noise drowned out the television evangelist.

Gamely, Virginia resumed massaging Douglas, as provocatively and as sympathetically as she could; for theirs was a bonded plight. She decided not to worry about the fever blisters, but kissed him full on the mouth. 'My love! Yes!' Quickly, Douglas became hard, and, like a man rushing with a glass of water filled to the very brim, desperate to spill not a drop, very quickly he pushed himself into her, where she was rather dry, and parched, and feverish, but ready for him — 'Oh yes!'

How long then they laboured together, like drowning swimmers, the roaring of the vacuum cleaner pervading the room and the shabby bed nearly collapsing beneath their exertions, neither might have said. Virginia stared open-eyed past her lover's contorted face, where droplets of sweat gathered like tears, seeing that the ceiling seemed to be lifting — floating. *Set so much in motion. Could not anticipate. Selfish, unthinking.* Was it so? Had their attraction for each other blinded them to others? Douglas' unhappy wife, her drinking, dependence upon a succession of therapists; the pretty daughter who dropped out of Bennington to live in a rural commune in Baja California where the principal crop was marijuana. Virginia's husband never knew that she'd been unfaithful to him for years with one of his most trusted friends, yet, shortly before his death (but what a triumphant death: on the golf course, having sunk a diabolically tricky putt, to the envy and admiration of three companions), he had accused her of being a 'promiscuous' woman — 'So unfairly!' In fact, Virginia had had few lovers in her life and of those Douglas had been the sweetest, the kindest, even as he'd been the first; certainly he'd been the one Virginia had most cared for.

The bed was jiggling so violently, Virginia didn't know if Douglas' accelerating pumping was causing it; or the damned maid, inconsiderately banging the bed with the vacuum cleaner nozzle. Maybe, when all this was over, Virginia *would* complain.

To encourage her lover, she began to moan softly. In pleasure, or in the anticipation of pleasure. Or in a fever-delirium?

Seeing then, vividly as if the girl were sitting at her bedside, her own daughter, a petulant, smirky high school girl of some years ago who had astonished Virginia by asking, suddenly, with no warning, one day when Virginia was driving her to a shopping mall, 'You and Mr Mosser — *did* you? When I was in grade school?' and Virginia blushed hotly, and stammered a denial, and her daughter interrupted her carelessly, saying, 'Oh hell, Mother! As if any of that matters *now*.'

Virginia wanted to protest, But doesn't everything matter?

She opened her eyes to see her lover's sweaty beet-red face contorted above hers, veins prominent in his forehead, eyes narrowed to slits. His breath was so wheezing and laboured, a dread thought came to Virginina: had Douglas died, too?

'No. It isn't possible.'

She shut her eyes quickly to dispel the thought, and saw, at once, the most unexpected, and the most beautiful, of visions: Douglas Mosser, aged thirty-five, in white T-shirt, shorts, sandals, leaning to her to extend a hand to her, Virginia, his friend's wife, to help her climb aboard his yacht; smiling so happily at her, his eyes shining; squeezing her fingers with such emphasis, she felt the shock in the pit of her belly. And she cried aloud, now, in room 555 of *The Paradisio* — 'I did love you! I still do! It was worth it!'

A fiery sensation immediately welled up in her loins, that part of her body that had felt nothing for so long; and shattered, yet continued to rise; and yet continued. Virginia clutched at her lover's sweat-slick body, weeping and helpless. As he groaned into her neck, 'Ginny! Darling! I love you too!'

The bed jiggled, sagged, clanged in a final shuddering spasm.

How embarrassing, their pooled resources came to only $44.67 – which they offered to the Hispanic maid, with trembling fingers; and which she contemplated, with suspenseful deliberation, weighing the bills and change in the palm of her hand.

Anxiously the lovers awaited her judgement. Was that bemused contempt in her face, or malice, or a wry grudging sympathy; was it pity; was it, simply, a look of finality – as if she too were eager to leave, after a long gruelling day at *The Paradisio*?

Until at last, to their infinite relief, she smiled, flashed a true smile, saying, shrugging, 'Eh, gratiás!' and closed her fist around the modest tip, and shoved it into her pocket.

THE ROCK

by

Melanie Tem

Melanie Tem's short fiction has appeared in anthologies including *Women of the West*, *Skin of the Soul*, *Cold Shocks*, *Snow White, Blood Red*, *Best New Horror*, *Final Shadows* and *Women of Darkness* and in magazines such as *Isaac Asimov's Science Fiction Magazine*, *Grue* and *Cemetery Dance*. Tem has had two chapbooks published by Roadkill Press. Her first novel, *Prodigal*, was co-winner of the Bram Stoker Award for Best First Novel in 1992. She has since published *Blood Moon*, *Wilding* and *Revenant*. *Making Love* and *Witchlight*, the first two in a series of collaborative novels written with Nancy Holder appeared in 1993 and 1994. Her next novel is *Desmodis*, which will be published by Dell/Abyss in 1995.

Many of Tem's stories are about intimate family relationships. 'The Rock' is more metaphorical than most of her fiction, and almost has the feeling of myth about it.

THE ROCK

Like a creature in heat, the rock lay exposed on the muddy hillside above John Paul Clarke's house. It had appeared a week ago, after exceptionally heavy spring rains had washed away the dirt around, over, and under it. That meant it had been there all along, under the surface, and John hadn't known. He liked that.

With what John considered gratuitous attention to detail, the authorities had estimated that the rock weighed well over four thousand pounds, and that the paperwork to remove it would require at least two weeks to complete. Sleep deprivation, overlaid with the mild state of sexual excitement that was constant these days, made him fantasize, briefly, that something actually might happen to him in the next two weeks that would hold his interest.

The window in front of him was, of course, spotless. After thirty-six years of his pipe smoke, the fingerprints of children and grandchildren and Los Angeles smog, Charlotte was an expert at keeping things clean. John respected and admired that. As he sipped at the drink in his hand and looked some more at the rock, it was possible to pretend that Charlotte's clear, clean glass wasn't there at all.

Since the emergence of the rock above his house, John had been hopefully noting freakish natural phenomena happening everywhere: blizzards in Texas, floods in Iran and drought in the Ukraine, tidal waves and earthquakes, meteorites and hurricanes and long-dormant volcanoes suddenly erupting. Maybe all this *meant* something, maybe the world was building up to some cataclysmic and miraculous change. In his lifetime there'd been other unsettled times like this and nothing had ever come of them, but he always hoped.

'We live in exciting times,' he'd said to Mara just last night. He said that to all the girls — not a line, exactly, but a way of intensifying mutual interest.

From this angle, the rock nearly filled the window. Another drop of rain, another breath of ocean breeze, some mysterious shifting of the earth and it might come tumbling down. The authorities admitted only the most infinitesimal possibility of danger to anyone.

The west side of the house, at his back now, was built out over the beach, supported only by heavy steel stilts with the sand steadily eroding under them. Observing and measuring the erosion of the foundation of his house was like standing at the edge of a cliff or just now discovering another pretty girl.

Years ago – long before Mara had started coming to him in the night, long before he'd met Susan; the name of the girl then had been Denise: lank blonde hair, grey eyes, rose perfume – John had had the entire west wall glassed, to bring the ocean right into the house. Charlotte hated it. Like him, she'd been born and raised in Ohio, where things for the most part stayed *still*; unlike him, she hadn't wanted to leave. And, besides, she was the one with all that glass to clean.

She'd moved her bedroom into their sons' old room in the northeast corner, tucked into the hill. When John woke up in her room he always felt vaguely claustrophobic and bored. He hadn't been there now since the rock had appeared, the same day Mara had started coming to disturb his sleep.

He'd been standing in the twilight rain on the east side of his house, looking at the rock, thinking how the landscape had fundamentally changed in the last twenty-four hours and wondering how long it would be before the rock became so familiar that no one noticed it anymore. A drink in one hand and a joint in the other, he'd been just starting to get high and enormously missing Susan, when the rock moved.

Then he saw that it was a lovely young woman coming down the hill towards him. From this distance she was imposing, tall and broad-shouldered. He was directly in her path. She was running, sliding in the mud; through the slight haze of the booze and the weed, John thought for a moment that she'd fallen and was rolling down the slope, as if the rock itself had dislodged. He squinted quickly and assured himself that the rock was still there, silhouetted against the darkening sky, and the girl was standing close to him, warm, smelling of earth and musk.

'Hi,' she said. 'You're John Paul Clarke.'

'Hi,' he said. 'Yes.'

He hadn't asked her name, but she said anyway, 'My name is Mara.'

'A pretty name for a pretty lady,' he said, which was what he always said, and, to some degree, it was always true. John had never met a young woman he didn't find attractive.

Up close, Mara was no taller than he was, and only ordinarily pretty. She was wearing some sort of coarsely-woven, diaphanous thing that seemed to dissolve when he touched her. And he touched her right away because she demanded it; she stepped up to him, put her arms around his neck and kissed him deeply. Her skin had an odd, gritty texture that John found extremely erotic. Her tongue coaxed him. She had nipples as sharp as chips of mica; he'd always been a tit man.

That first time, they made love at the foot of the hills. He'd never done that before. He'd seduced lots of girls on the beach, of course; it was so romantic. And so risky: Charlotte could look out the glass walls and see them – for that reason among many others he'd been disappointed when she moved her bedroom – and it would have been a little distressing for a man of his position to be arrested by the beach patrol for indecent exposure or contributing to the delinquency of a minor. When he thought about getting his picture in the paper because of some young girl instead of a housing development or a philanthropic project, it made him grin.

Making love with Mara among the hills had been a totally new experience. Other girls were attracted to him, because of his money or because he knew how to treat a lady, but Mara was hot for him, nearly insatiable. Afterwards he must have fallen asleep in the mud and loosening brush, because he'd awakened hours later, confused and still aroused.

The ocean was one of the things that had drawn John out of the Midwest to Southern California. Other lures were the San Andreas Fault and its less famous tributaries, the summer canyon fires and spring mudslides, the La Brea tarpits where sabre-toothed tiger fossils had been neatly landscaped into Hancock Park behind the L.A. County Museum, the imported palm trees and channelized rivers that locals now regarded as part of the natural landscape. And under it all, the lulling, deceptive, ironically pleasant climate.

John couldn't imagine a better place to live, although he'd been tempted by the Pacific Northwest after Mount St Helens. Now, finally, this boulder had worked itself up out of the ground to threaten everything he'd worked for, and at the same time Mara had emerged in his life.

There she was now, walking naked towards him along the beach.
Her aureoles glowed. Her pubic hair, two wings across the tops of her
inner thighs, glistened like the undergrowth on the hills after a rain.

John set his empty glass down and went outside to meet her. By
the time he got there she was already up on the deck, leaning back
over the railing, as close as she could get to the exposed edge. In fact,
he saw suddenly that both her feet – perfectly curved, the toenails
painted silver, sand glittering silver in the hollows of her ankles –
were dangling in midair, so that she was supporting herself only by
her elbows and her bare hips against the redwood rails. A breath of
wind, a subtle shifting of the structure under her and she might fall.

He rushed to catch her. Her body more than filled his arms, and her
mouth ground along the vulnerable hollow of his clavicle, making
him think of the trenches that appeared on the surface of the hill
after a mudslide. Those marks never lasted long.

Heart thundering, John turned his head and gasped for air while
still holding her as close as he could. 'What are you doing here?'

'I wanted to see you.'

'But my wife—'

'Might see us,' Mara whispered, rubbing herself so hard against
him that his chest hurt. 'Might find out. Yes.' She laughed.

Clutching each other, her hand around his penis and his under her
breast, they half-tumbled down the open stairway and rolled in their
own small avalanche among the stilts that kept John's house from
washing into the sea. The sand gave as Mara lowered herself on top of
him. Her muscles tightened around his penis; she pressed her fists
against his chest as she moved herself more and more rapidly up and
down, up and down. When she came she wailed, then flung herself
forward and covered his open mouth with hers so that he couldn't
breathe, couldn't cry out, was hardly aware of his own orgasm except
as a sudden and nearly total draining. He was sure he heard Charlotte
moving around in the house over his head.

Mara removed her mouth from his, released his now limp and sore
penis and crawled out from under the house. John missed her already
and, at the same time, was relieved to see her go. This time he
followed her a short distance and tried to watch where she went; she
ran easily up the muddy hillside to the crest where the rock was, and
then he couldn't see her anymore.

It took enormous, almost painful effort to get himself out from
under the house, dressed, and back up the swaying stairs. There was
no sound from Charlotte's room.

Early the first morning of the rock's appearance, before the minicam crews and the tourists had found it and before the authorities had fenced it off, John had climbed the slope. He hadn't done anything so physical in years, other than making love. He was quickly winded, his feet kept slipping in the mud, and there were no firm handholds.

Up close, the rock wasn't especially imposing. When he laid his palms on it, the surface was wet and gritty. When he leaned against it, even pushed at it and kicked around its base, it gave no signs of wanting to move. But John noticed scores of smaller rocks scattered below him, and the slope was trenched. He shivered pleasantly, patted the rock as if it were a pretty girl's rump, clambered and slid back down and went on to work.

'Hey, Mr Clarke.' The girl Tammy had approached him again that morning. 'You said you'd get me into school.'

Since he'd noticed Tammy working in his Santa Monica office, Charlotte had been pouting and Mara's sensuality had turned furious, almost vicious sometimes. Tammy had long red hair and fine legs which she showed off to every advantage; he was a leg man, too. And she treated him as if he were powerful, as if he could do things for her, some of which he probably could. He could not be expected to resist a pretty girl in need.

When he put his hand on Tammy's shoulder, he saw the quick hard light in her eyes and interpreted it as a signal of mutual understanding and respect. Each of them had something the other wanted. He tried never to think of these exchanges in terms of barter and price, although he knew, sadly, that other people did. Often – his hand on the belly of a girl he'd watched and wanted for a long time, his head between the legs of a girl he'd barely met – John's intense gratitude and excitement so fervent that he was often impotent.

He never had that trouble with Mara. Often she woke him out of a sound sleep and then stayed with him the rest of the night. Sometimes, waiting for her, he couldn't fall asleep in the first place. Even when he was so tired and spent that he could barely feel his body or hers anymore, even when he begged or ordered her in all seriousness to stop, he'd never once failed to respond to her. To her kisses, her tongue and teeth. To her touch, long sharp nails and slender fingers that stroked, massaged, pinched. To her moist labia and engorged clitoris and strong striated muscles pulling him in.

He'd been impotent more than once with Susan; at the time he'd thought it didn't matter. He'd thought both their love and their lovemaking were pure. He'd imagined that, when they walked together in public without touching, or when they sat up all night just talking over wine or hot chocolate, they were making love as surely and completely as when their bodies joined. Because he'd believed that he and Susan wanted nothing from each other but each other, he'd felt both free and compelled to promise her the world. It had never occurred to him that she would expect him to deliver.

'Why don't you and I go somewhere after work and talk about it?' he suggested now to Tammy, allowing his fingers to stray from her shoulder into her lovely hair. Maybe it was their hair that he noticed first. 'I'm sure we can come up with something.'

There was a silence, which John read as a deliberate pause for effect rather than a hesitation. This girl knew what she was doing, which pleased him as much as innocence in other girls. When she said, 'I can't tonight,' he was surprised and disappointed, and he removed his hand from her hair. Then, quickly, she added, 'But here, let me give you my home phone number. Maybe we can get together later in the week.'

The rock was driving Charlotte crazy. She would sit for hours at her window and stare out at it, listen simultaneously to the radio and TV news updates, and periodically call the authorities to tell them they had to do something. She said it to John, too, repeatedly and with increasing bitterness, which did not become her. 'Damn you, John Paul Clarke, you've got to *do* something.'

'There's not a thing I can do,' he pointed out with considerable satisfaction.

'You don't care about me! Our house will be destroyed! We'll be killed! That disgusting thing has no business in our lives!'

'Look, honey, there's no reason you should have to go through this. Why don't you go stay with your sister till it's all over?'

'I'm not going anywhere without you,' she informed him grimly, and turned back to the window.

John sighed and took her in his arms. After a while, as always, she relaxed and leaned back against him, and he tenderly kissed her ear.

John Paul Clarke loved his wife. After thirty-six years of marriage and seven children, they had a lot in common and he still recognized in her the comfort of the high school sweetheart waiting for him back home. He loved her. He was grateful to her. But she wasn't enough for him. 'They're making fun of you!' Charlotte had yelled at him after his break-up with Susan. He had needed her support then and eventually she'd given it, but he'd had to be patient. 'These girls, young enough to be your *grand*daughters! Everybody's laughing at you, John! And at me!'

'I didn't expect this to happen,' he'd protested miserably.

Charlotte had known about Susan from the beginning, as she'd known about all the others. John believed in honesty. 'Not that I wouldn't have done it anyway. Not that I wouldn't do it again.'

'She's young enough to be your granddaughter!' Charlotte had repeated furiously, as if that mattered. 'For God's sake, John, what *did* you expect?'

So many times Susan had told him, 'You're the best thing that ever happened to me,' taking his face in her hands, burying her curly head in his lap.

After a while he'd worked up the courage to say, 'I'm old enough to be your father. Your grandfather, actually. Doesn't that bother you?'

'*Bother* me? John Paul Clarke, don't you know that's one of the things I find so exciting about you? One of the reasons I love you so much?' And Susan would hide herself in his arms.

'What Susan and I had,' he told Charlotte when it was over, 'most people will never understand.'

'Oh, I understand perfectly. You think you're the first middle-aged man to make a fool of himself over girls young enough to be his granddaughters?'

Then, and again now, John put his hands on Charlotte's shoulders and looked deeply into her eyes. She'd never been able to resist that for long. In her bed on the hill-side of the house, whose stability had now been proven a ruse, John made sweet, familiar love to his wife, thinking of her, of Susan, of Mara and of the red-haired girl Tammy. He'd have enjoyed a glimpse of the rock through Charlotte's window, but she had her curtains drawn. When he kissed her good-night and left her, she was peacefully asleep.

Mara was waiting in his room. Moonlight highlighted her erect nipples, the undulation of her hip, her teeth. Her skin was multi-coloured, multifaceted, each facet catching the light in a subtly different way. He thought of her somehow as metamorphic: an amalgam of many substances, taking on the properties of each and making them her own.

She came at him, fists upraised and legs spread. 'You stay away from her! You belong to *me*!'

She pressed her open mouth hard over his and wrapped herself around him; her arms and legs were like stalactites and stalagmites, growing up and growing down. The force of her turned him around and pushed him against the glass wall, which bowed and creaked, but held. Her mossy hair was matted across his face, so that he could breathe nothing but her, her sweet fragrance and faint foul odour.

His erection was immediate and huge. Although it had been a long time since Charlotte had entirely satisfied him, no other woman had ever been able to arouse him like this so soon after he'd made love to his wife. He was gratified, and a little taken aback.

The odd reflections off water, through glass, off Mara's many surfaces, were making him dizzy. He tried to hold her head still so he could kiss her but she flung his hands away, then grabbed his wrists. Fleetingly, John was afraid of her, which increased his excitement.

'You stay away from that woman, John Paul Clarke! I'm all you'll need for the rest of your life!'

Assuming she was talking about Tammy, John said what he always said to Charlotte. 'Honey, she's just a kid. She's no threat to us.' Until Susan – until Mara – Charlotte had always believed that, and it had always been true.

'She's your wife!' Mara hissed. 'Of course she's a threat to me, and you damn well better believe I'm a threat to her. You stay the hell away from her!'

John was shocked. To all the girls, he'd made it absolutely clear that his marriage and family were sacred to him, inviolable. His relationship with his wife was a thing apart from any relationship with anybody else. Even Susan had known that.

But he couldn't think of how to make it clear to Mara. His mind was full of her, hot and slowly swirling, as if she were lava. His body was full of her and aching to explode. He came and cried out, couldn't free himself from her, came and cried out again. He wasn't entirely sure when she left him or how, but he knew she'd be back.

The next day, exhausted, he stayed in bed and watched the syndicated talk shows, which periodically were interrupted by local news updates about the rock; the authorities were still debating whether the rock was really a danger to anyone, and if so, what should be done. Charlotte brought him tea and soup, felt his forehead. He was vaguely grateful for her ministrations.

By late afternoon his head had cleared enough for him to get out of bed. Barefoot and in pyjamas, he crossed to the glass wall of his room. The ocean looked the same as it always had; its very unpredictability was becoming predictable. Hazily, John worried – not for the first time in his life – that he'd missed something, was at this very moment missing something fascinating.

He fumbled into his robe and slippers and made his way through the house to a west window, where he could see the rock. It looked unremarkable, as if it had always been part of the landscape – as, indeed, it had, although neither John nor anybody else had been aware of it. The sky was overcast, but it wasn't raining. He wished it would rain. He called for Charlotte but she didn't answer, and he didn't know what he wanted from her anyway.

Looking for his pipe in his coat pocket, he found instead the phone number for Tammy, and, hardly thinking about it, dialled. Her father answered. 'Good afternoon, sir,' John said pleasantly. 'This is John Paul Clarke. May I please speak to Tammy?' When she finally came to the phone, John tingled with sudden renewed awareness of her youth and availability. 'Hi, honey, how are ya?'

'Who is this?'

'This is John Paul Clarke.' Having expected her to recognize his voice right away, he was pleased by this little surprise.

'Oh, Mr Clarke.'

'How are ya?'

'Fine.'

'That's good, honey. I'm glad you're fine. Listen, I have a few ideas about your education that I'd like to share with you.'

'Oh, really.'

'Why don't you meet me at the Blue Room later tonight and we can discuss them. See if we can come up with anything we both find – interesting.'

There was a pause. John guessed she was figuring, and he liked that about her. Thinking he heard footsteps close behind him, he turned eagerly, but Mara wasn't there yet. Tammy said, 'I can't drink yet, you know.'

He chuckled knowingly. 'No, not legally.'

'I'm only nineteen.'

'No problem. The bartender's a friend of mine.'

'I don't want to get in trouble.'

His resourcefulness was as hardy as ever. 'Tell you what. There's no age limit on getting high. And I've got some fine weed.' She said nothing, and he understood he was to take that as assent. 'I'll meet you at nine o'clock at the Blue Room. You can get there okay?'

'Yeah.'

He would try to be home when Mara came tonight, but if things progressed nicely with Tammy, he had to be free to see them through. He'd missed kids' school concerts and business appointments that way; any number of times he'd been late for dinner. Charlotte and the kids got their feelings hurt but they always accepted him for who he was. He'd lost some money that way, but business associates also envied him his priorities. Mara would be furious. But John was invigorated.

Supper with Charlotte was a pleasant little interlude. Worry crossed her face, aging her, when he turned on the TV after supper in the middle of a news break about the rock. Several jurisdictions were arguing now over whose responsibility it was, and rain was in the forecast. He told her not to worry. Her eyes glazed with tears when he told her he was going out. He kissed her and said he wouldn't be late, and she smiled a little. Charlotte was a good woman, a good wife. She knew he loved her very much.

Whistling, John strolled along the beach towards the Blue Room. The sky was dark blue, the darkest it ever got this close to the city. There were lights everywhere, houses in the valley and up all the hills, planes across the sky. But he could no longer see the rock, not even its outline or its impression.

Remembering the countless other times he'd walked this way to meet a young lady at the Blue Room, he found himself unwillingly thinking of the last painful, bewildering months of his relationship with Susan. 'You promised!' she'd accused him again and again. 'You promised you'd set me up in my own store.'

'I meant to, honey. I still do. Things just haven't quite worked out yet.' The truth was, he'd forgotten he'd ever said that.

'I think I've already paid you pretty well in advance for any favours, don't you? I don't think I owe you anything.' She'd never again let him make love to her, directly or indirectly.

Tammy stood him up. He sat alone for a long time in the lounge of the Blue Room, drinking Scotch neat and chatting with the bartender, who'd been here for years and who always flirted with him. John was kind to her, of course, but did his best not to lead her on; she was easily his age.

Finally he sighed and went to call Tammy. The lobby was noisy and dim. He had to stand in line for the phone. Tammy's father answered. It pleased John to be talking on the phone to the father of a pretty girl whom he wanted to bed, whom he also wanted to help. 'Good evening, sir,' he said pleasantly. 'This is John Paul Clarke. May I speak with Tammy, please?'

'Just who the hell do you think you are?'

John blinked, and his heart speeded up. 'Pardon?'

'You're old enough to be her grandfather, for Chrissake. You just leave her alone, Jack, you understand? If you call here again I'll call the cops.'

'I don't understand—'

'Tammy tells me you've got daughters older than she is.'

John said proudly, 'Three of them.'

'How would you feel if some dirty old sonofabitch asked them out?'

Stung by the man's continual and unnecessary use of the word 'old', John nonetheless thought about the question, trying his best to be reasonable. He'd never considered it before. 'I don't think I'd mind,' he said truthfully. 'It's up to them—'

'Where'd you get this number, anyway? It's unlisted.'

'Tammy gave it to me.'

'My daughter tells me you got it from her personnel file. Those files are supposed to be confidential.'

'I'm afraid there's been some kind of misunderstanding here. This is John Paul—'

'I know who you are. Everybody knows who you are. My daughter's crying in her room right now because of you. She's afraid to go to work. She's afraid to walk home at night. Does that make you feel like a big man?'

'Afraid?' John was dumbfounded, and his voice broke. 'There's certainly no reason—'

The man was shouting now. 'Listen, you dirty old bastard, you stay away from my daughter or I'll call the authorities and plaster your filthy name all over the papers. You think you're such a hot shot, how'd you like a little free publicity? Huh?'

'I don't—'

Tammy's father hung up. John stood there for a moment with the receiver in his hand. Then, somewhat dazed, he went back to the lounge for another, stronger drink. He had totally misread this girl. She had wanted something from him and had never intended to give him anything in return. She'd led him on. She hadn't respected him. He was losing his touch, couldn't trust his instincts anymore. He was getting old.

During those last desperate weeks with Susan, when he'd known he was losing her, he'd sent her flowers every day. Yellow roses, pink carnations, orchids that looked artificial, even when they weren't. Frantically he'd imagined how they must be filling her apartment with fragrance and colour, and with sensual, unavoidable thoughts of him.

Susan had left him anyway, and he had no mementoes. He'd burned all her letters and photographs, given away or returned all her gifts, and he hadn't seen or heard of her now in years. Suddenly aware of himself, a balding and brooding old man sitting alone over too many drinks in a singles bar on a rainy night, John managed to finish his drink and stand up. He left a generous tip, even though his friend the bartender had practically ignored him all evening, and made his

way between tables, smiling and nodding in case there was anyone
he knew or anyone he might care to know in the future, some pretty
girl.

It seemed a long walk to get home. He was sick with fatigue and
his thoughts and impressions were distorted – from the drinks, he
supposed. Another sign of age. The beach sand shifted constantly,
affecting his balance and making it hard to tell whether he was
making progress in any direction. One spot on the beach looked like
any other – scallops of waves, footprints opening and closing, an
indistinct pattern of land and water and land becoming water. Many
lights had been turned off, apparently at random, so he couldn't use
them to orient himself. He couldn't quite make out his own house,
or the tasteful arrangement of streetlights he'd designed into the
development. He couldn't tell where the edge of the ocean was,
couldn't see the rock at all.

Frightened, lonely, so tired he could hardly move, John yearned to
be home. He would sleep all night tonight with Charlotte, his
beloved wife.

Hands came around his neck from behind. The instant he
recognized Mara – rough hands, with those sexy long nails, husky
voice whispering fiercely, 'I told you, you belong to *me*!' – his breath
came short and heavy, his flesh tingled, his penis hardened. Through
the fatigue which still enveloped him, he was aware only of desire for
Mara. He could not live without her.

She was riding him, long legs gripping his pelvis, long arms
encircling his chest. She was kissing and biting the back of his neck.
She was arching her back and pressing her groin into his spinal
column. He could feel the electrical warmth and wetness of her
through his clothes, through his flesh.

He cried out and collapsed, tumbling her off. In the split second
before she lunged at him again, muttering his name like an
imprecation, he thought wildly of Charlotte, thought of passers-by,
of the police, of the rock.

'You are *mine*!' Mara breathed, hot and sweet into his open
mouth.

She tore off his clothes with her teeth and nails and flung them
aside to be eroded with the sand. She broke his skin. She sucked his
fingertips, his nipples, his penis until they ached, and she bit into his
tongue. He ejaculated repeatedly onto the sand. Waves lapped all
around him, washing away what he'd emptied, and he heard Mara
panting and laughing. Then she was on him again.

'You don't need anybody else! You aren't *fit* for anybody else! I've marked you for my own!'

Easily she pulled him over on top of her and raised her pelvis hard. Although he'd have sworn he had no strength or energy and little desire left, he found himself thrusting. Her breasts and buttocks swelled in his hands, their surfaces gritty. When he climaxed this time, he buried his face in her exquisite, monstrous breasts. Salt water and wet sand seeped into his mouth and nose and ears, into all his body orifices, until he was drowning or being split apart.

'You're *mine*,' she told him again, and he believed her. Her tongue filled his mouth until he was sure he would choke, and then she was gone.

Eventually John's senses cleared enough that he could use them, and enough strength returned to his muscles that he could crawl out of the water, find his torn and dirty shirt and pants and struggle into them. Peering dazedly around, he finally realized that he was under his own house, among the stilts that held it up. The ocean lapped and, behind and above the opacity of his house, where he couldn't see it, the rock was still there.

Unless it had come down. If it had let loose and come crashing down its slope while he was making love with Mara, he might well not have known. His house seemed intact, but he had a terrifying detailed image of the hidden east wall ravaged, Charlotte crushed alone in her bed.

Swaying dangerously, missing more than one step, John climbed the teetering stairway and let himself into the house. Though the floor seemed stable enough, still he was careful where he stepped and how he distributed his weight. 'Charlotte!' There was no answer.

Cautiously he made his way through the skewed halls and rooms, unsure where steps would be, which room came next, where there would be windows. Lights had been left on for him and he was grateful. In all the dark glass, his reflection looked different every time, and when he tried to avert his eyes, vertigo swelled.

In the far northeast corner of the house, tucked into the traitorous hills, Charlotte's room was dark. As always, though her door was ajar, a signal for him to come in if he wanted to. He very much wanted to.

Someone was with her. A shape loomed over the bed. In the bed.

His first thought, ludicrously, was that the rock had in fact hurtled off its hillside and somehow lodged in Charlotte's bed.

Then he thought of Mara. She could well be waiting for him here, in his wife's bed, determined to make her possession of him complete. She could have hurt Charlotte. He could be too late.

But then, as he forced himself into the room, he heard the raspy breathing and his wife's panting, smelled the male musk, saw the enormous erect penis and her spread legs, and knew that Charlotte had taken a lover.

'You belong to *me*!' the intruder was shouting at Charlotte, murmuring to her. The voice was deep, rough, masculine, a stranger's voice, but oddly familiar to John. 'You'll never need another man for the rest of your life! You'll never be fit for another man! You're mine!'

John cried, 'No!' and lunged. The room tilted, there was a roaring in his ears like an avalanche or an orgasm, and he was on Charlotte's bed at the moment her lover entered her. Sinewy hands kneaded her breasts not inches from John's eyes. The hungry mouth sucked at her ears, at the hollows of her neck. The engorged penis thrust in and out of her, so close to John that their tangled pubic hair brushed his own penis, which was uselessly erect again and hurting. The room reeked of all their odours. Charlotte moaned, a long shuddering orgasm unlike any John had ever known her to have.

The intruder took his hand away from Charlotte to caress John. The rough fingers slid down the slopes of his body, making the flesh tingle as if it had been trenched. The intruder took his mouth away from Charlotte to whisper John's name. The intruder turned his face so that John could see, and it was a male version of Mara's face.

John must have passed out. Charlotte must have fallen asleep, satiated, or unable to make sense of what had happened except by calling it a dream. They awoke to grey morning light and the chatter of news on Charlotte's clock radio, reporting on the unchanged status of the rock. They lay silently in each other's arms; John thought of many things to say, but was afraid of them all. They heard the rain when it began again and held each other closer.

By nine o'clock the authorities were declaring that the required paperwork had been completed ahead of schedule, permits would be issued momentarily, and the rock could now be moved. By noon a crane had arrived at the foot of the hill. Workers in yellow slickers were attaching guywires around the rock's girth and to any protrusions that might hold. Wrapped in a quilt, his head and groin throbbing and his stomach queasy, John watched, while in her bed behind him Charlotte turned her face to the wall.

The rock refused to budge. In the steady drizzle the workers pulled and pried, the crane spun its wheels, the ropes and guywires strained and creaked, and nothing moved except a few clots of mud skittering down the slope. Newscasts began reporting that unexpected complications had developed.

Charlotte refused to get out of bed. Finally, dragging his quilt behind him, John went barefoot to the phone. 'This is John Paul Clarke. I'd like to speak to someone in charge of the rock.' He was put on hold. When the next girl finally came on the line, he tried to imagine her sweet, young face as he repeated, 'This is John Paul Clarke. I'd like to speak to someone in charge of the rock, please.'

'Which rock, sir?'

John was amazed. 'The two-ton boulder that has been threatening Ocean Hills. Surely you've heard of it?'

'Maybe I can help you.'

'Are you in charge of the rock?' he asked sceptically. She sounded so young. 'I want to buy it.'

'I beg your pardon?'

'When they finally get it off the hill, I want to buy it. Whole or in pieces.' Charlotte had turned over to stare at him. He smiled at her.

'Well, sir, I'm not sure it's for sale. I mean, it's a *rock*. It's probably public property. *Buy* it, sir?'

'Money is no object.' Finally, wearily, he left his name and hung up and went back to Charlotte's bed. Charlotte welcomed him silently, put her arms around him.

The rock finally came down the hill as the cloudy sky over the ocean was darkening for the night. Intact, the thing wouldn't budge. They had to blast it into pieces to get it loose, and John's house trembled on its stilts.

Once begun, the rock's descent was quick and simple. In just a few minutes, its pieces lay at the foot of the hill as if they'd always been there, and the drizzle had already smoothed any scars from the crest of the hill and the slope.

When John started to put on his raincoat and hat, Charlotte said, 'You're not going out there.'

'The rock's gone, honey. There's no danger anymore.'

'Stay here with me. Let the authorities take care of the pieces in the morning.' She sighed and shook her head. 'At least put your boots on. You'll catch your death.' He smiled at her gratefully, indulgently.

By the time he got out there, most of the workers had left. Two men, their yellow hats and slickers faded to grey in the gloomy twilight, were unrolling a chicken-wire fence. John hailed them and one looked up while the other kept pounding a stake into the soft ground.

The stake wouldn't hold in the mud. The worker swore and pulled it out, tried again a few inches away. He tested the give of the wire against his partner's stake. When it held, barely, he began to back up, with the wire unrolling crookedly in front of him.

John followed him. 'Why are you fencing it off now? What damage could anybody do to it now?' Wordlessly, the man shrugged.

Chunks of the rock had scattered very close to the east wall of John's house, in his backyard. 'My name is John Paul Clarke,' he began. 'I live here. I built this development. I have made arrangements to buy the rock.'

The man shook his head impatiently, spraying drops of rain from his hat brim into John's face. 'I don't know about that. All I want to do is get this fence up and get outta here.'

'It's not a very solid fence,' John said unhappily. The workers ignored him.

By the time John had trudged the short distance back to his door, he was weak from exhaustion. Charlotte tucked him into her bed with pillows, the paper and hot tea. Outside, the workers kept calling to each other. It wasn't until Charlotte came into bed and held him that he let himself fall asleep, as though they could protect each other.

He was awakened by the telephone. Bright sunshine outlined Charlotte's heavy curtains; the rain had stopped and it was morning. He remembered the harmless chunks of rock, remembered the fence and that Mara had not come in the night. Trying not to wake Charlotte, he answered the phone quietly, but cheerily. 'Good morning. This is John Paul Clarke.'

'Hi, Mr Clarke.'

It was the voice of a young girl, and John grinned. 'Hi there. To whom do I have the pleasure of speaking?'

'This is Tammy. Don't you recognize me?'

'I'm sorry, honey. It's early in the morning.'

She giggled, a nice sound. 'It's almost noon.'

He giggled, too. He didn't remember the last time he'd slept with Charlotte till noon. 'How are ya, honey?'

She took an audible breath before she answered. 'Could we get together tonight?'

He didn't even hesitate. 'Oh, I'm sorry, but my wife and I have plans.'

'Well, how about some other night this week? My parents are out of town.'

He tried to ignore the excitement low in his belly. Fondly, he suspected that Charlotte was only pretending to be asleep. 'I'll be in to work tomorrow,' he said as gently as he could to Tammy. 'Why don't you make an appointment to see me? Check with my secretary.'

There was a silence. Then she said in a small, furious voice, 'Sure,' and hung up.

He felt bad that he'd hurt her feelings. He regretted the obvious opportunity he was missing. But as he got out of bed and made his way very quietly to the windows, parted the curtains a little and squinted into the sun, he also felt freed.

Pieces of the rock were scattered all over the hillside, many more of them than John had imagined, all different shapes and sizes and colours. The wire fence had sunk onto its side, and two rock chunks – one the size of a beachball and nearly orange, the other considerably smaller and mottled orange and grey – had worked their way the last few inches downslope and were resting against the east wall of his house.

He glimpsed movement where the rocks lay against his foundation. A hand reached up between them, silhouetted against the sunny sky: long fingers, long nails. Waving at him. Beckoning him. Closing threateningly into a fist.

John dropped the curtain, and the room dimmed again. Charlotte stirred, pulled a pillow over her head. John stood there uncertainly for long minutes, watching her, then pulled on his robe and left the room.

He went out the east door and stood in the narrow space between the wall and the collapsed fence. The two orangish chunks of rock were at the far end of the house; he saw no movement there now, no hand, and he let out his breath and shook his head at the tricks of an old man's mind.

'John.'

John started and looked around, saw no one. But the hoarse, broken voice came again, rattled his name from a pile of rubble just on the other side of the bowed wire. He squinted in that direction and saw a head heave itself out of the pile and splat into the mud. Long thick hair like uprooted brush. Rough skin catching the sun on many fractured planes.

Taking a few unwilling, unsteady steps towards the head, John slipped and fell onto the fence. Wire scratched his flesh like fingernails. He peered at the ground and saw a penis hard as granite, labia like veins of ore.

He struggled to get to his feet, but the ground was slippery and shifting, and the fatigue had returned. He crawled towards his door, then realized he was headed eastward, towards the rock-strewn hills, up the slope. He couldn't stop himself. A tooth had lodged in his palm. A pebble like a tongue had entered the fly of his pyjamas and was caressing his scrotum.

He forced himself to turn around. He was sure he was going downslope, back towards his house, when Mara's call confused him again. 'Don't go away, John. You belong to me.'

Mara's magnificent breasts swelled out of the slope just ahead of him, aureoles glittering and nipples erect. He cried out and collapsed between them.

Then there was a rumbling like the building of an orgasm, and the ground quivered under him. John managed to lift his face to see the rock – intact, huge, multicoloured and multifaceted – rolling down the hill. He was directly in its path. His penis hardened in anticipation.

'I love you, John. I'll never leave you. You're *mine*.'

AN OUTSIDE INTEREST

by

Ruth Rendell

Ruth Rendell is a major writer of psychological suspense novels. She
has won three Edgar Awards from the Mystery Writers of America
and four Golden Daggers from England's Crime Writers Association.
Author of over thirty novels including *Going Wrong*, *The Tree of
Hands*, *The Killing Doll*, *Live Flesh*, *The Crocodile Bird*, a whole
series of Chief Inspector Wexford novels and six novels under her
Barbara Vine name. In addition she has published six collections of
stories. 'An Outside Interest' is reprinted from her *Collected Stories*.

'An Outside Interest' is a creepy tale of malicious mischief that
leads to disaster.

AN OUTSIDE INTEREST

Frightening people used to be a hobby of mine. Perhaps I should rather say an obsession and not people but, specifically, women. Making others afraid *is* enjoyable as everyone discovers who has tried it and succeeded. I suppose it has something to do with power. Most people never really try it so they don't know, but look at the ones who do. Judges, policemen, prison warders, customs officers, tax inspectors. They have a great time, don't they? You don't find them giving up or adopting other methods. Frightening people goes to their heads, they're drunk on it, they live by it. So did I. While other men might go down to the pub with the boys or to football, I went off to Epping Forest and frightened women. It was what you might call my outside interest.

Don't get me wrong. There was nothing – well, nasty, about what I did. You know what I mean by that, I'm sure I don't have to go into details. I'm far from being some sort of pervert, I can tell you. In fact, I err rather on the side of too much moral strictness. Nor am I one of those lonely, deprived men. I'm happily married and the father of a little boy, I'm six feet tall, not bad-looking and, I assure you, entirely physically and mentally normal.

Of course I've tried to analyse myself and discover my motives. Was my hobby ever any more than an antidote to boredom? By anyone's standards the life I lead would be classed as pretty dull, selling tickets and answering passengers' queries at Anglo-Mercian Airways terminal, living in a semi in Muswell Hill, going to tea with my mother-in-law on Sundays and having an annual fortnight in a holiday flat in South Devon. I got married very young. Adventure wasn't exactly a conspicuous feature of my existence. The biggest thing that happened to me was when we thought one of our charters had been hi-jacked in Greece, and that turned out to be a false alarm.

My wife is a nervous sort of girl. Mind you, she has cause to be,

living where we do close to Highgate Wood and Queens Wood. A
woman takes her life in her hands, walking alone in those places.
Carol used to regale me with stories – well, she still does.

'At twenty past five in the afternoon! It was still broad daylight.
He raped her and cut her in the face, she had to have seventeen
stitches in her face and neck.'

She doesn't drive and if she comes home from anywhere after dark
I always go down to the bus stop to meet her. She won't even walk
along the Muswell Hill Road because of the woods on either side.

'If you see a man on his own in a place like that you naturally ask
yourself what he's doing there, don't you? A young man, just
walking aimlessly about. It's not as if he had a dog with him. It
makes your whole body go tense and you get a sort of awful crawling
sensation all over you. If you didn't come and meet me I don't think
I'd go out at all.'

Was it that which gave me the idea? At any rate it made me think
about women and fear. Things are quite different for a man, he never
thinks about being afraid of being in dark or lonely places. I'm sure I
never have and therefore, until I got all this from Carol, I never
considered how important this business of being scared when out
alone might be to them. When I came to understand it gave me a
funny feeling of excitement.

And then I actually frightened a woman myself – by chance. My
usual way of going to work is to cut through Queens Wood to
Highgate tube station and take the Northern Line down into
London. When the weather is very bad I go to the station by bus but
most of the time I walk there and back and the way through the wood
is a considerable short cut. I was coming back through the wood at
about six one evening in March. It was dusk, growing dark. The
lamps each a good distance apart from each other, which light the
paths, were lit, but I often think these give the place a rather more
bleak and sinister appearance than if it were quite dark. You leave a
light behind you and walk along a dim shadowy avenue towards the
next lamp which gleams faintly some hundred yards ahead. And no
sooner is it reached, an acid yellow glow among the bare branches,
than you leave it behind again to negotiate the next dark stretch. I
thought about how it must be to be a woman walking through the
wood and, yes, I gloried in my maleness and my freedom from fear.

Then I saw the girl coming. She was walking along the path from
Priory Gardens. It came into my head that she would be less wary of
me if I continued as I had been, marching briskly and purposefully
towards Wood Vale, swinging along and looking like a man

homeward bound to his family and his dinner. There was no definite intent present in my mind when I slackened my pace, then stopped and stood still. But as soon as I'd done that I knew I was going to carry it through. The girl came up to where the paths converged and where the next lamp was. She gave me a quick darting look. I stood there in a very relaxed way and I returned her look with a blank stare. I suppose I consciously, out of some sort of devilment, made my eyes fixed and glazed and let my mouth go loose. Anyway, she turned very quickly away and began to walk much faster.

She had high heels so she couldn't go very fast, not as fast as I could, just strolling along behind her. I gained on her until I was a yard behind.

I could smell her fear. She was wearing a lot of perfume and her sweat seemed to potentiate it so that there came to me a whiff and then a wave of heady, mixed-up animal and floral scent. I breathed it in, I breathed heavily. She began to run and I strode after her. What she did then was unexpected. She stopped, turned round and cried out in a tremulous terrified voice: 'What do you want?'

I stopped too and gave her the same look. She held her handbag out to me. 'Take it!'

The joke had gone far enough. I lived round there anyway, I had my wife and son to think of. I put on a cockney voice. 'Keep your bag, love. You've got me wrong.'

And then, to reassure her, I turned back along the path and let her escape to Wood Vale and the lights and the start of the houses. But I can't describe what a feeling of power and — well, triumphant manhood and what's called machismo the encounter gave me. I felt grand. I swaggered into my house and Carol said had I had a Premium Bond come up?

Since I'm being strictly truthful in this account, I'd better add the other consequence of what happened in the wood, even though it does rather go against the grain with me to mention things like that. I made love to Carol that night and it was a lot better than it had been for a long time, in fact it was sensational for both of us. And I couldn't kid myself that it was due to anything but my adventure with the girl.

Next day I looked at myself in the mirror with all the lights off but the little tubular one over our bed, and I put on the same look I'd given the girl when she turned in my direction under the lamp. I can tell you I nearly frightened myself. I've said I'm not bad-looking and that's true but I'm naturally pale and since I'm thin, my face tends to be a bit gaunt. In the dim light my eyes seemed sunk in deep sockets and my mouth hung loose in a vacant, mindless way. I stepped back from the glass so that I could see the whole of myself, slouching, staring, my arms hanging. There was no doubt I had the potential of being a woman-frightener of no mean calibre.

They say it's the first step that counts. I had taken the first step but the second was bigger and it was weeks before I took it. I kept telling myself not to be a fool, to forget those mad ideas. Besides, surely I could see I'd soon be in trouble if I made a habit of frightening women in Queens Wood, on my own doorstep. But I couldn't stop thinking about it. I remembered how wonderful I'd felt that evening, how tall I'd walked and what a man I'd been.

The funny thing was what a lot of humiliating things seemed to happen to me at that time, between the Queens Wood incident and the next occasion. A woman at the air terminal actually spat at me. I'm not exaggerating. Of course she was drunk, smashed out of her mind on duty-free Scotch, but she spat at me and I had to stand there in the middle of the ticket hall with all those tourists milling about, and wipe the spittle off my uniform. Then I got a reprimand for being discourteous to a passenger. It was totally unjust and, strictly speaking, I should have resigned on the spot, only I've got a wife and son and jobs aren't easy to come by at present. There was all that and trouble at home as well with Carol nagging me to take her on a holiday with this girl friend of hers and her husband to Minorca instead of our usual Salcombe fortnight. I told her straight we couldn't afford it but I didn't like being asked in return why I couldn't earn as much as Sheila's Mike.

My manhood was at a low ebb. Then Sheila and Mike asked us to spend the day with them, Carol, Timothy and me. They had been neighbours of ours but had just moved away to a new house in one of those outer suburbs that are really in Essex. So I drove the three of us out to Theydon Bois and made my acquaintance with Epping Forest.

There are sixty-four square miles of forest, lying on the north-eastern borders of London. But when you drive from the Wake Arms to Theydon along a narrow road bordered by woodland, stretches of turf and undergrowth, little coppices of birch trees, you can easily believe yourself in the depths of the country. It seems impossible that London is only fourteen or fifteen miles away. The forest is green and silent and from a car looks unspoilt, though of course it can't be. We passed a woman walking a very unguard-like dog, a tiny Maltese terrier . . . That gave me the idea. Why shouldn't I come out here? Why shouldn't I try my frightening act out here where no one knew me?

Two days after that I did. It was spring and the evenings stayed light till nearly eight. I didn't take the car. Somehow it didn't seem to me as if the sort of person I was going to be, going to *act*, would have a car. The journey was awful, enough to deter anyone less determined than I. I went straight from work, taking the Central Line tube as far as Loughton and then a bus up the hills and into the forest. At the Wake Arms I got off and began to walk down the hill, not on the pavement but a few yards inside the forest itself. I didn't see a woman on her own until I had reached the houses of Theydon and begun the return trip. I had gone about a hundred yards up again when she came out of one of the last houses, a young girl in jeans and a jacket, her hands in her pockets.

It was clear she was going to walk to the Wake Arms. Or so I thought. For a while I walked, keeping step with her, but unseen among the hawthorn and crab apple bushes, the tangle of brambles. I let us get a quarter of a mile away from the houses before I showed myself and then I stepped out on to the pavement ahead of her. I turned round to face her and stood there, staring in the way I'd practised in the mirror.

She wasn't nervous. She was brave. It was only very briefly that she hesitated. But she didn't quite dare walk past me. Instead she crossed the road. There's never much traffic on that road and so far not a single car had passed. She crossed the road, walking faster. I crossed too but behind her and I walked along behind her. Presently she began to run, so of course I ran too, though not fast enough to catch her up, just enough to gain on her a little.

We had been going on like that for some minutes, the Wake Arms still a mile off, when she suddenly doubled back, hared across the road and began running back the way she had come. That finished me for chasing her. I stood there and laughed. I laughed long and loud, I felt so happy and free, I felt so much all-conquering power that I – I alone, humble, ordinary, dull *me* – could inspire such fear.

After that I took to going to Epping Forest as a regular thing. Roughly speaking, I'd say it would have been once a fortnight. Since I do shift work, four till midnight just as often as ten till six, I sometimes managed to go in the daytime. A lot of women are alone at home in the daytime and have no men to escort them when they go out. I never let it go more than two weeks without my going there and occasionally I'd go more often, if I was feeling low in spirits, for instance, or Carol and I had a row or I got depressed over money. It did me so much good, I wish I could make you understand how much. Just think what it is you do that gives you a tremendous lift, driving a car really fast or going disco dancing or getting high on something — well, frightening women did all that for me and then some. Afterwards it was like Christmas, it was almost like being in love.

And there was no harm in it, was there? I didn't hurt them. There's a French saying: it gives me so much pleasure and you so little pain. That was the way it was for me and them, though it wasn't without pleasure for them either. Imagine how they must have enjoyed talking about it afterwards, going into all the details like Carol did, distorting the facts, exaggerating, making themselves for a while the centre of attention.

For all I knew they may have got up search parties, husbands and boy friends and fathers all out in a pack looking for me, all having a great time as people invariably do when they're hunting something or someone. After all, when all was said and done, what did I do? Nothing. I didn't molest them or insult them or try to touch them, I merely stood and looked at them and ran after them — or ran when they ran, which isn't necessarily the same thing.

There was no harm in it. Or so I thought. I couldn't see what harm there could ever be, and believe me, I thought about this quite a lot, for I'm just as guilt-ridden as the rest of us. I thought about it, justifying myself, keeping guilt at bay. Young women don't have heart attacks and fall down dead because a man chases them. Young women aren't left with emotional traumas because a man stares at them. The oldest woman I ever frightened was the one with the Maltese terrier and she was no more than forty. I saw her again on my third or fourth visit and followed her for a while, stepping out from behind bushes and standing in her path. She used the same words the girl in Queens Wood had used, uttered in the same strangled voice: 'What is it you want?'

I didn't answer her. I had mercy on her and her little ineffectual dog and I melted away into the woodland shades. The next one who asked me that I answered with professorial gravity: 'Merely collecting lichens, madam.'

It was proof enough of how harmless I was that there was never a sign of a policeman in that area. I'm sure none of them told the police, for they had nothing to tell. They had only what they imagined and what the media had led them to expect. Yet harm did come from it, irrevocable harm and suffering and shame.

No doubt by now you think you've guessed. The inevitable must have happened, the encounter which any man who makes a practice of intimidating women is bound to have sooner or later, when the tables are turned on him. Yes, that did happen but it wasn't what stopped me. Being seized by the arm, hurled in the air and laid out, sprawled and bruised, by a judo black belt, was just an occupational hazard. I've always been glad, though, that I behaved like a gentleman. I didn't curse her or shout abuse. I merely got up, rubbed my legs and my elbows, made her a little bow and walked off in the direction of the Wake. Carol wanted to know how I'd managed to get green stains all over my clothes and I think to this day she believes it was from lying on the grass in a park somewhere with another woman. As if I would!

That attack on me deterred me. It didn't put me off. I let three weeks go by, three miserable yearning weeks, and then I went back to the Wake road one sunny July morning and had one of my most satisfying experiences. A girl walking, not on the road, but taking a short cut through the forest itself. I walked parallel to her, sometimes letting her catch a glimpse of me. I knew she did, for like it had been with the girl in Queens Wood, I could sense and smell her fear.

I strolled out from the bushes at last and stood ahead of her, waiting. She didn't dare approach me, she didn't know what to do. At length she turned back and I followed her, threading my way among the bushes until she must have thought I had gone, then appearing once more on the path ahead. This time she turned off to the left, running, and I let her go. Laughing the way I always did, out loud and irrepressibly, I let her go. I hadn't done her any harm. Think of the relief she must have felt when she knew she'd got away from me and was safe. Think of her going home and telling her mother or her sister or her husband all about it.

You could even say I'd done her a good turn. Most likely I'd warned her off going out in the forest on her own and therefore protected her from some real pervert or molester of women.

It was a point of view, wasn't it? You could make me out a public benefactor. I showed them what could happen. I was like the small electric shock that teaches a child not to play with the wires. Or that's what I believed. Till I learned that even a small shock can kill.

I was out in the forest, on the Wake road, when I had a piece of luck. It was autumn and getting dark at six, the earliest I'd been able to get there, and I didn't have much hope of any woman being silly enough to walk down that road alone in the dark. I had got off the bus at the Wake Arms and was walking slowly down the hill when I saw this car parked ahead of me at the kerb. Even from a distance I could hear the horrible noise it made as the driver tried to start it, that anguished grinding you get when ignition won't take place.

The offside door opened and a woman got out. She was on her own. She reached back into the car and turned the lights off, slammed the door, locked it and began walking down the hill towards Theydon. I had stepped in among the trees and she hadn't yet seen me. I followed her, working out what technique I should use this time. Pursuing her at a run to start with was what I decided on.

I came out on to the pavement about a hundred yards behind her and began running after her, making as much noise with my feet as I could. Of course she stopped and turned round as I knew she would. Probably she thought I was a saviour who was going to do something about her car for her. She looked round, waiting for me, and as soon as I caught her eye I veered off into the forest once more. She gave a sort of shrug, turned and walked on. She wasn't frightened yet.

It was getting dark, though, and there was no moon. I caught her up and walked alongside her, very quietly, only three or four yards away, yet in among the trees of the forest. By then we were out of sight of the parked car and a long way from being in sight of the lights of Theydon. The road was dark, though far from being impenetrably black. I trod on a twig deliberately and made it snap and she turned swiftly and saw me.

She jumped. She looked away immediately and quickened her pace. Of course she didn't have a chance with me, a five-foot woman doesn't with a six-foot man. The fastest she could walk was still only my strolling pace.

There hadn't been a car along the road since I'd been following her. Now one came, I could see its lights welling and dipping a long way off, round the twists in the road. She went to the edge of the pavement and held up her hand the way a hitchhiker does. I stayed where I was to see what would happen. What had I done, after all? Only been there. But the driver didn't stop for her. Of course he didn't, no more than I would have done in his place. We all know the sort of man who stops his car to pick up smartly dressed, pretty hitchhikers at night and we know what he's after.

The next driver didn't stop either. I was a little ahead of her by then, still inside the forest, and in his headlights I saw her face. She *was* pretty, not that that aspect particularly interested me, but I saw that she was pretty and that she belonged to the same type as Carol, a small slender blonde with rather sharp features and curly hair.

The darkness seemed much darker after the car lights had passed. I could tell she was a little less tense now, she probably hadn't seen me for the past five minutes, she might have thought I'd gone. And I was tempted to call it a day, give up after a quarter of an hour, as I usually did when I'd had my fun.

I wish to God I had. I went on with it for the stupidest of reasons. I went on with it because I wanted to go in the same direction as she was going, down into Theydon and catch the tube train from there, rather than go back and hang about waiting for a bus. I could have waited and let her go. I didn't. Out of some sort of perverse need, I kept step with her and then I came out of the forest and got on to the pavement behind her.

I walked along, gaining on her, but quietly. The road dipped, wound a little. I got two or three yards behind her, going very softly, she didn't know I was there, and then I began a soft whistling, a hymn tune it was, the Crimond version of *The Lord is My Shepherd*. What a choice!

She spun round. I thought she was going to say something but I don't think she could. Her voice was strangled by fear. She turned again and began to run. She could run quite fast, that tiny vulnerable blonde girl.

The car lights loomed up over the road ahead. They were full-beam, undipped headlights, blazing blue-white across the surrounding forest, showing up every tree and making long black shadows spring from their trunks. I jumped aside and crouched down in the long grass. She ran into the road, holding up both arms and crying: 'Help me! Help me!'

He stopped. I had a moment's tension when I thought he might get out and come looking for me, but he didn't. He pushed open the passenger door from inside. The girl got in, they waited, sitting there for maybe half a minute, and then the white Ford Capri moved off.

It was a relief to me to see that car disappear over the top of the hill. And I realized, to coin a very appropriate phrase, that I wasn't yet out of the wood. What could be more likely than that girl and the car driver would either phone or call in at Loughton police station? I knew I'd better get myself down to Theydon as fast as possible.

As it happened I did so without meeting or being passed by another vehicle. I was walking along by the village green when the only cars I saw came along. On the station platform I had to wait for nearly half an hour before a train came, but no policeman came either. I had got away with it again.

In a way. There are worse things than being punished for one's crimes. One of those is not being punished for them. I am suffering for what I did of course by not being allowed – that is, by not allowing myself – to do it again. And I shall never forget that girl's face, so pretty and vulnerable and frightened. It comes to me a lot in dreams.

The first time it appeared to me was in a newspaper photograph, two days after I had frightened her on the Wake road. The newspaper was leading on the story of her death and that was why it used the picture. On the previous morning, when she had been dead twelve hours, her body had been found, stabbed and mutilated, in a field between Epping and Harlow. Police were looking for a man, thought to be the driver of a white Ford Capri.

Her rescuer, her murderer. Then what was I?

AND SALOME DANCED

by

Kelley Eskridge

Kelley Eskridge lives in Atlanta, Georgia. She has published short fiction in *The Magazine of Fantasy and Science Fiction* and *Pulphouse* and has recently completed her first novel. Eskridge was the 1992 winner of an Astraea Foundation Writer's Award.

'And Salome Danced' takes place in the world of illusion – theatre.

AND SALOME DANCED

They're the best part, auditions: the last chance to hold in my mind the play as it should be. The uncast actors are easiest to direct; empty stages offer no barriers. Everything is clear, uncomplicated by living people and their inability to be what is needed.

'What I need,' I say to my stage manager, 'is a woman who can work on her feet.'

'Hmmm,' says Lucky helpfully. She won't waste words on anything so obvious. Our play is *Salome*, subtitled *Identity and Desire*. Salome has to dance worth killing for.

The sense I have, in those best, sweet moments, is that I do not so much envision the play as experience it in some sort of multidimensional *gestalt*. I *feel* Salome's pride and the terrible control of her body's rhythms; Herod's twitchy groin and his guilt and his unspoken love for John; John's relentless patience, and his fear. The words of the script sometimes seize me as if bypassing vision, burrowing from page into skin, pushing blood and nerve to bursting point on the journey to my brain. The best theatre lives inside. I'll spend weeks trying to feed the sensation and the bloodsurge into the actors, but . . . But I can't do their job. But they can't read my mind. And people wonder why we drink.

Lucky snorts at me when I tell her these things: if it isn't a tech cue or a blocking note, it has nothing to do with the real play as far as she's concerned. She doesn't understand that for me the play is best before it is real, when it is still only mine.

'Nine sharp,' she says now. 'Time to start. Some of them have already been out there long enough to turn green.' She smiles; her private joke.

'Let's go,' I say, my part of the ritual; and then I have to do it, have to *let go*. I sit forward over the script in my usual eighth row seat; Lucky takes her clipboard and her favourite red pen, the one she's had since *Cloud Nine*, up the aisle. She pushes open the lobby door and the sound of voices rolls through, cuts off. All of them out there, wanting in. I feel in my gut their tense waiting silence as Lucky calls the first actor's name.

They're hard on everyone, auditions. Actors bare their throats. Directors make instinctive leaps of faith about what an actor could or might or must do in this or that role, with this or that partner. It's kaleidoscopic, religious, it's violent and subjective. It's like soldiers fighting each other just to see who gets to go to war. Everyone gets bloody, right from the start.

Forty minutes before a late lunch break, when my blood sugar is at its lowest point, Lucky comes back with the next résumé and headshot and the first raised eyebrow of the day. The eyebrow, the snort, the flared nostril, the slight nod, are Lucky's only comments on actors. They are minimal and emphatic.

Behind her walks John the Baptist. He calls himself Joe Something-or-other, but he's John straight out of my head. Dark red hair. The kind of body that muscles up long and compact, strong and lean. He moves well, confident but controlled. When he's on stage he even stands like a goddamn prophet. And his eyes are John's eyes: deep blue like deep sea. He wears baggy khaki trousers, a loose, untucked white shirt, high top sneakers, a Greek fisherman's cap. His voice is clear, a half-tone lighter than many people expect in a man: perfect.

The monologue is good, too. Lucky shifts in her seat next to me. We exchange a look, and I see that her pupils are wide.

'Is he worth dancing for, then?'

She squirms, all the answer I really need. I look at the résumé again. Joe Sand. He stands calmly on stage. Then he moves very slightly, a shifting of weight, a leaning in towards Lucky. While he does it, he looks right at her, watching her eyes for that uncontrollable pupil response. He smiles. Then he tries it with me. *Aha*, I think, *surprise, little actor*.

'Callbacks are Tuesday and Wednesday nights,' I say neutrally. 'We'll let you know.'

He steps off the stage. He is half in shadow when he asks, 'Do you have Salome yet?'

'No precasting,' Lucky says.

'I know someone you'd like,' he says, and even though I can't quite see him I know he is talking to me. Without the visual cue of his face, the voice has become trans-gendered, the body shape ambiguous.

'Any more at home like you, Joe?' *I must really need my lunch.*

'Whatever you need,' he says, and moves past me, past Lucky, up the aisle. Suddenly, I'm ravenously hungry. Four more actors between me and the break, and I know already that I won't remember any of them longer than it takes for Lucky to close the doors behind them.

The next day is better. By late afternoon I have seen quite a few good actors, men and women, and Lucky has started a callback list.

'How many left?' I ask, coming back from the bathroom, rubbing the back of my neck with one hand and my waist with the other. I need a good stretch, some sweaty muscle-heating exercise, a hot bath. I need Salome.

Lucky is frowning at a paper in her hand. 'Why is Joe Sand on this list?'

'God, Lucky, I want him for callbacks, that's why.'

'No, this sheet is today's auditions.'

I read over her shoulder. *Jo Sand.* 'Dunno. Let's go on to the next one, maybe we can actually get back on schedule.'

When I next hear Lucky's voice, after she has been up to the lobby to bring in the next actor, I know that something is terribly wrong.

'Mars . . . Mars . . .'

By this time I have stood and turned and I can see for myself what she is not able to tell me.

'Jo Sand,' I say.

'Hello again,' she says. The voice is the same; *she* is the same, and utterly different. She wears the white shirt tucked into the khaki pants this time, pulled softly across her breasts. Soft black shoes, like slippers, that make no noise when she moves. No cap today, that red hair thick, brilliant above the planes of her face. Her eyes are Salome's eyes: deep blue like deep desire. She is as I imagined her. When she leans slightly towards me, she watches my eyes and then smiles. Her smell goes straight up my nose and punches into some ancient place deep in my brain.

We stand like that for a long moment, the three of us. I don't know what to say. I don't have the right words for conversation with the surreal, except when it's inside my head. I don't know what to do when it walks down my aisle and shows me its teeth.

'I want you to see that I can be versatile,' Jo says.

The air in our small circle has become warm and sticky. My eyes feel slightly crossed, my mind is slipping gears. *I won't ask, I will not ask . . .* It's as if I were trying to bring her into focus through 3-D glasses; trying to make two separate images overlay. It makes me seasick. I wonder if Lucky is having the same trouble, and then I see that she has simply removed herself in some internal way. She doesn't see Jo look at me with those primary eyes.

But I see: and suddenly I feel wild, electric, that direct-brain connection that makes my nerves stand straight under my skin. *Be careful what you ask for, Mars.* 'I don't guess you really need to do another monologue,' I tell her. Lucky is still slack-jawed with shock.

Jo smiles again.

Someone else is talking with my voice. 'Lucky will schedule you for callbacks.' Beside me, Lucky jerks at the sound of her name. Jo turns to her. Her focus is complete. Her whole body says, *I am waiting.* I want her on stage. I want to see her like that, waiting for John's head on a platter.

'Mars, what . . .' Lucky swallows, tries again. She speaks without looking at the woman standing next to her. 'Do you want . . . oh, shit. What part are you reading this person for in callbacks, goddamnit, anyway.' I haven't seen her this confused since her mother's boyfriend made a pass at her years ago, one Thanksgiving, his hand hidden behind the turkey platter at the buffet. Confusion makes Lucky fragile and brings her close to tears.

Jo looks at me, still waiting. Yesterday I saw John the Baptist: I remember how he made Lucky's eyebrow quirk and I can imagine the rehearsals; how he might sit close to her, bring her coffee, volunteer to help her set props. She'd be a wreck in one week and useless in two. And today how easy it is to see Salome, who waits so well and moves with such purpose. I should send this Jo away, but I won't: I need a predator for Salome; I can't do a play about desire without someone who knows about the taste of blood.

'Wear a skirt,' I say to Jo. 'I'll need to see you dance.' Lucky closes her eyes.

Somehow we manage the rest of the auditions, make the first cut, organize the callback list. There are very few actors I want to see again. When we meet for callbacks, I bring them all in and sit them in a clump at the rear of the house, where I can see them when I want to and ignore them otherwise. But always I am conscious of Jo. I read her with the actors that I think will work best in other roles. She is flexible, adapting herself to their different styles, giving them what they need to make the scene work. She's responsive to direction. She listens well. I can't find anything wrong with her.

Then it is time for the dance. There are three women that I want to see, and I put them all on stage together. 'Salome's dance is the most important scene in the play. It's a crisis point for every character. Everyone has something essential invested in it. It has to carry a lot of weight.'

'What are you looking for?' one of the women asks. She has long dark hair and good arms.

'Power,' I answer, and beside her Jo's head comes up like a pointing dog's, her nostrils flared with some rich scent. I pretend not to see. 'Her dance is about power over feelings and lives. There's more, but power's the foundation, and that's what I need to see.'

The woman who asked nods her head and looks down, chewing the skin off her upper lip. I turn away to give them a moment for this new information to sink in; looking out into the house, I see the other actors sitting forward in their seats, and I know they are wondering who it will be, and whether they could work with her, and what they would do in her place.

I turn back. 'I want you all to dance together up here. Use the space any way you like. Take a minute to warm up and start whenever you're ready.'

I can see the moment that they realize, *ohmigod no music, how can we dance without, goddamn all directors anyway.* But I want to see their interpretation of power, not music. If they don't have it in them to dance silent in front of strangers, if they can't compete, if they can't pull all my attention and keep it, then they can't give me what I need. Salome wouldn't hesitate.

The dark-haired woman shrugs, stretches her arms out and down towards her toes. The third woman slowly begins to rock her hips; her arms rise swaying in the cliché of eastern emerald-in-the-navel bellydance. She moves as if embarrassed, and I don't blame her. The dark-haired woman stalls for another moment and then launches into a jerky jazz step with a strangely syncopated beat. I can almost hear her humming her favourite song under her breath; her head tilts up and to the right and she moves in her own world, to her own sound. That's not right, either. I realize that I'm hoping one of them will be what I need, so that I do not have to see Jo dance.

And where is Jo? There, at stage right, watching the other two women, comfortable in her stillness. Then she slides gradually into motion, steps slowly across the stage and stops three feet from the bellydancer, whose stumbling rhythm slows and then breaks as Jo stands, still, watching. Jo looks her straight in the eye, and just as the other woman begins to drop her gaze, Jo suddenly whirls, throwing herself around so quickly that for an instant it's as if her head is

facing the opposite direction from her body. It is a nauseating
moment, and it's followed by a total body shrug, a shaking off, that is
both contemptuous and intently erotic. Now she is facing the house,
facing the other actors, facing Lucky, facing me: now she shows us
what she can do. Her dance says *this is what I am, that you can never
be; see my body move as it will never move with yours.* She stoops
for an imaginary platter, and from the triumph in her step I begin to
see the bloody prize. The curve of her arm shows me the filmed eye
and the lolling tongue; the movement of her breast and belly
describe for me the wreckage of the neck, its trailing cords; her feet
draw pictures in the splashed gore as she swirls and turns and snaps
her arm out like a discus thrower, tossing the invisible trophy
straight at me. When I realize that I have raised a hand to catch it, I
know that I have to have her, no matter what she is. Have to have her
for the play. Have to have her.

When the actors are gone, Lucky and I go over the list. We do not
discuss Salome. Lucky has already set the other two women's
résumés aside.

Before we leave: 'God, she was amazing. She'll be great, Mars. I'm
really glad it turned out this way, you know, that she decided to drop
that crossdressing stuff.'

'Mmm.'

'It really gave me a start, seeing her that day. She was so
convincing as a man. I thought . . . well, nothing. It was stupid.'

'It wasn't stupid.'

'You didn't seem surprised – did you know that first time when
he . . . when she came in that she wasn't . . .? Why didn't you say?'

'If I'm looking at someone who can play John. I don't really care
how they pee or whether they shave under their chins. Gender's not
important.'

'It is if you think you might want to go to bed with it.'

'Mmm,' I say again. What I cannot tell Lucky is that all along I
have been in some kind of shock; like walking through swamp mud,
where the world is warm silkywet but you are afraid to look down for
fear of what might be swimming with you in the murk. I know that
this is not a game: Joe was a man when he came in and a woman
when she came back. I look at our cast list and I know that
something impossible and dangerous is trying to happen; but all I
really see is that suddenly my play – the one inside me – is possible.
She'll blow a hole through every seat in the house. She'll burst their
brains.

*

Three weeks into rehearsal, Lucky has unremembered enough to start sharing coffee and head-together conferences with Jo during breaks. The other actors accept Jo as someone they can't believe they never heard of before, a comrade in the art wars. We are such a happy group; we give great ensemble.

Lance, who plays Herod, regards Jo as some kind of wood sprite, brilliant and fey. He is myopic about her to the point that if she turned into an anaconda, he would stroke her head while she wrapped herself around him. Lance takes a lot of kidding about his name, especially from his boyfriends. During our early rehearsals, he discovered a very effective combination of obsession and revulsion in Herod: as if he would like to eat Salome alive and then throw her up again, a sort of sexual bulimia.

Susan plays Herodias; Salome's mother, Herod's second wife, his brother's widow. She makes complicated seem simple. She works well with Lance, giving him a strong partner who nevertheless dims in comparison to her flaming daughter, a constant reminder to Herod of the destruction that lurks just on the other side of a single *yes* to this stepdaughter/niece/demonchild who dances in his fantasies. Susan watches Jo so disinterestedly that it has taken me most of this time to see how she has imitated and matured the arrogance that Jo brings to the stage. She is a tall black woman, soft muscle where Jo is hard: nothing like Jo, but she has become Salome's mother.

And John the Baptist, whose real name is Frank and who is nothing like Joe: I'm not sure I could have cast him if he had come to the audition with red hair, but his is black this season, Irish black for the O'Neill repertory production that he just finished. Lucky says he has 'Jesus feet'. Frankie's a method actor, disappointed that he doesn't have any sense memory references for decapitation. 'I know it happens offstage,' he says earnestly, at least once a week. 'But it needs to be there right from the start, I want them to think about it every scene with her.' *Them* is always the audience. *Her* is always Jo. Offstage, he looks at *her* the way a child looks at a harvest moon.

Three weeks is long enough for us all to become comfortable with the process but not with the results: the discoveries the actors made in the first two weeks refuse to gel, refuse to reinvent themselves. It's a frustrating phase. We're all tense but trying not to show it, trying not to undermine anyone else's efforts. It's hard for the actors, who genuinely want to support each other, but don't really want to see someone else break through first. Too scary: no one wants to be left behind.

There's a pseudosexual energy between actors and directors: there's so much deliberate vulnerability, control, desire to please; so much of the stuff that sex is made of. Working with my actors is like handling bolts of cloth: they each have a texture, a tension. Lance is brocade and plush; Susan is smooth velvet, subtle to the touch; Frankie is spun wool, warm and indefinably tough. And Jo: Jo is raw silk and razorblades, so fine that you don't feel the cut.

So we're all tense; except for Jo. Oh, she talks, but she's not worried; she's *waiting* for something, and I am beginning to turn those audition days over in my memory, sucking the taste from the bones of those encounters and wondering what it was that danced with me in those early rounds, what I have invited in.

And a peculiar thing begins: as I grow more disturbed, Jo's work becomes better and better. In those moments when I suddenly see myself as the trainer with my head in the mouth of the beast, when I slip and show that my hand is sweaty on the leash – in those moments her work is so pungent, so ripe that Jo the world-shaker disappears, and the living Salome looks up from the cut-off tee-shirt, flexes her thigh muscles under the carelessly torn jeans. We have more and more of Salome every rehearsal.

On Friday nights I bring a cooler of Corona and a bag of limes for whoever wants to share them. This Friday everyone stays. We sit silent for the first cold green-gold swallows. Lance settles back into Herod's large throne. I straddle a folding chair and rest my arms along the back, bottle loose in one hand. Lucky and the other actors settle on the platforms that break the stage into playing areas.

It starts with the actors talking, as they always do, about work. Lance has played another Herod, years ago, in *Jesus Christ Superstar*, and he wants to tell us how different that was.

'I'd like to do *Superstar*,' Jo says. It sounds like an idle remark. She is leaning back with her elbows propped against the rise of a platform, her breasts pushing gently against the fabric of her shirt as she raises her bottle to her mouth. I look away because I do not want to watch her drink, don't want to see her throat work as the liquid goes down.

Lance considers a moment. 'I think you'd be great, sweetheart,' he says, 'But Salome to Mary Magdalene is a pretty big stretch. Whore to madonna. Wouldn't you at least like to play a semi-normal character in between, work up to it a little?'

Jo snorts. 'I'm not interested in Magdalene. I'll play Judas.'

Lance whoops, Frankie grins, and even the imperturbable Susan smiles. 'Well, why not?' Lance says. 'Why shouldn't she play Judas if she wants to?'

'Little question of gender,' Frankie says, and shrugs.

Susan sits up. 'Why shouldn't she have the part if she can do the work?'

Frankie gulps his beer and wipes his mouth. 'Why should any director hire a woman to play a man when they can get a real man to do it?'

'What do you think, Mars?' The voice is Jo's. It startles me. I have been enjoying the conversation so much that I have forgotten the danger in relaxing around Jo or anything that interests her. I look at her now, still sprawled back against the platform with an inch of golden beer in the bottle beside her. She has been enjoying herself, too. I'm not sure where this is going, what the safe answer is. I remember saying to Lucky, *Gender's not important.*

'Gender's not important, isn't that right, Mars?'

Lucky told her about it. But I know Lucky didn't. She didn't have to.

'That's right,' I say, and I know from Jo's smile that my voice is not as controlled as it should be. Even so, I'm not prepared for what happens next: a jumble of pictures in my head, images of dancing in a place so dark that I cannot tell if I am moving with men or women, images of streets filled with androgynous people and people whose gender-blurring surpasses androgyny and leaps into the realm of performance. Women dressed as men making love to men; men dressed as women hesitating in front of public bathroom doors; women in high heels and pearls with biceps so large that they split the expensive silk shirts. And the central image, the real point: Jo, naked, obviously female, slick with sweat, moving under me and over me, Jo making love to me until I gasp and then she begins to change, to change, until it is Joe with me, Joe on me – and I open my mouth to shout my absolute, instinctive refusal – and I remember Lucky saying *it is if you think you might want to sleep with it* – and the movie breaks in my head and I am back with the others. No one has noticed that I've been assaulted, turned inside out. They're still talking about it: 'Just imagine the difference in all the relationships if Judas were a woman,' Susan says earnestly to Frankie. 'It would change everything!' Jo smiles at me and swallows the last of her beer.

The next rehearsal I feel fragile, as if I must walk carefully to keep from breaking myself. I have to rest often.

I am running a scene with Frankie and Lance when I notice Lucky offstage, talking earnestly to Jo. Jo puts one hand up, interrupts her,

smiles, speaks, and they both turn to look at me. Lucky suddenly
blushes. She walks quickly away from Jo, swerves to avoid me. Jo's
smile is bigger. Her work in the next scene is particularly fine and
full.

'What did she say to you, Luck?' I ask her as we are closing the
house for the evening.

'Nothing,' Lucky mumbles.

'Come on . . .'

'Okay, fine. She wanted to know if you ever slept with your actors,
okay?'

I know somehow that it's not entirely true: I can hear Jo's voice
very clearly, saying to Lucky *So does Mars ever fuck the leading
lady?* while she smiles that catlick smile. Jo has the gift of putting
pictures into people's heads, and I believe Lucky got a mindful.
That's what really sickens me, the idea that Lucky now has an image
behind her eyes of what I'm like . . . no, of what Jo wants her to think
I'm like. God knows. I don't want to look at her.

'Did you get my message?' Jo says to me the next evening, when she
finally catches me alone in the wings during a break from rehearsal.
She has been watching me all night. Lucky won't talk to her.

'I'm not in the script.'

'Everybody's in the script.'

'Look, I don't get involved with actors. It's too complicated, it's
messy. I don't do it.'

'Make an exception.'

Lucky comes up behind Jo. Whatever the look is on my face, it gets
a scowl from her. 'Break's over,' she says succinctly, turning away
from us even before the words are completely out, halfway across the
stage before I think to try to keep her with me.

'Let's get back to work, Jo.'

'Make a fucking exception.'

I don't like being pushed by actors, and there's something else, too,
but I don't want to think about it now, I just want Jo off my back, so I
give her the director voice, the vocal whip. 'Save it for the stage,
princess. You want to impress me, get out there and do your fucking
job.'

She doesn't answer; her silence makes a cold, high-altitude circle
around us. When she moves, it's like a snake uncoiling, and then her
hand is around my wrist. She's *strong.* When I look down, I see that
her hand is changing: the bones thicken under the flesh, the muscles
rearrange themselves subtly, and it's Joe's hand on Jo's arm, Joe's

hand on mine. 'Don't make me angry, Mars,' and the voice is genderless and buzzes like a snake. There is no one here to help me, I can't see Lucky, I'm all alone with this hindbrain thing that wants to come out and play with me. Jo's smile is by now almost too big for her face. *Just another actor*, I think crazily, *they're all monsters anyway*.

'What are you?' I am shaking.

'Whatever you need, Mars. Whatever you need. Every director's dream. At the moment, I'm Salome, right down to the bone. I'm what you asked for.'

'I didn't ask for this. I don't want this.'

'You wanted Salome, and now you've got her. The power, the sex, the hunger, the need, the wanting, it's all here.'

'It's a play. It's just . . . it's a play, for chrissake.'

'It's real for you.' That hand is still locked around my wrist; the other hand, the soft small hand, reaches up to the centre of my chest where my heart tries to skitter away from her touch. 'I saw it, that first audition. I came to play John the Baptist, I saw the way Lucky looked at me, and I was going to give her something to remember . . . but your wanting was so strong, so complex. It's delicious, Mars. It tastes like spice and wine and sweat. The play in your head is more real to you than anything, isn't it, more real than your days of bright sun, your friends, your office transactions. I'm going to bring it right to you, into your world, into your life. I'll give you Salome. On stage, off stage, there doesn't have to be any difference. Isn't that what making love is, giving someone what they really want?'

She's still smiling that awful smile and I can't tell whether she is talking about love because she really means it or because she knows it makes my stomach turn over. Or maybe both.

'Get out of here. Out of here, right now.' I am shaking.

'You don't mean that, sweet. If you did, I'd already be gone.'

'I'll cancel the show.'

She doesn't answer: she looks at me and then, *phht*, I am seeing the stage from the audience perspective, watching Herod and Herodias quarrel and cry and struggle to protect their love, watching John's patient fear as Herod's resolve slips away: watching Salome dance. When she dances, she brings us all with her, the whole audience living inside her skin for those moments. We all whirl and reach and bend, we all promise, we all twist away. We all tempt. We all rage. We stuff ourselves down Herod's throat until he chokes on us. And then we are all suddenly back in our own bodies and we roar until our throats hurt and our voices rasp. All the things that I have felt about this play, she will make them feel. What I am will be in them. What I have inside me will bring them to their feet and leave them full and aching. Oh god, it makes me weep, and then I am back with her, she still holds me with that monster hand and all I can do is cry with wanting so badly what she can give me.

Her eyes are too wide, too round, too pleased. 'Oh,' she says, still gently, 'It's okay. You'll enjoy most of it, I promise.' And she's gone, sauntering onstage, calling out something to Lance, and her upstage hand is still too big, still *wrong*. She lets it caress her thigh once before she turns it back into the Jo hand. I've never seen anything more obscene. I have to take a minute to dry my eyes, cool my face. I feel a small, hollow place somewhere deep, as if Jo reached inside and found something she liked enough to take for herself. She's there now, just onstage, ready to dance, that small piece of me humming in her veins. How much more richness do I have within me? How long will it take to eat me, bit by bit? She raises her arms now and smiles, already tasting. Already well fed.

THE DISQUIETING MUSE

by

Kathe Koja

Kathe Koja is the author of *The Cipher*, *Bad Brains*, *Skin*, *Strange Angels*, and *Famished*; she was co-winner (with Melanie Tem) of the Horror Writers of America's Bram Stoker Award for *The Cipher* (best first novel) which also won the Locus poll in the same category. Author of many short stories, several of them have appeared in Best of the year anthologies. She lives with her husband, artist Rick Lieder, and her young son in a suburb of Detroit.

Most of the stories in this anthology are about losing control in some way. Sometimes this loss is liberating, other times merely terrifying, as the protagonist of 'The Disquieting Muse' discovers.

THE DISQUIETING MUSE

They sat in a circle around him, in the room as white as a block of
salt, as Lot's pale wife turned from defiance to thoughtful critique of
humours no less stringent than her own: and they listened; anyway
he thought they were listening, sometimes it was hard to tell.
Debbie, arms folded, head cocked like a clever pet; Mrs Wagner who
had trouble keeping her mouth closed; Mr Aronson who would not
stay still.

'We're going to work,' he said, using his doctor's voice, calm and
pleasant, was it pleasant? 'in red this time'. Red, the tricksy colour,
blood and guts and resonance all the way back to the womb, like
echoes, breadcrumbs left to mark the trail of an access forever now
denied. Rubbing at his nose, half-unconscious and then consciously
stopped; too much like a tic. Daily surrounded by movements
deliberate and not, he kept his own affect even, his motions minimal
and serene; a berg of calm in this endlessly juddering sea.

'Red today, to help us feel our emotions.' No one said anything.
'Does anyone need any additional materials, any paint? Mrs
Wagner? Debbie? Mr Aronson, are you going to join us today?'

'Fuck off.'

'You know, Mr Aronson,' Debbie's petulance, that false gentility
behind clown's eyes, the yellow curve of nail so long it was hard for
her to hold a brush, a piece of chalk, a pencil stub, 'you know I asked
you not to use that word. I mean I asked you not to use that—'

'You fuck off too, lardass.'

'Dr Coles,' immediately, lips around the word like food; not
enough art therapy in the world to help Debbie, not enough therapy
period. 'Doctor, I have *asked* him not to use that word because it's an
ugly word, Doctor, and we're here to create beauty, isn't that what
we're—'

'Oh for fuck's sake,' and Mr Aronson out of the chair, Mrs

Wagner's big mouth bending in that deep unnerving smile that
always made him think of animals, big wet animals down in the
mud, look at the slouch of those breasts, big breasts, her back must
be killing her. Something wet, not paint, across her dirty blouse, red
and gold windmills and Debbie was still going on about beauty,
beauty, and Mr Aronson grabbed his crotch and said, 'You make me
sick right here, you know it? You and your fucking beauty,' and
behind his own eyes, his careful noncommittal frown, he felt
nothing; not even annoyance; nothing at all.

'Dr Coles!'

Like voices from a painting; he had been an art major. Last night
Margaret had asked him about *Guernica*, did it feel like *Guernica*
every day, did it feel like Bacon or Bosch? No, trying for lightness, no,
it feels like a painting of a clown. Her smile against his neck,
reaching around to feel for his cock; her fingers were always so cold,
cold now and 'Black velvet,' she said, 'a black velvet clown.' The
head of his cock was red, a royal colour against the elegant bleach of
her hands, her red nails, red as the paint they were using today and
now Mr Aronson had consented to sit, Debbie was still talking but
Mr Aronson had consented to sit and Mrs Wagner was smiling now
down at the colours, red on the floor and between her knees and red
on the backs of her hands.

It took him a minute to realize it was not paint.

Sometimes, it was *Guernica*, after all.

He went for a drink, wanting to call Margaret, not wanting to stay in
his office long enough to make the call; more than usually tired, of
course it had been an ugly day. He had three drinks almost before he
noticed, three small squat glasses of Scotch; he did not like Scotch,
hard liquor, secretly preferring fruity drinks, rum and pink froth, but
he felt like an asshole ordering them here, anywhere, wanting
Margaret to order one first so he could say I'll try that too, what is it?
Knowing what it was. Margaret knew he knew, too, but didn't care,
or said she didn't; Margaret said he should drink what he wanted.

He was rubbing his nose again, made himself stop again and then,
suddenly angry, rubbed hard, faint oil beneath his fingers and he
could rub his own fucking nose, couldn't he? Tics; *shit*. You make
me sick right here. He left the fourth glass untouched; a headache
and he went home, the message light on and Margaret's voice, sweet,
light as pink froth saying I can't come tonight, there's a meeting,
marketing and so on and on, he closed his eyes halfway through. Her
voice; her white fingers on his cock. His erection was flabby and

small, tired. It had taken over an hour to clean the room after what Mrs Wagner had done. At least she was out of the group now, back to the wards, sixty days minimum like a reward; maybe it was. It was for him, anyway.

Among his colleagues he was unique; and always uncomfortable, did they know, could they smell it on him? Art therapist, but forever more art than therapy; he had never had grand plans, saving the world, saving the sick from themselves, Art's white knight with the key to free expression in his warm collegiate hand. He had been an art major first, but so unconnected, so thoroughly lost amid the rush and thickets of images caught and captured — too large for him, he knew it the way the ant fears the spider and his advisor had recommended a change in venue.

But I love art, he had said. You can love it there too, the advisor said, you can help other people love it; and then there was a link, a proven bridge between creativity and, say it, madness. Craziness. The crazies always get there first, his instructor used to say; listen to them. Jeremy, listen: her gaze on his, big Teutonic blonde with a handshake that could crush rocks. You've got to learn to listen.

His own aptitude had surprised him; his first client had been an even bigger surprise, noisy and stinky, he would never forget her smell if he lived to be a hundred. Piss smell, people said, Margaret said when he told her the story. They don't wash, they pee themselves. But it wasn't that, he couldn't explain, it was something cellular, something to do with the way her eyes had rolled in her head, rolled like a horse's eyes, the way her fingers closed around the stem of the brush as if she held the tube of his windpipe in that moist considering grasp, he could hardly breathe, he could hardly wait until it was over.

But she made *progress*, that woman, her psychologist had told him so. Cornering him outside the therapy room, glorified holding tank but 'It's really incredible,' smiling, 'she's finally coming along. You really opened her up,' and he, small Judas smile of incomprehension both utter and dire; the curse of luck: oh God I am good at this, oh God. A roomful of newsprint paintings in wet blues and stinky blacks, she talks, it's terrific; oh God.

Two years past and he was still helping them, luck's blind hand in his own, unsure how someone like Mr Aronson, say, or fucked-up Mrs Wagner could take anything from what he gave, or rather lay out for the taking: there was, he thought, no active sense of giving, he put the tools before them, they had to want to be helped. To change. To use art itself as a catalyst for self-expression and through self-expression find the freedom to free themselves; he told all this to Margaret and she laughed, head on his chest and she laughed, her fingers curled loose about his own.

'You sound like a course description,' she said, 'a brochure,' but she was smiling, holding his hand and smiling and he smiled back at her. What did she know, she wasn't there, she had no idea. Clean Margaret with her hands cold as a clinician, cold as the hands of the clock. He had not told her, finally, of Mrs Wagner, fresh new sense of failure, of luck denied; but now, two days later and Long John was grabbing him in the hall, like a principal collaring a tardy student: 'Nice fucking work, Jer. Nice fucking piece of work.'

Staring up at him but not straight on, six feet four and yardstick arms even longer in that white coat, dirty collar, it smelled faintly of sweat. And gravy, cafeteria gravy. Is he happy? Is he angry? Nice piece of work, Jer. 'I don't—'

'Mrs Wagner, you know, Mrs Out-to-Lunch? Cut herself up in your playroom, *you* know. Anyway today's my day with her and out it comes, big problems, she hates her husband, she hates her kids. Hates everybody, me, you, herself for putting up with it. Mad, and screaming like hell. She's ready to talk, now.'

'That's—I didn't know, that's really—'

'Maybe I ought to invest in some crayons, huh. Lucky you,' and gone, still smiling and he left behind to adjust for himself a smile, he had done it again; how? Mrs Out-to-Lunch; blood on her hands and his hands in his pockets, white coat clean as a piece of new paper, as an unmade wish and in the end what difference did it make, she was Long John's problem now and they would be sending him a new one, another one to take her place. Maybe today, maybe next session; what difference did it make?

That evening Debbie cried, and Mr Aronson called her a lardass and drew a picture of a big black bird pecking out her eyes before relenting enough to admire her drawing, of a box of chocolates and a sweetheart bow, she was really a terrific draughtsman, Debbie; the bow looked completely real, down to the dust in its creases; it was an old box of chocolates, she said. He himself sketched loops and circles, long lines, geometries in spiral like fractals split down their bloodless middles and left to dry in logic's light, and Mr Aronson squinted over his shoulder and said, 'Hey Debbie, look at this—he can't draw.'

That evening Margaret came to him, soft smile and a half-drunk bottle of margarita mix; her panties were as pink and shiny as her vulva, but it took him almost half an hour to come. She said, still smiling, that it didn't matter; she did not stay the night.

Her name was Ruth, and she smelled like all the others only more so; like milk and cloudy water, like some fish caught dying in a frozen lake. Albino eyes and a file made heavy with page after page of recommendations, half-sure diagnoses like a map of a land unseen. At the bottom someone had written SCHIZOAFFECTIVE? in heavy red ink; it was crossed out in black, the pen strokes light and thin as hairs.

She would not sit by Mr Aronson; Debbie went not ignored so much as unnoticed, it was as if she did not actually see Debbie at all. Bare white arms crossed across the hospital gown; the chart said she refused to wear street clothes, underclothes. Her hair was incredibly dirty, a thin and gummy blonde. When he tried to speak to her she ignored him too, so he turned instead to the others, told them they would be working in pencil again today, told them to express what they felt to be their worst conflict this week, whether with the staff, or other clients, or themselves.

'How about you?' Mr Aronson said. 'What if it's with you?'

'Then express it,' half-listening; he was watching her, was she going to ignore this too? But no, she had pencil in hand, bent so close to the paper her dirty hair brushed it, was she nearsighted? Perhaps she had broken or lost her glasses, perhaps they had been stolen, it happened all the time. Short definite strokes, the pencil wearing down; sharpened but not sharp, he had learned not to make them too sharp. Mr Aronson was complaining about the light so he turned on all the overheads, grainy fluorescence, it made her look more pasty-green than ever. At the end of the hour Debbie and Mr Aronson had expressed their conflicts with the staff, both over the issue of smoking in the dayroom; Ruth was still working, but set the pencil aside as he approached.

'Ruth?' pleasantly, he always tried to be pleasant. God did she smell. Leaning over her shoulder, careful not to touch, to see centred on the page before her a correct and detailed drawing of a large flayed penis, spread like a flower, delicately pinned.

'It's a horse cock,' she said. 'I hope you like it.'

That night he read through her file again, sure and slow like a man wading through a swamp. No firm diagnosis, neuroleptics had been tried without result. No auditory hallucinations, although a psychologist at Busey had speculated she might be hebephrenic; she had been hospitalized here for three months, had done poorly since admittance, at least they could all agree on that. One of the attendants had found her drawing with lit cigarettes on the grey linoleum of the dayroom floor, and so they had sent her to him.

Debbie did not like her, nor Mr Aronson; they both seemed, if not afraid, then studiously wary, careful to keep their distance. They sat almost together, chairs an inch from touching, as Ruth in grimy isolation dipped her brush like a sixth finger, one heavy spot of blue acrylic shiny as a bruise on her white knee. Through the soiled drift of her gown he could see, if he looked, the firm shapes of her breasts, conical breasts bigger, say, than was proportionate, bigger than Margaret's.

If he looked.

He knew he wanted to look, he wanted to *see*: past the dirty hair and smelly skin, track where the attraction lay: for there was attraction, he was honest enough, bewildered enough to admit it.

Why?

Her silence was peculiar, not the leaden quiet of depression nor the blank affect of incipient catatonia; it was not anhedonia, for she was capable of pleasure: she enjoyed her food, according to the file. Did she enjoy her art therapy? Who knew? She did not yell like Mr Aronson, or bitch like Debbie; she rarely volunteered remarks. Once or twice he thought he had caught her looking at him, a gaze studied and cold as a reptile's; but nothing she did seemed to indicate that she gave him more notice than the chair she sat on, the easel she used to paint.

She had been with him nearly a month now, once a week her drawings, paintings and always one a session, never less or more; after the horse penis (and what fun he had had logging that in his notes) came a headless female torso covered in slit-pupilled eyes, its hands fisted and firm on the lapping head of the male figure between its legs; a pair of three-armed women locked in some strange hybrid of combat and sex; a blindfolded prepubescent girl about to penetrate herself with what looked like a broken baseball bat; she had titled that one, called it THE DREAM OF REASON. Did she dream? She would not say, would not answer when, to draw her out, he talked of his own dreams, lightly, lying; in reality they were simple sex-dreams, fantasies made figment in the empty sweaty dark, but lately in waking it was as if her drawings, or their shadows, lay caul-like across the innards of his eyes; he had to sit up in bed, turn on the light like a child in a nightmare, ignoring his erection the way you ignore the unpleasant, a street person on the corner, a dead animal splashed on your turning wheels.

He had made photocopies of the drawings for his files; alone in the bedlamp light he now took them out, feeling absurdly like a boy with a girlie magazine; remembering, like a book read, his first time masturbating to *Penthouse*, he had come all over the magazine, his brother's magazine and his brother had teased him, but kindly, he was in the fraternity now. Drawings in his hand, wondering again how to reconcile that vast technique with the impenetrable fact of her silent physical self, the sloppy swing of her breasts beneath the gown; how to interpret the power of those images, their brute sexuality; their affect on him.

But it was natural, wasn't it, to be affected, they would affect any man, they were so detailed, so frankly sexual and she . . .

Was so very sick.

So very sick and helpless.

He slept with the drawings spread across him like limbs; and woke to dreams of nothing that morning could recall.

Today it was acrylics again, Mr Aronson vocal about his dislike for painting, Debbie listless with blues and purples and off in her corner Ruth, hands in constant motion, her blank face still. He found within himself a kind of new impatience, a wish for the others somehow to be still, to be gone; it was Ruth he wanted to study, Ruth he wanted to see. Standing silent beside her in the surrounding atmosphere of her smell, it was like standing next to a statue for all the interest she displayed, bending close now to see better and suddenly she turned, turned on him in complete distilled awareness and he stepping back in almost comical alarm brushed with the back of one moving hand the side of her breast, half-visible, big and white beneath the gown.

He said nothing, did not apologize, at once beside Debbie and her sloppy cornflowers and he was hard, shamefully hard, he could not look at Ruth again. Discussing at length Mr Aronson's work, Debbie's, the session was nearly over when he went at last and slowly to her side.

The paper was full, dire blue background bisected by a pair of byzantine highways, intricate and red, both dead-ending in a grim little house with broken windows; beneath, in her stylized printing, she had lettered MARGARET'S FALLOPIAN TUBES. He felt her watch him read the words, her gaze all arctic composure, her slippered feet crossed lightly at the ankles like a duchess at a drawing-room tea; when he asked her (still hard; oh God that smell) some standard questions she ignored him as thoroughly as before.

He omitted the name's coincidence in his notes, in his conscious thoughts, but making love to Margaret in the night's dry-furnace air the image found him, red roads like snakes, like wires, like vast veins feeding and writhing and between the veins the image of Ruth unbidden, pulling up her dirty gown to show him, *oh show me* and 'What are you doing,' her sweet voice blurry, now, raising up on her elbows, 'Jeremy, what are you doing?' and looking down between them saw like a peepshow stranger the tilted gush of his orgasm on her belly and her thighs.

'I don't know,' and then in a rush, as if in waking, 'Oh God I'm sorry, Margaret, I'm sorry,' but she was sliding out from under him, she was wiping herself with his shirt, expensive green linen but he said nothing, she was angry, she had a right to be. She stayed the night but slept cocooned, her back to him as smooth and martial as a blade exposed. In the morning she smiled, but evaded his kisses; I'll call you, she said. Not tomorrow, but soon.

He had a day off coming; he took it, spent it like a sentence served at home with her file. Page after page, it was as if he could smell her there, her dirty skin, her drawings between them like challenge and tease. He was not helping her; she would not speak, perform simple tasks of hygiene; in her psychotherapy she was if not actually regressing then certainly making no progress at all. Perhaps he should ask for a change, to have her transferred out. But if he did they would want to know why, they would ask for an explanation and instantly, absurdly, the defence, a guilty anger: I haven't even *done* anything, I haven't even touched—

Oh yes you have.

—and angrier still, shoving the file away; he was doing the best he could, all that he could. He would give it another month, and if he had had no luck by then he would ask for a change; he would tell them it was in her best interests, it was best for both of them, it was the best that he could do.

The white room abysmally cold, and emptier by one: Mr Aronson had pneumonia again, his smoker's lungs invaded, exacerbated by the daily failures of the heat. In Mr Aronson's absence Debbie was tearful and hard to handle, she kept accusing him of complicity with her mother, of taking phone calls from her mother behind her back. In her drawings she caricatured him as the devil, fat strokes, big goatish hooves; still weeping she left early fleeing to rec therapy, leaving him alone with Ruth.

Who did not seem to notice the cold, still in her gown, same gown, same steady hand on the pencil. His promises, his firm inner precepts now seemed less stringent, less worthy of resolve in this moment of watching her, greasy hair and the sway of her breasts as her arms moved, he was watching her, doing nothing but watching her: busy hands now choosing among the pencils, new pencils, and he seeing as if in a light removed the fact of her absolute availability, yes call it helplessness, call it sickness, spread and gleaming and her hands now on the thick stems of the pencils, black graphite shine down the planes of her thighs: 'I'm drawing my veins,' she said, quiet in the quiet around her, turned to face him and he saw spit on her lips. 'I'm drawing how it *goes*,' and as loose and careless used her hands to pull aside entirely the gown, show herself, spread herself with the pencils in a grotesquerie acrobatic, it reminded him of the laboratory, pins, an anatomical drawing and he was so hard it hurt, ached like skin pulled to bursting and she saw or seemed to see because she smiled, smiled straight into his eyes as she slipped one pencil deep inside her; and pulled it out to sign her name across the bottom of her paper.

And left; and he behind, moving to pick up the pencil by its dry eraser tip and hold it, close to his nose and breathe; his hands were shaking, he felt as if he was going to come, to be sick, both. Closing his eyes to open them to the drawing, lines and shading and this time she had drawn herself, head back and naked, raised legs like a whore's and past her spreading fingers the fact of eyes, staring out from her darkness, staring at him.

Drawing and pencil wrapped in two quick motions, stuffing them both in his case and he was pulling on his gloves, his hands were shaking and shaking as he drove, home and the house warm around him as he took the drawing to the bathroom and masturbated, crying out as he came, no name, no sound, nothing more human than the whuff of air back in lungs tight as Mr Aronson's, strangled tight and over his breathing he heard Margaret's voice on the machine, cool and sweet and distant as a face in a magazine.

He took another day off, a personal day; he was sick, he said, lying, maybe he had caught Aronson's bug. Dry cough like a phony adulterer, hanging up to stretch back down, shirt and tie, he had tried to get up, to go; but could not go. Not today. You're the doctor, aren't you? Aren't you? Shaking his head in the blind-drawn light, no; no to what? He was trying his best, wasn't he; or was he, subtly, in ways he did not recognize, encouraging those drawings, that illness, using strategies that on the surface were both rational and defensible but when viewed another way, turned right-side up, were nothing but yet another narrowing and easing of the way, the way *in*, the one path and the hunger thoughtless as a rock, a cock, his own hard cock like a breathing animal; using his power to help instead to damage and damage ineffably, brutally, fierce infection of desire meeting head-on the infection of her illness; and she was very ill, there was no question of that, no question at all.

Confusion like a migraine, his hands damp on his temples; he had seen patients sit this way and in that thought stopped at once; stop it. It all had to stop. He had to make a change; he must admit he could not help her. Notes on the back of other notes, structuring a memo, discontinue art therapy. Why? Because I want to fuck her, that's why, because fucking her is not in her best interests. The memo written he felt somehow easier, he would hand it in tomorrow, he would be grave and composed. She could switch over to rec therapy – bouncing in her gown, that cold empty face and legs spread in calisthenics, oh God let it not be his problem, I never wanted to do this and he was talking out loud, talking to the drawing of Ruth, the eyes that seemed to see him even more clearly here, in his home, in his room, see and know more clearly than he the wet clarity of his wants: the dirty, the bad, the wrong and infinitely wrongful, the stink of the toilet in his nose and every time he saw her it was as if he committed anew some warm atrocity, her slack passivity a goad and her hand between her legs, the clenched drawing like kissing dry lips and his belt undone and jingling absurd as spurs, he was going to come, here and now and in frantic haste he pushed the drawing against his body, her pencilled legs open, gluey and sticky and the angle was wrong, all wrong and oh God it was already over, down his legs the river translucent as a stream of cloudy tears, heat turned cold in an instant and he was breathing like a horse, like a beaten animal—

and she was there

—there in the room, wearing her gown, smiling beneath those cold white eyes. Tangled hair and gritty feet, her slippers a colour like dirt against the muted blue plush of the carpeting, her edges hyper-real and clear as a drawing; he could even smell her, that milky musky stink like an animal in oestrus. It was like the hallucinations his patients reported: so real they couldn't be real.

'I'm your charm,' she said, her grin in his face, hands beneath her breasts in proffering pose, black parody of a stripper, of a dancer in a bar. 'I'm your *luck*. You didn't think you could do all this without luck, did you? You didn't think that, did you?'

He was breathing so hard his chest hurt, his lungs beneath the bone as strictured as ligaments, as muscles torn and he could not stop, breathing as loud as some misfunctioning machine. His cock had shrunk to a limp purplish smallness, as if it too were a muscle now deprived of strength; the semen was cold. His arms against the bedclothes trembled, as if he were really ill.

'Because there's nothing warm in you,' her voice so calm, pleasant as his own when he addressed a crying Debbie, a raving Mr Aronson, bleeding Mrs Wagner and all of them, all of them, her hands like spiders at her sides. 'Nothing warm at all but the place for luck, and that's *me*,' really pleased now, really smiling. 'That's me.'

Closer, her hair a special grey with grease collected and it was past imagining but he was getting an erection, she was close enough to touch and 'I'm your charm', she said again, 'your lucky star,' and with one contemptuous hand reached to squeeze his cock, her hand as big as his own, squeeze it to the cusp of pain and he said her name, Ruth, said it once and twice, Ruth, head down and eyes as empty as any patient's, RUTH and she squeezed him harder, RUTH and she squeezed him again.

Margaret left four unanswered messages on his machine before she stopped calling entirely.

HOLES

by

Sarah Clemens

Sarah Clemens lives in Florida where she works as a legal medical illustrator and writes movie reviews. Her first story was published in 1988 in *Ripper!* edited by Susan Casper and Gardner Dozois. This is her second.

Body modification is currently *the* hot trend in the United States. Individuals have myriad reasons for getting themselves tattooed, pierced or scarred. In 'Holes', the protagonist goes through a process of liberation.

HOLES

When she sat down to get her nipples pierced, she felt a jumble of emotions. In a few minutes jewellery would be nestled in her body. It was a beginning, an action of her own choosing, and more than anything it made her chaotically happy.

'Just sit back, Beth, relax.' Bridget the piercing artist was in her forties, professional, sympathetic.

Relax? Most people would fear the pain, seeing it as something to get past. Not Beth. She sat back in the old dentist's chair, trying to calm the coursing of her blood. She was in a small cramped room containing a table with an autoclave, other sterilizing equipment and a box of disposable surgical gloves. The mirrors had swatches of memorabilia taped around the edges, old photographs of satisfied customers baring pierced and tattooed body parts. She heard the murmur of gossipy voices in the showroom outside where she had bought the two bead rings. Everyone here was pierced somewhere and she was amid kindred spirits she hadn't even known an hour ago. Now, warmed by Bridget's lamp, she settled in and waited while Marty's face loomed over the piercer's shoulder. He had the knowing look of someone who had been through it, but she couldn't explain to him that pain could be as real or distant as she chose.

Bridget swabbed Beth's breasts with Betadine and squeezed one of her nipples with a surgically gloved hand. It shrank back and hardened and Bridget made dots with sterilized ink, carefully, on either side.

Marty smiled a lazy smile. She had discovered a lot about him in the one night they had been together – that he knew, for example, when to get involved and when to let her do things for herself. He was the only man she had been with since Gary.

Pennington forceps were squeezing and pulling her nipple. It hurt. But as much as what? As much as rose thorns pricking her arm? As much as Marty twisting her between his fingers during rough foreplay? She loosed her grip on the spidered network of nerves, swam slowly away inside herself and watched Bridget push the needle into one side of her nipple. The pain, red and full, shot through her body, contained in its hull. She watched serenely, for only the skin, not she, could feel the needle lancing its way through. Suddenly her face flushed as if a hot wind had blown straight through her. The sensation was over in as much time as it took for the needle to emerge from the other side. Bridget inserted the ring into the end of the needle, pulled it through and clamped it shut. All done. Beth was left with only a warm watery pain as she lay back lightheaded, her skin clammy. A tear of blood oozed from the ring. Bridget padded it up and smiled.

'Let me know when you're ready for the second one. By the way, I really like your tattoo. Where's it from?'

Oh, yes, the tattoo on her shoulder blade. Just far enough down to be out of her sight, but never out of her thoughts. 'It's Micronesian,' she said perfunctorily, and the subject dropped.

The second piercing made her gasp involuntarily. She could actually feel her veins and arteries vibrating, plucked from within like a tight, wet harp. In that dark chasm where she separated herself from pain, she was not alone. There was a voice, keening. Her vision grew dark and sparkled and as she struggled to clear her head, she realized the voice had stopped as soon as the pain had, as if only able to harmonize with the highest intensity of her body's sensations. Cautiously, she moved back to the outward reaches of her skin. Felt both rings in place.

Bridget was collecting her implements and Marty moved in. Tanned and sun-beaten, wispy blond hair just a little too long, eyes very pale and blue. Spawn of Georgia crackers.

'Congratulations,' he smiled.

'I'm tired,' she said and surrendered herself to Marty's care. When they got back to their hotel room there was a message from Gary. He had called all the way from Kyoto to see how the convention was going. Why did he yank at emotional cords she had severed? More now than ever, it was over and with each piercing he would fade further from her consciousness. She lifted one nipple ring and brought it back down gently. The pain was dull, not worth masking.

Marty sent down for food and they ate with no clothes on.

'Who's Gary?' he asked.

'A former boyfriend who hasn't gotten the message yet,' she said, unable to take her eyes off his extraordinary body.

They had been talking shop the first evening of the rosegrowers' convention. Comparing notes on how roses fared in different climates. Which root stock they preferred. Effortlessly, their words spiralled off into the realm of the personal.

'I need to change the subject,' said Marty gently. 'I have to tell you something.'

His eyes were direct and clear and she knew he wasn't being coy or conceited.

'You're married?' she said idiotically.

'Not even close.' He laughed quickly. 'I, uh, collect body jewellery.'

She stared uncomprehendingly.

'My nipples and genitals are pierced.' He mistook the look on her face. 'I'm sorry if it bothers you . . .'

'Show me!'

They took the world's slowest elevator to his room, turned on one soft lamp and he began by pulling off his tie and shirt. Each of his nipples was pierced twice, a small steel ring nestled inside a larger one. She touched a nipple, curved her finger inside the rings.

'You can pull on them. It doesn't hurt.'

She tugged gently, stretching the nipple away from his chest. A primal feeling was stirring, beyond the warmth and tightening of her clitoris.

'Want to see the rest?' he asked her.

'Oh, God, do I.'

He stood and unzipped, stepped out of his pants and underwear. His penis fell lazily from confinement, already semi-erect. Beth drank in the sight of all that steel jewellery nestled in his most sensitive flesh.

'What do you call this?' she said in a small voice.

It was a barbell, running horizontally through the head of his cock.

'An ampallang.' He sank onto the bed next to her. 'Popular in areas around the Indian Ocean. This loop running under the head is a frenum, it's pierced through the glans. . .'

His penis pulsed towards erection, twitching as she touched him and ran her fingers over the rings and studs. The rings in either side of the scrotum were hafadas, Arabic in origin. The guiche was a ring back under the scrotum, very sensitive. She trailed her hand over the ridges in his shaft, front and back, where bars were lodged under the skin, the studs at either end shining. She squeezed him, felt the jewellery move with the soft skin, riding over the hardness. She heard his quick intake of breath, and it brought her around.

'I'm sorry,' she said.

'Sorry?'

'I'm being selfish and playing with you.'

'It's okay. Does it turn you on?'

How could she even begin to tell him what it did for her? Her desire to pierce her own body was overwhelming. Marty kissed her, focusing her needs on more immediate cravings. Their lovemaking was intense. The sensation of the studs easing in and out of her was like nothing she had ever imagined; a little pain with the hardness of the jewellery, bridging to amazing pleasure. They made love all night, ate breakfast the next morning, she couldn't remember what. She wanted to start with piercing her breasts. There was nothing to attend that day at the convention, so they set out for a place he knew.

And now Marty sat facing her and her new piercings, wanting to know who Gary was.

'I had a very bad relationship with him,' she told Marty. 'I don't want to talk about it now.'

He smiled his lazy, knowing smile. There was a lot he hadn't asked her, and she was grateful. She wanted to tell him she could separate herself from the pain, but she was afraid to.

'When you had your piercings, did you feel that sort of screaming inside you?' she asked, smiling an initiate's smile.

'Screaming like how?'

'I don't know exactly. It was pretty fast . . . in the same way the pain is really sharp for a second, then it's gone.'

'You've got me on that one. Usually it just hurt like hell, then settled down to something more manageable.' He flicked his penis idly.

'Can I ask you . . . what made you get all your piercings?'

'People always ask me. If they don't just run the other way.' He paused a moment 'It's a matter of uniqueness. We all experience the same movies and television, read the same books . . . an individual experience is hard to come by. So I get a couple of piercings a year. There's nothing as unique as pain.'

'But you don't like the pain.'

'No,' he admitted. 'But I like the fact that I went through it. And no one else, no matter how many piercings they have, has a body just like mine.'

If only the horticulturists at the convention knew. The next day was like an inside joke for Beth, who went to grafting seminars with her nipple rings gently taped so they couldn't jostle. She sat with southern lady gardeners who had known her mother, women who talked about their grandchildren and the latest bestsellers over lunch. She spent time with representatives from other nurseries, touting her own's latest national winner, 'Summer Love', a bland hybrid tea rose with no scent. She resented the task. She was a rose breeder, not a saleswoman. But as long as she was attending, the front office suggested, mentioning 'Summer Love' to the right people wouldn't be too much trouble, would it? Beth would think, in the middle of it all, *I've got nipple rings*, and it seemed incredibly funny. When she thought about Marty's steel shafts and rings riding with his genitals as he did such simple things as walking and sitting, she would shudder with excitement. Occasionally their eyes would meet and he would give her a knowing grin.

'Come to Florida,' he said to her that night. 'I could always use one of the best rose breeders in the country at my nursery.'

'This is too soon,' she said lamely. 'And it's not that easy.'

'North Carolina has a nicer climate than Florida,' he admitted. 'But if you ever yearn for intolerable heat and humidity, let me know. Besides, there's an excellent piercer in my area.'

They kissed, and her breasts pressed against him, hurting a little, feeding her hunger. They came together quickly, moving in breathless rhythm, but she realized after the first flush of pleasure that the jewellery in his penis was clawing at her, scoring dark red furrows and crashing up against her with a terrible echoing noise. She was being raped by someone – not Marty – who was tattooed all over, and his thick body was rancid with lust. Like a wound, lips inside of her screamed, though her mouth only shaped the sound. And pain, if only there were pain, it would have been better, more real—

Marty rolled away from her, crying out. He looked terrified.

'What happened?' he gasped.

The tattoo on her shoulder tingled and she wondered what it meant. They huddled on the same bed until they could face each other.

'There's probably some blood on your chest. I'm bleeding a little.' She gently cupped her breasts, as if to shield them.

'What did you feel?' he asked her.

'It was like an hallucination,' she said lifelessly. 'The jewellery in your penis was clawing at me. And somewhere inside of me was something screaming.' The rest of what she remembered she couldn't bear to say.

'I felt – well, I didn't feel pain, but you seemed empty, like something had eaten you from inside.' Marty looked down at his penis, which had shrunk back from its erection. He held her and smiled at her, but there was fear around his eyes. Was he telling her everything he had seen? They slept scarcely touching.

The next day she went back to North Carolina. She would have to call Gary. The horrific images, the feeling that something was dwelling inside her, she was sure now that somehow the tattoo was doing it.

Marty crowded her thoughts. How he looked at her, made her feel special, wanted. The feel of his body and his directness about his piercings. Her pulse quickened whenever she thought about him, intoxicating her so that the air itself seemed richer, each breath more delirious. She pressed her hands to her breasts when she was alone, feeling the hardness of the nipple rings, tempting pain by pushing harder. He was her gateway to everything Gary told her she didn't deserve.

She threw herself into her work, tending her new seedlings. Rose hybridizers work on a yearly schedule, fertilizing the anthers of one rose with the pollen of another, then waiting for the hips to swell with seeds. Only a few out of hundreds or thousands might show the promise of becoming a marketable hybrid. In all, ten years might pass before a new rose becomes commercial viable. The isolation of such a quest gave Beth time to think.

Unbidden, came a memory of her mother – lovely, southern, Victorian. The day, when she was about ten years old, that her mother had found her calmly putting a sewing needle through the web of skin between her thumb and forefinger. The look on her mother's face, the torrent of words so out of place in that beautiful and controlled presence.

'Beth! Don't ever do that again! Not ever!' It was the way Mother had yelled at her, losing control. Not even when her father died had she seen her Mother like this. As a little girl she had cringed in horror and the memory of that moment, haunted her for years. She inherited little from her mother, besides the house, which had been in her mother's family for generations, a grand antebellum mansion full of china and flowered wallpaper and antique furniture, all Victorian, all heavy Cuban mahogany. Beth could stand in the front hall and hear the murmur of southern voices, lonely for company in a house built to embrace as many people as it could hold. There was only Beth now, alone with all the grandeur. Her mother had held court here, entertaining in her perfect home while Beth hugged the banister overhead, listening to the music and the laughter of people who treated her with perfunctory courtesy. Beth had none of her mother's overwhelming beauty and composure. No one ever told her this, it was simply the message her mother delivered to her every day. All they shared were the roses. Her mother taught her how to tend them and the passion was passed on.

In a special plot forbidden to the estate gardeners Beth kept antique roses, mostly dating back to the nineteenth century. They were the greatest of all, the Old Garden Roses like Souvenir de la Malmaison and Tuscany and Fantin-Latour. They bristled with thorns. They only bloomed once a year and the flowers fell apart after one day in a vase. But when their time came, they burst forth in many-hued effulgence, heavily petalled with fragrances so intoxicating they were nothing short of decadent. The Austin roses were not like them, nor the Hybrid Teas nor the Floribundas. She kept them as a reminder of how much roses had changed. So many now were scentless, identical in shape. Since meeting Marty she had found special meaning in a hybrid called Bed of Nails, which she had bred from some of the strangest roses in her private garden. It had started as a joke in college, a reaction against the stifling uniformity of the modern rose, and perhaps against her mother as well, who considered only modern roses acceptable. Beth had bred Bed of Nails to sport the most vicious thorns in existence. She crossed *Rosa rugosa* with *Rosa sericea*, both cultivars of ancient and thorny lineage, and the final result after years of refining was a bush festooned with wicked spikes alternating with red hooked thorns nearly an inch long. It was almost painful to look at, but she was proud of her monster. She lavished as much attention on it as she did her blue-blood antiques and it rambled happily along the back fence, repelling all intruders and once a year making pale little bunches of sweet-smelling flowers, almost as an afterthought. It struck her that not many things, certainly not her work with hybrids, brought her the satisfaction she had gotten out of breeding Bed of Nails. As she carefully trimmed its canes, Beth thought of pain and how strong she had felt during the piercing. Empowered.

She held a bristling, spiked cane from her rose and removed one gardening glove. Her mother had been wrong. This was not bad, this was an extraordinary gift, to be able to curve her bare hand around the cane and watch the thorns penetrate the skin of her palm. Elated, she opened her hand and saw that no blood was coming from the punctures. In all the tests Gary had performed on her, this had never happened.

Suddenly, unbidden, came the wailing, writhing sensation from within, and she hurled the cane away, the pain and the blood welling out at the same time. A tumult of images flashed through her consciousness; of dark-complexioned bodies, Pacific Islanders with tattoos, native women screaming at horrible, swollen genitals. The tattoo on her shoulder was stinging hard as the deluge of images subsided.

That night she thought about Gary. She remembered how he exuded strength and confidence. How perfect and hard his body was. How white his teeth were when he smiled. How his tan never went away in the winter, as if all those years of sun in Micronesia had physically changed him. Beth took a course from him as an undergraduate, 'Polynesian Societies', to fulfil some sort of credit requirement for her degree. Why had he singled her out when there were so many more attractive women in her class? They went on a date and he dominated the conversation because what he had to say was so much more important than anything she could tell him about roses. He talked about the South Sea Islands and primitive natives sophisticated in ways Westerners couldn't even grasp. He had once seen an old man lie down and will himself to death.

'Their mastery over their bodies is something so alien to us,' he said. 'Their control over things like pain. After all the years I spent there, I never even came close to understanding.'

And then, foolishly, she had shown him. She so desperately wanted to impress him, this lauded and published anthropologist. She took the hatpin she always carried from her purse.

'Like this?' she said, and drove the pin through the centre of her hand.

Beth shook herself from the memories and went looking for her old hat pin. She kept it in a carved wooden box studded with cowrie shells that Gary had given to her. She lifted the lid and took it out. It was nothing special, just a long needle, very sharp, with a mother-of-pearl head. She had started to use it in college. A child might put a needle through the skin of her hand, a young woman drove it through her breasts, through her labia, her clitoris. And always, behind locked doors. Like a sacred, primitive rite, she tested her capacity to probe her body, to enjoy enduring the hurt, then releasing herself from it.

She knew why she had let Gary know about her gift. The elation she felt in the way he looked at the needle in her hand, then at her – in their whole time together she never felt that good again.

When she got home from work the next day Gary was waiting in the gravelled driveway that curved past the colonial columns flanking the front porch. She clenched her hand, the one she had lanced with the thorns, and let herself feel the pain. Anger blossomed forth.

'Hi, Beth,' he said, getting out of his car.

'I thought you were in Japan.'

'I took a break.' He was holding her and she bore his kiss to the lips as a liberty not granted. She could control her repulsion until she knew more about why he was here. Perhaps he would unwittingly tell her what she needed to know about the effect the tattoo was having on her and how to drive it out.

As an anthropologist Gary had the detachment to document primitive cultures. It was a gift, his ability to sit unbiased in the middle of a group of people and witness everything without getting involved. His papers were never haunted by the judgmental spectres of western civilization. But conversely, this meant that he was unable to take Beth into his life without trying to change everything about her, blaming her for every character quirk. So she left, then realized later that that showed the good sense he said she didn't have.

'I thought I'd come around and see how you were doing,' he said, bounding up the steps after her. 'You frosted your hair. It looks more blonde.'

'Sorry I didn't write for permission.'

'You don't have to be that way with me.' He was inside now, and as she threw her purse at the hall tree, he touched her shoulder blade. A soft touch, of two fingers pressed over the tattoo he had forced on her, and the feeling drained her, as would a kiss. She stood, just barely, as he gathered her to him, his dark hair smelling so different from Marty's, his hands, his compact body, the thick feel of the saliva on his tongue. She tried to think of Marty as Gary's hands flowed over her lines, making her need of him unbearable. She could hear the soft creak of the oak floor under them echoing up the front staircase.

More dimly she remembered kissing him and saying from a great distance, 'Why are you doing this to me?'

He smiled with his mouth, but not the rest of his face. 'I just wanted to be with you tonight. Do you hate me so much?'

Beth felt lost, unable to tie the pieces together. She folded her arms across her breasts. 'You don't care how I feel about you.'

He brought her wrist gently to his mouth. 'You need me more than you think.' His kiss drew her in more deeply. He put his mouth over her thumb and curled his tongue around it, and she gave in, wanting his body so badly it blotted out her anger. Just so she could feel him inside her, expunging the terrible memory of that last time with Marty. Her hunger for him, for his penis almost overwhelmed her. Then she opened her eyes to see Gary looking down at her, observing her coldly, confidently, and the dizzying lust vanished. She thought of Marty again. Not of that awful last session, but of how naturally he smiled. How little he asked of her.

'Leave me alone,' she said. 'Don't ever come back.'

He gave that exasperating smile that stretched over his teeth. 'You'll want me back.' He touched her tattooed shoulder and looked at her expectantly. And, yes, feeling came upon her again, the wanting, the craving. Then the rage caught up with her and she knocked his hand away.

'You know why you want me so much?' he said. 'You haven't had anyone since I left, have you? There's no way you can have anyone but me. I told you that, but I bet you tried anyway.'

'What are you talking about?'

'Well,' he said, moving away from her to lean back against the panelled wall and plant a foot against it. He had never respected her house. 'You just don't remember as well as you should. When we got tattooed we became faithful to each other for the rest of our lives. Bad things happen if you try to fool around, and I know you tried, Beth. I felt a tingling on my shoulder while you were at the conference. Just like the old man said it would. There's a spirit that goes with the tattoo, and it will keep all men but me from making love with you.'

'Oh, right.'

'But you did try to fuck someone, didn't you?'

'You realize, of course, if this nonsense is true, you can't be with anyone else either.

'Why would I want to? It's you I want.' He moved towards her.

She backed away and went to the door, holding it open, and he left without a word.

She closed the door and curled up on the huge couch in the front parlour, aching with memories. Her mother had never let her into this room as a child, so with deliberate intent she used it as her personal living room.

Unbidden came the memory of Gary saying, 'Does this hurt?'

Yes, that's how his litany went.

Gary became obsessed with her special talent. His experiments seemed justified at first. She was so unique, so gifted. Had she developed this ability?

No, it had always been there.

Can I try some tests? We have to find out everything we can about this.

Well, I guess.

First, she told him everything she could about how she lifted herself away from pain. Over and over, she told him, in every way imaginable. He listened so hard. He tried so hard, but he never got past the fear of marring his skin or feeling even the smallest agonies. He got as far as putting a pin through the web of his hand and yanked it out, hissing through his teeth.

In her eagerness to please, she hadn't realized how much he envied her. All that time studying primitives, doing nothing but reporting their behaviour, understanding so little. Perhaps it wasn't such a small step, from watching her pierce herself to putting the needle through her skin himself. And that is how she learned about agony, because as much as she wanted to help, to earn his approval, she didn't want him to do this to her. And that mattered. She cried out the first time and jerked back from the needle. He grabbed her hand and slammed it down, ramming the needle through it, the way she had shown off the first time. This time she screamed at the uncontrollable pain.

It grew dark as she lay balled up on the couch, her fist clenched. That Gary had tried to force himself on her and left his smell on her was unbearable and she found herself running for the shower. Being clean, wet, helped take the throbbing edge off the memories. She had made love to Marty before her piercing and nothing terrible had happened. Why? The terrible things had happened after she had been pierced. The pain had awakened it. She pushed herself to remember; what had Gary done to her after running her hand through? First, he had apologized profusely, with tears in his eyes. Then left, saying he had to be alone. Came back after a weekend and humbly asked her to forgive him. Would she just come over for the weekend? He had a house guest she would find interesting. A friend from Hawaii.

She said yes. What could it hurt?

Gary's guest's name was Howard Oyami. He was part Hawaiian, part Japanese, with skin the colour of teak and full, sensuous lips. His eyes were dark and liquid and unsettling because they never crinkled at the corners when he smiled. Sort of like Gary's. But he watched everything around him like an alien visiting a different world, one he felt contempt for. After dinner they made casual conversation, drank coffee. Beth felt relaxed.

They went to the living room and sat, basking in the pleasant feeling that follows a good meal, and then Howard brought out a long, flat box. Gary opened it and swivelled a bright lamp to shine on it. Inside, stretched out on a frame, was a long, uneven piece of leather. The painting on it was magnificent. In dark, soft blues it showed a great dragon, surrounded by decorations that crowded but didn't fight with the central figure.

'Like it?' Gary asked, taking her hand. 'Have you ever heard of the Yakuza?'

'No,' she said, her face open, curious.

'In Japan, they're like the Mafia. They go back a long way, like so many things in Japan, and they have traditions. One of those traditions is to get tattooed all over the body.'

What he was saying sank in slowly. 'This is—'

'The skin of a Yakuza, removed when he died to be preserved as a work of art . . .' His words became shapeless sounds and she felt as if she was sinking inside. In the brilliant lamplight the skin seemed to grow smaller, and she thought of the tiny bright light that comes through a keyhole and lets you peer at a ray of truth. Gary's hand on hers grew tight.

'Does this hurt?'

Gary was so much stronger than she was. He could hold both her wrists together with one hand as she writhed and jerked. He threw her on the floor as if she was nothing, held her down and tied her.

Howard spoke up. 'She'll never sit still for it, man.'

'I gave her something in her coffee. She should calm down pretty soon.' Gary sat comfortably on her back. She could hear the rustling of a piece of paper as her heart raced on, pumping whatever it was through her system. 'Here's the design.'

'Okay,' she heard Howard say. 'It's not one of my people's. I'll do it.'

'What are you going to do?' she whispered. She had never been so afraid in her whole life.

'Give you something special. See this?' Howard handed Gary back the paper and he held it where she could see it. The sleepiness was setting in, but she could recognize what she saw. It was an abstract tattoo design that would have been beautiful under different circumstances, one of interwoven spikes, concentric squares and lines. He explained that it was an ancient design from a Micronesian culture, a symbol of mutual love.

'Sick . . .' she gasped into the carpet.

'I'm getting one too, Beth, because I could never bear to lose you. You're special. I may never learn to control pain the way you can, but I learned a few things in the islands. An old man told me what this design could do. He was going to take it with him when he died, because his people didn't believe in magic the way they used to. But he gave it to me because he liked me. Beth, we belong together and this tattoo is a symbol of all that.'

She tried to tell him she didn't want it, but the words blew soundlessly through her mind. Gary couldn't hear her.

Howard was crossing the room, he was out of her sight, then she could see him again, carrying a small case. He set it down and brought out the oddest collection of things, which he proudly explained to her. The tattooing was done with an au, a fine comb made from a boar's tusk sharpened with a sea urchin's spine. With the skin stretched taut, the au is dipped into a homemade ink and pulled across her shoulder and tapped repeatedly, driving the ink into the indentions.

As she drifted in and out, she was scrubbed with antiseptic and the design was transferred to her shoulder blade. As Gary smoothed her skin, pulling it tight, Howard went to work, relentlessly tapping with his tools, working the details indelibly into flesh. The pain went much deeper.

Beth jerked away from the memory. The drugs had blotted out everything else, but in her dreams that night she could see herself getting tattooed, see Howard tapping over and over again as the black pattern emerged, couched in dots of blood that welled up in protest. The tattoo gradually swirled, writhed and seemed to lift from her shiny taut skin then sink in, swallowed by her muscle and bone. She could feel the terrible sensation of the pattern unravelling itself around her lungs and heart. She breathed hot spikes from the tattoo and the pieces burst into her breasts, swelling them at unnatural angles, then oozing out around her pierced nipples. She woke trying to pull air into her chest, screaming on the intake. She was clutching her breasts as if to hold something in. The nightmare evaporated, leaving her curled and crying in the dark swellings of her sheets.

She felt herself rise numbly the next morning, go to work. She couldn't call Marty yet. She let it wait a day and when she dialled his number that evening her hands no longer trembled.

'Marty, I have to see you. Can you get a couple of days off or shall I?'

'I'll be there tomorrow.'

She gave him directions and, true to his word, he pulled into her driveway soon after she got home from work. He was sitting in the driver's seat gaping when she came out onto the portico. Then he saw her and got out of the car without even bringing his keys with him. Such a small act, to come to her without even securing his car, but it touched Beth like a clear light. *I love this man.*

'Come in,' she said. They held each other softly, experimentally, then he looked up and around at the front staircase and the stained glass windows on the landing.

'My God, Beth. You never said you lived in a place like this.' He smiled selfconsciously. 'And I asked you to move to Florida.'

'I inherited it.'

'It's . . . nice. Could I see the grounds?'

'Spoken like a true gardener,' she smiled. They went out her favourite way, through the French doors in the dining room. She led him slowly past the flowerbeds and goldfish ponds, enjoying the way he would stop and touch a plant with such a knowing hand. Finally she showed him her garden. He went straight to Bed of Nails, touching it in a strangely intimate way and turning to smile at her.

'This is one of yours, isn't it?'

'My masterpiece.'

'I want a cutting,' he said.

In the evening warmth they stood close for a long time.

'Let's go in,' she said at last.

They went up the back stairs to her room, the only one in the house with modern furniture and plain white walls. They settled on her bed.

'I said I would tell you about Gary. He was here a couple of days ago and tried to get me to sleep with him – no, wait, let me start again; I want to get this right.

'Ever since I was very little, I could control pain. I can just . . . distance myself from it.' She picked up her hat pin, which she had placed close by earlier, and watched Marty's face as she pushed it smoothly through the centre of her hand. 'It doesn't hurt.'

She pulled out the pin and felt the rush of wailing voices inside. She could feel emotion from . . . the spirit of the tattoo? Its voice was confused, malevolent, and – most strangely – impotent in some way. Her vision cleared and she could see Marty's stunned face.

'Marty, believe me, I can feel some pain. I can't control it all.'

'My God.' He took her hand, looked at the palm and turned it over. 'No bleeding either.'

'There's more.'

He smiled fleetingly. 'Getting pierced really means something to you, doesn't it?'

'More than you know.'

She told him how she had played with needles and how she

learned to keep her secret until Gary came along, then about the tattoo. 'The last time you and I tried to make love, the tattoo did something to us – you know what I mean. And when he came here the other day, all he had to do was touch me on the shoulder blade and I felt like I couldn't stay away from him. And then I got mad and threw him out – and it . . . the feeling went away.'

Marty looked overwhelmed. As if he was close to believing.

'He touched my shoulder *deliberately*. Like he was jerking a string on a puppet'.

'Anything else?'

'Yes, a lot.' And she told him about Gary's confidence in her not having slept with anyone because of the tattoo. He had been wrong, but the next day she got pierced.

'I want to see that tattoo again,' said Marty.

She pulled off her shirt and turned her back to him and he touched her gently.

'Feel anything special?'

'Nothing.'

'No naked lust?'

Her spirits lifted as she grinned and shook her head.

'It's a neat tattoo. I have to admit that. When you called me, I thought it would be about what happened that last time in New York. But what you're telling me . . .'

'I'm sorry . . .'

'Just give me a little time. It's all so—' He shrugged and wiped a tear from her face. He kissed her, asking, not taking. It was she who wanted more, who pulled him to an embrace and rubbed her hand against his shirt, pulling at his nipple rings. He leaned back and looked at her, his eyes clear and cautious.

'Let's try,' she said. 'It's one way I can prove it to you.'

They went slowly, as if to delay penetration. The touch of his mouth against her skin was soothing, exciting, and she remembered with fleeting hilarity that his keys were still in his car as he finally moved on top of her, guiding himself in. It was wonderful to move with him, to feel the studs of his ampallang—

—it happened quickly, the sharp onset of revulsion, that his penis was tearing and ripping her. Her perception became more clear and she gripped him hard so he couldn't withdraw. She was seeing a completely tattooed face with wild bright eyes. It was inside of her, screaming in its alien tongue and showing her the suffering it had visited on others, the images that had driven centuries of other men and women apart. Like an obscene climax, they caught their breath together shuddering in each other's arms. 'Marty,' she said at last, 'I don't think I could stand it if we can never make love again.'

Marty reached for her and held her so that she could feel his emotions through his skin, through his mouth and the taste of him.

'I'll hold out as long as you can,' he said.

His lovemaking was gentle at first, then the rhythm of their bodies grew tighter. She could feel Marty gasping as she closed her eyes and looked within. It was a face she felt/saw, crazed with tattoos that radiated out from the eyes and mouth. It spoke and she couldn't respond to the strange language. Alarmed that it had no effect, the face flew apart. Spikes of black snaked out from the visage and into her pierced breasts, her vagina, her clitoris. Marty grasped her breasts, curved his fingers through her rings and pulled hard. The pain shot through her, and she let it become the pinpoint centre of her wet-red consciousness. The rings strained against her raw nipples, they oozed pain, blood. She reached for his chest, pulling as hard as she could at his rings. His toughened piercings stretched away in peaks as their rhythm grew tighter, faster. The apparition could scream inside her and create its rending ephemeral visions, but she and Marty bathed in pain that left no room for anything else. More intense than anything she had ever known, an orgasm built, crested and carried her violently as the demon tasted and fled from what it had no power over. Its visions weakened and shadows of the tattoo flew through her skin like ghostly knives. They entered Marty, screaming as they wove through his many piercings. He shuddered in her arms and cried out as they lanced in and streaked back out, unable to find purchase in a body with so many piercings. She felt him growing wonderfully hard as he climaxed, driving deep inside her.

The demon hovered and dissolved like so much dust and she buried her face in Marty's neck, seeing nothing but dark.

They spiralled down together. At some point he weakly withdrew from her and they huddled together and slept. Beth finally woke, her nipples crusted with savage usage. She needed to shower, but there was something else that would need taking care of very soon. It was early dusk and she eased from Marty's arms. In the old bathroom mirror she looked at her nipples, cleaned them, then on impulse looked back over her shoulder.

She had to reach for the sink for support. The tattoo had grown pale, like frozen branches trapped under thick ice. She showered and went out to her garden. The air was redolent with the scent of roses, shadowed in the dusk. Gary would be here soon. His tattoo must have stung plenty while she and Marty were in bed together.

Ignoring her gloves, she headed for Bed of Nails, seeing in her mind where she would cut canes, how the new shoots would grow. She grasped the first cane, the thorns caressing her skin and pressing to gain entrance. Some of the thorns glided in but there was no pain, no blood. Making her cut, she lifted away a long cane. A soft change in the darkening air made her turn, and Gary was there.

'How dare you try to fuck that yahoo?'.He gripped her arm very hard and she fleetingly considered plunging her shears in his chest.

'I told you what would happen if you tried,' he told her. 'You stupid cunt.'

The air was very still, heavy with deep hues.

'I made love with him in New York,' said Beth. 'It made me wonder why the next time was so terrible. How could that first time be so good? It has to do with getting hurt, I think. Pain woke that thing up.'

'What are you talking about?'

'Who knows?' she mused, 'maybe the spirit, or whatever it is, could only be summoned with pain. After all, Gary, what do you really know about the spiritualism of some tribe on a Pacific Island? Why would an old man give you any of his magic if he wouldn't pass it on to his own people?'

'He gave it to me as a gift before he died.' Gary didn't sound convinced. He reached out in the gathering darkness and touched her shoulder. Pressed it. She smiled and shook her head.

The thing that had fled from her and Marty settled on Gary's shoulders unnaturally, like cinders falling in the twilight.

'You've done it all wrong,' she said, feeling the black sparkle and malevolence of a force that didn't want her any more, but hovered near the one who stole it from extinction. 'You had the gall to tattoo us with something that doesn't belong to us, you had it put on by a man from another tribe, because a Micronesian would have refused.'

Gary was waiting, listening. He didn't feel the membrane of the curse drifting down on them, but Beth could feel its yearning to enter Gary.

'I think the old man had something else in mind. Let me show you,' she said. 'Put my hand on your tattoo.'

He took her hand and brought it to his shoulder. She could sense his arousal.

'No, Gary. Take your shirt off. It'll work better.'

He was silhouetted in the falling darkness, feverishly jerking at his shirt.

'Just turn your shoulder this way,' she whispered.

He turned and she lashed out with thorned cane. It whistled through the air but landed with the curiously blunt noise of a blow softened by hundreds of spikes impacting flesh.

'SON OF A BITCH! WHAT ARE YOU TRYING TO DO?'

He grabbed for her, but she stepped away, whipping at him again with the cane. His hands took the brunt of the attack, and he drew back, breathing heavily. Then the demon came out of the blackness, descending hungrily on the holes in his flesh and on his pain. The tattoo sliced into him, as if its strands were cleaving their way through bone and tendon. He fell to the ground, shuddering and struggling for breath. Kneeling beside him, she gently laid down the bloody cane. Touching him, she could feel the spectre of the tattoo under her hands, resting in the core of a man who understood so little. It wreaked havoc in his body, feeding off pain that he couldn't translate to ecstasy.

Beth rose and went to Marty. They would sleep together, then talk of many things, perhaps about where she would pierce herself next.

She would never see Gary again. Perhaps he would work it out one day, how to exorcise the demon from his consciousness, but she doubted it. The tattoo's spirit would only make its presence known to him as long as pain lasted. Any pain.

THAT OLD SCHOOL TIE

by

Jack Womack

Originally from Lexington, Kentucky, Womack now is happily ensconced in New York City. He is the author of the novels *Ambient*, *Terraplane*, *Heathern*, *Elvissey* and *Random Acts of Senseless Violence*. He makes his friends watch very bad movies, and has a large collection of very odd books.

Womack has only written a handful of short fiction but each piece has been a gem. Unlike his longer works, which some critics place in the cyberpunk subgenre, his short fiction focuses on dysfunctional intimate relationships. Each story is like watching a traffic accident – what's happening is horrible but you just can't look away.

THAT OLD SCHOOL TIE

Charles spun webs of charm and guilt around his friends, entwining them tighter if they tried to wander, loosing them once they drew near. The resulting networks were so complex that it was impossible for onlookers, or even participants, to discern who might be spider and who, fly.

We met at college and grew closer over the years, as people do when they have nothing in common but the length of time they've known one another. He taught English at NYU and wrote several books about lesser figures of the Romantic period, who seemed all the lesser once he was through with them. I'd been in pre-med until discovering how readily I weakened at the sight of real blood, and so I edited medico-legal textbooks instead; forensic pathology was my *métier*. Call it slumming amid the stews of human behaviour, if you like; Charles once did. The manuscripts arrived in my office exclusive of their photographs – cake without frosting, as it were.

Charles and his wife Elaine, a divorce lawyer, lived on Riverside Drive, in a long-hall apartment overlooking the shadier side of 99th Street; their six-year-old daughter, Cecily, attended a good school, though one unblessed with alumni of more than moderate renown. I lived alone, on 95th Street.

They rented a house in Springs every other August; he invited me out one weekend, the summer before his final semester. On Saturday we went to the beach, smothering sandfleas beneath our towels as we roasted ourselves; Cecily begged her mother to put away the phone she'd brought along.

'Charles,' Elaine said, pressing her palm over the mouthpiece. 'Put some sunblock on me, please. I'm burning already.' While she consulted with her client, Charles rubbed oil into his wife's shoulders until they shone. His own were as muscular as they'd been in college, when he was on the crew; I was never one for sports,

myself. Rubbing his hands dry against his plaid swim trunks, he
reached into Elaine's bag, extracted a cigarette and lit it.

'He's got nothing to go on, believe me,' she told her client. 'Give
him enough rope, they always use it—'

'*Mommy*—!' Cecily said; Elaine lifted a finger, shushing her. She
shook her father's arm as if to break it off, and whispered into his ear.
'You take me swimming.'

'Mom's a better swimmer,' Charles said, gently pushing her aside.
'She was on the team at Vassar. Want to go to Vassar?'

'Take me now.'

'Shouldn't complain until you have something to complain about,
honey.'

'*Now!*'

He looked at his daughter, appearing to love her. Charles's parents
held old Yankee notions of appropriate behaviour, and drummed
into him the belief that revealing one's emotions to a feckless world
is a shameful act. While young, he perfected an impenetrable façade
– bland half-smile, eyes lowered but alert – that served him in every
situation, however pleasant or grotesque. The structure was unimportant to the facing; the person, superfluous to the mask.

'*Cecily!*' She quieted.

'The writ's in order. Don't worry, I said. Call you Monday.'

Elaine put away her phone and stood, dropping the towel with
which she was swathed. Her bathing suit, a white maillot, sheathed
her torso with a condom's snugness. None of Elaine's physical
attributes would have been unattractive had they appeared, singly,
on other women; the ensemble as presented was sadly discon-
certing. Her suit rode up her hips with every step as she led Cecily
toward the sea. Charles stared at his wife, evincing no more emotion
than when he'd watched her talking on the phone.

'Doesn't she look good in that?' Charles asked, his tone assuring
me that he'd served as fashion advisor. He snuffed his cigarette in a
tuffet of sand, and as speedily lit another.

'She seems uncomfortable,' I said. Elaine left Cecily to play near
the shoreline; eased her suit over her buttocks before plunging
headlong into a wave.

'First thing she told me was take it back. Said she was too old for it.
Got her to reconsider. Told her to give it a spin, she agreed. Never
guess she was as insecure as she is, would you?'

Elaine and Charles were married twenty years; they had a
competition, rather than a relationship, throughout. I declined to sit
as judge, however often he handed me the gavel. 'When's class start?'

'Two weeks,' he said.

'Anticipating or dreading?'

'Got to look at it as a challenge. How long will it take to find the one who stands out from the crowd? If I find them, they make up for the rest. If not, so be it.'

'You've still got freshmen courses?'

He shivered; I gathered that the breeze chilled him. 'Only one. Up for tenure in January. No more after that. Rest are juniors and seniors.'

'Better informed?'

'School's out even when it's in, these days. Not when we were going.' He sighed; eyed Cecily as she dug a hole. 'What've you been working on?'

'*The Pathology of Trauma.*'

He frowned; his eyelids crinkled as he confronted the sun. 'The usual?'

'Nothing unexpected,' I said. 'One fascinating case study. Suicide by dynamite.'

'What did they do? Blow up the house?'

'Used a stick as a cigar, sort of. Astonishing results.'

Charles grimaced. 'Don't you think you'd ever want to get into the general field? Don't see how you can keep your head on straight, editing what you do. Not healthy. I know people, I could call around. Never too late.'

'Sometimes it is,' I said. 'I like what I'm doing, Charlie.'

'I can help,' he said. 'Trust me.'

'Believe me.'

Charles's sense of *noblesse oblige*, also grafted onto him by his parents, was as genuine as it was fulsome; still, little disgruntled him more than to have his proffered altruism declined – save when his help was accepted, and the gratitude resulting struck him as incommensurate with his beneficence. 'You don't get out enough,' he said. 'Haven't I always told you that? You're not getting younger, you know.'

Charles was my age. 'I'm content.'

'Fine, then,' he said, his expression unchanged, his words rich with hints of disappointment. For a minute he said nothing, containing unseemly emotion; then he changed the subject, lowering his voice, as if afraid that fellow beachgoers would dash off to enter marks into his permanent record if they cared to overhear. He was accomplished at drawing out the guilt in others for having felt its *frisson* so keenly, so often, himself. 'Remember Gail Hamilton?'

'Why?' I asked.

'Ran into her on Lexington. Held up pretty well. Told me I'd held up better.'

Had his hair still been brown he would have looked two or even three years younger than he was. 'I wasn't aware she lived here.'

'Moved back from San Francisco in April. Divorced, lives at Second and 68th. Told her we should get together for lunch one day.'

'You going to?'

He shook his head. 'Been so long. Too many questions. What's she been doing? Why'd she get divorced? Looks fine, but who's to know?'

'Any reason to think that she's not?' I asked. 'Is she all right?'

'Says so. They always seem all right at first. Why do you care?'

'Why'd you suggest lunch, then?'

He slipped on his sunglasses. 'Have to be polite.'

Elaine, treading water beyond the breakers, called to Cecily, who then ran up to us, sprawling herself in the dunes at our feet. 'Mommy wants her towel,' she told Charles. 'She wants *you* to bring it to her.'

'Why me?'

'Mommy says just bring it.'

He stood up, hoisting his trunks above his deflating waistline. Retrieving Elaine's towel, he followed his daughter to the water and walked in up to his knees. Elaine swam inland; leapt up and took the towel from him. Her suit's fabric, when wet, became so translucent that she appeared to be naked. Cloaking herself, she emerged from the ocean and strode across the sand as if into court. 'Excuse me,' she said, picking up her bag with one hand, securing her towel with the other. 'I have to put on my sun suit. I'll be right back. Charles, watch Ceese.'

Charles called after her as he ascended the dunes, 'Could wear it at home.'

'Give it to one of your students,' she muttered, walking away. His smile flattened; he sat down. Cecily slapped his knees with her plastic bucket; then she wandered a few feet away and started filling it with sand. While waiting for Elaine to return we watched a speedboat roar by, scarring the water. He said something I didn't catch.

'Pardon?'

Charles examined his knees closely, as if fearing his daughter had bruised them. 'Beautiful day, don't you think?' I couldn't disagree.

Two or three times a month Charles and I met after work for drinks and dinner. After a point in the evening our conversation revolved, inevitably, around our old college days. If our memories differed, it was expected that I support his version, which he felt suffered less from time's numberless rewrites. Often – more often, of late – we'd read obits of acquaintances from school who'd died of coronaries or cancer, and mourn them as we remembered them, their collegiate portraits blurry with thirty years' distance. Charles grew uncomfortable, considering the oft wayward course of postgraduate lives.

Once I was positive that a remarkable case study I'd proofed was one of our housemates during our sophomore year; I told Charles. 'Wasn't him,' he insisted, with uninflected voice. 'If he was going to die, he wouldn't have died that way.' I avoided trifling with my old friend's preferred realities, and so concurred in his opinion, without belief. Change didn't disturb him as did unpredictability; one of many talents on which Charles prided himself was his ability to foresee situations early enough to benefit from their results – in truth, he rarely did.

The first time we got together, that semester, Charles raised an unanticipated subject, and told me he'd already encountered the student who stood out. 'A brilliant young woman,' he said, intoning his new mantra while his fettucini cooled. 'Brilliant. Audited my poetry class on the second day. By the end of the hour she was the only one participating. Class was full, but I pulled some strings and got her in. Simply brilliant.'

'How brilliant?' I asked, trying to decipher his face; his expression was as he moulded it each morning, though I thought he might be on the verge of allowing his smile to wax gibbous. 'What's her name?'

'Valerie,' he said. 'She's twenty-one. We spoke after class. She's formulating her own critical theory. Non-traditional, perhaps wilfully so, but that's half the pleasure of it. And it works. Only meet students like her once in a lifetime.'

'Where's she from?'

'Shaker Heights. Left Swarthmore to come here.'

'Why?'

He shook his head and chuckled. 'Swarthmore didn't get the concept of chaos philology at all.'

'Excuse me?'

'Her critical theory,' Charles said. 'Takes semiotics one step beyond.' As he spoke his smile broke loose of its moorings, curling into an unsettling rictus; his eyes shone as if they'd been moistened.

'How?'

'Ask her,' he said, rising. 'Valerie, like you to meet—'

'Charmed,' she said, taking my hand before I offered it. Charles provided her with a chair expropriated from another group's table. Valerie wore a cashmere turtleneck, striped leggings and yellow running shoes; at first glance she looked slim enough to slip through a mail slot. Her ivory skin possessed the matte finish older women sometimes develop when their features are annually updated. She had a child's smile, a doll's eyes; her hair was black as the wing of a carrion crow. Valerie was beautiful, though her beauty was of a sort often attainable only through compulsion. Taking a roll from his plate, she bit into it with sharp little teeth.

'Charles was starting to tell me about your theory—'

'Which?' Seizing a knife, she smeared butter over the remains of the roll; crammed it into her mouth as if she were starving.

'Chaos philology,' Charles said. Valerie grinned, and snatched the fork from his plate, wreathing its tines in chilled fettucini.

'Did he explain it?' She brushed her hair away from her face and sucked the fork clean. 'The bottom line is that unravelling always works, even where deconstruction doesn't.'

'Unravelling what?'

As Valerie reached for another forkful, she overturned my glass, baptizing the table with barely-sipped bourbon. 'Whatever's communicated,' she said, ignoring the spillage. 'Written or verbal narratives. Like this. One, unravel the text as presented. Two, reweave into a turbulent pattern of discourse. Three, examine the new design. Chaos philology allows deepest penetration into auctorial intent.'

Charles slid his plate in front of her so that she could reload her fork with less collateral damage. 'Could you give me an example?' I asked.

'Sure. Let's stick to Romantics. His favorite.' Charles smiled. 'Take a typical passage from Shelley's *Adonais* such as, "Peace, peace, he is not dead, he doth not sleep."' From her backpack Valerie took a pen and notebook and began writing, dripping strands of pasta onto the paper while she ate. 'Start simple, finish big,' she said, presenting it to me. On the page I read *Sleep doth not peace dead not peace is he he*. Each word was harnessed to its mates by curves, lines and arrows; singly, in pairs and as *ménages à trois*.

'Remarkably subtle patterns,' I said, regarding the fetishistic intricacy of the lacings.

'They leap out at you, after a while,' said Charles.

'If you desire, you can defer the critical climax indefinitely,' Valerie continued. 'If not, bang and run. Strip sense from nonsense. See what fantasies the author tried to hide. You understand how it works? It's so obvious that what Shelley is doing in that particular line is laughing at the prospect of his own predictable death.'

'I wish I'd taken more lit courses,' I said. Charles beamed, and gave her a look that gave me a toothache.

'Wouldn't have helped,' she said. As she lay down her fork I thought I glimpsed a tattoo of a green butterfly on her left wrist. 'Authors never mean what you think they're saying. You have to find a quick way to get them to confess. Chaos philology may seem violent, assaulting the author from behind as it does, but how else do you get to know what's really there? Nothing wrong with that. Nothing's wrong as long as it doesn't hurt someone you don't know.'

Valerie slumped, as if her air had run out; she looked at Charles, seeming hungry to hear not only agreement, but approval.

'Method broadens the range of readings,' he said. 'Makes what's obvious to me obvious to anyone tying themselves into the network. The Romantics always lied about what they were really up to, for example.'

'Downright morbid, most of them. If you hadn't had Romantics, you wouldn't have had Hitler,' Valerie said. Charles nodded. 'Chaos philology is usable in unravelling any fantasy in any field, the more I think about it.'

'I'm completely lost,' I admitted.

'You're unravelling,' she said, bouncing up and down in her chair as if it were hot. Charles interrupted, keen as ever to assist the unassistable.

'Not everybody gets it,' he said; his smile reset itself into a shallow, upturned arc. 'Try again some other time.' He looked at my emptied glass. 'When we're more sober, perhaps.'

Valerie's nipples rose, appearing as beads underlying her sweater. She rested her chin in her palms; her sleeves drew up as she moved her arms; seeing her wrist more plainly, I realized that the greenish blotch wasn't a butterfly, but a bruise. 'You and Charles went to school together?' she asked, seemingly to confirm what he'd earlier told her. 'Nothing like an Ivy League man.' She caressed my silk tie with her fingers, oiling it nicely. '*These* aren't the school colours.'

'Chaos haberdashery,' I said.

Valerie laughed again, and then jumped to her feet as if she'd been pricked. 'I've got to pee. Be back.' Turning away from us, she bent over double and fumbled through her backpack until she found an unlabelled bottle. Her leggings were split along the inseam; she wore no more underwear below than she did above. Reattaining the vertical, she swallowed a pill with a gulp of my water and bounded off.

'She's a corker, isn't she?' Charles said, tapping the table with his fingers, watching me straighten my tie. 'Overexuberant, sometimes. Excuse.'

'Genius knows its own etiquette,' I offered. 'How's the family?'

'Fine,' he said, staring at the ladies' room door, appearing ready to lunge for it. 'Fine, fine, fine.'

I supposed his deeper involvement with Valerie began about a month into the semester; suspected that one evening, they'd forged bonds that were other than intellectual – but he didn't tell, and I didn't ask. He'd had an affair once before while married to Elaine, alluding to it only after he'd broken it off, and only to me. Afterward, having confessed, he was able to pretend it never happened. Years later I asked him her name, but she no longer had one.

Throughout the fall Valerie came with him each time we met. They sat on either side of me at the table, rambling about her unorthodox theories, the elaborate projects they dreamed of shortly undertaking, the officials at Barnard he'd contacted, using such pull as he had to grease her way along her chosen path. At no time would it have appeared to anyone who didn't know Charles that anything was ongoing between him and his new associate but a mutual fondness for the workings of the mind – the interest they seemed most deeply to share, as long as theirs were the minds involved.

One afternoon in late October, he called me at work. 'Meet me at my office instead of the restaurant, could you?' he asked. 'Something I think I want to talk about.' Possibly he intended a fresh confession; a moot concern, as it developed. When I arrived, the secretaries were closing up for the night but allowed me to come in. I strolled down the hall to his office; his door was shut. As I prepared to knock, Valerie's voice came from within, rising over the building's white noise; she gasped as if she were hyperventilating.

'Tight enough?' she asked. 'Is it? Is it?'

I returned to the reception area without waiting to discover if it was. Ten minutes later they emerged, donning their coats, appearing no more dishevelled than if they'd been unravelling one of the thornier passages of Byron. 'Look who's here,' Charles exclaimed; his evident surprise could have been no greater had I plunged out of the sky to settle on his shoulders. 'Thought you'd be at the restaurant already. Hungry?' I nodded. She shook her hands as if something clung to them. 'Let's go.'

We went. When, later, Valerie made for the facilities, I asked

Charles why he'd wanted to talk to me. He closed his eyes while answering, as if to channel an entity better equipped to respond.

'Why do you say I wanted to talk?'

'You called me this afternoon. You said you had something to talk about. Don't you remember?'

'Misunderstood me,' he said, slipping his smile into place. 'Meant you should meet us there, have more time to talk. Weren't waiting long, were you?'

'Not long. Why'd you seem so surprised to see me?'

'Thought we'd meet out front. Didn't know the building was still open.'

'You didn't want to talk?'

'Talking now, aren't we?' Charles concluded. Valerie returned. She scoured her chin with a tissue, studying it as if fearful she'd drawn blood.

'You haven't said anything about Charles's tie,' she said, pitching away the tissue. Hooking his repp, she reeled him in. 'School colours.'

'Out of the closet,' he explained. 'Dad made me buy one first day we went up. Told me I should wear it once a week on Sundays. Went right to the Co-op, bought it. Never wore it a time after that.'

'Because he told you to,' Valerie said, releasing her grip. She shook one of her pills from her bottle. I'd earlier asked Charles what she was on; an assortment of the milder antidepressants, he told me. 'I tied it for him. He's all thumbs.'

Charles shifted his head, swivelling it a fraction of an inch away from me; frowned at Valerie, making a moue so understated as to be almost nonexistent. 'Bit more conservative than what you usually hang around your neck,' I commented; he blanched, as if nauseated by memories of those accoutrements of his he hadn't purchased from Brooks Brothers. The dimple in the tie appeared mathematically centred; the knot, too, was perfect, though no wider than my thumb, and fitting against his Adam's apple so closely it might have been glued there. 'Isn't that awfully tight?'

'You'd be surprised,' he said, stretching his neck as if to free it from a trap.

'Cocteau used to tie his neckties as tight as he could, to lessen the flow of blood to his brain,' Valerie said. 'He claimed it helped him think.'

'Penny for your thoughts,' I said to Charles; they looked at one another and smirked as children would, satisfied to have hoodwinked their parents again.

'Thinking about our work,' he said. 'Going to do a book explaining her theories. Should turn a few heads. My ideas tally well with Valerie's, as it happens'.

'We're two of a kind, in our own ways,' she said. 'In a lot of ways. We've been testing dozens of new concepts. Just wait. We'll hear what they have to say about us, once the book comes out.'

Not long after, tiring of their increasingly exclusive camaraderie, I excused myself and went home. Elaine called, soon after.

'I have to ask you something,' she said. 'When do you think you'll be finishing up this project you and he are working on?'

'Project?'

'I'm only asking because I'm rarely in before ten during the week and I'm going to advertise for a full-time governess for Ceese if you think it'll be much longer. I've asked Charles but he's so vague about these things. Can you give me an idea?'

'Better place an ad,' I said.

'That's what I thought.'

By morning I'd almost convinced myself that I hadn't lied to her.

Several evenings later Charles called me, sounding considerably more frantic than had Elaine. 'I'm at Valerie's apartment. Get over here, fast.'

'What's the matter?'

'We're at Broadway and 86th, southwest corner. Number 5E. Please.'

In ten minutes I reached the building and rushed upstairs. Charles opened the door as I rang the bell. A lone ribbon of gauze was wrapped around his right hand; a dab of blood marred its whiteness. 'It's okay now,' he said, aiming his stare at me, allowing his smile to flicker along his face. 'Come on in.'

Valerie's studio was the size of my living room. Rain blew in the open windows. Notebooks and papers were stacked upon the kitchenette's table, near two uncleared dinner plates. A pair of wire clippers lay atop an unpacked box of dishes. Six hanging baskets brimming with unwatered ivy dangled from hooks in the ceiling, swaying as if they were pendulums. Clothing and linens blanketed two filing cabinets. In the bathroom was a metal wastepaper can split open along the side seam. Hundreds of books, their titles facing inward, were shoved onto the shelves of three bookcases. The décor could have been called Chaotique Moderne.

'Hi,' Valerie said; she lay on her futon. Gilt-framed photographs of Houdini and Isadora Duncan hung on the wall behind her. 'Thanks for coming by.' A thin quilt covered her from neck to knees; her bare calves appeared more muscular than they did in the leggings she usually wore. She breathed heavily, as if she'd been running. The room's single lamp shadowed her face, making her eyes appear deep-set within her skull. The tip of her nose and her forehead bore fresh abrasions, as if she'd fallen and scraped them on the sidewalk during her sprint. She'd smeared vaseline or another soothing ointment on her cheeks and beneath her jaw.

'You have an accident?' I asked her. 'What happened?'

'Damnedest thing,' Charles said. 'Valerie asked if I'd take the garbage down the hall to the compactor. Sliced my hand open on the door. Thought I'd need stitches. Closed up fast enough, though. Here, I'll show you,' he said, motioning as if to unveil his wound.

'That's okay,' I said. 'So you're both all right?'

'Sorry to make you run over here like this. Tell you what, I've got to be going. Walk you home?'

'Sure.' Recalling the panic in his voice, I wondered why he hadn't phoned 911; then realized he'd surely feared that any higher authority upon whom he might rely would notify his wife as to where he'd been found. I still thought it possible that he and Valerie might have been working; Charles always seemed most guilty when he had the least reason. Valerie watched him as he took his raincoat from the closet.

'You can't stay?' she asked, rolling over. Her quilt fell away as she shifted onto her side. Valerie's body was as toned as her legs; she trimmed her public hair into a tufted mohawk; thin bruises resembling calligraphic designs laced her ribcage, above and below her breasts. 'Get home safe,' she said, covering herself, behaving as if neither of us might have noticed her *déshabillé*.

'Got to go. Lock yourself in,' he said as we stepped into the hall. 'Call you tomorrow.' She nodded, staring at the door until it slammed shut. While walking to the elevator I looked for the trash compactor, but saw neither area nor room marked as such.

'I didn't know she lived in the neighbourhood,' I said as we descended.

'Close to Barnard,' he remarked, though Valerie presently attended NYU.

'Elaine called me the night we went out,' I said. 'She mentioned something about a project we were working on?'

He wore his school tie; he must have knotted it himself this time, as its four-in-hand seemed tied by one unused to opposable thumbs. 'We're busy putting Valerie's ideas into shape for publication. Get together sometimes to work on it.'

'Who are you talking about?' I asked, believing the confusion deliberate. 'Me and you, or you and Valerie?'

'You know how Elaine gets sometimes. Been worse, lately. Started seeing chimeras. Imagining situations. Getting to be that age, you know.'

'She's two years younger than us.'

'Came in later one night last week than I expected. Had to improvise.' He seemed enormously pleased – as if, having daily told himself that the sky was orange rather than blue, he'd awoken one morning and discovered he was right. 'Romance at short notice. Got to admit I'm good at it.'

'Too good,' I said. 'What did you tell her?'

'That you're helping me edit my new book as I'm writing it. Kills two birds with one stone. Improves my text, helps you out. Gives you a real book to edit.'

'But I'm not editing it,' I reminded him. 'What do you mean, real book? Don't patronize me.'

'That didn't come out right. Of course you edit real books. Too real, if you ask me, but that's not what I meant. You ought to think about why you get so defensive about your work, if you're really satisfied with what you're doing.' He slipped on a new look; the exaltation seen moments before was supplanted by an expression suggestive of unassuageable pain.

'If you'd warned me of what you'd told her before she called, I wouldn't have minded,' I said. 'Not as much.'

'My intention. Didn't have the chance. Of course you were upset when she called you, I don't doubt it.'

'Is that what you wanted to talk about when you phoned me?' I asked. 'Why didn't you tell me at the time? Or when I asked you, later that night?'

'Couldn't say anything in front of Valerie,' he said. 'She doesn't need to be involved in this.'

'She wasn't there when I asked.'

'Valerie's young, and hasn't had an easy life, however it may seem,' Charles said. 'No need to hurt her unnecessarily.'

He veered away, seeming to lose his balance, eyeing the closed stores we passed as if windowshopping. There was no reason to belabour the point; Charles remembered the evening differently than I did, and that was that – once his revisions were made the text remained inviolate, whatever the fact-checkers said.

'You two getting along well?' I asked.

'We mesh. Same channel, great minds.'

'I hadn't realized she was so athletic. She looks so petite, clothed.'

'Did gymnastics in junior high. First rate, I'm sure. Gave it up. It's a shame.'

'What happened?'

'Balance beam accident. Made the best of it.' Lifting his arms, he snatched at air with his hands; such intensity, in Charles, made him appear to be having a convulsion. 'It's impossible to say where she could go if she gets the opportunities. All I'm trying to do is make sure she gets them.'

'If she only had some redeeming faults,' I said, wishing to lighten his mood.

'Valerie'll do anything.' He spoke so softly that I wouldn't have heard him had I not seen his lips as they let the words slip loose; the intonation, and phrasing of his declaration belied that the fact excited no less than it terrified. 'Could do anything.'

'It's a shame some people get the wrong idea.'

'Who?' he asked, nodding sharply as if expecting me to hand over a list.

'Elaine,' I said. He frowned. 'At least that's what I'm inferring, from what you're saying.'

'Elaine's imagining a rival where there is none,' he said. 'Reality's got nothing to do with it. Wouldn't think she could be jealous of a dream.'

'Much gossip at school?'

'Told there's some, around the department. Nine-tenths of it's intellectual envy. Got no desire to know what anyone's saying.'

'Is anything they're saying true?'

He didn't respond at once; for an instant I dreamed that I'd draw out a sort of confession. 'Troubles me you feel you have to ask that,' he said. 'Where's your mind been? You hear anything I've said?'

'What's the matter with you?'

'No need to ask, then.'

'Charlie, I only wanted—'

We reached 99th Street 'Give you the benefit of the doubt. Don't have to, but I don't think you meant to upset me.'

'That's big of you,' I said, irritated as much by his professorial condescension as by his manipulation of event.

'Situation should be obvious. Just what I've told you, nothing more.'

'I was only saying you've got to expect people will think—'

'Doesn't matter. People'll think what they want to, whatever the truth is,' he said. 'Let'em.'

He glared, as if daring me to acknowledge what I thought, if I still fancied I knew. I tired of his games of trick or treat. 'It upset me when Elaine called, Charlie. I'm not as good at lying as some people.'

'You're not lying,' he said, walking toward Riverside, calling back over his shoulder. 'Remember that.'

In the third week of November he left a message on my machine, asking if I wanted to get together with him before Thanksgiving. When I phoned his apartment, Elaine answered; I hadn't expected to find her at home so early in the evening. 'Charles isn't here at the moment.'

'Think he'll be in soon?'

'Depends,' she said. 'How late are you two working tonight?'

No matter how quickly I could have reacted, it wouldn't have been quick enough. 'I hadn't heard from him. Thought I should check.' The silence following lasted much longer than I'd have preferred.

'Should I say you were looking for him? I suppose I will,' she said, before hanging up.

The next morning Charles called me from his office, asking if I was available to see him later in the day; he thought it would be good if we talked. 'Be by myself, Valerie's at class,' he said. 'Don't worry about Elaine. Everything's under control.'

'What did you tell her this time?'

He gave no indication of hearing me; deafness at command was an ability to which he had no objection as long as he was the one so conveniently handicapped. By five that afternoon I was at our chosen rendezvous, a coffee shop on 86th near Columbus, and waited outside until he arrived alone, ten minutes later. Charles carried a small suitcase; he sagged, seeming to melt. His eyes were pouched as if lined with sand; his face had more new wrinkles than a floater's. He'd lost weight, but not where it mattered, and coughed with a junkie's rasp. Though he avoided artificial stimuli – save for the three packs of cigarettes filtered daily through his lungs – his ravaged look warned of a dilatory concern for the more mundane aspects of life, as when what was once thought an idle distraction proves addictive unto death.

'What's in there?' I asked, pointing to his bag.

He flashed his demi-smile. 'The cat.'

'What'd Elaine say when you got home?'

'Taken care of,' he replied, his gaze drifting to the mirror affixed behind the counter, perhaps suspecting his wife of lurking beyond the cereal boxes and coffee urns. 'Told her we were supposed to hook up last night. Had to go to an emergency department meeting, wasn't able to call.'

'That worked?'

'Why wouldn't it?' he asked, seeming baffled as to why I should be unaware of plans I'd not been told.

'I wish you'd tell me what was going on if you plan on using me as an alibi. I don't like it.'

'You're right,' he said. The waiter brought our coffee; I had no appetite and declined a menu. Charles ran his fingers through his hair, as if combing it. 'You're absolutely right.'

'Why are you hiding if you've got nothing to hide?'

'That's what you'd call it?'

'If all you're doing with Valerie is working, why do you tell Elaine and God knows who else that you're out with me?'

'You're assuming I was with Valerie last night.'

'Weren't you? Is it so hard just to say?'

Charles lifted his cup to his mouth. His hand shook; he splashed coffee on his sleeve. 'No need to be hostile,' he said, allowing the stain to soak in. 'Your work getting to you? Knew it was only a matter of time. Don't get out enough.'

'She knew I was lying. I didn't want to lie to her.'

'Your decision.'

'I've had it, Charlie.' Tossing my napkin on the table, I started to get up; he scanned the restaurant to see if anyone was watching. 'You got me involved in this and I don't even know what I'm involved in. Tell me what's going on or I'll go home and call Elaine at work and ask her.'

'That's unnecessary,' he said, grabbing my arm, gesturing that I should sit down. 'Get control of yourself. Hadn't realised you were so angry.'

'Give me a straight answer and I won't be.'

'I can understand transference,' he said. 'I'll try to explain.'

'Fine. Why all the secrecy?'

'It's a private matter, but I'll share it with you if you insist,' he said. 'You know Elaine's not the easiest person to get along with. Going through a difficult time in her life right now. The woman thing. Up some days, down the rest. We've had more than our share of disagreements since Cecily was born.'

'You've never said.'

'Nothing to talk about. Cecily's a beautiful child, we love her dearly, but she was an accident, after all. Didn't expect to have one so late. Bad timing. Knocked Elaine right off the fast track at her old firm. Wasn't in the forefront on parental leave. Now she's got her own office, has to work twice as hard. Not many women want to be new mothers at forty-two.' Charles shook his head as if reshuffling its contents to see what settled where. 'Elaine didn't.'

While speaking he tightened his old tie's knot, aligning it precisely between his shirt's frayed lapels. 'Didn't please her. Started transferring. Thank God she takes it out on me, not Cecily. Came to an agreement before it went too far, for Cecily's sake. Had upper and lower bunks in the marriage bed since. Get along, though. You have to get along. You have to.'

'Both of you always seemed happy.'

'Essential precept of chaos philology, remember. Nothing's as it seems,' he said. 'Situation like ours doesn't make anyone feel secure. And she's always been a worrywart. Insecure, like I've said. Won't surprise you to hear she's never thought much of my students. Early on, I introduced her to Valerie. It was the right thing to do, and it wasn't.'

'They must not have much in common.'

'Both need my time.' He watched the restaurant's entrance as if expecting them to arrive simultaneously. 'That's my excuse, take it or leave it. Something about her just sets Elaine off. If she knew I was working with Valerie and not you, she'd eat us alive. No real person threatening her, but Valerie serves as the best model she's found'.

'Does Valerie know how she feels?'

'She's perceptive enough, I haven't seen the need to tell her. Call me overprotective, but I don't want to involve her in our problems.'

'How can she not be involved?'

Charles sighed, as if accepting that he'd again have to explain the difference between noun and verb before the class could start in on the syllabus. 'Questions like that complicate a simple situation. I try to help her, she helps me.' Forcing his fingers underneath his collar, he scratched his throat. The skin on his lower neck was inflamed, as if badly sunburned. 'Valerie comes on strong because she's so defensive. She's really very insecure. Thinks I'll stop helping her if they keep saying things. Couldn't do that, you can't abandon people. She'd never polish her theories on her own. Valerie needs a certain discipline. I'm able to provide it.'

Between sentences he drifted, at moments appearing unaware of my presence. His explanation had been more straightforward than any he'd given me before; he'd revealed nominal truths shorn of convenient tangents. Nevertheless, I saw no reason to entirely believe him. 'Charlie, if you were having another affair, what would you want out of it at this point?'

'Why do you say another affair?'

He tapped his spoon rapidly against his saucer as if testing how many strokes it could sustain before shattering. His eyes could have been glass. I had neither the desire nor energy to hurdle another series of circumlocutions, and so reworded my question. 'An affair, I mean. What would you want it to be?'

'What if you ever had a relationship? What would you want out of it?'

'That's not important, Charlie.'

'I've known women. Have a good marriage. Few problems, not many. Young women like Valerie want to work with me. Why would I have an affair?'

'Hypothetical question. Forget it.'

'Average person has an affair to have sex, I think.' he said, peering into his coffee as if cribbing from notes earlier taken; staring at me when he found the answer sought. 'Having sex's a given with most people.'

'I wasn't asking about most.'

'Ever imagine you're in school again?' he asked, his eyes half-shut. 'Remember what it was like then? How you'd dream of having sex with a beautiful young woman. One who'd do anything. *Anything*.'

'That was a long time ago, Charlie—'

'Imagine you're twenty, and with her,' he said. 'She's naked. Squeezes your chest between her thighs till you can't breathe. Drowns you when she sits on your face. Rides you like a horse and whips you to the finish. Rolls on her stomach, spreads her legs. Says do what you want, she can't get away.' His voice never rose above a stage whisper. 'She screams your name.'

'Charlie, stop.'

'You'd like that, wouldn't you?' he asked. 'Wouldn't you?'

'Stop it,' I said, more loudly than I would have wanted; he fell silent, and lit a cigarette. 'Please stop.'

'Why's that make you uncomfortable?' he asked. 'You brought it up.'

'Why did you do that?'

'Have to be careful applying chaos philology to anything other than a text,' he said. 'Finding out what's what can be as hard on the one unravelling as it is on what's being unravelled.'

'I don't know what's the matter with you—'

'Why do you distance yourself so fast whenever something takes a sexual turn? Always have. Ever wondered why? People don't live up to your fantasies? Afraid somebody else's doing better than you? Is that it?'

'Leave it at that,' I said, picking up my jacket.

'Understandable how people might get the wrong idea about you if they were to only go by your behaviour.' As I stood I looked at the floor, so he couldn't see my face; I noticed that he wore only one sock. A furrowed black bruise encircled the exposed ankle. 'Be realistic. My business is mine, yours is yours.'

'I've got to go.' I threw a dollar on the table. 'If I don't talk to you before Thanksgiving, give my love to your family.'

'Just my family? You sure about that?' A semblance of avuncularity reappeared on his features; his smile remained embedded in his face. 'Thanks for your help with Elaine,' he said. 'I mean it. Have a good Thanksgiving.'

'Don't tell her you're with me when you're not,' I said as I left. He had no further response; he'd probably stopped listening. Some texts defy unravelling. Upon reaching my apartment I discovered that Elaine had left a message on my machine.

'Are you there, Charles?' her voice asked. 'Charles? Charles?'

Two weeks before Christmas, they had their annual party. For days I debated whether or not I should go, finally deciding on the afternoon anteceding the event. I worked late, editing manuscripts; by the time I arrived, everyone else was there. Half of those attending were Charles's friends, half Elaine's; there was little commingling of subcultures beyond the initial encounters.

'Good to see you,' Elaine said, greeting me by kissing the air in the vicinity of my cheek. Strangers might have imagined we'd only met once before, and not by choice. 'Charles is in the kitchen. I told him to bring in more eggnog if he thought he could handle it.'

'How are you?' I asked.

She glared, as if offended by my question. 'Have the man fix you a drink. You're usually thirsty.'

The caterers had the setups in the library; they performed their duties with the enthusiasm of galley slaves. Cecily wore a red velvet party dress and spent the night believing that she entertained the guests. An eight-foot Norwegian pine bedizened with white lights and blue balls was in the living room; the soundtrack from *A Charlie Brown Christmas* played mercilessly over the stereo. The press of the crowd was so great that had it not been for those yuletide touches I should have imagined that a celebration of the Black Hole of

Calcutta was underway. I shoehorned myself in near a group that appeared no less lawful than they did academic, and eavesdropped.

'Is she here?' asked a man whose eyebrows resembled caterpillars. 'Tell me she's not.'

'She is,' said an older woman with a forbidding mien. 'Arrived with Lit's Derridadas. They got away from her as fast as they could.'

'He got her away from them,' said a woman wearing red-rimmed glasses. 'Shook them off like flies. I just can't see the attraction.'

'I'd hope it's other than physical,' said the scary woman.

'Or intellectual,' said caterpillar eyes. 'Ah, there's Columbine and Pantaloon now.'

They ploughed separate paths across the room, so intent on ignoring each other as to be unignorable. Charles wore a black pullover with oversized turtleneck. Valerie, perhaps believing the event a masquerade, came as a party favour, enshrouded in green ruffles. She'd wrapped a red silk scarf around her neck and carried a tureen of eggnog. 'Match made in heaven, if you ask me,' said the scary woman.

With deliberate steps Charles inched into the dining room, schmoozing briefly with those he passed. He reached the breakfast table; commandeering two empty chairs, he sat in one and placed his drink on the other. A sheet draped over the table and the legs of the guests sitting around it was imprinted with the phrase BAH HUMBUG! several thousand times. Valerie materialized so immediately at Charles's side that she might have been teleported from space. Academics from departments other than theirs hovered buzzard-like around them; his cigarettes smouldered in the ashtray while he declaimed opinions.

Charles and I hadn't seen each other since our contretemps; we'd spoken, once or twice, but the memory of his assault remained and I wasn't anxious to talk to him. I squeezed down the hall toward the library, feeling as a clot travelling through a clogged artery. After refreshing my drink I lingered, casting glances in the direction of the momentarily distracting. Lawyers so often approached me that I felt I'd been in an accident. Returning to the dining room, I encountered Elaine. She stood in the doorway, watching her husband and his comely protégé.

'You're not leaving yet, are you?' she asked me.

'Not for awhile.' She was smoking; I remembered how much trouble she had quitting while pregnant with Cecily, and I'd not expected her to backslide. Her gown sagged around her waist; I estimated she'd lost twenty pounds, either by accident or design, since August.

'You've said hello to Charles?'

'Hard to get his eye.'

'Depends, don't you think?' By her intonation I could tell she expected no answer. 'Go talk to him, why not? I'll be over shortly.'

Valerie waved briskly as I approached. 'You've got a school tie, too,' she said, recognizing my cravat, having seen its mate often enough around Charles's neck.

'I didn't know if you were coming or not,' he said, smiling. 'You know the chairman of the English department? Doctor Buebenhofer?' The doctor, bald and dowdy, lounged in a chair across the table; looking up at me from behind the bowl of eggnog he grunted, as if to be polite.

'Mutual,' I said.

'His latest project's a video for the MLA,' said Charles.

'Doctor, let me tell you about something.' Valerie said. He seemed nominally more interested in her than he had in me. 'Charles and I are developing a new critical approach.'

'I've heard,' said the chairman.

'Like to hear it from people who know what they're talking about?'

'No one works at a party,' Charles said, interrupting. 'Some other time.'

'This isn't work.'

'*Valerie!*' He spoke her name as he would have called Cecily's. Tapping me on the arm, he gestured that I should lower my head, to hear something he had to say. Valerie scooted her chair forward, and then she reclined; with movements as obvious as they were subtle, she took his left hand in hers and pulled it off the table.

'Having a good time?' he asked, his mouth at my ear. 'You're not still mad at me, are you?'

'I don't understand why you acted as you did.'

'There're reasons,' he said. 'We should talk. We should.'

'Well?'

'Not here. Later.' His gaze fixed itself upon the ceiling, as if he saw heavenly hosts hung from above. Valerie stared ahead, appearing hypnotized by the candelabra's electric flames. Bringing up her hands, she fondled her scarf; loosening its knot, she retied it tightly, drawing the silk around her throat. 'Shame to have trouble over the holidays,' he muttered. Elaine smiled, sidling up to her husband.

'Charles,' she said. 'I need to ask you something.'

'Be right with you, dear,' he said, not moving.

'It won't take a minute.'

'After the party, Elaine.'

Bending down, she seized the tablecloth's hem in her hands. With effortless motions she whipped it away; glassware and crockery shattered against the floor. Eggnog drenched the doctor's tweed. Through the glass-topped table all saw Valerie's panties hanging loosely around one knee, resembling a loosened restraint. Her feet were braced against the table legs as the curtain rose; at the instant of exposure she clamped shut her thighs, entrapping Charles's hand within her dark curls. He couldn't immediately free himself; when he did, jerking back his arm, his ring rapped sharply against the glass, concluding the cacophony, calling the company to attention with a resounding chord as if announcing a toast.

'Are you moving in with her before or after Christmas?' Elaine asked, her attitude preternaturally calm. She left the room, pushing Cecily back from the door. Her supporters hastened after her. Charles's associates glanced at one another before filing into the hall, refusing to look behind them. The doctor rushed to the bathroom to see if his suit might be salvaged.

Valerie looked at me as she stood; matching my stare, she lifted her dress and pulled up her underwear with the aplomb of a bather preparing to leave the beach. Charles looked to have had electroshock, if not a lobotomy; he clasped his hands before him as if to say grace.

'Honey?' he called out. 'It's not what it seems.'

In February I ran into Valerie as she emerged from a drugstore on Columbus. 'Got a few minutes?' she asked, entwining her arm with mine. We went to the coffee shop on 86th. Valerie left her muffler on; the fluorescent glare illuminated a dime-sized bruise on her forehead.

'Charles misses you,' she said. 'He'd never say, but I can tell. Half a dozen times I've tried getting him to call you, but it's like talking to the wall.'

'We argued the last time we got together before the party. Right here, in fact.'

'I know. He felt bad about it, once I told him he should. Keep in mind he's been himself more than he's not been himself, lately.' She dumped seven packs of sugar into her coffee and stirred it into a whirlpool. 'You probably just misread each other's texts, though I wonder for how long.'

'The longer we were friends, the less I knew him.'

'The first time I met you I thought you two were lovers once,' she said, slipping off her shoes, lifting her legs onto the booth's seat. Contorting herself into a variorum lotus position, tucking her feet beneath her, she began rocking back and forth, as if hearing music. 'Your body language fooled me. But I can't figure out why you've stayed friends so long. Do you know? Would you say, if you do?'

'We went to school together.' I hadn't better reasons to offer.

'Do you like me?' Valerie asked. 'I mean, you don't dislike me, do you?'

'Why do you ask?'

'Most of his friends think I'm bad for him. Elaine does, certainly.'

'You're surprised?'

'We've had an equal relationship,' she said. 'I was sure you liked me. I'm glad you admit it. Men your age usually don't talk at all. Ones my age never shut up. Are you as close-mouthed about yourself as Charles is?'

'Different reasons.'

'He's better, but it's still like pulling teeth. Ask me anything and I'll talk about it, I have neither pride nor shame.' Valerie patted her muffler while she bobbed in place; sighed, as if relieved it was there. 'He talks about you.'

'What's he say?'

'You care? You disappointed him. He thought you'd understand.'

'How could I? Wouldn't tell me what was going on—'

'Charles said that's what you should have understood.' Valerie swept her hair from her face. 'He told me he wanted to be closer to you, but you wouldn't let him. When you think someone's getting too close, you run. That's what he said.'

'Distance myself if something's too painful. Sure not alone in that.'

'When you kept pressing him that time, he told me he blew up.' Her body's rhythm counterpointed that of her speech. 'Said he knew how to drive you away. That's what he did, obviously. I don't believe he knew how upset you'd be.'

'What'd he expect?' I asked. 'Don't know if I'd talked to him, even if he'd called.'

'I doubt it,' she said. 'Otherwise you'd have called him. I gave you my number once, and you could have guessed he was staying with me.' She drank her coffee in two swallows and signalled the waiter for more. He served her at once. 'What got you so upset?'

'He did something, reminded me of something he did before.' Resting her elbows atop the table, moving her body as before, she reached up and wound her muffler once more around her neck. 'Doesn't bear repeating,' I concluded.

'That's what he'd say. You two are more alike than you'd ever admit.'

'How is he?'

'Could be better. NYU might let him return for the summer semester but tenure's a moot point. He's told Elaine she can have everything, but that's not enough. She won't let him see Cecily. His wife's so insecure. I think they stayed together because each reminded the other of their least intimidating parent.'

'What's he doing?'

'Hangs around the apartment. Rewrites our notes. My ideas were easy to understand until he improved them. I write a sentence, he rewrites a chapter. He puts masks on, I try to get them off.' Her eyes widened; they were bluer than I'd remembered. 'Charles thinks nothing's academic if you understand it.'

'I know. That causing you trouble?'

'We have our disagreements,' she said. 'I'm not sure we bring out the best in each other, but we have brought out what's really there. That's as much as you can expect in a relationship. Too much for most people. I don't know if he'll be staying with me after March. Couldn't stand many more rewrites.'

'You and Charles have been having an affair, haven't you?' I asked.

'He wouldn't call it that.' She rocked more slowly; her muffler slipped away from her throat, which was as red as his had been. 'He never expected to have this kind of relationship, so he thinks of it as being something apart. If you asked do we fuck each other, there's no denying. How did we seem when you saw us together?'

'Isolated.'

'I asked him why we had to pretend we were Warren Harding and niece around you. He said it would make you uncomfortable if we didn't, and you'd run.'

'No,' I said. 'He's hurt everyone, the way he's acted. Needlessly hurt himself. It's masochistic.'

'You think so?' she asked, holding her muffler against her neck with her hands. 'It's as much deliberate as needless. Not entirely masochistic.'

'Masochists love the sin and hate the sinners. That's Charles.'

'Not in every situation,' she said. 'You can't be happy without pain. Charles does what he can.' I nodded. 'Do you know anything about his childhood?'

'His parents were old guard. That's all he's said.'

'Something happened to him back then that he won't let me unravel. May not have been anything major. You never know what'll affect you most, years later.' Valerie returned one of her feet to the floor, resting it alongside mine. 'But he won't tell me what happened,' she said. 'I could tell you a horrible thing that happened to me.'

'Some people have no trouble doing that.'

'That's what Charles told me,' she said, closing her eyes. 'It was in junior high. One afternoon I was practicing gymnastics after everyone else had left.'

'Valerie, if it's something I don't need to know, don't—'

'Maybe you do,' she said, her movements more deliberate. 'Two girls jumped me while I was in the shower and dragged me into a practice room that was being redone. They jammed an empty paint can on my head. They bent me over a balance beam and tied me to it. They held my legs apart and then their boyfriends came in. First one, then the other.'

Valerie told of what was done to her as if recounting the plot of a movie she'd seen, weaving the narrative with such precision that I would never have attempted an unravelling. The flat manner in which she related her story assured me of its essential truth; the details, almost lovingly expressed, led me to believe that her remembrance had been told not infrequently but many times, if only to herself. Perhaps the act of continual revision enabled her to tell it at all.

'My coach came back to get something and heard me trying to get loose. He untied me but I couldn't get the can off my head. I was suffocating. When I passed out I relaxed, and he was able to work it loose. When I came to he was standing over me, looking. I was still naked.'

Letting go of her muffler, she stopped rocking, opening her eyes as if she'd been screamed awake; her body shivered, her face flushed. At first I thought she was going to cry; then realized her tears wouldn't have flowed in sorrow. No one was watching; Valerie moved the foot upon which she'd been sitting down to the floor, where she prodded my shoe with her toes.

'I was fourteen,' she said.

'Are you all right? I mean—'

She smiled. 'It affected me, but I deal with it.'

'The boys and girls who hurt you,' I said, convincing myself that I shouldn't find an excuse to leave. 'You reported them? Were they arrested?'

'They were on the team. They knew people. Knew my coach. I was suspended. They went to good schools.'

'That's—'

'Typical,' Valerie said. 'I dealt with it. Stare at a wound long enough and it doesn't hurt anymore. You'll see its beauty, eventually.' She studied the table's surface, as if becoming aware of something previously unseen. 'Has part of your problem been that you're attracted to me, too?'

Caught unaware as I was, I'm uncertain of what I showed; Charles once told me my face was as readable as a cheap novel. Valerie must have inferred much from my hesitation. 'You're beautiful,' I said. 'You have a remarkable mind.'

'Charles said that when I asked him what he thought of me. Were you two ever in love with the same woman?'

The nature of his response to Valerie was clear to me that afternoon – it was fascination as well as attraction, as when a deer freezes, seeing oncoming lights. Either of us would have confessed to anything if she said we should. 'It's more complicated than that,' I said.

'What was her name?'

'Gail,' I said. 'We were together through our junior year.'

'What happened?'

'I don't think about it.'

'Except when you do,' she said. 'Tell me. We'll keep each other's secrets.'

'We argued, one night,' I said. 'About what, I don't remember. Charles saw I was upset. He told me he'd talk to her. Smooth things over. Next night he went to her apartmmet. She lived off campus. Valerie, I don't think—'

'What did he do?'

'He was still asleep when I woke up. I called Gail. She hung up when she heard me. Wouldn't let me in when I went to her apartment. Stood at her door and asked her what happened. She said go ask your friend. When I got back to the house Charles was having breakfast.'

'Keep talking. It's all right. What did he say?'

'He told me she was drunk. One thing led to another. When she woke up, he said she got weird and he left.'

'You didn't believe him.'

'I kept saying tell me what really happened. He started telling me what they'd done. What she did to him. In detail. Smiling the whole time he told me. Finally said if Gail and I ever slept together again he wouldn't be surprised if she called out his name instead of mine.'

Valerie stroked my face with her hand, caressing my cheek, pressing her fingertips under my ear. 'She was your first girlfriend?' she asked. 'Only girlfriend?'

'She thought I sent him over to her. I did. He offered to go, I said yes. It was my fault too.'

'It wasn't,' Valerie said. 'It's all right. It is. What happened to Gail?'

'She didn't report it. No one did, back then. We didn't get back together. Month later she transferred to Berkeley.'

'And you stayed friends with Charles after that?' I nodded. She petted my ear; ran her tongue along her lips, as if they were dry. 'I guess you do understand masochism.'

'Getting late, Valerie,' I said. 'I better go.'

'But you don't have to run, do you?' she asked. 'Not this time.'

'Give my best to—' She slapped my face, as if in play. 'Get home safe.'

'He's home, or I'd say walk me there. I keep telling him he doesn't get out enough. I'm glad you live close by.' She watched me rise. 'We should start hooking up more often.'

'I'll call.'

'Charles gave me a lot of new material,' Valerie said, smiling. 'I could use a good editor.'

FORWARD TO: Editorial Production
Legault & Van Gelder/Adv Forens Compan/JANUARY

The following account appears to be the only case in the literature involving joint participants in what has been recently (Hazelwood, Dietz, Burgess, 1983) termed Kotzwarraism, [FLAG 32] or hypoxyphilia. The diagnostic criteria for these paraphilia include the acting out of masochistic fantasies involving torture, abuse or execution and a desire for sexual arousal through risk-inherent situations, being generally in these cases the employment of a preferred mode of self-induced (or, induced through the agency of others; op.cit. Asa and Burroughs, 1978) sexual excitement by means of mechanical or chemical asphyxiation. This case should be considered sui generis but the patterns are unmistakable.

129. The victims were a fifty-year-old Caucasian male and a twenty-two-year old Caucasian female. A good state of preservation was observed, the temperature within the female deceased's studio apartment being forty degrees Fahrenheit [FLAG 33].

Both victims were nude, obliquely reclined back to back in arched positions, touching only at the head and heels. An electrical cord was attached at one end to the female deceased's neck by a slip knot, and tied at the other end around the male deceased's ankles. Another cord interconnected her ankles to his neck in like manner. Both victims were also tied together at the neck with a blue and white repp necktie looped and knotted around the throats of the victims [FLAG 34]. Commercial lubrication cream was detected in the rectum of the female deceased. A small pink ribbon was tied in a bow at the base of the male deceased's penis. No signs of struggle were noted. Neither a suicide note nor any writings indicative of depressive states were found.

The positioning of the victims assured that the leg movements of one would exert increasing pressure upon the neck of the other, compressing the carotid baroreceptors, slowing the heart rate, within a short time causing unconsciousness. The male deceased died of asphyxia due to laryngeal ligature. The female deceased died concurrently through vagal inhibition. Examination of the slip knots, in these cases often serving as a self-rescue mechanism, revealed that the female deceased's hair had become entangled in her cord's knot, precluding release. It was not evident that such release was attempted.

Six metal hooks had been installed in the ceiling to facilitate bondage activity. A dented metal wastepaper can showed signs of having been recently worn on the head by the female deceased as an entrapment device. Thirty-nine standard school notebooks kept in file cabinets were found to contain variant texts of a masochistic fantasy written in the hand of the female deceased.

Prescriptions for Stelazine and Tofranil in the name of the female deceased had been recently filled. The male deceased's evident possessions consisted of a travel-size toiletry case. Among the female deceased's possessions were a braided leather whip of the type known as a cat o'nine tails, lengths of 3/8" diameter hemp rope, three spools of cloth twine, two children's red jump ropes, twenty feet of clothesline, a roll of piano wire, a pair of wire clippers, battery cables, two Polaroid SX-70 cameras and eight boxes of film, seventy-three developed Polaroid photographs depicting the female deceased in earlier asphyxial episodes, battery-operated vibrating devices of assorted sizes including one capable of ejecting warmed fluids, six books on yachtsmanship and sailing, a sculler's oar, two wooden paddles of a model used frequently in fraternity/sorority initiations, scrotum weights, a penis vice, and a leather belt studded along its inner length with carpet tacks [FLAG 35].

Smiles noted on the faces of both deceased were ascribed to rigor mortis until investigators ascertained the estimated time of death [FLAG 36].

32 Correct? Not in Stedman's.
    OK.
33 Dangling.
    Not unexpected in these accounts. Fix.
34 Hard to picture as described.
    Photo en route to Art Department should clarify.
35 Authors as obsessional as victims. Cut?
    List already trimmed by half.
36 Necessary?
    Stet.

ICE PALACE

by

Douglas Clegg

Douglas Clegg was born in Virginia, but has lived in Los Angeles for nine years. He has published the novels *Goat Dance, Breeder*, and *Neverland*. *The Dark of the Eye* is just out from Pocket Books in the United States. His short stories have been published in the magazines *Cemetery Dance, Deathrealm* and *The Scream Factory* and in the anthologies, *Love in Vein* and *Best New Horror*. He has an upcoming story in my untitled cat horror anthology.

When I joined a sorority in high school my initiation consisted of a 'Hell Night'. I remember dressing up in a silly outfit and rolling a raw egg down the street with my nose. It was terrific fun. So when I read in the news about young men dying from their 'hazing' and initiations in college or military academies I always find it a somewhat alien concept.

'Ice Palace' brought me a little closer to understanding some of the psychological dynamics of these rituals.

ICE PALACE

1

I once helped murder a boy when I was nineteen, only we didn't think of ourselves as boys back then. It was in college, at a university in the mountains of Virginia, when the snow had piled up and the parties were in full swing. I lived with my brothers — we weren't blood relations, except through the college fraternity system. It was February, and certain aspects of fraternity hazing were not yet complete. It was always in the harshest part of the season that the sadistic rituals took place on campus, from paddling to raiding to a particularly cruel torture called Ice Palace.

I was just buttoning up my shirt, about to start shaving, when Nate Wick, known as the Wicked Wick or the Flaccid Wick, grabbed me by the collar and slammed me against the wall; the whole world shook and I cussed him out something fierce; his face was all scrunched up like he was about to cry. He had hair growing from his ears even at twenty-one, and fat cheeks like a cherub gone to seed. I socked him in the jaw, 'cause he could be crazy sometimes, even if he *was* my fraternity brother. He took the blow pretty good, and my fist ached like a son-of-a-bitch, and he dropped on my bed, right on the wet towel, so it made a smack kind of sound, and if he hadn't been naked I'd've grabbed *him* by *his* collar and heave-hoed him right onto the balcony where it was twenty below and iced smooth.

'Damn it, Wick,' I said, 'you drive me, you know that? You drive me, Christ.'

'Drive you what? Nuts?'

'You just drive me, that's all,' I said, finally catching my breath.

Nate said, slyly, 'I know what you want, Underdog. I know what you want.' I felt my face going red. Something disturbed me about his comment.

'What the jizz you shittin'?' Stan, ever the poet, said from the doorway to my room. Stan was naked, too, which was pretty much how the guys went around on a Saturday morning in February when the nearest open road to the girl's college was ten miles away. It was funny, being as generally modest as I was, how I'd got used to all this flaunted nakedness in the ice cold mornings. I never got out of the showers myself except with a big blue towel around my waist, and never left my room except with a shirt and khakis on.

Nate began laughing and I figured, given his jug face, that I hadn't even caused him a moment's pain; but I was still mad 'cause I hated being surprised like that. Everything in that frat house was a surprise attack, especially on Big Weekends. Nate was on edge on account of his girl might not be making it down for Fancy Dress, so there was a chance he might be the dateless wonder. Nate said, 'Look, Underdog, we got the pledges coming over for Ice Palace, and you look like a queer from Lynchburg.'

'If that's what you think, jerk-off, then you better not lie naked on my bed too long with that come-hither look on your face,' I said. I went back to shaving in the bowl I'd put beneath the mirror in my room for privacy; it saved me from running to the communal and much-pissed-upon bathroom every time I needed to shave or wash.

Stan said, 'Fuck the fuck it very.' It was a line he said often, sober or drunk, and I couldn't figure it out for the life of me. He had patches of hair up and down his body, armpits to knees, like he had some ape pattern baldness problem. 'I can't wait for tonight, girls, I'm gonna get me some fine pussy, fine pussy.'

'Underdog,' Nate addressed me in his usual manner, 'the hose queen's coming down tonight. You want to get laid?'

'No thanks, and get out of here, willya?'

This particular winter semester, my second year, Nate, who was my Big Brother in the House, wanted me to learn how to be a man as only Nate knew how. It wasn't enough that I was flunking Physics for Poets because of the mid-week grain parties, nor that I had no interest in cow-punching or whore-hopping. Nate was a wild man and rich redneck from Alabama, and his life was something to marvel at. He had learned the ropes of human sexuality at twelve from his babysitter; at seventeen, he'd saved an entire boat-load of immigrants off the coast of Bermuda – losing three toes in the process. He *knew* life, how to live it, what paths to go down, when and where to get a hard-on and what to do about it and with whom. The bizarre part was, he was an honours student, his old man ran one of the growing tobacco companies, and he never, *ever* had a hang over.

*

Somebody stuck a condom in the scrambled eggs that morning, a typical frat joke, so I passed on breakfast and headed up to the Hill to do some studying on campus. I didn't have a date for the Fancy Dress Ball that night, even though I'd bought two tickets well in advance thinking this girl I knew from high school, named Colleen, might want to go, or maybe I'd meet someone else last minute. But Colleen was not to be wooed down to what she called the Last Bastion of the Old South. I called three girls I knew Down The Road, but each had a date since October. One of them was kind enough to say she could set me up with this really homely girl who was a Chem major. I passed, and figured I'd get some studying done for once, and let them all go to hell. I was determined to spend the day studying not scrounging for dates or hazing freshmen.

But Nate was not one to give up easily in his quest to keep me from doing anything productive. He hunted me down on campus, shut my American History book for me, sat on the edge of my desk and said, 'you missed Ice Palace.'

'Big deal. Jesus H., quit following me around like some kind of retriever.'

'Jonno told a good one. Got us laughing right off. BugBoy practically froze to death, we had to let him off after about half an hour just 'cause we were getting bored watching his lips turn purple. Only one part left,' he said.

I groaned. 'Yeah, yeah, the crowning of the King. It's like being with Nazis in kindergarten.'

'Hey, it takes a special kind of guy to be King of the Palace.' Nate Wick had a snarly way of talking, that was both seductive and distancing, as if he were an untamed dog waiting for the right master. 'Ice Palace is almost as good as fish dunking.'

'I hate the whole thing. Ice Palace could make one of them sick.'

'You liked it well enough last year.'

'Well, I was drunk last year. I liked lots of things then.'

'Well, piss on you, Underdog. Sometimes I wish the old you would come back, the one that would stay out all night and really howl.' But his mood changed again. 'We're gonna kidnap Lewis,' he said, like he was planning out the day in his head. He grinned so bright I thought the sun had come out from the grey sky outside the window.

'When?'

'This afternoon. Few hours.'

'Shit,' I said, 'Jesus, of all days. He's your King? Christ, Wick, that poor son-of-a-bitch won't last three hours in the cold. He's got bronchial asthma, he'll come down with something.' The truth was, I was protective of Stewart Lewis, who didn't even have the hapless luck to be a brain, for he was skinny and homely and not too bright; if he hadn't been a Legacy, he would've gotten blackballed by sixty per cent of the House. But his old man was a major brother back in the fifties, so the frat had no choice, because it was in the charter to take Legacies no matter what. I had known Stewart Lewis back at St Sebastian's, the Episcopal school I'd gone to before college. Lewis was always a weenie, always sick, always a mama's boy, always something not so good.

Nate dismissed Lewis with a snap, and then a slap on the desk. 'He's a Spam, don't worry about him. We're gonna take him to Crawford's Dump, stick him in the snow, pay Donkeyman to watch him, tie him up, nothing bad. We won't leave him there all night, you fiend. Just a couple of hours, and then I'll go get him in time for Fancy Dress. I doubt he's got a date, though. He's such a Spam. Maybe we'll write on him. The usual. Scare the kid a little. Just a shit speck. He'll get to wear his Jockeys, whatta you want? Whatta you want?'

'You always sound homo to me when you talk about it,' I said, hoping to get him angry. I was only a sophomore, but I'd hated hazing so much from the year before – I'd been too blotto to protest too much – that I felt very protective of the poor freshman pledges who went along with any idiotic torture that seniors like Nate devised.

'Maybe I am homo, Underdog. Wanta suck it to find out?' Here he whipped out his thing, which was not the most unusual sight between frat brothers, and was, perhaps, a big reason why we were all so homophobic. Then, he put it back in his trousers, zipped up, and said, 'you gonna go tonight?'

'Why? You want to buy my ticket?'

'Just wondering. I'm not always as insensitive as I seem, buttface.'

It started to snow again, and the wind picked up outside, whistling around the old brick and columns along the Colonnade; feather flakes seesawed beyond the bevelled glass of the windows. It was an ancient campus, from the 1700s, all columns and Greek parthenons and mountain vistas, and I wished I was somewhere, anywhere, else.

'Look,' Nate said, 'Helen's coming up from Hollins. She likes you. She said she wants to see you.' Helen was his girlfriend, a pretty girl who, for some reason, idolized Nate, possibly because she was more unbalanced than she seemed – there was a hint of this in her Sylvia Plath-like scribblings. I thought she was too good for him.

'That's nice,' I said, and then, 'look, Nate, I don't want Lewis to go to Ice Palace. He'll get sick. If Dean Trask hears about it, we could get shut down. Think about that. I mean, a half hour of Ice Palace is one thing, but three or four hours, and it's snowing . . . it's not that funny.'

Nate laughed, drumming his fists into the desk. I'd seen him pummel a stray dog like that once, just because the dog was in his way. That was how he used his fists most of the time. He said, 'I think it's a goddamn laugh riot.'

I avoided the frat house until six, when hunger got the best of me. I was wary of most of my brothers, because I wasn't good at taking any kind of teasing, and that seemed to be their primary business in college. When I entered the foyer, I smelled the steaks — it was a special night, Fancy Dress Ball and all that, and so our cook was doing it up good, steak and asparagus and biscuits and potatoes and fruit and jello and apple pie. Most of the brothers had taken their dates out to dinner, but the poorer among us sat at the long tables, not yet dressed in black tie, with dates astride hard-backed chairs. Plain girls, too, for the most part, until, upstairs, in a guarded bathroom, they would make-up and spray, vaseline their teeth for smiles, and later, for other, more urgent desires; spruced with expensive, oversized gowns, and their mothers' Shalimar or L'Air du Temps; transforming from ordinary faces and bodies to creatures of unconscionable beauty; perhaps gaudy in the garish light of the upstairs bathroom, but almost mythic, the Woman In All Her Glorious Aspects, in the dimmed, squinting light over at the student centre, where the Ball would be held.

Nate called out, 'Underdog!' He was at the last table, with Helen at his side. She looked up briefly, and then down at her plate again; flash of curiosity about me, about what I'd been up to since last summer, dying in her face. She was skinny — looked like she had starved herself for this one night — and she'd greased her hair back around her ears with some sort of conditioner.

I went over and took a chair, grabbed some slop and lopped it on my plate. 'Helen,' I said.

'Hey, Charlie,' she said, sweetly, her accent growing more Southern with each year she spent in Virginia. She did not look up from her plate, but it was obvious she hadn't eaten.

Nate lip-farted, 'Call him Underdog. Humble but lovable.'

I smiled at Nate. 'Things go okay with Lewis?'

Nate winked, 'Fine, fine.'

'He around?'

'Yeah. I don't know. I guess he was upset.'

I wasn't sure whether to believe Nate or not, but Helen must've detected my doubt. She said, 'He said he was going to a movie. He was very upset. Y'all are so dang insensitive. It's what I hate, absolutely hate, about y'all being in a fraternity and all.'

'Helen's on the rag,' Nate half-whispered loud enough for all six tables to hear.

I looked to Helen, and reached my hand across to touch hers because I felt so bad for her at that moment, stuck with Nate, Nate who bragged about doing her on his waterbed, about muff-diving her in the backseat of her father's Continental, taking her every which way but loose up in the carillon tower of chapel when she didn't want it but loved it anyway. I didn't know Helen well, but I wanted to touch her more than anything.

Helen glanced up at me, her eyes dry. Nate was clanking his fork on the side of his plate. He was always jealous when it came to Helen, and he must've seen the way she looked at me.

'Why don't you just fuck her?' he asked, shoving himself away from the table, his chair falling backwards. He was drunk; so that was it. He stomped across the room, and went upstairs.

Helen said, 'I hate him.'

'Nah,' I said, 'he's a jerk sometimes. But he has his good side.'

Helen laughed, 'No, he doesn't. I don't know why I'm even here.'

'Okay,' I agreed, willing to go with the flow, 'why are you here?'

She shut her eyes, her face taut, her hands in fists. Then, she opened her eyes, unclenched, and said, 'Because I'm a good girl. Because I do what I'm told.' She said it like it was taking her medicine, an antidote to some other, more profound venom. And then, 'Will you go with me tonight? I don't want to go with him.'

2

There are certain humiliations we will withstand when we are young, if it means that we can become part of something bigger than just ourselves, by ourselves. This notion upheld all the tortures of hazing.

Ice Palace was a peculiar ritual, in which a tunnel was dug out in the snow, at least the length of a man's body. The pledges had to dig it, for they were virtual slaves to the upperclassmen, and it always reminded me a bit of stories I'd heard about the Jews digging their own graves before the Nazi guard. Then, one at a time, the pledges were stripped down to their underwear. Each was then hosed down with water, and sent into the tunnel which was now deemed the Ice Palace. The pledge had to sit back in the freezing ice and tell a joke until every upperclassman present laughed. When I had gone through Ice Palace, I had got them laughing within ten minutes, so it hadn't been too hard on me. There had even been something of a respite from the outer world when I had crawled back into that ice cave, shivering for sure, but also experiencing a strange pleasure, as if I were protected in a way I didn't quite understand. Some pledges could not tell a joke to save their lives, however, and so it could be a painful, if not simply chilling experience. This was one of the least pleasant aspects of hazing. The other rituals (egg-yolk-passing from mouth to mouth, or fish-dunking in a toilet) were disgusting, but essentially harmless. Even paddling was child's-play, with the only casualty being a sore butt for a few days.

But Ice Palace . . . I thought of Stewart Lewis, with his taped-up glasses on his beaky nose, his small peapod eyes, that squirmy way he had of moving as if he had worms or something, and of the humiliation of the whole ritual, particularly of being chosen to be the King of Ice Palace, as he had been. King of Ice Palace: the honour at the shit end of life's stick. The pledge got chosen basically because he was commonly known as the Spam, the Nerd, the Loser, the Meat. There was always one pledge who fit this bill – almost as if, each year, the brothers decided to admit someone they could torture, someone who was so desperate to be accepted that he would take it.

The King's hands and feet were roped together and he was to be sealed up in Ice Palace until someone came to get him out. Cold water was hosed over the entire tunnel in order to truly give it a thick layer of ice. Then, after a set period of time, the Brother High Alpha, which in our case was Nate, would break open the door to Ice Palace. The King would come forth from his white chamber, freezing and cursing, yet somehow stronger, and more part of the group than he could ever be through ordinary means. If the chosen one tried to get out early, there was Donkeyman, the local wino. He was as scary as any nightmare, his face elongated, his ears out and pointy like a mule's, only three teeth in his head, and barely a nose at all, just two flared nostrils exhaling frosty clouds of carbon dioxide. The freshmen weren't familiar enough with the university to have seen Donkeyman yet, for Donkeyman was a creature of alleyways and dumpsters. He was perfectly harmless, but he looked like the demon lover of donkeys.

Ice Palace was a fraternity secret and, by all accounts, illegal, at least as far as the college went. If it had been known that it was an

ongoing ritual, the entire fraternity system, which was then enjoying a rebirth in popularity, would have been shut down.

There was a story that, back in the late fifties, a boy had died in Ice
Palace.

3

'That's the boy,' Helen whispered in my ear. We were slow-dancing,
off the dance floor. She had abandoned Nate to his drunken fury
earlier in the evening, and, because I owned my own tux, she had
grabbed me and driven me up to the student centre and the Ball
before I could protest too much. I felt a little guilty for snaking my
Big Brother's date, but she was pretty and he was acting like an
asshole anyway.

I glanced up from her shoulder, for I had been watching the bone
there, beneath the skin, so delicate, so feminine. Smelling her, too,
like jasmine with the snow just on the other side of the walls, and
here there were flowers and sandalwood. 'Huh?' I asked.

'That boy,' she said, dreamily, 'the one they put in the snow.'

We stopped dancing, and I turned around to look at Stewart Lewis.
'I didn't know he was going to be—' I said, but then, there was no
Stewart.

Just Stan The Man, who came over and slapped me on the back,
'Fuck the fuck it very,' he said, his breath, stinking of whiskey. 'So,
Underdoggie, you got Nate's squeeze, bravo, good job, didn't deserve
her, the Flaccid Wick didn't, my god, this wine tastes like cow jism.'
His eyes barely registered either of us; his date, Marlene, stood off to
the side, avoiding just about everyone.

'Stan wasn't Ice Palace King,' I told Helen. 'Is that who you saw in
Ice Palace?'

'I didn't see him,' Helen turned away from me, waved to a friend.
'Nate told me, it was him. Isn't that Stewart,' and then, to Stan,
'aren't you Stewart Lewis?'

'The Spamster?' Stan guffawed, 'lawdy, no, Miss Scarlett, I don't
no nothing about birthin' no babies.'

'He's too drunk to make sense,' I said. 'Nate told you?'

Helen shrugged. 'I thought this guy was Stewart. You boys all look
alike with your khakis and down jackets. Are you sure you're not
Stewart?'

Stan grinned, but wobbled back to Marlene, who apparently
scolded him for something.

'Jesus, I wonder if he ever let Lewis out,' I said. 'Look, Helen, you wait here, I'll be back in a while.'

'Charlie,' Helen said, not even startled. 'Charlie.'

'What?' I snapped, and then blurted, 'My god. My god. It'll kill Lewis. It'll kill him.' I left her there, and ran through the make-out room just beyond the dance floor, out through the French doors, down the icy steps, almost slipping on the concrete pavement. The town was a small one, almost a town in miniature, and I didn't own a car. It would be a ten minute jog down Stonewall Drive to get to the House, and to Nate, if he was still there. The night was a furious one, for while the snow had quieted to shavings from trees, the wind had picked up and had dropped the temperature at least twenty degrees. I was a decent runner then, but I had had two beers and this, with the wind, seemed to slow all motion down by half, so I felt like a half hour had passed before I was coming into the frat house from the back entrance. The lights were off in the kitchen; I flicked them up. The place was a mess, like a child's giant toybox overturned, but this was usual. What was unusual were the marks on the wall, as if someone had tried finger-painting with bacon grease – which there was plenty of around, for it was stored and used in another hazing ritual.

'Nate! Wick! Where the fuck are you?' I took the stairs two at a time, and came to his room on the second floor.

He lay in bed, with the light on. He was wearing his tux. He opened his eyes. 'Underdog.'

'Where's Lewis?'

'Lewis? Who the fuck cares? That human spittoon. You stole my girl, Underdog. You stole my girl.' He rolled over, away from me, facing the wall. 'You stole my girl. But fuck it. Like Stan says, fuck the fuck it very.'

I couldn't believe that even Nate would leave Lewis in Ice Palace for the eight hours he would've been in it by now. I almost laughed at myself for worrying. I caught my breath, my hands on my knees, bent over slightly. I looked at the poster of the naked girl with the snake that Nate had on his wall. She was some movie actress, I don't remember who, but her belly seemed to meet the boa constrictor in an almost motherly caress. 'Whew, Nate. Whoa, boy. You almost had me going. You know, you miserable – you know I ran all the way down here from Fancy Dress, just to – just to—'

'He's still in it.' He didn't turn to face me, but his voice was smug. 'And I'm the only one who knows where he is.'

'You're joking.'

'I'm joking, but the joke's on Lewis. Or should I say, you can now find Spam in the freezer section of your local supermarket.'

I went over and grabbed him by the back of his collar and hauled him off the bed. When he turned to face me, I slapped his face four times. 'Where is he?'

Calmly, Nate said, 'What the hell do you care?' There were tears in his eyes. 'What the hell do you care? It might as well be me in there, for all any of you care. Why don't you like me, Underdog? Why?' His tears were both a shock and a revelation to me: he was only a nine-year old in a twenty-one year old's body, the jug face was a mask, the rough talk, a cover, the attitude, a sham.

And I said what I felt, although I regretted it within the hour.

I said, 'Because you're not even human.'

4

We took his car, but I drove. 'You said you were doing Ice Palace at Crawford's dump,' I said, 'so we'll go there first. You better hope to God Lewis had the sense to break out of there.'

'I don't know,' he said, a sing-song to his voice. 'I gave Donkeyman some Chivas to do double-duty. I told him to hit Spam on the head with the shovel if he tried to get out. We hosed it down pretty good. Twenty below. Nice thick ice. Ice you could skate on. Ice *Palazzo*.' Nate was still crying, bawling like a baby, and singing; he had cracked; he was drunk; he kept trying to grab the wheel while I was driving.

Crawford's dump was the old graveyard just outside town, but there were few markers and even fewer showed through the heavy snow. I skidded the Volkswagen to a stop on the slick shoulder of the pot-holed, salt-strewn road, and left the headlights on. We tromped in our tuxes through the styrofoam crunch of snow, and each time Nate tried to pull away, I socked him in the shoulder and cussed him out. The snow and a clouded moon provided a soft light, making the dumping ground of the dead romantic, beautiful, sublime. Even Nate, when I spat my fury at him, looked beautiful, too, with the tears streaming, and his eyes always on me. The dump descended into a brief valley, where the entire cemetery spread out all around us.

'Where?'

Nate shrugged. His tears ceased. The wind, too, died, but we heard it howling around us, up the hill. Trucks out on the interstate blew their horns, one to another, and even the music from the Fancy Dress Ball, playing *The Swing*, could be made out.

'Where, Nate? Tell me.'

'Wherever Donkeyman is. You stole my girl, Underdog.'

'Look, asshole, Lewis is going to die. You hear me? You will have murdered a human being. Don't you get it? You tell me where that stupid Ice Palace is, or I will kill you with my bare hands.'

Nate blinked twice. 'Suck my dick.'

I got a good clear shot at his jaw, my second in one day, and then a knee in the groin, before he swung back; he clipped me, but I was off balance, and fell into the snow.

I thought for a second, just a second, I felt a gentle tugging.

There, in the snow.

Like a soft mitten, pulling me down.

Nate jumped on top of me, spitting all over my face as he spoke, 'You are my best friend, Underdog, you are my best friend in the world. Who the fuck cares about Lewis? Are you in love with him or something? Are you? Is that all you want? Lewis? Why are you doing this to me?' He began boxing my ears with snow, until I felt them go numb; I tried to heave him off me, but the mother was heavy; I felt that gentle tugging again. Soft. Like kittens on my back.

And then, something I had always known would happen, did happen. I just had never had a clue as to the form it would take.

Nate Wick kissed me on the lips as warmly and sweetly as any lover ever had.

Something clicked for me then, and for the longest minute in the world, I shut my eyes and just felt the warmth of those lips and the even tempo of my own breathing through my nostrils. I was somewhere else, and the cold of the snow was almost burning now, like a bed of warm coals against my tuxedo. His hands remained around my ears, and the sound of distant music, and trucks, too, their own music, voices up on the hillside, passers-by to whom we were invisible. The whiteness of snow; the indigo sky, all there, but without me seeing or hearing. His lips were rough and chapped, and I felt my own opening like a purse that had been kept too long shut; his upper lip grazed my teeth. His breath was a caustic brewery, but I held each one for as long as I could. I hated this boy, this man, so much, I hated him, and yet tied like this, together, unnaturally if we were to believe those who ran the world, we were perverse brothers, children playing. The blood rushed to my face, an unbearable burning sensation. I opened my eyes. His remained closed. I kissed a corner of his lips, and then the other. He made a deep noise, a churning machine somewhere within his gut, or igniting along his spine, as he rose and fell again, softly, like the tugging I felt in the rabbit-fur snow beneath my back. The knob of desire, or prick, or dick, or wang, whatever we had called it through all the shared moments of college life, pressed from his pants against mine. I shivered as much from embarrassment as from lust; but there was no one around, you see, no one within miles. I remembered him in the showers, soaping his underarms like he was scrubbing a saddle, tender and quick and then sandpapering at the last; the tumescence he had, which I noticed only peripherally. I hated him, I hated him.

He pressed the side of his face against mine and it was like holding someone for the first time, this boy, this innocent, angry, drunken boy, I wrapped my arms around him. 'I love you,' he whispered, and even though I smelled the alcohol, I sighed.

He said, 'Lewis was nothing. He was nothing.'

And then, my mind came back to me, through this physical revelation, through this lightning swift understanding of all I had done before in my life, as well as much of what Nate himself had done.

Lewis.

Stewart Lewis. The freshman that Nate Wick had chosen as King of Ice Palace.

'You fucked Lewis,' I said. 'You fucked him and then you buried him. Get the fuck off me!' I shoved hard, and he rolled back.

'No,' he said, rather meekly, not breaking eye contact with me. 'I didn't. He wouldn't let me. He . . . he didn't want me.'

I would've liked to have died right there, my secret self that I had worked so hard to hide buried forever in snow, but I was worried about Lewis. The kiss had made me forget him, briefly, but the reality of who and what Nate Wick was came back to me, a sour taste in the back of my throat. 'Get up, get up,' I stood, kicking him in the side. But he looked forlornly up at the moon, which had swept off its clouds, the lover's moon, I thought, the horny poking male moon, the prick of light, the howling desire of man's madness. I felt dirty, and picked up fresh snow and rubbed it on my face, my lips, to get that awful taste of *him* off me.

'It's so white,' Nate said, snow in his hands, too, packing a snowball which he threw at me as I wandered the valley.

At last, I saw a solitary figure, a minute man standing guard: the illustrious Donkeyman, his shovel struck firmly into a heap of snow. He was the whitest man I had ever seen and even at night, the pink eyes, the white hair, the chin stretched like putty, the ears, demonic. Blubbery lips, nostrils drippy with snot. He grinned, and brayed some greeting – the bottle of Chivas Regal lay empty beside him, along with several piss-stains at his feet. 'Preppie boy, how you?' he asked, congenially, waving the flashlight that he held tight in his gloved left hand. He had a hunter's flapdown hat on and an oversized tan duster around his shoulders, one that one of my frat brothers had no doubt loaned him for the night. 'King a Ice Palace, in there. I done my job. Got you another bottle?'

I took the shovel up and asked, 'Where?'

'I said, got you another bottle? Donkeyman done his job. Icy Palace, nobody goes in, nobody goes out,' he was pleased with himself, for he took pride in such work.

I threatened him with the shovel, until he pointed out the mound, not three feet away. I tapped it with the edge of the shovel. Hard as a rock. The ice of its outer layer gleamed, for Donkeyman shone his flashlight upon it.

'Lewis?' I shouted, 'Lewis!'

I listened, but there was only the adenoidal sniggering of Donkeyman as he lit himelf a Camel and puckered his lips at the first puff.

'King a Icy Palace ain't been talkin' since about six, seven. Done a good damn job. Best. You boys know it, too,' he spat a brown lungie in the snow.

I took the shovel up, down, up, down. The blade struck the outer edge of the Ice Palace. It was like breaking rocks in two. The ice finally creaked and cracked where I struck and snow began to fall rapidly as I worked.

5

I looked through the opening I had dug. Nate was already there at my side, perhaps sobering up a bit, because he seemed nervous and worried. Donkeyman patted me on the back now and again in my labour, cheering me onward. We were some crew.

'Lewis? Stewart!' I shouted into the tunnel.

Silence.

'I only had him make it maybe six feet in,' Nate said, with some regret.

I grabbed Donkeyman's flashlight, and shone it into Ice Palace. The tunnel in the ice and snow did go about six feet or so, but then there seemed to be a twist. Handprints in the ice, too, along the shiny white and silver walls. There were the ropes. 'He got out,' I said, almost relieved. 'He got out.'

'He got out,' Nate said, solemnly.

'Thank God, thank you God for saving Lewis' life,' I stood, leaning against the shovel.

Donkeyman said, 'He got out?'

'Underdog. Charlie,' Nate said.

'Thank God, you better thank God, Wick, because if he had died in there . . .well, you are one lucky s.o.b.'

Nate looked stunned, 'He didn't get out, Charlie.' Finally, for the first time in his life, calling me only by my real name.

'What do you mean?'

'I mean what I said. He didn't get out.'

'He must've. See for yourself.' I showed him the tunnel, and swirled the flashlight around to show the shape of the curve, to the left, barely visible. 'He got loose and dug around that way. The lucky bastard must've gone for about six yards or something, and then tunnelled up.'

'He didn't get out,' Nate repeated. He shoved me aside, and crawled into Ice Palace. I watched his ass shimmy through the thin tunnel, blocking my light.

'Nate, get out of there,' I called after him.

I heard his words echo through Ice Palace, 'I'm telling you, he didn't get out, I put him here, Charlie, I put him here, so I should know.'

'What's he mean by that?' I asked Donkeyman, as if he would have a coherent answer.

Donkeyman scratched his scalp beneath his cap and said, 'Don't know. The boy already done got Icy Palaced by the time the Donkeyman show up.'

I crawled in a ways, shining the flashlight first up ahead, and then to the frozen walls. Lewis' handprints, as if he'd pressed against the snow to try and push his way out here. But he must've realized that this end of the tunnel would be iced over from the water that Nate would toss over it. So Lewis — you smart dog — you figured on digging further, I thought, you miserable lucky nerd! Nate turned left, at the twist in the tunnel. I noticed a certain indentation in the inner ice wall. Letters of a word. I held the flashlight at an angle to make them out.

R E S U R

Then, a hint of red. A bit of fingernail. Lewis had cut his fingers in the stiff snow. He had stopped writing.

'Nate?' I called, but there was no answer, so I shuffled on my hands and knees, my back low but still pressing the ceiling, to catch up with him.

I turned the corner to the left, and stopped, for something was different.

I shone the flashlight all around.

I couldn't see Nate at all, anywhere, on top of which, the tunnel seemed to descend at the turn, rather than do the logical thing, which was to move forward and up. If Lewis were to escape, surely he would've tried to push *up?*

'Nate?' I cried through what now seemed an eternal tunnel of ice. 'Nate!'

My voice echoed.

There were other handprints there, in the ice, none of them the same. All were smeared, and some seemed impossibly thin; in one indentation, I saw what might've been a silken patch of the thinnest skin. I began to back up, to get out of the tunnel. As I reversed as far as I could, I turned a bit, shining the flashlight back toward the entrance.

It was once again sealed.

'Donkeyman!' I shouted. 'Donkeyman!'

I thought I heard him laughing, but perhaps it was not on the outside, but within this chamber, this tapeworm that had no end. This chamber of ice. I slammed my fist into the ceiling, but succeeded only in skinning my knuckles. Somehow, Donkeyman had sealed us in there again. I moved forward, the only place to go, past the hieroglyphs of hands and the sides of smooth bony faces, a thread of skin here, a spray of torn hair under my knees. The tunnel descended and then widened so I could move about a bit more; there was less air here, and what there was of it began to stink like sewage.

And then, something grabbed me by the wrist, and shook the flashlight out of my hand. It rolled to the side, shining its light against the wall, casting grey white yellow shadow.

I was in a room with others.

Nate whispered, 'I killed him, Charlie. I killed Lewis.'

I was too numb to be shocked by what seemed inevitable, for I had had a feeling from the beginning of the day that Nate would kill Stewart Lewis.

Nate leaned over and kissed me gently on the cheek, then my right ear. Something moved in front of us. 'I love you, Charlie. I'm scared. I mean, I'm really scared. I never been this scared.' His face shuddered, and I drew away from his caress.

I leaned forward, picking up the flashlight and shot its beam directly in front of us.

'Oh God,' Nate said.

It was Stewart Lewis, hunched in a wider chamber, his white oxford cloth shirt torn and bloody, with red and black slices through the skin of his chest. His khakis were muddy and soaked. I had never seen him without his glasses, but he seemed handsomer, with his hair slicked back, and a pale cast to his face. Around him, others, young men all, young and decayed, slashes along their arms, or blue flesh as if their blood were frozen, half naked, tendons dangling from some, others as beautiful as if they were alive, and in some respects I knew they were, and in some respects, they had not lived in a very long time.

Nate said, 'King of Ice Palace.'

Lewis grinned, naughtily, and leaned into us, until his lips were practically an inch from my face. 'Pleasures beyond life, Charlie, beyond the snow. The warmth of life, the sun within the flesh.'

Lewis turned his face towards Nate, who clung to my sleeve. 'One of you,' he said, his voice the same hopeless soprano of an undeveloped choirboy, but the face, full of fiercer authority, his lips drawn back, his eyes ice, ice, ice. 'One of you,' he said, 'is mine.'

Nate let go of my arm recoiling from me, and said, 'Him. Charlie. You can fuck him. You can do whatever you want to him.'

'Oh, Nate,' Lewis said, 'you wanted me, in the woods, you held the knife to my throat because you wanted me.'

'I'm not like that,' Nate said, pressing himself back against the wall. 'He is. Charlie's like that. It was because you wanted me to do it. That was all. I have a girlfriend. *Charlie*, tell him about Helen. *Tell him*.'

'You miserable—' I said, pushing at him. And then, I turned to Stewart Lewis. 'Lewis, what happened, what – what – are you?'

'King of Ice Palace, Charlie, just the way Nate wanted me. Frozen, consenting, helpless, Nate, give me your tongue, give me your wet sweet tongue, give me the fire of your breath, give me the secret you.' Lewis leaned into Nate, and I moved to the side, but could not get too far from them. Lewis and Nate had locked mouths, and I heard a gurgling, but not of terror or pain. It turned into a tender moan, like a kitten searching for its mother's milk. I watched in the white chamber as Nate's colour changed to a peach on his face, for this love was being passed between them, this frozen and glorious and fearful love.

All the young and dead men in the chamber watched as Nate pushed himself against the wall as if trying to break out of there. His hand traced a line along the shiny wall, gripping, becoming a clench of delight as Lewis leaned forward into him. Stewart Lewis was only newly resurrected, but it made me think how beautiful physical love could be, between two people, a doorway between two separate entities, that submission on both parts, that surrender to the warmth and the gasps of physical contact. I knew then why men enjoyed watching the sexual act almost as much as participating in it.

Because it is a celebration of the perverse, no matter the context, the thrusting buttocks, the muscular legs tight and kicking as if in combat, the slobbering mouth, the exquisite beauty of lost consciousness.

That can happen to me, yes, and that, too, you think when you watch one enter the other, one clasp his hands around the other's shuddering flesh.

I loved Nate Wick, and I loved Stewart Lewis, and I loved the boys who had died, for the ritual of the ice had been known since before I came into the world.

All of them, crowned for a season through years of winter, Kings of Ice Palace.

6

Leaving Ice Palace, while difficult, is not impossible, for the King is not a tyrant, neither is his court a prison. Nate never followed me out to the other side when the morning broke, but I think he was safer in there. I did not run from that place, but departed after having left my own handprints along its white walls.

I helped murder a boy once, or perhaps he had just become a man that night and did not want to return to the warming climates. He was my brother, although he was no blood relation. I do not believe that he is, in any real sense, dead, although his family has given up on him, as has his girlfriend, Helen.

Ice Palace: I do not wish to live there, not yet, although I venture into its white, secret chamber often on dark winter nights.

It is a secret chamber, Ice Palace.

Ice Palace.

But, even so, it is never as cold or as lonely as my days in the world above.

SERIAL MONOGAMIST

by

Pat Cadigan

Pat Cadigan was born in Schenectady, New York and now lives in
Overland Park, Kansas with her husband. In addition to being one of
the original 'cyberpunks', Cadigan has been writing an amazing
array of fantasy and horror stories throughout her career. She has
been consistently nominated for the sf field's top literary prizes and
won the Arthur C. Clarke Award for her novel *Synners*. *Fools* has
just been published by Harper Collins. In addition, Cadigan has
published three story collections: *Patterns*, *Home by the Sea* and
Dirty Work. She is currently collaborating on a novel of the
supernatural with Storm Constantine and working solo on *Woman
in Red*, a horror novel.

'Serial Monogamist' is a vicious little dish with plenty to offend
both sexes. Enjoy the feast.

SERIAL MONOGAMIST

Some people are serial monogamists the way others are serial killers.

Think about it: first, they stalk their prey, then they entice it. Then they do the deed and when it's over – when they decide it's over – they bury the bones and never look back.

When my sister left her husband, she came to stay with me. I'd been expecting this practically from the day she and Richard got married, so it wasn't a big surprise to me. Of course, considering Richard was her third husband, this shouldn't have been a big surprise to anyone, least of all Richard himself. But apparently he was sitting back there in their nice, big, comfortable house with a bottle of Absolut and ESPN on the big screen TV, still trying to figure out what had hit him.

'That's what he was doing when I left,' Julie said, plopping one of her suitcases onto the middle of the bed in my second bedroom. 'Watching motocross and getting shitfaced.' She flicked the locks open and tossed the lid back. Her clothes had been thrown in carelessly; now she shook them out, frowning at the wrinkles and glancing at me in that expectant way that meant, *Well, can't you tell what I need right now?* What the hell; her first day in, I would indulge her. I brought her some empty hangers from the closet.

'Thanks. Is there a place to hang these in the bathroom?'

'Just hang them up for awhile and let the worst of the wrinkles fall out of them,' I said. 'Then if any of them need the steam treatment, put them in there when you shower tomorrow.'

'I was going to take a nice long hot shower tonight,' she said, sounding just a little petulant.

'I ran the dishwasher *and* the clothes washer today. My hot water heater won't take that kind of burden. You'll have to wait till the morning.'

The disadvantages of leaving another husband were setting in early this time. She gave me that look that meant I had just denied her the one hope that had kept her going up till now and she might not be responsible for what her disappointment could make her do. In that way, disappointment and love were alike for her.

'Unless you have a hot date you need to clean up for,' I added.

Julie shook her head. 'No. No date,' she said offhandedly and brushed at the wrinkles in a jade green silk blouse. And right then, of course, I knew she'd left Richard because she'd found someone else. My sister never sounded that blasé about not having a date on any particular night, even on the night she'd left a husband. A serial monogamist's nose is always open for prey and none is ever comfortable without that scent perfuming each inhalation.

I watched her ferry clothing from the suitcase to the closet and resisted saying *So, what's his name?* – though it took a fabulously super-human effort. Calling her on it would only force her into a charade in which she acted out just 'bumping into' someone she'd been sneaking around with for weeks or months behind the unsuspecting Richard's back and I didn't care to have to watch this guy, whoever he was, awkwardly try to follow her script: 'So as not to scandalize my sister, who doesn't, you know, understand how these things can happen between two people.' Julie could always act rings around her leading man because she could make herself believe whatever she was saying at any given moment; the guy, on the other hand, believed in what she was saying at any given moment but since this was often contradictory from one occasion to the next, he would become completely disoriented. Julie would then teach him how to live from moment to moment – a favourite occupation of lovers, I've heard – and then suddenly he'd come to the moment when he'd find himself sitting alone in front of the TV with a bottle, watching a sport he'd given up out of deference to Julie's boredom, or sex drive, or both.

But I couldn't resist making her a *little* uncomfortable. She was imposing on me for the umpteenth time – this was only her third marriage but I'd lost track of her less-formal commitments, and I felt like exacting a little rent. It was the only kind of payment I was going to get.

'Look,' I said, 'why don't you call Richard tonight and ask him if this can be a trial separation for you. A cooling-off period. Then just hang out, get a job here through my temp service. I can even help you find a place that will given you a month-to-month lease—'

She shook her head. 'I think I'm experienced enough to tell the difference between a relationship that's just going through a rough patch and one that's dead. This one's cold and in the ground. And it makes me sad, it really does, because I was so sure that Richard was the man I was going to spend the rest of my life with.' She paused, hugging a white blouse to her front. 'Maybe *you* can't understand wanting to devote yourself to one person.'

I shrugged. 'Lots of things I don't understand. But I've decided to keep busy while I'm waiting for enlightenment.'

Julie sighed again. 'I've *been* busy, working my tail off at this marriage. Now enlightenment has come and I'm worn out. All I want to do is rest. I'm tired. I need some r-and-r.' She crawled onto the bed and lay down next to the suitcase, which still had a layer of underwear (or something) in the bottom. 'Don't worry,' she said, nestling her head on the pillow. 'I'll finish putting this stuff away later.'

'Good,' I said and left her there, lying under the overhead light on our grandmother's chenille bedspread and sniffing while she mourned the death of her latest marriage. Julie was always careful to mourn anything that died; as she had told me so often, it was very important to recover and go on with your life.

About fifteen minutes later, she was snoring. I shut off the phone ringers, put on the answering machine, and left.

I suppose I could have stayed out all night just by phoning my own number and leaving a message on the answering machine for Julie to pick up in the morning so she wouldn't worry. Except I really couldn't be sure that Julie would know how to work the answering machine correctly, because it was built into the fax machine – just the sort of technology that Julie found both frightening and offensive. *Big Brother* she would say knowingly.

Of course she said the same thing about programming the VCR, too. But then, Big Sister knew whereof she spoke better than even she herself realized – her presence cramped my style. I decided I'd save a night for later, when I'd want it more. Maybe Julie would be gone by then, too.

'You can only hope,' Fay said as we pulled up in front of my house at three a.m.

In the back seat, Carol and Pilar roused themselves from semi-sleep. 'Hey, if she's not gone in two weeks, do what you did last time,' said Carol with a yawn. She sat forward, poking her fuzzy head through the gap between the seats. 'Pretend to hire Pilar as your illegal alien minority cleaning woman.'

'Hey, get someone else this time,' Pilar said. 'I *actually* had to clean the whole refrigerator before she left and I've got to tell you, B.J., your sister is a *pig*.'

'You're telling me?' I said. 'Thank God I had a cleaning woman to take care of it.'

We all squealed with laughter at that one. 'So,' Fay said, wiping her eyes when we quieted, 'does this mean you're sitting out tomorrow night?'

'No way,' I said. 'I'll put sleeping pills in her Ovaltine if I have to, but I'll meet you at the usual place at the usual time. Don't forget the pheromones. And if you leave without me, I'll have you *all killed*.'

We all laughed again and Fay leaned over to give me a kiss good night.

'Dykes,' said Pilar.

'Lesbos,' Carol jeered.

'The word is *thespian*,' Fay said and I almost fell out of the car. Their imitations of the guys at the bar were just too perfect.

I was still giggling to myself as I tiptoed through the house. Everything was quiet and dark and Julie was sound asleep when I looked in on her. But she'd obviously been active since I'd gone – the suitcase was put away and I could see where she'd shut some of her underwear carelessly in the dresser drawer. Also, the scent of my SunSpray bath gel permeated the room; she'd had her shower after all. Well, I thought, that would probably mean she wouldn't be asking too many questions about where I'd been.

In fact, it was the first thing she asked me when she came stumbling into the kitchen at the crack of noon looking for something to eat. That would teach me to underestimate my sister's chutzpah, I thought while she helped herself to a large bagel.

'All night grocery store,' I said grumpily, watching as she found the extra-fancy lox in the refrigerator.

She paused to look over her shoulder at me sceptically and knocked over the open box of baking soda. 'Oh, yuck. What a *mess*,' she said, pulling the lox out and bumping the door closed with her hip. 'You ought to get one of those baking soda holders with the holes like I have, instead of just keeping it in there with the top torn off. Now it's all over everything.'

I laughed with disbelief. 'Aren't you going to clean it up?'

She gave me a look as she unwrapped the lox on the counter. 'In a minute. I didn't want to keep the door open and refrigerate the entire kitchen. It's so hard to find anything in there. Do you have any cream cheese?'

'*I'll* get it.'

I managed to have some of my own lox. We finished it off while she gave me a catalogue of Richard's sins, offences and shortcomings, all the reasons she'd had for throwing up her hands and deciding the marriage was past salvaging. It was all very diisheartening and I told her so.

'If you think you're disheartened, you should have tried living with it,' Julie said bitterly.

'No, thanks,' I said. 'It sounds like single is better.'

'But it isn't. People aren't meant to be alone.'

'Doesn't sound like they're meant to be married either.'

'Well, then, what's *your* definition of a good relationship?'

I made a face, pretending to think hard. 'Let's see . . . hours of screaming sex and when you're tired of him, he disappears without a trace.'

Julie blinked at me several times. 'What about intimacy, friendship, companionship? You know – a *relationship*?'

'That's what my women friends are for, of course.' I kept a straight face for about fifteen seconds. Then we both laughed.

'No, really now, B.J.—'

'No, *really* now, Julie.' I tossed the wrapping paper from the lox in the trash and grabbed some paper towels. 'I find as I get older that my women friends fill a lot of my emotional needs.'

'You haven't gone gay on me, have you?' she said, sounding a bit nervous.

'People don't just *go gay*, you idiot.' I opened the fridge and started cleaning up the baking soda spill.

'Then what's your problem with men?'

'I don't have a problem with men. Men are fine, I enjoy a man whenever I have a yen for one.'

'God, B.J., that is *so cold*.'

'Not as cold as the water was in the shower this morning.' I closed the refrigerator door again. 'You wouldn't know anything about that, would you?'

She sighed. 'I'm sorry. When I woke up, I felt so icky and sweaty and awful, I just automatically went for a shower. I was really more asleep than awake and you were out and by the time I remembered, I had to rinse off anyway. I'm sorry. It's just water, it'll heat up again.'

'Well, that's true, Julie. I have noticed that.'

She started to say something and then thought better of it. 'You never did tell me where you went last night.'

'Yes, I did. All-night grocery. Schnuck's. I'll take you there sometime, it's a pretty fabulous place. Open twenty-four hours and they've got everything except a golf course and a wet bar. And always so clean, I don't know how they do it.'

Julie planted herself directly in front of me frowning. Big Sister was a head taller than I was as well as three years older, but annoyingly, she didn't outweigh me. My only comfort was knowing that she always put on weight when she stayed with me.

'Don't bullshit me, B.J. Where *were* you?'

'Why do I have to answer to you? This isn't *your* house, I'm not staying with you, you're staying with me.'

Now she looked hurt. 'Hey, you don't want to tell me, fine, but I don't see what you have to hide. Or why. We're *sisters*, for chrissake. I told you all my stuff, so it's not like I'm being unfair. You could at least catch me up on what you've been doing since I saw you last.'

I smiled. 'Oh, this and that.'

'What?'

'What I've been up to.'

'Thanks, that's very forthcoming.' She sat down at the kitchen table and put her chin on her fist, the better to have the sulks with.

'I keep busy,' I told her wearily. 'I've got some friends I hang out with and temp work never dries up so I can work when I want to, save up, and not work when I don't want to. Like now.'

'When do you think you'll go back to work?' she asked.

I shrugged. 'When I get bored. And I'm sorry, but I don't have any projected date for when I'll be feeling bored enough to do that.'

My sister pressed her lips together just the way our mother used to do. 'You're really starting to worry me, B.J.. You seem to have no ambition, no goals, and no interest in acquiring any.'

I shrugged. 'Can you explain how you're any different?'

'I've been trying to build a life for myself. I want a family. A *real* family, with two parents. I don't care to be a single parent, thanks all the same.'

'Maybe you should concentrate on a career for a while,' I said.

'Oh, I am,' she said quickly. 'I didn't tell you I'd gone into graphic design, did I?'

'No,' I said, 'you didn't.'

'Well, I have. I took this course in desktop publishing and I discovered I have a knack for laying out pages of things – books, magazines, things like that, you know?'

I waited.

'And I ended up getting some freelance assignments to design some newsletters for some local organizations.'

I kept waiting. Irritation pushed Julie's forehead into furrows.

'It was through the instructor, in case you want to know. He was *so supportive*, right from the very beginning.'

Bingo, I thought, feeling mean.

'Richard just ignored me, he was all wrapped up in that tiresome programming garbage and it was like *my* interests had just stopped existing or something. He simply ignored the fact that I'd uncovered this incredible talent I'd never known I had. But my teacher was a *real* teacher. He brought me along, kept encouraging me to push myself, challenge myself.'

'Well,' I said. 'I didn't see any desktop publishing stuff in your luggage. Did you leave it behind with Richard?'

She actually blushed. 'I don't have any – I haven't been able to afford to buy any yet. First I used one of the classroom computers, but now Stan's been letting me use his system.'

'Stan's the teacher?'

'Right.' She dimpled to show me she was pleased with my powers of deduction. 'He's got all the state-of-the-art software and enough memory to handle an entire publishing company. Which is what he really wants to do – start this specialty press that publishes high-quality books for specialized markets, poetry, or travel books, other things. He's trying to save enough money from teaching and he told me that when he's ready to start up, he wants to hire me right off to do all the designing.' She took a moment to be proud. 'So you see, B.J., I *may* be on my third divorce, and I *may* be temporarily living with my sister, but I've *still* got my sights set on tomorrow. Bloody but unbowed. Life goes on.'

I felt like sending Richard a card.

I caught them together, of course. Now that Stan's name had been mentioned, I knew it wouldn't be long before the man himself appeared, but as I said, I was tired of the charade and I decided I'd just fix it so we all knew where we were and where everyone else was. So I told Julie I was going to a movie and then out to dinner afterwards with some friends, ran down to Schnuck's for half an hour and made it back in time for her first orgasm.

Either Stan was some kind of high-powered and unstoppable sex machine or Julie had got better at enjoying herself. The thought that my sister might be faking it crossed my mind a few times in the past but I decided it was highly unlikely. Making Julie come was probably the entrance exam, if you'll pardon the expression; anyone who couldn't qualify in the Big O event didn't advance to the serious relationship stage. As a standard, it wasn't so bad, I guess, and maybe better than just judging them on the size of their bank accounts – more personal, anyway. And as Julie herself had said once, *I hate to think of all those other women out there who put up with worse than I have and don't even get to have an orgasm.* In her own hinky way, she had a point.

Anyway, there I was in my own living room, listening to my sister and her latest victim going at it and feeling like that scene from *The Stepford Wives*, where the women go into their neighbour's house and hear her telling her husband how great he is. Except Julie didn't sound anywhere near so submissive. It was all give-it-to-me-show-me-right-there-go-go-do-it and so forth, right out of *How To Be An Assertive Sex Partner.*

And I had to admit, as hinky and perverted as it might sound, it was a turn-on. I'd have been better off in my own bedroom but there was no way I could get there without walking past Julie's open door and alerting the lovers, so I just lay down on the couch.

The most fun was imagining what Stan looked like – skinny or muscular, or even a little plump, dark or fair, much younger or somewhat older. He sounded like the macho type in that he had a lot of requests of his own and tended to make them all in a sexy growl. I imagined his hands everywhere at once, urgent but very sensitive, as if he were searching for the exact location of the very best point . . . and then when he found it, pressing his mouth against it in a long, ornate kiss, while his hands and his fingers began to prepare for what was next. I imagined he was quite talented; he certainly sounded talented, Julie's back-up singing aside.

Eventually, I just stopped hearing her. It was good; for awhile, I almost believed that old Stan and I were making a real connection. He and I finished together, anyway; Julie screamed on and off for another half an hour. It gave me time to pull myself together, more or less. I started counting and when I finally got to a hundred and twenty without hearing her give another howl of ecstasy, I opened the front door, slammed it hard, and yelled, 'Julie, I'm home!'

I went straight to her room, blathering about how movies these days just really sucked and I'd suddenly got so tired of having my intelligence insulted that I'd just walked right the hell out and the hell with dinner, I decided I'd just come home and fix myself a—

'Sandwich?' I said, standing in the open doorway. My surprise was genuine, in that I was just finding out what Stan really looked like. 'Uh, Julie? Did I, uh, show up at an inopportune moment?'

From where she was lying on Stan's shoulder, my sister blew out a noisy breath. 'You could say that, B.J., though I have to say your timing isn't quite as bad as it could have been.'

'Oh,' I said. 'Well, does this mean I should fix *three* sandwiches instead of just one?'

'*B.J.!*' Julie said, mortified.

'What?' I said. 'We've got a guest, I'm just trying to be a good host. Ess.'

During this exchange, I hadn't actually looked at Julie at all. It was hard to see anyone else with Stan in the room. He was a knockout. That's the only way I can describe him – maybe *breathtaking* for a variation. He had thick black hair just a little long, pale green eyes and the kind of masculine features that would go a bit craggy with age but would never lose their sex appeal.

Then there was his body. The sheet was pulled up to hip level so I could see he'd been taking good care of himself; he wasn't a bodybuilder but his muscles were firm and well-defined in a way that I personally have always found irresistibly touchable. *Wait till I tell the gang about this*, I thought.

'*B.J.!*' Julie yelled and I realized this was the third time she'd said it.

'What?' I said brightly.

'Will you for chrissakes get the *hell* out of the doorway so we can get dressed? Then I'll introduce you two.'

'Oh. Sure.' I smiled at Stan. 'So, you want a sandwich?'

Stan's smile broadened and I got the feeling that he did. 'What have you got?' he asked softly.

Julie opened her mouth to scream at one or both of us. 'I'll get it out and you can see for yourself,' I said quickly and escaped to the kitchen.

I put out all the sandwich stuff, enjoying the jittery sound of Julie's voice in the bedroom. I couldn't hear what she was saying but I was pretty sure she was trying to explain to him why I wasn't acting all shocked and scandalized after all, and when she got through ascribing mood swings and unpredictability to me, I was going to sound like Sybil on an especially bad day.

I put some Genoa salami and provolone on a kaiser roll, poured myself a beer and waited.

Julie came out in her bathrobe but Stan was fully dressed, shoes and all. 'Gosh, I hope you're not leaving just because I have a lousy sense of timing,' I told him, gesturing at the food laid out on the counter next to the refrigerator.

'No, he's leaving because he has a lot to do,' Julie said. 'Don't you?' she added as he turned to her with a sweetcakes-don't-answer-my-questions-for-me look.

'Hey, anyone's got time for a sandwich,' I said innocently.

She did her best to look affectionately bothered while he fixed a corned beef on rye and raised his eyebrows at my beer.

'Help yourself,' I told him without moving from the stool by the breakfast bar (that was what the real estate agent called it when I bought the house). As he stuck his head into the refrigerator, Julie gave me a murderous glare. I just shrugged at her and tried not to laugh out loud.

That was the problem with going to bed with Julie – well, one of the problems, anyway: afterwards, you were supposed to lie there and talk about what a great lay she was and how she could get thousands of dollars a throw for this if she ever decided to turn pro. In return, she'd tell you how great you were for saying that. Food and drink didn't enter into it, unless, half an hour later, you got the urge to take her out for an expensive meal before you did it again.

Well, I never cared much for guys who hopped out of bed a split-second after the grand finale and locked themselves in the bathroom for an hour myself, so maybe I couldn't blame her there. I also couldn't blame her for getting mad at me for intruding like that, though she'd have been a lot madder if she'd known the truth, and maybe a little bit scared besides. Because she wouldn't understand, of course, that it wasn't the fact that she was my sister that had turned me on.

And what she *would* understand wouldn't make her any less angry, so all I could do was sit there stuffing my face and hoping that she had no idea right at that moment exactly how terribly and powerfully much I wanted her new boyfriend.

'Oh, baby, oh, *baby*,' said Fay as we watched Stan leaving my house and walking down to his car parked at the curb. Julie dragged along with him, hanging on his arm and adoring him. We all ignored her.

'That's the infamous Stan, huh?' said Pilar. 'Wow, you were right, B.J. I'm making pheromones *this minute*.'

'Did you look him up in the city directory?' Carol wanted to know.

'Sure did. Stanhope Lloyd O'Brien,' she read from a printout. 'Address over on West 39th, registered *Republican*—' she looked up from the paper, watching him kiss Julie good-bye 'Stan-baby, *boo hiss*. Instructor in computer design and desktop publishing at the local community college. *Un*married. No divorces, just plain *un*married.' She gave a short laugh. 'Lives alone. Will someone explain to me how he can be more perfect?'

'He could be rich as Croesus and take us all to the Bahamas,' Fay offered.

'Strike one,' Pilar said. 'But it takes three strikes for an out and remember, with enough balls, we can walk him.'

We all fell out for awhile over that one. Fay was alert and let him go only half a block before starting the car and going after him.

'Stan? It *is* you, isn't it?' I stood next to him at the bar, smiling up at him. There was half a second when he didn't recognize me out of context and then he was effusively glad to see me. No, Julie wasn't with him, he'd come out to get some fresh air and a change of scene before going back to work grading some student assignments. Actually, Julie had got rid of him early so I couldn't walk in on them again – I'd done it twice more since the first time and done my gracious any-lover-of-my-sister's-is-OK-by-me act each time, and once he'd gone, Julie had chewed me out for being insensitive. This time, she'd no doubt sent him off with a promise that soon they could be together uninterrupted at his place, as her divorce from Richard was coming right along, though she didn't want to jeopardize what little of Richard's goodwill she had by going public before everything was final and blah-blah-blah.

I didn't have much trouble persuading him to join me and my friends in the dining room for a bite to eat and some harmless, undemanding companionship – the keyword there being *undemanding*, something my sister was not. Then there was the fact that none of us are so terribly hard to look at, even me though I know I'm not as pretty as Julie. But the four of us together make a fairly good-looking party, and of course, we're good company, too. Especially when we're loaded with pheromones, the way we were then. I could tell old Stanhope liked us pretty well and wasn't allergic to pheromones, like one unfortunate and too-memorable case we had.

He lingered over his empty plate talking movies with Fay, books with Carol and politics with Pilar, while I made wisecracks. Pretty soon it was two hours later and we were into after-dinner drinks and looking at the dessert menu. I thought about my sister alone in the house, having the post-traumatic post-coital-stress blues and phoning her beloved for a little emotional pumping-up, only to get his answering machine for hours and hours, even though he hadn't said anything to her about having to be out.

We managed to make dessert and coffee last an hour and a half, and when we finally let him go, I'm not sure which one of us he was in love with. Maybe all of us; he was a man with a hearty appetite.

Julie was in a full-blown hissy-fit when I got home. I pretended not to notice and put *The Beguiled* on the VCR. For awhile, I thought that was going to push her right over the edge into total panic hysteria, and I suppose if you count eating a barrel of popcorn by yourself in a frantic, mechanical way, perhaps it did.

If she'd ever offered to pay me some rent to help with the mortgage, or taken on the housework, it all might have been different. But that wasn't the way my sister worked, so I had to figure out other ways to make her pay. Her room had begun to smell like one I'd lived next door to in my first college dorm – the two guys had turned it into a frank and unapologetic sex pit they had christened *The Hot Spot*.

I started referring to her room by that name – the Hot Spot – and she got greatly offended, though the gang thought it was hilarious, if inaccurate.

'If he thinks *that's* a hot spot, he's got some surprises coming when *we* take him to the *real* hot spot,' Fay said.

'All of us together?' Carol pretended to be shocked. 'Dykes.'

'Lesbos,' Pilar said.

'Oh, you *fags*,' Fay said, and nearly drove the car off the road. What *wasn't* funny was that it seemed like the only times when we didn't have some hockey puck making remarks at us was when we were with Stan.

We didn't start bumping into him regularly right away. We let him go on by himself for awhile, let him hang out alone after a session in the Hot Spot, so he could feel the difference. Then the next time we ran into him, we were all loaded with pheromones again and boy, had he missed us.

If it had just been me by myself, I probably would have got impatient and rushed things. Though sometimes I think my purpose in life is to keep Fay, Carol, and Pilar from dragging stuff out until everyone involved is old and grey. Things *do* take time if you're going to do them right, but if the others had just let me hurry things along a little more, Julie wouldn't have caught us.

Of course, I have to recognize that it was probably due to us that three months went by and she still hadn't moved out of the Hot Spot. These days, Stan would come over to the Hot Spot, get his ashes hauled, and then run down to the local bar and grill to meet us for dinner and drinks. And pheromones, of course. The pheromones were the big thing, though it certainly helped that Julie was all wrapped up in her troubles these days – neither her divorce nor her new career as a graphic artist were going well and she couldn't figure out why. And she didn't say so, but I suspected that old Stan had gone from passionate to perfunctory: *here's your orgasm, gosh, look at the time.* Carol maintained that it would have gone this way even if we hadn't intervened but Fay said we speeded it up some and made it all inevitable besides. I was inclined to agree with Fay, and to add that without chemical enhancement, we couldn't have done it at all. This wasn't just some guy we picked up, after all – this was some guy who was screwing my sister, and supposedly in love with her. Definitely a harder case than your typical meatball but, we were hoping, a much greater reward.

It was the night we were going to settle it that Julie caught us, so it would seem that timing was something that ran in the family. But then, it was a very odd night all the way around; it always is when we do it. But what it was on this particular night was that Pilar had got attached, and was talking about *keeping* him.

Now, the rest of us weren't totally unsympathetic but we had to talk sense to her. 'How could we keep him?' Fay said as we bounced along the interstate, heading south from the movie theatre downtown; she needed new shocks. 'You know you don't have room at your place and I sure don't have room in mine. Carol, how about you – you have a toolshed in your backyard, right? Or maybe B.J. wants to put him in permanent residence at the Hot Spot?'

'I know, I *know*.' Pilar sighed again. 'I just *like* him, is all.'

'I don't blame you,' I said. 'I like him, too. He's very likeable. But you know the rule. It's a sacrifice, but then, it's *supposed* to be.'

'I know, I *know*.' Pilar sighed again. 'He's so *fine*, though.'

'Which is *exactly* why we have to do this.'

Then she started talking about maybe we could do this or that or something else, and I could tell she knew everything she was saying wouldn't wash, but she just had to get it out of her system. So we let her go on and on, till we got to the restaurant and we even let her go on a little there.

When Stan got there, we let Pilar do a lot of the talking and pheromone-spraying. I think Stan sensed that something was up, or at least wasn't as usual with us, and even though we didn't leave him an opening to ask any questions, he might have forced one anyway if Julie hadn't shown up.

When I looked up and saw her all in black with what seemed to be every piece of gold jewellery she owned coming through the dining room at us, I thought of a battleship at ramming speed. Julie was livid, but with this peculiar *Aha-Gotcha!* smile, her black hair standing out like a mane or a halo. She was all dressed up, I realized, all dressed up and all made up, ready to take on anyone. This was Julie in her game face.

I stood up just as she moved up behind Stan's chair. 'Well, *what* a coincidence!' she said, so loudly that the entire dining room turned to see who was experiencing synchronicity. Stan jumped and almost fell under the table trying to get up without pushing the chair back into her. Julie smiled at him, jingled the six dozen bracelets on her left arm, and didn't move. 'Can you *imagine* this?' she said. 'There I was, sitting home alone, *by myself*, and it suddenly occurred to me that I felt like going out, only there was *no one* around to go out with. So I go out by myself and who do I run into but the *very people I would have wanted to go out with in the first place.*' She frowned at Pilar, Fay, and Carol, who were all still sitting at the table, holding their menus like shields. 'Only I don't think I've met you ladies. You must be my sister's accomplices. Ha, ha, friends, I mean.'

'Accomplices will do,' Pilar said. I could tell by the way she jerked that either Fay or Carol had kicked her under the table.

'Gosh,' Julie said, 'table for five. I guess there isn't room for a sixth, is there?'

Some reshuffling and Julie and I were crammed in side by side along one edge of the table. Stan had made room for her but she'd ignored him and sat by me; the better to force him to compare the two of us. Good old Julie, always ready to pull out all the stops, though she'd have thought better of it if I'd looked like Pilar.

We put in our drink orders and waited in silence until Julie took out a pack of cigarettes. 'This is the non-smoking area,' Fay said, not bothering to smile. Julie hesitated and then decided she didn't want to take on Fay, which almost had me revising my estimate of her intelligence upward. Almost – it only took half a brain to know better than to go up against Fay. As soon as she was done fidgetting the cigarettes back into her purse, I pushed back from the table. 'Going to the restroom,' I said.

'Good, I'll go with you,' Julie said, and practically chased me to the back of the restaurant.

Julie bashed the restroom door open half a second after I slipped inside. 'All right, *sister*,' she snarled at me. 'What the *fuck* is going on here?'

'Nothing,' I said, pausing to look at us both in the mirror before I went into a stall. She followed me so closely I had to slam the door in her face to keep her out.

'*My* boyfriend with *four* other women is *not fucking nothing*!'

A toilet flushed, followed by two seconds of complete silence. Then there was the sound of hurried high heels tapping over the tile floor and out the door without stopping at the sinks.

'How long has this been going on?' Julie demanded.

'Just a minute. I can't talk and pee, you know that.' I watched Goofy's seconds hand go round three and a half times.

'God*damm*it, B.J.!' Julie banged her fist on the stall door.

'Hey, I'm sorry. Now you've made me pee-shy.'

'If you want to stay in here all fucking night, B.J., we can do that. It'll be weird, but I can stand it if you can!'

I gave it another thirty seconds and then opened the door. 'Back up. I mean it, Julie, don't crowd me. I didn't steal your boyfriend—'

'Oh, no?' She stuck her fists on her hips. 'For weeks, he's been practically jumping out of bed the minute we finish making love and rushing out the door. I *thought* it was because he didn't want you embarrassing him the way you were by barging in on us with all that 'Hey, want a sandwich?' bullshit – which I *thought* he was taking you up on just to be nice to *me*, to my sister, to show me that he accepted my lunatic family. And instead—'

'Instead you found out he was really hungry,' I said. 'Jeez, Julie, I guess you should have fed him, huh?'

She actually raised her fist to me.

'Julie! Over a *guy*?'

She froze and then lowered her hand. 'He's not just a *guy*. He's special, really special.' A pause while she calmed visibly. 'I *still* want to know what's going on here. And for how long. And *why*.'

'Dinner and a little conversation. Did you have any idea that he was *that* deep?'

'Well of *course* I did, you imbecile. That's why I fell in love with him. He was my teacher and my mentor as well.'

'Oh. I thought you fell in love with him because Richard was such a loser.'

She looked bewildered. 'I've never married a loser. I mean, Richard wasn't a loser when I married him.'

'But a few years in your hands turned him right around, eh, Julie?'

Her pretty face contorted so painfully that I could feel myself echoing her expression. 'Why are you doing this to me? Is it because of something I've done, or because I'm . . . ' she floundered for a few moments, 'your big sister or you think I'm – I'm – doing better in some way than you are, or . . . or . . . I don't know, B.J. I'm at a real loss here.'

I sighed. 'No, I don't hate you because you're thinner. Okay?'

'I didn't *say* that,' Julie said resentfully.

'You didn't *have* to,' I said, echoing her tone back at her. 'But the truth is, I really *don't* hate you because you're thinner. Sometimes I'm angry at you, but I don't hate you. Look, these things have a way of happening that nobody asks for, nobody looks for, and that nobody would even imagine. I thought *you*, of all people, would understand this.'

She should have, since she'd said those very words, more or less, to me about every one of her relationships at one time or another.

'*But* – and here's the big but, Julie, bigger than mine—' I slapped my haunch and smiled 'I swear to you I've never touched him. None of us has, not Pilar or Carol or Fay. We've just been hanging out chewing the fat – you should pardon the expression – shooting the shit, and having some laughs. And that's all. I swear.'

Julie looked grim. 'Uh-huh. And no one knows better than I do that you can achieve real intimacy with someone without ever touching them in just that very way. How *could* you? My *own* sister.'

'Come *on*. You mean to say you've never noticed how much this man enjoys *female energy*?'

She blinked at me. 'What?'

'He's a woman lover. Not a woman*izer*, but a woman lover. He loves women. He loves the whole idea of women. He loves them as a concept, he loves them as a reality, and he loves them individually and in groups. This guy is one hundred percent pro-female, and you should count yourself blessed.' I grinned. 'Why else do you think he's so willing – and good – at cunnilingus?'

Julie's face got so red I was afraid she might have a nosebleed or cry blood or something. '*B.J.! Have you been spying on us?*'

'No,' I lied, 'I just know you. You wouldn't bother with a guy who wouldn't. Or who wasn't any good at it.'

She put a hand over her mouth as if she were shocked and then suddenly started to giggle.

'Only men who really love women will do that,' I said confidently.

Julie giggled some more. 'Who says'

'Women who get it.'

'B.J.!'

'What the *fuck* are you acting shocked about. We're both over thirty and in case you didn't know, I'm not a virgin either.'

Julie's giggles trailed off. 'Actually, B.J., I've been kind of waiting for you to tell me that you're gay.'

'You know, that's the second time you've brought that up. Why do you keep saying that? And why would you think it's your business?'

She floundered some more.

'Never mind,' I said. 'I don't need your permission to have a sex life of my own.'

'Well, I'd be supportive, you know. No matter what you are.'

'Gosh, thanks, it's nice to know I have your blessing. Never *mind*,' I added as she started to say something. 'Do you want to stay in here all night? Or would you like to go eat dinner with your boyfriend?'

She followed me out of the bathroom and by the time she sat down she was almost all smiles. This didn't make Pilar, Carol, and Fay any too happy, as I'd known it wouldn't and I had to let Carol get me alone in the bathroom after the next round of drinks.

'I know, I know,' I told her. 'If she doesn't trot off on her own, we'll have to give her a shot of the pheromones. And I have to tell you, she's not too likely to trot off on her own. I mean, if he were your boyfriend, would you?'

Carol ran a hand through her short blonde hair, making it stand wildly on end. 'How are we going to manage with her along for the ride?'

'With a few pheromones in her, I don't think that'll be the problem.'

'And what about after?' Carol asked evenly, folding her skinny muscular arms. If there was anyone I was going to hate for being skinny, it would have been Carol because she had the athletic wiry body I'd always wanted and could never get, except I liked her far too much.

'OK, that could be troublesome, but I'll take care of her. You know that saying – my sister, my problem.'

Carol smiled at the joke. 'She'll freak out, you know.'

I nodded. 'Yeah. Then she'll sleep it off and after that I'll tell her Stan left town or eloped or went gay.'

'People don't just *go gay*.'

'Sh. Julie doesn't know that.'

After the appetizer, Carol took Fay to the bathroom, and in the middle of the entrée, Fay took Pilar. I had to go myself by then but I didn't dare – I had nothing more to tell anyone, but not knowing that, someone would insist on going with me, and then the whole cycle would have to go round again just so everyone could be notified that I'd really had to pee. Stan was boggled enough.

'You know,' he said chattily as Fay and Pilar came back, 'we used to joke about the real reason women always went to the bathroom together was so they could pass on vital information they all needed for world domination. But the way you all go, I'm beginning to wonder here.'

'Don't wonder,' Fay said, waving one hand like a flamenco dancer. 'Have another drink, think about dessert, but don't *wonder*. You could strain something you'll need later.'

We all laughed. Stan glanced at Julie; she smiled enthusiastically at him while he looked tentative. No, it wouldn't have lasted, I thought, watching him decide to break up with my sister. She'd have *needed* the living daylights out of him and he just wasn't up to her. He'd had no idea what he was taking on when she'd walked into his life. Now he was starting to get an idea, and he saw us four as the rescue squad that had saved him from making a serious mistake. *Well, Stannie, guess again – but we promise it'll be good to the last drop.*

Sometime before dessert, I got Julie with a dose of pheromones and watching her cope, or try to, was both amusing and alarming. My sister wasn't familiar with the phenomenon of naked libido; she'd been dressing hers up in emotions for so long, she thought it came that way naturally.

Now, she looked as if she were on a rollercoaster. Stan's proximity was making her crazy, which made all of us just as crazy. Except for Stan, of course, who still didn't have a clue; he stayed bewildered, but that was all right. It kept him off balance, and with a lot of food and drink dulling his senses as well, he'd be going over the brink before he understood what was happening.

By the time we decided to give up the table, both he and Julie were pretty drunk, which was perfect. Fay wouldn't hear of them driving and shoehorned them into the backseat of her car with Carol and Pilar. Carol planted herself on Stan's lap, to his everlasting delight, while Pilar made the sulking Julie sit on hers. There was only one bad moment, though, and I think that was more due to Fay's bad shocks than anything else – halfway over to Carol's, Julie mumbled something about being sick, which had us all holding our collective breath, but fortunately, nothing came of it.

Carol's house had once belonged to a musician who had sound-proofed the finished part of the basement – very nice. Carol had added some improvements and while they weren't enormously innovative – mirrors on the ceiling, great big pillows instead of a sofa and chairs, a small wet bar with a Rubenesque nude on the wall behind it – we'd found that the surroundings only needed to be suggestive and comfortable.

Stan was very comfortable. He went right down on the pillows and settled in with a big smile. Julie picked her way around the room unsteadily as if she were searching for something but couldn't quite remember what it was. Carol let her wander for a while before she put on some music, and Fay and Pilar got up to dance.

Julie came stomping over to me at the bar, where I was setting out glasses and looking for the absinthe. 'B.J., are you nuts?' she whispered. 'Let's get out of here. Obviously these people are *weird*.'

'Not hardly,' I said. 'Come on, give it a chance. You might find you like this sort of thing.'

'Yeah, I just might,' she said, looking troubled. 'That's the problem. I don't *want* to like it. I want things the way I've always had them.'

I found the absinthe. 'Well, you can't. Not tonight, anyway. Come on, don't embarrass me in front of my friends?'

'*Embarrass you in front of your friends!!*' she shouted, and then turned to look at the rest of the room. Fay and Pilar stared back at her but didn't stop dancing. Carol turned the music up and Stan lay on the pillows without trying to conceal the fact that all this had given him a world-class hard-on.

'Oh, *God*, B.J.,' Julie whispered, turning back to me. 'This is *so sleazy*.'

'Yeah,' I said, handing her a glass. 'And without sleaze, we'd be no better than animals. Remember that.'

She automatically took a sip from the glass and then frowned, holding it up to eye-level. 'What's *this*?'

'Makes your heart grow fonder. Does wonders for your other parts, too. Absinthe,' I added as her expression became even more confused.

'Jesus!' She put the glass down on the bar as Fay and Pilar danced over to get theirs, Fay taking a second glass and dancing over to Stan with it. 'B.J., absinthe is poison!'

I chuckled. 'Not to us, it isn't.'

'Or you,' Carol put in as she leaned past Julie and took a glass for herself. Julie stepped back and glared at her. Carol laughed. 'Oh, calm down, Snow White. Nobody here is going to do your fair young body until you beg for it.'

My sister looked to me again and I shrugged. 'House rule – nobody does anything they don't want to.'

'Well, don't tell *me*, tell *her*,' Julie said, gesturing at Carol as she moved away from us.

'She knows. It's her house, after all. She just thought you might need the hint.'

Julie made a revolted face. 'Me? Why?'

I looked over at Stan. Carol was curling up next to him on the pillows.

'Great,' she said. 'You wanted to prove you could steal my boyfriend, you proved it. You wanted to show me that everyone's got a streak of low-life in them, you showed me. Now I know how sick people can be. Now let me out of here.'

'I would,' I told her, sipping my absinthe, 'if you really wanted to go.'

My sister crossed her arms protectively over her chest. She looked prim and nervous, but she was still holding her absinthe in one hand. 'Are you one of those crazy women who thinks "no" sometimes means "yes"?'

'No,' I said. '*You're* one of those crazy women who thinks every time her libido wakes up, she's in love. You're the one who's sick, Julie, but don't worry. Tonight, you're getting the cure.'

She looked scared. 'What are you going to do?'

'To you? I don't know. The night is young. Oh, calm *down*,' I added as she started to go over the brink to panic. '*I'm* not going to do anything. *You* are. Nobody can do anything to you that you don't do to yourself, don't you know that by now?'

Stan and Carol had put their glasses aside and were stretched out facing each other, touching only their fingertips together. I couldn't really tell whether he was being patient, or just shy. Fay danced over behind Julie and gave her a nudge. 'Why don't you go over and ask him if he wants a sandwich?'

'Yeah,' said Pilar, chuckling a little, 'it's not like he just ate or anything.'

I poured some more absinthe into her glass. 'This'll help.' It wasn't, strictly speaking, absinthe. Or rather, it wasn't *only* absinthe.

She looked down at the glass and I could see how the fumes alone were getting to her. Extra-sensitive, she'd never had this stuff before. 'I don't know . . . ' she said, mostly to herself.

Pilar gave her a little push. 'Go on. People don't usually get to find out what they *really* want.'

Suddenly, she drained the glass in one gulp, handed it to me, and went over to where Carol and Stan were still teasing each other's hands. Pilar and Fay looked at me.

'Vanilla,' I said, 'but she enjoys it.'

Julie lay down behind Stan, moving in close. Carol gave Stan a small push so that he fell back on top of Julie, who slipped one arm around his chest, holding him tight. He squirmed against her, enjoying the sensation and, coincidentally, blocking her view so that she didn't know what Carol was doing until it was too late to object or stop it.

Carol really was athletic and quite limber; watching her was like watching Olympic-level gymnastics, or state-of-the-art ballet. She primed him, more with the sight of herself than anything, stretching up over him, muscles moving and flexing under her skin. Her nipples came up slowly, darkening as they crinkled – Carol claimed she could consciously control her heartbeat, too, and I didn't doubt it. As he reached up for her, she slipped away and Pilar took her place. Julie still hung on, looking again as if she were on some wild carnival ride, the scariest rollercoaster in the world, trying not to like it, refusing to stop. Her bent knees came up between his legs from behind, which made him move more urgently, arching his back and lifting up until Pilar pressed him down again with her body.

Barely thirty seconds later, Pilar looked over her shoulder at me and Fay and there was no mistaking her expression. Apparently we were all just too good for him; Julie must have gotten more perfunctory than passionate as well. Pilar pulled away from him; Fay and I moved in and lifted him off Julie, who didn't have to be told what to do next.

She was on him immediately and without preliminaries; this wasn't the sort of serial she was used to, but then she was no longer perpetuating the love fiction, either. She was vocal this time, but there not being any lies to tell, there were no words, just noises.

He tried to rise up under her to meet her every movement but she was driving and she pushed him down further into the pillows. His clothes had been undone and disarranged; now she tore them off and her own as well. We were already stripped, waiting for the sign. Deep inside me, the absinthe burned, a private star, as we twined our arms and closed the circle around them.

The sound of his breathing changed suddenly and that certain smell came to us, unmistakable and potent, but we waited until Julie lifted her face and we saw the blood shining on her mouth.

As I'd expected, when Julie came out of it and saw what had happened, she passed out immediately. I put her in Carol's tub and hosed her down while Pilar and Fay took care of the mess. There wasn't much left this time – it had been quite a while since our last party and with an extra person, there had been barely enough to go around. Nobody said anything about feeling shorted, though Fay had the most right. I knew she was refraining out of respect to me.

I, on the other hand, felt no such compunction, since Julie *was* my sister and this was just more of her usual behaviour – being a hog and not cleaning up any of the mess she made.

In the middle of the second rinsing, I could feel the new tension in her body that meant she was actually awake but pretending to be asleep. I switched the spray from gentle to needle and the temperature from hot to cold before taking the shower massager off the handle and pointing it right at her breasts.

She screamed as if I were doing to her what she'd just finished doing to Stan with the rest of us. (Stan himself hadn't screamed; he'd been too busy coming.) Then she started getting hysterical so I had to give her a faceful of cold water. I knew this was probably my way of getting back at her for using up all the hot water when I'd told her not to, so I changed the water to easy-going and blood-warm and kept it on the back of her neck until she stopped crying.

I got her into one of Carol's muumuus but it took all four of us to get her into Fay's car, and I seriously considered Pilar's suggestion that we just use the trunk. Everyone else would spend the night at Carol's while I borrowed Fay's car and came back the next day. Truthfully, I would much rather have stayed there with them the way I always did, but Julie would have thrown a hissy fit.

She started crying again on the way home; this time, I figured the best thing to do was just let her go till she wound down, and I was right. By the time we got to the front door, all she had left in her were some sniffles.

After I got her inside, though, she wound up again and started ranting about group sex and how *she* wasn't kinky or deviant, *she* never did that kind of thing, *she* didn't like that kind of thing—

'Dear Julie, always in denial,' I said. 'You're forgetting the part where we tore him to pieces and ate him.'

She froze in the middle of my living room and stared at me with her eyes bulging. '*That was an hallucination!*'

'No, that was real, actually.' I chuckled. 'Everything else that happened up till tonight – all *that* was a hallucination.'

She shook her head clumsily and suddenly her face looked terribly old. 'Who *are* you?' she said. 'I don't even know you, I don't know what you've become—'

'Yes, you do, Julie,' I said. 'I'm your sister, and I'm just like you. A little variation but really, the same tune. Only there isn't as much evidence left afterwards.'

'You *monster*—'

'Knock it off. I do what my nature tells me to do, the same you do what *your* nature tells *you* to do. And it's *all* Nature, Julie, Nature with a capital N: Pilar, Carol, and Fay and me, we're the latest in a long line of tradition, a tradition that predates just about everything historical. And you see, you're obviously part of the tradition, too, except you buried the feeling under a pile of niceties and outright lies until it got all twisted. *You're* the pervert, Julie, because you won't face the fact that you're not supposed to let them live afterwards!'

She was completely flustered. 'You . . . you . . . you *serial killer!*'

'Actually, I think the closest thing would be the black widow spider. Of course, the spider's imperative is blind Nature, without intelligence, neither conscious nor diabolical. But she goes at it with such relish that it is tempting to believe that somewhere inside whatever passes for a spider brain, there emerges something that is the arachnid equivalent of *God, how I love this!* before she passes out, or spins more silk, or whatever spiders do in their equivalent of afterglow.'

'*I'm not a spider, goddammit!*' she screamed at me.

'No? Fay found this guy at another place across town. Plays tennis, great ass, same colour eyes. Says he'd like to get married if he could find the right woman.'

Julie stared at me in silence.

'Come on, someone who's just been through her third divorce should still have her sights set on tomorrow. I've still got *my* sights set on tomorrow. Bloody but unbowed? Life goes on? Remember?' She still didn't say anything. 'Come on, Julie. If you don't insist on some kind of big fancy church wedding, I'm sure Fay and Carol and Pilar would be willing to work something out. Bridal party dresses are just like costumes. *Lots* of people like to do it in costumes.'

'You're on,' said my sister.

BLACK NIGHTGOWN

by

K. W. Jeter

―⁂―

K. W. Jeter is the author of several novels, including his early precursor to the cyberpunk movement (which coincidentally contains a nice dollop of sexual horror), *Dr Adder*. Other of his novels are *Soul Eater, Farewell Horizontal, Madlands* and *Wolf Flow*. He has agreed to do a two volume series called *The Deckard Chronicles*, based upon the characters and concepts of Philip K. Dick's novel *Do Androids Dream of Electric Sheep?* and has just finished *The Kingdom of Shadows*, a major novel that he has been working on for the last few years.

Jeter's rare short stories have appeared in *Omni, Midnight Graffiti, Alien Sex* and *A Whisper of Blood*.

'Black Nightgown' isn't as overtly horrifying as 'The First Time' (from *Alien Sex*) but like that story it is about a kind of sexual initiation.

BLACK NIGHTGOWN

Everyone knew.

Everyone knows, he murmured to himself. His lips brushed across the white skin of her neck, the soft region between her throat and ear, when he spoke aloud, a whisper, her name. His lips brushed across the delicate strands of hair that trembled with the exhalation of his breath. He breathed in her scent that wasn't roses but just as sweet. He murmured her name, he couldn't stop himself, and she shifted in his arms but didn't wake.

They all knew, but he didn't care. Not here in this world that he wrapped his arms around and was held by at the same time. A world bound by her scent and their mingled warmth, caught by the tunnelled sheets and the white-tasselled covers. Her breasts encircled by his arm . . .

Outside, in that other world, the streetlamp's blue merged with the faint shadows of the moon. The thin light slid around the edges of the curtain, made empty shapes of her bedroom dresser and the door that led to the rest of the empty, silent house. She moved in his embrace, eyes closed, her mouth parting slightly, her breath a sigh.

'They all know.'

Another's whisper. His sweat felt cold upon his naked shoulders. He turned his face away from hers and looked up at the figure standing beside the bed.

Her dead husband could see through the drawn curtain and through the walls of all the houses lining the street, the lights left on in kitchens and sleeping hallways shining through the red bricks as though through glass. 'Your mother . . . your sisters . . . even your father.' The dead man looked away from the window and everything beyond, turning toward his sleeping wife. 'They all know.'

Of course his mother and sisters would know. He brought his face back down to hers. They had known before any of this had ever come about. He closed his eyes, lashes brushing the curve of her cheekbone. His father would never speak of what he knew. He kissed the corner of her mouth.

They all know . . .

And now he did as well. He knew; he knew something.

He held her fast in the night of their small world. Held her, and felt her dead husband watching them. Watching them in the great night's world.

The women spoke the old world's language. The mothers less than the grandmothers, and the daughters only a few words. But they all knew, and understood. The grey-haired poked their tree-root fingers through the shelled peas, the bowls held in their laps as they sat gossiping to each other or murmuring to themselves; the youngest turned their dark-eyed gaze at him as he stepped into the street to pass by their jump ropes slapping the cracked sidewalk. Whisper into each other's ears, laugh and run away, their white anklets flashing like the teeth of an ocean's waves.

He asked his father what women talked about.

'Christ in his fucking Heaven – who knows?' Sweating through his undershirt as a cleaver snapped free the ribs of a dangling carcass, the knotted spine turned naked as a row of babies' fists. In the store's glass-fronted cabinets, the mounds of beef liver glistened like soft, wet rubies. 'Ask them and get told what a fool you are.' Drops of blood spattered the sawdust and the broken leather of his father's boots.

Outside the door, with the slow overhead fan trying to keep the flies away, the little girls' ropes had been left behind like shed snakeskins. He rang open the cash register and sorted out the dollar bills that the neighborhood housewives had paid him for their deliveries. His hands still smelled like raw sausages and the red water that had leaked through the wrapping paper.

Later, he took a beer from the case kept just inside the door of the meat locker, a privilege he'd earned when he'd started shaving, and sat in the alley doorway. He tossed his stained white apron across a hook on the rail that the slaughterhouse trucks backed up to, and tilted his head to drink the bottle half-empty. He could watch, undetected as an evening ghost, as the married women walked by the alley's mouth, flat summer sandals and arms shining from the tarry pavement's heat. The shy, pretty one who had married last autumn bent her head over her newborn. All their voices were like the sounds of nesting birds, too soft to tell what they were saying.

He rolled the bottle between his wet hands. He knew that they were probably talking, among other things, about him and the widow.

'She oughta wax that upper lip of hers.' That was what his oldest sister had said, not because the woman had a moustache, but because she was so dark and wore hollow gold bracelets on her wrists like a gypsy. She looked like their grandmother's wedding photograph, the framed sepia oval in the hallway. His other sisters had giggled behind their hands, though the widow wasn't any darker than any of them.

She hadn't been a widow then. Her husband was a Cracow dandy and still alive. That was what his mother called a man who wore a pinstripe suit with a waist nipped in like a woman's. A hat and a red silk tie that turned black around the knot, like a hummingbird's throat. It must have been winter when he'd heard his mother call the man that, because he remembered the kitchen window being covered with steam from the pots upon the stove. His father had sat at the table eating, his suspenders hanging loose from his waist, his big-knuckled fists swallowing the knife and fork. She'd glanced back at his father, her husband, then leaned across the sink to look out the part of the window she'd wiped transparent with her hand, looking out at the men talking under the streetlight, the shoulders of their thin jackets hunched up against the cold, their breath silver mingled plumes.

'A Cracow dandy,' she'd said again, her voice filled with the same terrible empty longing it held when she spoke of her dead father. It must have been something she'd heard from her dead mother; she'd been born here. What did she know of the old world? Nothing but the old language, and less of that than her mother and her grandmother had known.

The last of the beer had warmed between his hands; on his tongue, it tasted sour and flat. He leaned forward, elbows against his knees, and watched the little girls run past the alley, called to set the tables for their fathers and older brothers who would be coming home from work soon.

He had wondered if the widow still set a place for her dead husband. And then he had found out.

Before that, he could have asked his mother – he would have, regardless of his father's warning – if it was something women do. Were supposed to do, an empty plate in front of an empty chair. He would have, except that he knew his mother and all his sisters were on the other side of the blood feud that had broken out in the parish church. It was doubtful if his mother would say anything now, good or bad, about any of that tribe, the widow included.

Something about the altar flowers; those were all women's doing, their world, so he could never be sure of the exact details. The priest had told the women to make room in the flower rotation for the newcomers, the ones who'd come to live in the parish only a few years ago, arriving with all their children and husbands and sons, bringing with them the air of the old world, the one that has been left a generation before. The newcomers' presence could be endured in silence, but the priest's order had caused grumbling among the women.

He took another sip of the beer's dregs and wondered how many languages the priest spoke. Not the languages that changed from place to place, but the other, the secret ones. The priest was like some black, slightly threadbare angel, neither man nor woman, occupying a barren holy ground between them. Perhaps he knew what women talked about, understood what they said; perhaps he had talked about the altar flowers in their own tongue.

Grumbling, then bad words in a language anyone could understand. He remembered his own mother muttering something under her breath as she'd passed by one of the newcomer women in the street – not the yet-to-be widow, but one of her cousins – her eyes narrowing as though the bell-like rattle of the other woman's gold bracelets made the fillings in her teeth ache. It could only get worse, and did. Especially after the toad crawled from the chalice at the altar rail.

He heard his father calling him from inside the shop. The last of the evening's customers would have come and gone by now; it would be time to close up and make their own way home.

Everything in its appointed time. The gears of this world's machinery meshed with the other's.

He would have to eat something of what his mother put on the table, or pretend to, pushing things around on the plate with his fork, knowing all the while that he wasn't fooling anyone. Just as he wouldn't be fooling them later, when the summer night was finally dark, and he would walk past his mother and father in the living room, pulling on a thin sweater as he stepped toward the front door without saying a word. As though he were going to do nothing more than sit out on the stoop, to catch a cooling breeze. At his back he would be able to feel, as he did every night, his mother looking up from the sewing basket on her lap, his father's glance over the top of the newspaper. Everybody knew – why he didn't eat, where he was going, even when he would be back, in the cold pearl light before dawn.

He could hear his father rummaging through the cash register, scooping the coins out of the little trays, bundling up the dollar bills with a rubber band, dumping everything into the little drawstring bag that he'd carry home inside his coat. One night a week – not this night, but another – he'd sit at the bare kitchen table and sort out the bit that would be placed inside a simple white envelope, to be left on top of the shop's counter. The widow's husband used to come in to pick it up, with a smile and a nod and a few overly polite words that the butcher had acknowledged with a simmering anger in his eyes. Now one of the other Cracow dandies came in every week to pick up the money.

His father called his name again, louder. He drained the last weak taste of beer and pitched the empty bottle in among the waste bin's red bones. He pulled the apron down from the hook and walked inside with it in his hand.

'You were thinking about that silly animal, weren't you? That toad.' She sat on the other side of the table from him, her bare elbows on the white cloth, holding a glass of wine in her hands, rubbing the corner of her brow with it. Her face was shining, the loose curls of her tied-up hair dampened against her neck and by her ears, from the steam off the pots on the stove. 'That was stupid, it spoils your appetite.' The widow smiled, eyes half-lidded, as though there were some indefinable pleasure in watching him eat. 'Think about things like that, a frog will grow in your belly and your eyes will bulge out. All the time.' She lowered the glass and sipped from it.

He looked up from the plate, not sure – never sure – if she was joking or not. They knew so many things, all women did; maybe that was one of them, a true thing. How would he know? Then he caught the lifting of one corner of her mouth. 'Bullshit.'

'Bullshit, he says.' She gazed up at the ceiling. 'I fix him dinner, he picks at it like I'm trying to poison him, then he says *bullshit* to me.' Her gaze, still smiling, settled back upon him. 'What would your mother say if she heard you talking like that?'

He had to wonder. Not about what his mother would say, but about the possibility of some conspiracy between her and the widow, a dealing in confidences that ran beneath the little feuds and hushed glares on the ordinary world's surface.

'I don't know.' No man did. He laid down his fork, a garlic clove and a bite of mutton – it hadn't come from his father's shop, he knew that at least – speared upon it. What they told each other, what all women shared amongst themselves, even the little girls with their jump ropes and knowing laughter. 'I mean, I don't know what she'd say.'

He looked down at the plate, at the speckled grease congealing, a scrap of bread as white as the underside of her breasts. As dark as she was, how shining black her hair and eyes . . . he'd laid his hand upon skin as pale as glass, beneath which the trembling of her veins could be seen, blue ink written on milk. He'd been rendered wordless by how that soft curve had fitted its cloudlike weight into his palm, an event foreordained by dreaming prophets.

Now he bit and chewed, laying the emptied fork back down, the motion of his jaws massaging the brain. To thoughts unbidden, still the blasphemous toad. He hadn't even been in the church that day, but he'd heard – everyone had; they all knew – and he could imagine the woman's cry as she'd fainted from the rail, the chalice rolling through the blood of Christ spilled upon the floor, as clearly as though he'd been in one of the pews. One of the altar boys had scooped up the toad to keep it from being trampled upon in the uproar or beaten to death with a broom-handle by the verger who saw Satan in every unusual thing. The toad was let go by the boys, with a degree of fearful reverence – it did, after all, count as some kind of miracle – in the tangled weeds behind the rectory. Nothing that had happened had been the toad's fault; everyone knew the ones responsible. The newcomer women had sat together, a long row of them wearing the old-fashioned black clothing in which they came to church, bits of their gold ornaments gleaming out through the stiff black lace at their wrists and throats. Through all the crying and shouting, they had passed a smile both secret and public amongst themselves. He knew that the widow-to-be had been there with her sisters and cousins, the grandmother with gold in her mouth as well, all of them; because they had known what was going to happen. All this over the altar flowers.

'Such a little thing,' she said. The widow gazed into her wineglass as though a mirror were there. 'What a thing to worry about. And let it spoil your appetite.'

He swallowed, the lamb sticking in his throat for a moment. He hadn't come here for dinner; he never had. He closed his eyes to see better, just what he was thinking of.

'You're so stupid.' She said it with great affection, the way she might have said it to her husband when he was alive. She laid her hand on top of his beside the plate. 'A toad – what's that?'

He shook his head. That she could tell what he was thinking of, he couldn't doubt. But never exactly; always a little shifted in focus, the circle around the bull's-eye. He supposed that was another difference between men and women, one that made all the other differences bearable.

Not *that* toad, but the other. A story that was not even whispered about, but which everybody knew somehow. That the men knew something of, enough to keep their silence, and the women, even the little girls, knew everything. Because it dealt with the business of women, even more than the altar flowers had.

Eyes closed, he felt the soft weight of her hand upon his. The widow must have leaned closer to him, across the table; he could smell her scent, both her perfume of ancient roses and the other, that would taste of salt when he kissed her brow.

'You're so pretty.'

He opened his eyes. 'No, I'm not.'

'Don't be mad. I just meant I like to look at you. That's all.'

Her eyes were so dark, he could have fallen inside them. That was a scary enough thought – scary that he would want to – he had to turn his face away from hers.

'Why do you think about these things?' Her scolding voice touched his ear. 'If they make you feel so strange?' Then softer: 'Better you should think about *me*.' Her fingers closed around his wrist. 'Here.' She had undone the buttons of her throat. She pressed his palm against the skin; he could feel her pulse echoing among the small bones of his hand.

He looked round and saw the whiteness caught beneath his fingertips. His skin was already chafed and hardened, like his father's, from the knives and icy flesh of the butcher shop.

'Nobody was hurt.' She whispered to him now; he could feel the words move inside the widow's throat. 'What happened had to be done. And the girl's fine now. Isn't she?'

He nodded. Everything she said was true. The war that had started with the altar flowers had come to an end, not by the parish women admitting defeat, but by their recognizing that the dark-eyed newcomers hadn't left their skills and secrets in the old world. That, in fact, what they knew was a worthy match for those who had come over generations before them. For everyone to know that was enough.

And the girl, the one who had taken the newcomers' flowers, roses dark and red, and dumped them in the battered trashcans behind the church hall's kitchen – she was just fine now. Or as well as could be expected. She was actually some second or third cousin of his, in

those ways that could only be figured out by his grandmother or one
of her sisters poring, mumbling, over a sepia photograph album, was
just fine now. Or as well as could be expected. The girl had come
back, tanned and loud-voiced, from a long vacation with her aunt
and her uncle who ran a construction business in far-off Tempe,
Arizona. The girl had only stayed around long enough to show how
healthy she was now, that none of what had happened to her really
mattered, that everything, her brief marriage and pregnancy and
what had happened in the delivery room, that had all been
something like a dream. From which she had wakened with a Reno
divorce certificate and a canteloupe webbing of stretch marks across
her stomach, that just meant she couldn't wear two-piece bathing
suits any more. Then the girl had gone with her barking, brittle laugh
into the city, to work as a secretary in another uncle's import-export
company and sleep with negro musicians. There were enough of her
friends left behind who envied her, that the widow could say now
that no one had been hurt and it would be true enough.

It was only the men who knew, and the older boys who knew, and
those like himself who were caught between those estates, who
dreamed and let their waking thoughts be troubled by such things,
that were women's business and none of their own. They all knew,
even though they had seen nothing of what happened to the girl.
Fool that he was, fool that both he and the widow knew him to be, as
all women know all men are; he could close his eyes, like the point of
his tongue unable to resist prodding an aching tooth, and see a
chrome and white-tiled room, the girl's feet up in the stirrups, a
hospital-green sheet over her enormous belly. And then another
tongue poke, and he would see more of what he didn't want to see
and couldn't keep from seeing: the doctor's sweat soaking through
his mask as he shouted at the nurses and anaesthesiologist to get out,
to get out of the delivery room and leave him alone here. Then the
doctor had turned back to his task, lifting the sheet above the girl's
spread-apart knees with one gloved hand, while the sharpest scalpel
from the tray glittered in his other hand. Bringing the metal close
enough to reflect the idiot round eyes peering from the small
darkness, the webbed claws braced to keep it inside the wet sling of
flesh it was so reluctant to leave.

How did these pictures get inside their heads, if they were of
things the men had never seen, never been told about? But they all
knew, after a night of bad dreams they could see it in each other's
eyes; he had seen it in the way his father had bent over the broom,
sweeping off the sidewalk in front of the store, counting the money

into the till to get ready for the morning's first customer. And silence, the silence that lay behind the words even when someone spoke, silence that had looked at and then turned away from the cruel necessities of women's business. All the men, the priest included, had been grateful that the war of the altar flowers had ended, that this truce both grudgeful and admiring had been achieved.

And he, the butcher's son, had been grateful, because by that time he had already begun sleeping with the dark-eyed widow.

In her kitchen, the night velvet behind the steamy windows, he sat leaning across the table toward her. She loosened another button at the front of her dress, and his hand fell of its own weight, almost without will, to cup her breast.

'You're so stupid,' she murmured and smiled, her own eyes half-lidded now. He knew she meant not just him, but all of them.

There was one more picture inside his head, that he turned his face down toward his plate to see, as though ashamed of this weakness. But he had to, so he could forget for a while, or long enough. Her heartbeat rocked inside his palm even louder now. His arm felt hollow into his chest, where his own pulse caught in time with hers.

Inside his head, in that other night, the doctor still wore his surgical scrubs from the delivery room. As he walked across the field behind the hospital's parking lot, the high grass silvered by the moon. Carrying something wadded up inside the green sheet, something that leaked through red upon his bare hands. Until the doctor flung open the sheet from where he stood upon the high bank of a creek, and heard a second later the pieces drop into the water. He threw in the red-edged scalpel as well, and it disappeared among the soft weeds like the bright flash of a minnow. In that picture, the doctor looked over his shoulder at the hospital's lights, face hardened against what he'd come to know about the business of women. The doctor and the priest were brothers apart from other men, and the same as all men. They all knew, but could not speak of these things.

He felt the widow kiss him on the side of his face. He looked up and saw her, and nothing else. Nothing at all.

She wore a black nightgown to bed, or what would have been black if her skin hadn't shone so luminous through it. To him it looked like smoke in her bedroom's darkness, smoke across a city of a thousand doors, the shadow across the crypt deep in the white stone where Our Redeemer was both born and buried.

The black nightgown felt like smoke as well, if smoke could have been gathered into his hands. He lay with her in his arms, her eyes closed now, the sheets moulded with sweat to his ribs.

'She likes it very much that way.' Her husband's awkward English came from above them, from the side of the bed. 'To be held, and held. Just so.'

He turned his head and looked up at the dead man. The Cracow dandy. Half of the man's face was gone, from the first bullet that had struck him in the eye, then the rest that his murderer had poured like water from an outstretched hand, feet spread to either side of the man's shoulders upon the pavement. Not murder really, but a business disagreement between the Cracow dandy and his dark-eyed brothers; it was the business of men to know the difference. Just as it had been the business of the butcher, every other Friday, to ring NO SALE on the cash register and count again the thin sheaf of fives and tens in the plain white envelope that he set beside the Saint Vincent de Paul charity jar. So that the Cracow dandy, when he'd been alive, or one of his elegantly tailored associates, could come in, smile and talk to the butcher, and buy nothing and leave, the envelope somehow magically transported into the dandy's coat pocket without his ever having shown his soft, manicured hands. Then nodding to the butcher's son with the pushbroom and smiling, all of them knowing that this was how the business of men was done. So much so, knowledge passed from one generation to the next, from the old world to this, that he had known what to do without being told, to wait upon the rest of the day's customers, to wrap chops and stew bones, and make change and finally lock the shop up, turning the sign in the door from OPEN to CLOSED, all while his father sat on the alley stoop and knocked back thimbles of schnapps with a heavy, brooding scowl on his face.

'I know,' he told the dead man. 'I know what to do next. You don't have to tell me.'

'You know . . .'

But that wasn't the dead man who spoke, who whispered, it was the widow with the dark eyes and the black nightgown, the stuff of smoke and silk, pushed above her hips. His hand passed from there to the curve of her thigh, and it felt like laying his palm upon his mother's stove, if anything in the world could be both that soft and yet as hot as heated iron. Hot enough to burn the tongue in his mouth until he was as mute as dead men should be.

'Like this . . .'

He knew that her dead husband stood by the bed, an angel in an elegant suit. A Cracow dandy, a rose with splinters of bone for white thorns where his right eye and cheekbone had been. He felt the dead man's fingers curve around his hand, the way his father's had when he had first been shown how to bring the cleaver between the compliant ribs. Now he let the dead man cup his palm around the widow's breast.

I'm not such a fool, he thought. *I know all this. I was born knowing.*

But he let the dead man show him anyway. Because that was what she wanted. He knew that as well.

'Kiss her.' The dead man whispered in his ear. 'While you hold her. Press tight and don't be afraid. Be a man . . .'

I'm not afraid. He hadn't been afraid the first time he had been in her bed – their bed – and he had looked over his shoulder and seen her dead husband with the ruined face. How could anyone lying in bed with a woman ever be afraid? And with her clad only in a nightgown of black smoke and silk . . .

That was what women didn't know. For all their mysteries and secrets, for even the youngest girls' knowing smiles – they didn't know that when men trembled in this place, in the grave of desire, it was not from fear.

He opened his eyes and looked down. Looked down and saw what the dead man above him saw. He saw her with her eyes closed, lips slightly parted, her naked arms reaching . . .

For her husband.

His face burning with shame, he looked over his shoulder to the one who the dark-eyed widow loved, who she would always love.

'Don't feel bad.' The Cracow dandy's voice was the kindness of one man to another. 'It's not that she doesn't care for you. She might even have loved you, or someone like you, if she hadn't loved me first.'

'I know. I know that,' he said. 'It doesn't matter.'

Here . . .

He no longer knew whose voice it was, that told him what to do. It could have been his own.

Like this . . .

Or hers. He watched his hand, or that of her dead husband, stroke her dark hair upon the pillow. She turned her face toward that touch.

And smiled.

'You see?' said the dead man. 'Just like that. Just like that. Just like that.'

He closed his own eyes. And kissed her. The tear between his lashes and her cheek burned like fire, if fire were salt.

As he knew would happen – as none of them told him, but he knew anyway – a year passed, from the time a sealed coffin was lain in earth, to the time when he knocked upon her door, his hands smelling of blood from his father's shop, no matter how much he scrubbed them with soap and vinegar. A year passed from the Cracow dandy's death, he knew it had, but he still came and knocked at her door.

The dark-eyed widow opened the door just wide enough that he could see the others inside, the bottles of wine upon the table, and hear their bright laughter. She looked out upon him, standing there in the darkness that came so early in the winter. She smiled with enough sadness to break his heart, then shook her head and silently closed the door. He could still hear the laughter and singing on the other side.

He turned away and saw the cardboard box at the curb, the box of her old clothes, for the trash collectors to pick up and carry away. All the black dresses that she had worn for the last year. The black with which she had mourned her dead husband. A year had passed and she didn't need them anymore.

He knelt down and pushed his hands through the contents of the box. Until he found, at the bottom, something of silk and smoke. He drew it out and helt it against his face, breathing in the scent that was part her and part the perfume of ancient roses that she had used.

He knew. He had always known. A year would pass, and she would forget about both of them, the butcher's son and the Cracow dandy. She was still young, and a year had passed.

He heard steps running on the sidewalk. They halted, and he looked up and saw one of the youngest girls watching him without smiling, a coil of jump rope in her hand. It got dark so early, this time of year.

The little girl ran past him, toward her home and supper. He let the nightgown slip from his hands, drifting across his knee and a corner of the box like smoke, if smoke could fall.

MÉNAGE À TROIS

by

Richard Christian Matheson

Richard Christian Matheson is a novelist, short story writer, and screen writer/producer. He has written and produced more than 500 episodes of television for over thirty prime time series. He also has played with the writers' band 'Rock Bottom Remainders'. He is considered an important writer of short horror fiction, having published fifty short stories in such diverse magazines as *Penthouse*, *Twilight Zone* and *Omni*. His stories are collected in *Scars and Other Distinguishing Marks*. His first novel *Created By* was published by Bantam and he is working on his second, *Leading Man*, which will be published by Bantam in 1995.

Matheson's forte is the short-short. His choice of the perfect image can evoke in shorthand more than many writers do in lengthier works.

MÉNAGE À TROIS

_12:38 A.M._

Heat.
Midnight fingers.
They wipe warm metal. She reaches with needful tears. He gently takes her in his arms. Her back arches. Nipples lift. He stabs her. She shudders, Clutching air.
'Yes,' she moans, crying; helpless.

_2:15 A.M._

She awakens, gently kisses his fingers.
He opens eyes. Feels it cut his chest. Feels wetness slither down ribs as it opens strands of perfect muscle.
'Deeper,' a groaning whisper.
She pushes it, harder, placing her ear to his skin. Listening to it tear open, more. They hold hands. Smile softly.
The two bodies braid, sleep.
Bleed.

_3:40 A.M._

He wants to watch. Just the two, doing it for him. She lowers eyes, lips a vulgar bow. He waits, fixed. She spreads, runs the bevel along her inner thigh; makes ghastly red licorice.
Again. Illegible. Running onto sheet. Legs an obscene note written with private ink.
He kneels, gripping himself. Breath speeding. Her teeth part, tongue reaching. His eyes close in soundless convulsion. He collapses.

She strokes his hair. Holds him close. Cuts his face open. 'I love you.'

He clings like a baby, soaking her breasts red.

4:14 A.M.

They hold each other in candlelight. Sweet body oils; their personal sea, seeped into sheets.

The knife rests, between them.

They take it together, run lips over it, faces touching. Lick mirror sharpness, kiss thick stem; ecstatic slowness.

Their tongues spread open and bleed.

They giggle.

6:35

The candle burns.

They moan. Turn to face each other. Both want more.

He begs with sounds; eyes. She sits on his chest, raises it over him and his eyes close, letting it happen.

Hot-red freckles them and he smiles up at her, as she slices him.

6:50

They sleep. Huddled. Bloody blade nestled between his stomach, her back.

She stirs. Can't sleep. Something is wrong. A feeling. She begins to resent them as three.

The rivalry. It's become ugly. Obscene.

She quietly turns, takes the knife lover, moves it to his throat.

THE LAST TIME

by

Lucius Shepard

Lucius Shepard burst onto the science fiction and fantasy scene in the early 1980s and became one of the most prolific and influential writers of that decade. In 1987 he won the Nebula Award for his novella 'R & R', in 1988 he won the World Fantasy Award for his collection *The Jaguar Hunter*, and in 1993 he won the Hugo Award for his novella 'Barnacle Bill the Spacer'. He is the author of three novels, *Green Eyes* – an sf/zombie novel, *Life During Wartime*, and his most recent *The Golden*, a brilliantly fresh take on the vampire.

'The Last Time' seems an appropriate closing to *Little Deaths*, as it describes the arc of a doomed relationship that is obsessive in its all-consuming fire.

THE LAST TIME

1

These new drugs separate me from madness by the thinnest of chemical partitions. Normally I sit in my room with the weather of madness – I picture it as a ceiling of turbulent, lightning-filled clouds – seething about me, lowered to cover my skull, my eyes, occluding all my senses; but now it is as if that ceiling has lifted to inches above my head, and though I can hear the thunder and smell the ozone, I am sufficiently lucid to participate in life, rather than, as has been the case for almost three years, to sit and stare as the minimal operations of my existence, baths and feeding and such, take place around me.

My doctor, who under most circumstances is an enthusiastic sort, a cheerleader among psychiatrists, cannot assure me that the drugs will be permanently effective, but he suggests I proceed as if they will; and since I refuse to discuss the events that led me to this pass, he encourages me take advantage of my newfound lucidity and write about them. I have decided to follow his suggestion. Writing, I've found, tends to assuage feelings of guilt and anguish, and to render somewhat abstract the memories that afflict me, whereas talking only serves to exacerbate them.

And yet how shall I explain what on the surface appears inexplicable?

The magic of love, the illusion kindled in the warmth of lovers' beds that they are becoming a single ecstatic creature.

The all-consuming power of sexual desire.

Certainly these principles were involved in all that happened, but from the beginning, desperate to win at love, I resorted to prayer, to oracles, to palmists and spiritual readers, and eventually to *santeria*, and while I did not believe in any of these things in the specific (I often felt foolish, in fact, for seeking such implausible consolations), I did allow myself to believe that, taken all together, they were creating a climate for success, concocting a psychic potion, a blending of obsession and unsavory arts that would enable or entice some unfathomable force to forge an unbreakable bond between me and my lover. I doubt that what I write will shed much light on these matters, but in documenting them perhaps I can reach a small accommodation with the past. That would be a consolation, indeed.

This, then, is the story of my affair with Kathleen Cardoza, how it began and how it thrived, and the terrible, sad thing that came of it. In it is almost everything I know, all that is left for me to know. I suppose it is a love story.

2

I met Kathleen in the summer of 1988 at a cocktail party given by my editor at the *New York Times* to celebrate my release from prison in Guatemala and the publication of my series on the politics of terror in that country, an event that everyone told me was sure to herald a Pulitzer nomination. She was a recent hire at ABC News, just up from the affiliate in Boston, where she had served as co-anchor on the Eleven O'Clock Report for the previous three years. Rumour had it she was being groomed as a replacement for Joan Lundun, but I thought this unlikely. Redheads of her stamp, those with pale coppery hair and milky skin, were not considered particularly telegenic, and her curious imbalance of Irish and Italian features, large blue eyes and prominent nose and full mouth, had too much character and earthiness to conform to the airbrushed look that network executives preferred for their hostess slots. She had an overbite I found sexy, but that at certain angles, in combination with her high cheekbones, lent her face a horsey cast; there were faint lines at the corners of her eyes, and when depressed she would often look sullen and puffy and very young, rather like a plain child. But all these flaws seemed interesting to me, part of her unique beauty.

As I recall, we were not introduced, but gravitated together in a corner of the apartment, where we remained talking, just the two of us, for more than an hour, a difficult feat considering that we were both in demand. But we managed it, and what ensued was less a flirtation than a feeling-out process. Within fifteen minutes or so we had established that she admired my work (always a good sign), especially my Guatemalan series; we had exchanged backgrounds, phone numbers, and a few fundamental prejudices; and she had made it clear through intimation and body language that she was unhappily married: throughout our conversation she twisted and tugged at her wedding ring as if it chafed and she were about to wrench it off and hurl it out the window.

I had been involved with another married woman several years before, a brutalizing experience that had ended unhappily for all concerned. So, although I could not help responding to Kathleen's signals, I wasn't sure how far I wanted things to go. But before I reached a decision as to whether to call her or not, my uncle, the man who had raised me from the age of six following the death of my parents, was diagnosed with terminal cancer, and I took a leave of absence from the *Times* and returned to his home in Cartersville, Virginia to care for him.

For the better part of the next ten months I lived in my uncle's two-hundred-year old farmhouse, changing his bedpans, bathing him, giving him injections, and whenever I could, working on a book describing my prison experiences – a project whose materials did nothing to alleviate the depressing circumstances. I was given intermittent relief by a private nurse, but my uncle was not at ease alone with her, and I was able to escape only rarely. And when I did succeed in getting time to myself, there was nowhere to go: Cartersville consisted of a general store, a post office and several hundred members of what Richard Nixon had once described as the Silent Majority. Eventually, however, I learned that there was a roadhouse in Goochland, some twenty miles away, and I began spending my off-duty hours drinking in a dingy room furnished with pool tables and digital beer signs in the shape of waterfalls and Poulan chainsaw calendars, surrounded by plump, loud women and surly, rawboned, weathered men in hunting caps and denim jackets whose stares seemed as alien and coldly calculating as had the stares of Indian whores in the little jungle towns of the Petén. But I was myself at heart a redneck, at least I could play the role, and before long I was accepted as a kind of prodigal cousin returned from the Great Deviant Beyond, from the dimension of homosexuals and the Democratic Party. I was, after all, Roy Dean's Boy . . . 'Y'know, ol' Roy Dean Autrey lives out past Spanky's store over in Cartersville? This here's his boy, Michael.'

'Hell, yeah! I know Roy Dean. Been huntin' over to his place many a time. Y'all gettin' any birds this year?'

For a time I thrived in this atmosphere. Quite probably I would have thrived in any atmosphere a degree more life-affirming than that of the ancient house where my uncle lay wasting away; but be that as it may, and despite the occasional suspicion that I was hobnobbing with examples of inbreeding such as could be seen each afternoon screeching at one another on the Maury Povich Show and Sally Jesse Raphael, I came to renew my affection for these country people. For all their prejudice and ignorance, they had good hearts, and the kindnesses they did my uncle upon learning of his condition, the little gifts they sent, brightened him and made both our lives easier. For one thing, it pleased him to think that I might stay on in the farmhouse after his death, and he began encouraging me to go out, hoping I would deepen my attachment to Cartersville and its environs. But each night, driving home drunk through the black, winded emptiness of rural Virginia, I grew more and more to dread the sight of the farmhouse, the smell of cancer and its antiseptic consolations, and to resent the protracted process of my uncle's dying. As a foster parent he had been generous and loving, and to feel this way about him now bred in me a tumultous guilt. I drank to greater excess than before, I brooded, I shouted at the nurse, and finally, in a pathetic attempt at evasion, I took up with Evelyn Cobb, an attractive, thirtyish divorcee whom I had met at the roadhouse.

During our first night together Evelyn was thoroughly uninhibited, more so than I had any reason to expect. It became apparent that she, like myself, had not had sex for a considerable while, and she went at it with almost demented ferocity. The instant I came she would set herself to arousing me again, and once I was hard she would impale herself upon me and bring herself off within a few minutes. I doubt we exchanged more than a handful of coherent sentences the entire night, and then only to say, 'Let me get on top' or 'Roll over' or some equally clinical instruction. This is not to suggest that Evelyn was in the least demure. When she was not occupied in screaming, she carried on a breathy prattle of OhJesusyesses and fuckmeharders and similar encouragements, a trait that I found distancing. We engaged in juicy, thrashing, calisthentic sex, an activity wholly at odds with the white four-poster and heirloom-filled china closet and doily-strewn settee and portraits of her prudish, witch-killing ancestors gazing balefully down from the moonstruck walls upon the unregenerate lusts of their great-great-great-granddaughter.

Over the next few nights Evelyn grew markedly more restrained in both the frequency and stridency of her outcries, and her sexual spectrum narrowed somewhat, though she remained healthily responsive. Then on the sixth night she stopped me as I was about to enter her and confessed a deep and abiding faith in Jesus Christ, and said that what we were doing was wrong. Lord, she loved doing it with me, it wasn't that, you understand, she just didn't think she could go on this way. Because it was wrong. Against God's law. The lustful bed, she told me, is Satan's playground. Okay, I said, fine, how about let's talk about this later? After I had finished fucking her she burst into tears and asked me to pray with her, which I pretended to do, kneeling naked by her side at the foot of the bed, a prayer that degenerated into a doggie-style fuck on the floor and more weeping.

I am certain that Evelyn was not trying to coerce me into marriage, that she was undergoing an actual moral crisis. And I doubt that marriage would have resolved the crisis. She never made her state of mind clear to me, but I believe the main problem for her was not that we were having sex out of wedlock, but was instead related to the alarming new depth of her sexual responses, the effect of the hormones that were starting to kick in now she had hit the big Three-O. Whatever the case, our nights took on a dismaying therapeutic intensity, bouts of weepy self-abnegation and hysteria on her part, weary tenderness on mine, interspersed with sex that, for all its physical fervour became less and less involving. Given everything else that was going on, I was ill-equipped to handle anyone else's problems, and after a couple of weeks I broke it off with Evelyn. She was disappointed, but – I think – even more relieved.

A few days later I telephoned Kathleen and we began a long distance relationship. At first the calls were brief and only marginally personal; but I could tell she was happy to hear from me, and within a few weeks we were talking several hours a day, mostly on her dime – she, after all, had ABC to foot the bill. As a result we became close in a short period of time. Our conversations ranged from politics to art to the news business, but always centred about one or other of two topics: my loneliness and her unhappiness. We consoled each other. She assured me that things would turn out all right; I would return to New York, get into my work again, finish my book. I, on the other hand, acted as a marriage counsellor, encouraging her to talk about her husband Darryl. Not that she needed encouragement; she was bursting to tell me about him. Darryl had disappointed her in every way. They rarely slept together. He was insensitive, compulsive, immature, a racist, a fool – essentially a child – who knew nothing yet made his living writing self-help books. She had married him, she said, not for love, but in a fit of existential panic brought on by the sudden death of her mother and her twenty-ninth birthday, which had followed hard upon that event. She had known the marriage was a mistake, but she had been unable to stop the momentum of the proceedings and had gone through with the ceremony. Almost immediately after the wedding she had entered into two short-lived affairs, scarcely more than one-night stands; it had been, she thought, her way of establishing that the ceremony had not really taken, that she was still free. Now, however, she felt trapped. Guilty at the idea of leaving Darryl. I used my experience with my former married lover to show her that she should not settle for loveless security. To do so, I said, was to condemn both parties in the relationship to unhappiness. I discussed the worthlessness of guilt, its relation to one's duty to one's self, and how a lack of self-esteem sometimes governed our life choices. I knew I was not truly advising her, I was trying to seduce her; yet I also knew that she wanted to be seduced, and I believed this mutuality was based on a friendship that had been nurtured by months of intimate conversation. But even had I not believed that, I would have tried to seduce her, because I had become reliant upon her calls. They were ropes dropped down to me from a better, happier world, and I thought that by clinging to them I would be able to haul myself out from this place of death, this moribund old house haunted by the barely human spectre that my uncle had become. I imagined Kathleen's face, her body. I fantasized about her. At night I would sit listening to my uncle moan, and I would come as close to prayer as I had since childhood, squeezing my eyes shut, clenching my fists, wishing the days would pass quickly so I could join her in New York. There was no god who could serve as a suitable receptacle for my prayers. I had seen too many desolated Christians to give credence to Jehovah. Too many mutilated Mohammedans, starving Buddhists, and so forth. And so, in an act half desperation, half delirium, I conjured a new god from the pit of my imagination, from the misery around me, from cancer and country nightmares and all the bleakness and savagery of my recent past, a dark Guatemalan god, mangy and bestial, with just a hint of the Catholic for atmosphere, and I poured every ounce of my obsession into him, demanding that he bring Kathleen and me together, that he join us inseparably forever and ever. I never pictured him, never gave him a face, yet I could have sworn that I felt something come near, something heavy, heated, and grim, a black gravity grumbling in a voice like the end of metal.

Desperation, I thought at the time. Delirium.

The evidence of my senses, naturally, can no longer be considered credible, but it seems to me now that I did not stop feeling that presence until nearly two years later, and as I sift through the passionate wreckage of the affair, through the twisted shapes of my faith, looking for answers, I can almost believe – in fact, it is very hard to disbelieve – that some vile, bloated, fleck of negativity, itself almost an absence, smelled my terror and shuffled up to me from the back end of damnation and so as to satisfy some evil whim granted all my wishes.

One bitterly cold morning Kathleen phoned to tell me that she wouldn't be calling anymore. She had just finished being dressed down by her immediate superior for the thousands of dollars of calls she had made to Virginia; he had not threatened to fire her, but she knew she was on probation. 'I can't believe I risked my job,' she said tremulously. 'I want to talk with you, but I don't know how I can manage it.'

I told her it wasn't a problem, that in the future I'd pay for the calls, and that I shouldn't have let her assume all the responsibility in the first place.

'It's not your fault,' she said. 'You've got so much else to deal with, I just wanted to help.'

There was a moment here, I realized, one I had been waiting for, if I only had the courage to seize it. I was sitting in the kitchen, a drafty place with an immense black iron stove, an overflowing woodbox and rippled linoleum with a faded floral pattern on the floor; through the frost-edged window I spotted a deer poised on the crest of a low, brown, snow-dappled hill that divided two strands of leafless trees behind the house. I focused on the scene outside, imagining that I was only rehearsing what I intended to say to Kathleen, hoping this would make me feel less foolish.

'Have you got a minute?' I asked her. 'I'd like to talk to you about something.'

'Sure. What is it?'

A handful of seconds passed without either of us speaking, and at last she sang out brightly, nervously, 'Hello-oh?'

'Look,' I said, 'I've been under a lot of stress, and when that happens people tend to blow things out of proportion. But I don't believe stress has anything to do with this.'

There was another prickly interval, and then she asked if I was ill, if that's what was wrong.

'No, no,' I said. 'I'm fine, I'm . . . I'm just having a little trouble getting this out.'

As I screwed up my nerve, feeling as anxious as a teenager, it seemed I could sense her anticipation in the faint hum of the long distance wires – I had the idea she knew what was coming.

'The thing is,' I told her, 'I'm falling in love with you. It's been happening for a while now. Maybe I shouldn't tell you. The way everything is, it's probably ridiculous. But I can't go on talking to you like this without saying it. I can't talk about your marriage with you . . . not with any degree of impartiality. I probably shouldn't ever have talked about it.'

'It's all right,' she said – I couldn't read her tone, except to the extent that she sounded distracted, and that worried me.

'I mean I'd hate to lose these phone calls,' I said. 'But I've got to be honest.'

'Don't worry. You're not going to lose me,' she said after a few beats; her voice was small and, I thought, a bit depressed, as if my not losing her was something to which she had been condemned. 'It's the same for me. I think about you all the time.'

I thought she was going to say something more, but she fell silent. I was so giddy with relief, I was unable to muster speech. Finally, trying to lighten the mood, I said, 'I guess this is where we're supposed to throw our arms around each other and kiss.'

She gave a rueful laugh. 'I wish.'

I heard shotguns in the distance and thought about the deer. There was no apparent end to hunting season in Cumberland Country.

'I want to see you,' she said with a sudden increase in energy.

'Me, too. But there's no way I can get out of here right now.'

'I might be able to come for a weekend,' she said. 'I could tell Darryl I'm going to visit my dad.'

That brightened me, but then I thought about trying to start things with her while my uncle was dying in the background.

'It's getting pretty rough around here,' I said. 'My uncle hasn't got a lot of time left. Maybe only a few weeks. I doubt we could have much of a visit.'

She said, 'Oh,' sounding disappointed.

'I want you to understand something,' I said. 'I'm not after a fling. I'm dead serious about you. I know we have problems to overcome, and maybe I'm hoping for more than is reasonable . . . but I'm hoping for it just the same.'

She made no response, and I asked, 'You okay? Did I say something wrong?'

'Oh, no!' She gave another laugh. 'You're saying all the right things. Believe me.'

There was something in her laugh that puzzled me, an undertone of bewilderment, as if she couldn't quite trust the fact that I was saying the right things. I heard an engine and looked out the window that faced the road. A battered grey pick-up was bouncing along the driveway toward the house – Walter and Red, two men who did occasional work for my uncle. In a minute they would be all over the kitchen, loose and sloppy as hounds, breaking out a bottle of sour mash, talking about the weather and what they'd shot recently in accents as thick as Gomer Pyle's. I always looked forward to their visits, and this was no exception – I was afraid that I might screw things up if I talked any longer to Kathleen, and I wanted to celebrate what had happened. I would check in with the nurse, then have a few drinks with Walter and Red.

'I gotta go. Some people are here,' I said. 'But let me finish first. I don't want to start things with you and have anything else on my mind. You understand? I want to make a good, clean beginning. If you came here now . . . I don't know. It'd be great to see you, don't get me wrong. But there's no way it could be a good beginning.'

'I understand,' she said. 'It's just going to be even harder waiting for you now.'

'Is that what you've been doing? Waiting?'

'It feels like it,' she said. 'So I guess I have.'

Walter and Red were walking toward the kitchen door, red-faced and seedy-looking in their worn coats and orange hunting caps, blowing exhausts of frozen breath. Judging by their unsteady gaits, I figured they were each about a pint into a drunk.

'I gotta go,' I said. 'I'll call you tomorrow.'

'Michael?'

'Yeah.'

'I love you.' She said it with such calm, quiet assurance I had no reason to doubt that she understood everything the words portended.

3

Three days later I received a card from Kathleen saying once again that she loved me, and that she knew I was going to get through the next part with my uncle in fine shape. She closed by saying, 'Whenever I think of us together, I experience an unmistakeable physical reaction', a confession that stimulated me no end. It was the first of many notes and cards I was to receive from her, a correspondence that continued even after we were living in the same city. I was always happy to get them, but there came a point when I began to wonder if this need to document her feelings and replay her erotic moments did not reflect a perverse level of voyeurism, something that might have signalled to me, if I had stopped to think, a dangerous (dangerous to me, in any case) capacity for compartmentalizing her emotions, for viewing her life in an unhealthily abstract context. Indeed, she mentioned such a tendency in the long, explicit letter I received following our first night together, speaking of the 'voyeuristic delight I felt in watching myself surrender to you so completely'.

That first night took place nearly a month after my uncle's death, on a train between New York and Montreal, where we had arranged to attend a conference on Ethics in Journalism, and if one is to believe Kathleen's letter it was among the central moments of her life:

'If any of my friends had described responses similar to the way I was responding to you, I would have laughed at them, I would have said they'd been reading too many romance novels. Yet there I was, lost with you. Sometimes when I opened my eyes I wouldn't recognize you, I'd see the face of a bearded stranger caught in a freeze frame of white light coming through the sleeping car window, and then a moment later I'd look at you again, and you'd seem wholly familiar and loved. And sometimes I'd hear myself saying things to you, foolish things, making promises that I would have considered impossible to keep at any other time, with any other man, but now struck me as being utterly reasonable and right. And the things we did . . . God! I hope I don't sound slutty talking about all this, but I want you to know everything about how I feel. I never let anyone come in my mouth before that night. You were the first. I'd always thought it would be awful, but it wasn't, it was wonderful. I loved how you tasted, and how your cock pulsed when you came, and how odd it was to feel submissive and at the same time in control. It may seem foolish to you, but it made me feel virginal again.

'Afterwards, lying there with you, I felt perfectly wanton, perfect in abandon. The slack rhythms of the coach and the racketing of the wheels, they seemed to reflect my own slackness and disarray, and all the disordered universe beyond, the trillions of inconsequential lives and stars whose centre had become the mystery of our sweaty, lurching little bed. It was incredible how much I felt, not just the sex, not just the love, but everything, all the nuances of feeling, the sense of being completely open and vulnerable, and not worrying about it. It seemed even more incredible that I could have gone for thirty-two years without knowing any of this existed.

'We started talking, then. I can't remember about what, but the words sounded vulgar to me, all except 'I love you', and even they barely passed muster. Love must take place mostly in the silences, I think, because everything we said seemed to diminish what I felt. But I suspected you were worried that I was feeling guilty, that I was thinking about Darryl, and you were trying to soothe me. Which was ridiculous, because I hadn't thought about him since we began planning the weekend. But at any rate, we were talking, and the noise of the wheels suddenly intensified, and white light came crashing through the window, and I could see our hung-up clothes, the mirror on the door, my purse. The smallness of the compartment startled me. It seemed I'd been living in this infinite place, a place without walls, and even though the notion was totally unreal, it made me uneasy to imagine that I'd been suspended in all that black turmoil with only your arms to support me. Your hand was on my breast, and my heart was throbbing against it. It was as if I'd had a mild fright, an anxiety attack or something. But then your erection came back, and all I could think was to get you inside me again. That was when I rolled over and got up on my hands and knees for you. Do you remember? Once again, that was something I'd never enjoyed, that position, but I wanted to do it like that with you. I wanted to do everything with you.

'I can't tell you how strange it was to feel that way, to act that way. It wasn't like me at all, or rather it was an entirely different me from the one I was used to, and I didn't quite know what to make of it. I'm still not sure I do. Anyway, there I was with my butt up in the air, just begging for it, and instead of fucking me, you began running your hand along my flank, and then you put two fingers in me. You worked them inside me so slowly and carefully, it put me in mind of a surgeon inserting his hand into a rubber glove. I asked what you were doing, and you said, 'Just playing.' In retrospect it seemed so clinical, I should have found it off-putting, but I didn't, because I was completely in league with you, with the requisites of your desire. I loved what you were doing. Your fingers felt so good! And when you did start to fuck me, I know I came unglued. You were so deep inside me, all through me. I couldn't believe how quickly I came, I couldn't believe I came at all in that position. I guess orgasms really are 90 per cent mental. But the hardest thing for me to believe was how much pleasure I took from your pleasure. I loved how you handled me, not roughly, not too gently, as if I was breakable, but like you were handling a strong, young animal, gripping me firmly and battering into me from behind, and I just rested there, staring out at the rattling dark and the stars, and every once in a while I'd reach back and touch the sticky, complicated place where you entered me and feel how hard you were.

'The train began slowing down, pulling into a station. I saw the station walls and the roofpoles of the waiting area passing by, but I didn't try to stop you or pull the curtain. You were so close, and I wanted you to come in me. Even when I saw people standing outside, I didn't interrupt you. I didn't care if they saw us. In fact I wanted them to see you come in me, I wanted them to know how thoroughly possessed by love I was, and I rolled my hips more quickly, trying to bring you off. And after you had finished, after you'd collapsed beside me and the train had stopped, I lay there for what must have been almost a minute, just staring out at the people staring in, not because I had an urge toward exhibitionism . . . I don't know why exactly. Maybe simply because it didn't matter if they saw, because what had happened between us made ordinary concerns irrelevant. And when I finally did pull the curtain, it wasn't out of embarrassment or prudishness. I only wanted to be alone with you . . .'

The intense sexuality that informs this letter was a mirror image of my own, and my memories of that night were no less commanding than Kathleen's. Before we became lovers we had discussed how things might go for us, and we had agreed that everything depended on chemistry. We need not have been concerned. In fact, there were often times when I thought that the powerful chemistry between us actually harmed our chance to win at love, causing us to neglect other facets of the relationship – the friendship, our mutual interests, all those things that were our foundation. But what struck me as curious about Kathleen's letter, about all of her letters, is that there was never a single mention of tenderness, of sweetness, of any of the qualities that served as the setting for our passion, qualities that women generally prize above the basics of sex. We were in love, she with me and I with her, completely, all-consumingly in love, and when we were together we lived in a world of whispers and caresses, of small, delicate behaviours and quiet joys. Yet in her correspondence Kathleen was absorbed by the flamboyant aspects of sex, by the number of times we made it and the duration of each encounter, and by the exotic deployment our bodies. This is not to say that such an absorption was unnatural, but it puzzled me that she was absorbed by these things to the exclusion of everything else. Then I remembered Evelyn Cobb's alarm at her awakened sexuality, and I had the thought that Kathleen might be similarly alarmed, and that her fascination with our sex life was concentrated on her lack of control. She had spent her entire adult life in cities, mostly alone, involved in the paranoid wars of the corporate world, and she had never been in love before; her previous relationships with men, including that with her father, had been problematic at best, abusive at worst, and thus she required a certain measure of control in order to feel secure. Now, though she exulted in her newfound liberation, she was also frightened by it, distrustful of it. All this is there in her letter, but at the time I could not see its importance.

Kathleen moved out of her husband's apartment three days after our return from Montreal, and for nearly a year thereafter, though we kept separate apartments, we were essentially living together. I suppose that for the most part we were happy. Certainly we were excited, alive, bright with who we were and what we might achieve. We were both successful, we had love and enough money so that we did not have to think about it, and we were living in the most thrilling of cities, at the confluence of sewage and great art, of politics and business, of bloody murder and sublime grace. We talked about marriage, children. We made plans to make plans. Yet I never felt that anything in the relationship was a *fait accompli*. Indeed, there were signs that gave me cause for doubt and inspired me from the very beginning, as I have already mentioned, to exercise my superstitious nature, to buy charms, to consult psychics, and so forth. For one thing, she had not told her husband about me, claiming that she didn't want him to think she had left him for someone else, but rather because the marriage had failed. It's kinder this way, she said. Yet it appeared that nearly everyone else in New York had heard about us. I found it annoying that so many people to whom Kathleen introduced me wore knowing smiles, it seemed that her penchant for confessional gossip signalled a shallowness that I had not noticed before, to reflect her desire to be a luminary among her friends, to have her brilliant life outshine their drab ones. But perhaps, I told myself, all this was merely a product of her excitement, her enthusiasm.

In the end I could never understand how we had gone so wrong, how everything that in the beginning seemed so clean and strong had been twisted and defiled. But perhaps my perceptions of the beginning are faulty; perhaps those early signals of wrongness were not mere harbingers, but symptoms of an already terminal decay. Whatever the case, I analysed our failures incessantly. I knew I had made my share of mistakes with Kathleen. I had pressured her too much at times, I had not been the neatest of housekeepers, and I had drawn her into a wilder orbit of people and drugs and music, something that initially pleased her but that she came to use as evidence we were not suited to each other. Yet I had done so many things right, and my mistakes were not the crucial sort her husband had made and continued to make, particularly the irreparable mistake of being someone whom she did not love or respect. Even more significant was the recognition that my sloppiness, my aggressiveness, my lifestyle, these were all qualities she had originally treasured because they were in opposition to Darryl's compulsiveness, temerity, and conservatism. It appeared that she was rejecting me now for the very same reasons she had embraced me, and this made me realize that my flaws were not driving her away so much as were her lack of trust in her feelings and her failure to come to terms with her loss of control.

Of course it was not that simple. I did not, for instance, incorporate into my analyses the fact that Kathleen was a liar of almost pathological proportions; I was unaware of it then, and so was unaware that much of the information she relayed to me was useless. Because of her lies, I will never be able to understand it, but this was how I understood the situation on the night she told me she was going back to her husband.

'Just on a trial basis,' she said. 'I've got some feelings about him I need to resolve. The only way I can be sure they're just reflex, just habit – and that's what they are, I'm sure of it – is to move back in.'

We were sitting in a rear booth at the Lion's Head on Christopher, surrounded by tables packed with chattering, wine-sipping yuppies, and when she told me this, a terrible flush came to my face, hot as a fever, and the babble and the colours of the place seemed to dim and waver like things in a dream.

'Don't worry,' she said, putting a hand on mine. 'I'm not going to sleep with him. I'm not going to do anything with him except coexist for a while. I know I won't be able to take it for more than a month . . . if that.'

'Then why do it at all?' I asked her, still so shocked I could barely get the words out. 'What's your therapist have to say about this?'

'She's disappointed in me, but she thinks this'll prove her point.'

I pulled my hand back from hers, had a swallow of vodka. I thought about giving ol' Darryl – who was still and would always remain in the dark – a call and clueing him in that little Miss Demeanor here had spent the better part of the past year with her feet waggling in the air. But all that would achieve would be to cause an explosion. 'Fuck it,' I said. 'I can't go through this again.'

'What do you mean?'

'You know what I mean. I've been through this before, I know what's going to happen. I'm not going to sit back and watch my life unravel again. You move back in with him, and that's it. I'm leaving you to it.'

'You waited for *her*.' She looked glumly down at her wine glass. 'You must not love me as much.'

'How much I love you's got nothing to do with it. I just know what's going to happen. I'm not going to hang around and take a beating for no good reason.'

'You can't do this!' she said angrily. 'You can't make assumptions about me based on what happened to you with another woman. It's not fair. I'm not her!'

It had been raining when we entered the Lion's Head, and I could smell the rain in her hair, along with the smells of wine and perfume. The mixture of scents made me dizzy. She looked radiant, all the fineness of her face, the high cheekbones and parted lips, unusually articulated, polished to a rare splendour. I felt sick at heart.

'No,' I said weakly. 'You're not her.'

She took up my hand again, playing with my fingers; then she leaned forward and slipped my index finger into her mouth almost to the knuckle, caressed it with her tongue. 'It's going to be all right,' she said, leaning back again. 'I love you, Michael. Keep that in mind. Even though I'm back there, I'm still going to see you.'

'See me? You mean we'll have lunch, shit like that?'

'No! I don't want anything to change between us while I'm there. My commitment is to *you*. This is just something I have to do so I can be with you all the time.'

One of the yuppies at the adjoining table was staring at us. I scowled, made my hand into a fist and let him see it. I wanted him to say something, but he turned back to his friends.

We continued arguing for a while longer, but although I believed it was the beginning of the end, in truth it was not an argument I wanted to win. I was too much in love with her to walk away. I did, however, insist upon one thing, a codicil to our agreement. 'If you decide to stay with him,' I said, 'I want to have one last time with you. A weekend. We'll go up to Connecticut. A country inn, maybe. Just to say goodbye. Just to make an ending. That's important.'

'It won't be like that. I'm *going* to leave him.'

'Maybe so,' I said. 'Maybe it's all going to work out. But the worst thing I can think of is to have something like this end without really ending. To have it just fade away. I won't do that again. It's too much pain. If I have to wait out here in the cold while you get your head straight, I need you to promise that if you stay' – she tried to offer another protest, but I cut her off – 'in the unlikely event that you stay, you'll come away with me one last time.'

I felt a strange confidence then, not one grounded in the belief that she would leave Darryl, because I no longer believed that . . . or rather, if I did believe her, it was in the prayerful, clinging way that a sick man turns to God. Perhaps my confidence was simply delusional. Or perhaps I had an intimation of the future, perhaps I knew in my secret heart the strength of my obsession, the lengths to which I was prepared to go in order to achieve my ends.

'It's not unlikely, it's impossible.' Kathleen leaned close again and kissed me with her mouth open, her tongue flirting with mine; she put my hand on her breast. 'But I promise.'

That night was the only time I ever had difficulty in achieving an erection with Kathleen. I was still shocked, still poisoned with anxiety, and lying on her bed, watching the slices of light that fell through the blinds jiggle atop the blankets, listening to car horns making a hot, brassy, incoherent music, to sirens and shrieks and curses, to all the traumatised animals of the New York night, I felt

distant from everything, helpless and adrift, as if the bed were a shoal
in the midst of a black and troubled sea. But Kathleen would not let
me maintain a distance. She lay down beside me and began stroking
my cock, gently at first, but with increasing vigour, whispering as
she did. 'I want you to come in my mouth,' she said, brushing her lips
against my neck, my chest. She pitched her voice softer, lower, so it
was scarcely more than a sibilant breath. 'On my face,' she said. 'I
want some on my face. All over my face . . . and my breasts.' Her
tongue traced a line of wetness down past my navel, and her warm
mouth engulfed me for a moment. 'And in my pussy. I want some in
my pussy, too.' This whispered to the head of my cock, held a
fraction of inch away from her lips. Then she moved back up beside
me, continuing to work me with her hand and to list all the things
she wanted me to do, the cadences of her voice as steady and
hypnotic as those of a snake charmer.

This was new for her, this kind of seductive intensity, and I
wondered how much the evolution of her sexual aggressiveness had
to do with what she had asked of me back at the Lion's Head. Then
the thought occurred that maybe fucking me over was a turn-on for
her, maybe the power she was beginning to use on me was directly
related to the new condition of our relationship, to the fact that she
had put herself in a position to control two men. I doubted that she
was aware of this, but I was convinced that the recognition of the
circumstance and opportunity was operating in her on an unconscious level and was at least partially responsible for her behaviour. I
could not see her in the darkness, and I imagined that her face had
been replaced by that of a witch, a woman with human eyes and a
cruel, curved beak flecked with shreds of flesh, whose whispers were
an evil incantation. But I was hard now, hard as a spike driven
through her fist, inflamed by her hand and her voice, and it really
didn't matter which sort of magic her words were, whether a lover's
enticement or the wicked spell of my imagination, because they had
done their work, neutralized all my bitterness and transformed
anger into lust.

I rolled Kathleen onto her back and spread her legs and tasted the
damp, musky place between them. Her breath caught, and she
caressed my hair, encouraging me. I slipped my hands under her ass,
lifted her to a better angle, and probed with my tongue until I found
the little nub of flesh that cued her gasps. She bridged up from the
mattress, her thighs clamped to the sides of my head. She was
already so close to coming that when I breathed in I breathed her
spend. Like water thickened with pungent oils. Her belly spasmed,

her hand tangled in my hair. I felt wild, lapping at her, an animal driven mad by some vile nourishment. Her hips churned, and my own hips pumped in reflex, my cock butting at the sheets. I heard her cry out, a single, sharp cry cut short, like the cry of someone who had taken a heart wound, and she began to thrash about so fiercely, I was nearly tossed aside. Then the tension that had flooded her abdomen ebbed, flowed into her thighs, and she held me so tightly I couldn't move, couldn't use my tongue, my mouth pressed to her in a still kiss.

'God, Michael,' she said feebly. 'Oh, God.'

The city sounds had receded, as if all the hornblowers and shriekers and profaners had stopped to watch us. I came to my knees and lifted my head, feeling solitary and vaguely triumphant, vaguely predatory, rather like a wolf standing over his kill and scenting the air. The only smell was the smell of her sex. The wetness on my face was cooling, drying.

'Come here,' Kathleen said, pulling at me.

My eyes had adjusted to the weak light, and I could see her. With her narrow hips and smallish breasts, the merest convexities when she lay on her back, like overturned saucers, and the pink candy of her aureolae, the sparse red tuft between her legs, her body had an almost childlike aspect, as if not quite finished, and it was that unfinished quality, that simple pale softness, that I found so desirable, so precious in its apparent vulnerability, so surprising in its passionate strength, in its wonderfully adult capacity for giving and receiving pleasure.

'What're you doing?' she asked, groping for my hand.

I wished I could tell her what I felt, the mixture of delicacy and lust she aroused in me, but I couldn't have framed the words just then.

'Just checking you out,' I said.

'And?'

'If I hadn't already eaten, I might just gobble you up.'

She giggled. 'I hear it's like Chinese food. Twenty minutes later and all that.' She left a pause. 'I'll still be here in twenty minutes.' Then her smile faded a bit and she reached out for me with both arms. 'Come here,' she said. 'I want you here.'

I gripped my erection in one hand, and put the other hand between her legs. Her cunt was so wet, when I rested my thumb against it, just that slight pressure caused it to sink into the folds of her labia. I planted my hands, palms flat, on either side of her head, and when she had fitted me to her, I went all the way inside with a single, slow thrust. The tight, hot, silky feel of her took my breath, and I hung my head, eyes closed, phosporescent blooms printing on my lids.

'I love you,' she said, drawing up her knees, starting to rock beneath me. 'Oh, God, I love you so much.'

As we moved together, I had the impression we were becoming a single entity, a dark red shape wrapped in skin, four-armed and four-legged, the whole of it pulsing like a heart, a great man-and-woman-shaped heart through which pumped blood and all the steamy, beasty juices of desire, an immense circulatory system that allowed us to share everything, every thought, every nuance of emotion, every nervy shock and thrill. Fucking her, I was fucking myself, we were almost that close, and growing closer with each passing second, permeating one another, and it seemed I could feel myself plunging into myself, the plush muscles rolling and pushing and tightening around me were mine, and there were voices, hers and mine, our voice, whispering, cajoling, demanding, a confusion of heat and breath so profound that when I began to come, when I straddled her chest and pressed my cock against her lips, her cheek, letting the semen smear across her skin, I was no longer certain whose demands I was responding to, and even separated from her, I had a muddled sense of identity. Then she slipped me into her mouth, and I felt irrationally aloft, unnaturally apart from her. The feel of her tongue going at me made me faint, and I had to put a hand on the wall to keep my balance. But then a few moment later, lying beside her, kissing, a salt taste in both our mouths, I began to lose myself once more, to yield up what was mine to the configuration of that larger being we comprised, and when I grew hard again, when she lifted her leg and let me come inside, joined like that, with our sticky faces and sweaty skins glued together, melting one into another, growing dim and thoughtless in that dissolute embryonic warmth, I realized that this weird, perfect unity, this sweet glide into non-being, this was what I refused to give up, this was what I desired most of all, the pure centre of love, the force that compelled me to obsession, that made me willing to do whatever was necessary in order to preserve it.

4

Six weeks after Kathleen returned to her husband, I lost my sublet and, unable to find a new apartment in Manhattan, relocated to Brooklyn, to the second-floor of an old brownstone at the grafitti-festooned gangster end of Park Slope, a neighbourhood whose ruinous appearance and violent populace provided an environment that accorded with the progressive deterioration of my life. I have always considered myself to be a strong person, and it seems unreasonable that love, or rather the apprehension of its loss, should have so deranged me that I fell into a state of collapse. And yet it's true, as my doctor has pointed out, that other factors were involved in my pathology. I had spent the past six years enduring abnormal stress, beginning with my first unhappy affair, proceeding through Guatemala, prison, and my uncle's illness; perhaps my affair with Kathleen was simply the nudge that sent me falling off the precipice of those years. But be that as it may, my level of derangement would have been extreme under even the most fortuitous of circumstances. I slept fitfully if at all, I neglected to eat, I drank to excess. I managed to keep up something of a schedule of work on my prison book, but as had happened in Virginia, its dark materials conspired with the darkness that was accumulating in my head, and accelerated my depression, and I was subject to horrible dreams in which Kathleen and I were lost inside the prison walls, assaulted by guards, by demons, by mentally deficient prisoners. To keep at it I began dosing myself with increasingly large amounts of cocaine, which I bought from one or another of the legion of drug dealers who frequented the streets. Over the nine months I lived there, my abuse became so monstrous that when I told my favorite connection, a dreadlocked Jamaican by the name of Rickey, I was thinking of quitting, he said half-jokingly, 'Michael, you quit doin' cocain, an' you t'row de whole neighborhood into a recession.'

This deterioration was not lost on Kathleen. My doctor is of the opinion that this may have served to make her even more reluctant to leave her husband. I will admit to the possibility, for it's evident that the self-destructive side of my nature was dominant during that time, which is the point the doctor wishes to establish; yet I feel my self-destructiveness was called into play by the black forces that were gathering about me, those same forces that had caused me to lose my sublet and move to Hell on the East River so as to effect their dire purposes, and while my deterioration gave Kathleen ammunition to use in argument against me, I am certain now that she would have stayed in the marriage even had I been a paragon of stability – she had her own mysterious agenda in all this, and it was those concerns, not my frailties, that informed her various modes of indecision.

We saw each other often during the first seven months of her return, at my apartment, at her father's house in New Jersey where she would frequently spend weekends, in bars and clubs, in the homes of mutual friends. I knew she was displeased by my drug usage, but she joined me in it nevertheless; and though she commented negatively upon my appearance, my decaying health, and similar matters, she remained as ardent as ever. We made love when- and wherever we could, and when the opportunity did not arise naturally, we contrived an opportunity. Buses, both Greyhound and Trailways; taxis; trains; airplanes; the only form of transportation that did not at one time or another function as a bedroom for us was the subway, and we nearly managed that. Once when we had not made love for almost a week, Kathleen suggested we visit a friend of hers, a film editor at the network, and the instant we were inside the door, she announced brightly to the woman that we had not had sex for some time, could we use her bathroom? Yes, we could. The bathroom was scarcely bigger than a broom closet, but for the next forty-five minutes we engaged each other in almost every possible way, employing position after position, ending with Kathleen bent over the toilet while I took her from behind. The perfunctoriness of this encounter, which seemed a kind of sexual sampler from our salad days, devoid of all emotion except that of lust, distressed me; but I was so weak, so full of longing, I would have done it again without a second thought.

Even when sex was impossible, we approximated it. Kathleen would meet me for lunch and say that she was not wearing a bra or panties so I could touch her more readily, and we would spend the entire hour in secretive foreplay beneath the tablecloth. And then there were her phone calls, during which she would inform me how much she loathed Darryl and what foul thing he had recently done, and how she was almost ready to leave. She never slept with him, she told me; she dressed in the bathroom and ignored his attempts at seduction, most of which involved pornographic videos and masturbation. Then in a loving tone, she would shift the subject to us. Typical of these moments was a call I received around Christmas time. She was in a nostalgic mood, her voice soft as she reminisced about a Sunday night we had spent at her father's several weeks before, and how on her way to work after making love early Monday morning, she had enjoyed the feeling of my come leaking from her.

'It made me feel you were still with me.' She paused, dropped her voice to a stagey whisper. 'I get so wet when I think about it.'

My body reacted uncontrollably, and half my mind was swept away in a rush of arousal; but at the same time I was furious with her. What the hell was she doing? Teasing me? No, she wasn't that cruel, she was simply missing me, missing sex, and wasn't considering how her reminiscence might affect me. Which was, of course, every bit as cruel as teasing would have been. But it was the sort of cruelty I had learned to accept from her, the childlike cruelty that accompanies self-absorption. Perhaps she believed she was consoling me by saying these things. And in a way it was a consolation to have even this much evidence that nothing had changed for her.

'I wish I could see you,' she said wistfully.

I wanted to shout at her, to tell her this was bullshit, that we should be together, but all I said was, 'Maybe soon.'

'Maybe.' Her voice was frail, without conviction. Then in a more assured tone, a tone designed to give me hope – because, I knew, she still wanted me to have hope – she added, 'I love you, Michael.'

Afterward I remained seated for a long time, less thinking about the call than immersing myself in it, recalling every inflection, every shift of emphasis, trying to interpret word choices and turns of phrase that to anyone else might have seemed plainspoken, but that to me seemed marvels of intricacy and innuendo.

Even more problematic were the calls I began to receive in February from her apartment. She had told me previously that she had bought a vibrator, and now, when Darryl left her alone while he took his shower and she thought it safe, she would call with the vibrator in hand and talk dirty to me while she brought herself to completion. Sometimes I would join in. These techno-fucks, albeit perversely satisfying, left me feeling wildly agitated, and following them I would go for long, perilous walks through the neighbourhood, striding like a madman into the midst of streetcorner brawls set to screams and boombox salsa, past rock-smoking villains and shadows with knife hands, saved from injury or worse, I assume, by a principle similar to the one that caused the Crow tribe to refrain from scalping pioneer nut cases during the days of Westward expansion.

At this juncture, in late winter, I began to ask Kathleen – no, let's be honest – I began to beg her to tell me it was over. She had to tell me, I said, because otherwise I wouldn't have the strength to walk away. But she would not speak the words. Don't worry, she'd say. Just give me a little longer. We'll spend next Christmas together, I promise.

Next Christmas, I thought on hearing this. Fuck, I'll be dead by next Christmas. Can't we make it the Fourth of July, can't you show up on my doorstep dressed as the fucking Easter bunny with a basket full of eggs, or how about Arbor Day? We'll plant a goddamn tree together and experience Druid joy. But I never said these things, I only rarely expressed any rancour, and usually I would tell her, okay, all right.

My obsession with Kathleen had grown so all-pervasive by this time that I was, I believe, insane. My doctor denies the legitimacy of the term and offers instead a number of politically correct labels; but I must insist on my choice of terms. Insane, with its connotations of Bedlam, of dark nightmare wings lifting from the back of a tormented skull, of hallucination, delirium, and violence, is the only one that fits. As evidence of my condition, I offer my change in attitude towards Kathleen's husband. I had never met Darryl, though I had often heard his petulant voice on Kathleen's answering machine, and I had never been able to feel much more than distaste for him; yet in my heart I understood that he was not to blame for any of this. He, too, was a victim, as perhaps we all were. Now, however, I contemplated killing him. I did so quite calmly and methodically, and I devised several workable plans, several of which I took so far as to perform walk-throughs, making certain of his schedule, his habits. Darryl's pathetic stance had come to reflect my own, and aside from the satisfaction I would get from the deed, I thought it would be something of a mercy to let the breath out of him; that way, only one of us would have to suffer. Sometimes to entertain myself I would imagine a meeting on a dark street, a series of swift, sure blows or a single knife stroke, and then I would stroll off without a care, leaving his Gucci-clad feet sticking out from a dumpster. There were also moments when I was very close to ringing their doorbell and saying, 'Howdy hi, folks! How 'bout we have us a little chat?', thinking that by doing so I would goad Darryl into initiating violence. But I recognized that any attack I made against either Darryl or the marriage would in effect be a violence against Kathleen, and I could not bring myself to hurt her. God knows why. Kathleen, who on the surface was charming, charismatic, smart and professional, had proved to be a saucily packaged bundle of neuroses, and on those infrequent occasions when I was honest with myself, I realized I did not have the slightest idea who she was anymore. Nothing could ever be the same between us. But I wanted her. I no longer knew what it was I wanted, I only wanted it with frightening intensity, and Kathleen, whom I loved, hated, needed, despised, exalted, and wished to profane, seemed the nexus of all my hopes and desires.

Early in my durance on Park Slope, Ricky the Jamaican drug dealer introduced me to *santeria*. I had told him my story . . . I had told my story to everyone in the neighbourhood who cared to listen; I preferred the passionate advice the gangbangers gave me: 'Kill the muthafucka!' 'You gotta steal her, man!' 'I know somebody fix the cocksucker for fifty bucks!' 'Can't let no bitch fuck you up like that, man. You got to slam the bitch around so she understand what's going on,' and such — to the bland counsel of my friends and colleagues, who unanimously told me to get on with my life, a homily whose absurdity more often than not provoked me to rage.

Get on with what life?

This sickhole black absence with rotten gums and six OZs of Mistress Cocaine stored under the fridge roach-infested nightsweat baddream convulsion of a life with typewriter and tape recorder in Bongoland where the seven hooded shadows stand, man, I got no fucking life without pretty Miss Bitchtoes Lovestar Wetdream Kathleen the Great and her tight little pussy, and her sucky little mouth, and her big white butt, don't you understand, I got to have it, ain't nothing going to be right til I fly through her window and seize her up in my jaws and swoop down the thirteen alleys to the holy rooftop where we can do the messaround forever and ever, and you know the last time we fucked at my place, we left a wet spot on the grey sheet in the shape of a slightly-darker-shade-of-grey eagle, now what do you figure that means?

Ah, lucidity! What a trip.

I saw everything so clearly when I was angry. My doctor maintains that lucidity cannot be abnormal, but I submit that extraordinary lucidity is the true province of the insane. The problem is, it's impossible to sustain. If I could have remained in that state of feral lucidity for even an hour, I would have savaged whatever feelings I had left for Kathleen and thus saved us both. My troubles always began when I allowed myself to sag back into that sappy, dreary, mooning condition I knew as love, but had long since become something much more destructive.

But as I was saying, I told Ricky my story, and he said, 'Listen up, you gots to see de witch mon. He don't like white people very much, but he deal wit' you, 'cause he religion say he must.'

'Who's the witch man?'

'Dis Sponnish guy name Beltran. Got a *botanica* sells remedies and shit over on Twenty-Third. He's a *santero*. *Santeria*. Like a preacher, y'know. 'Cept he gots spells he can work get you woman back.'

Santeria, I thought. Animal sacrifice. Voodoo gods. Shango, Ogun, spirit possession. Cool. Just what I fucking need.

And underneath those thoughts was a deeper current of thought, a wordless stream of compulsion, of superstitious fascination, of manic hope that maybe this would be the key.

But I had my doubts.

'I'm not into joining a church,' I said.

'You don't hafta join, mon. *Santeria* ain't like dat. You just go ax de mon to help you, and you pay him for what he do. Then maybe t'ings work out, you want to join.'

'Sounds like a fucking fast food religion,' I said. 'Sounds like shop 7–11 and go straight to heaven.'

'Dere's more to it den dat,' Ricky said. 'I'm tellin' you, mon. Better you check dis out.'

I mulled it over, but not for long. 'Twenty-Third and what?' I asked.

I am unwilling to assign to *santeria* or to Sebastian Beltran the lion's share of blame for what happened – that I must accept myself. It may be that my imperfect usage of it came into play, or that the Beltran's ethnic bias caused him to lead me astray. But at heart I believe that *santeria* was merely the capstone of my obsession, the final piece in a monstrous mosaic. At the very least it provided a colourful focus for my obsessiveness, appealing in its vivid imagery, its mixture of animism and Catholic pageantry. Yet I cannot state that the rituals I participated in and the sacrifices made on my behalf had no effect whatsoever. During them I sometimes felt curious stirrings in my flesh, in the air, and sensed invisible presences close by. Of course I felt similar things on other occasions due to bad health, drug abuse and mental instability, but those occurrences seemed of less moment.

Beltran himself was difficult to dismiss. He was an unprepossessing sort, a sinewy little man with a pumpkin-coloured complexion and a pinched, bespectacled face and long grey hair worn back in a pony tail; yet he had a distinct personal force, and whether by virtue of occult powers or the exercise of simple common sense, he gave the impression of having great insight into my situation. When I approached him in his *botanica*, telling him I had woman trouble, he said with studied disinterest, without even glancing up from the paperback he was reading, 'Find another woman.' But after I had pled my case further he stared at me searchingly and said, 'This woman is not for you. She is a silly woman, a liar. Her love for you is the love of a child for a precious toy. Stronger, perhaps. But of no more depth. Still,' he shrugged, 'if she is the one you want . . .'

I made no reply, unable to deny the truth in what he had said, yet at the same time unwilling to accept it, and I looked away from his stare. On every side were glass cases filled with figurines, bottled herbs, amulets, charm sacks; above our heads hung strings of painted bean pods and gourds, and the walls were decorated with vivid representations of the *santeria* pantheon, beautiful, powerful-looking black men and women contemplating or wielding the staffs and spears and mirrors that were their arcana. But for all the exotic clutter there was an air of peacefulness about the place that seemed at odds with the drum-beating passion and savagery I associated with the religion.

'Very well,' Beltran said. 'We will begin. Things will go badly at first. Prepare yourself for that. You will see the woman less and less during the weeks to come. But there are measures you can take. You must persevere in them. If you do, at the end, in what seems the final moment, you will succeed in your purpose.'

I maintained my silence and he asked what I was thinking.

'All this makes me a little nervous,' I said. 'I'm not comfortable with things I don't understand.'

'I would imagine you are often uncomfortable.' He gave a snort of disdainful laughter. 'The only way you will ever understand the *orishas*,' he gestured at the paintings of the gods on the walls, 'will be to slice your wrists and let all that white blood drain out.'

I ignored this and asked about payment.

'There are certain purchases you must make. You will buy these things from me and from shops whose addresses I will supply. And once the woman is yours, you will bring flowers and food for a month to my altar for my *santos*.'

The following day Beltran performed a *despojo*, a cleansing designed to drive away the evil spirits that he claimed had gathered about me. He passed bundles of herbs over various portions of my body, lashed me with a tied-up bunch of long grasses, all the while singing with convincing occult passion in Spanish. Afterward he provided me with a foul-smelling herbal potion that he called an *omiero* and instructed me to drink it every day; he also gave me another, less noxious potion that I was to slip into Kathleen's food whenever I could manage it. For $86 he sold me two ceramic figurines, one depicting the goddess of beauty and female sensuality, Oshun, a voluptuous, brown-skinned woman clad in bright African dress, and the other an image of Shango, the god of fire and lightning, of male potency, a powerfully built black man wearing a straw hat and carrying a bloody spear. He then commanded me to construct an altar for the figurines in my home and to make daily sacrifices of

flowers, fruit, rice, and candles, some of which I was to buy from him
and the rest from merchants who apparently had been stamped with
the *santeria* seal of approval.

When I left the *botanica* that day with my merchandise in hand, I
had no faith in anything that had transpired, nor in the future of my
association with Beltran; but over the weeks, as Kathleen fell further
away from me, even as Beltran had predicted, I began if not to believe
in *santeria*, then at least to fixate upon it, especially upon the altar I
had built: a coffee table draped in a red cloth, surmounted by the
figurines and, at all times, an assortment of wilting flowers, plates of
rotting food, and burning candles. Fruit flies made a faint haze above
it, and sometimes the haze gave the figurines the illusion of a non-
ceramic vitality, making it appear that they were wavering, just
beaming in from another plane. Though they bore not the slightest
resemblance to Kathleen and me, I came to see in their exaggerated
forms, in Oshun's torpedo-like breasts and earth-mother hips, in
Shango's muscled chest and bloody spear, the equally exaggerated
forms of our sexuality, the archetypal roles we assumed in sexual
congress; and I would imagine our souls embedded in those timy
ceramic skulls and invent conversations between the figurines that
Kathleen and I might have engaged in had we been such divine
primitives. Once I actually thought I saw them fucking, saw them
shimmer and grow real and make it in the cusp of a watermelon rind
(during an abstracted moment I had eaten part of that day's sacrifice),
aping Kathleen's-and-my lovemaking in style and fervour, the artful
gleams supplied by the ceramic glaze slipping along their limbs as
they moved, Oshun's robe draped over a rotten pear and Shango's
spear stuck quivering in a slice of pineapple. I did not place much
stock in this hallucinatory interlude, but neither did I reject it out of
hand. The brightness of those dark bodies captivated me. They were
brightening further, I thought, gaining vitality with every passing
second, drawing energy from the room, an impression that gained in
credibility whenever I looked at the area about them, an expanse of
worn brown rug given ruinous perspective by a litter of Chinese food
cartons, crumpled beer cans, balled-up sheets of paper, a mummified
steak still encased in its shrinkwrapping, scatters of useless coins,
dead shoes, a crippled pair of trousers, a guitar that played nothing
but dirges, all the sour relics of my ex-life. No, there was no doubt
about it, Shango and Oshun were increasing in strength, acquiring
the vigour of the real, more than could be said for their ribbed
originals.

Several days before Kathleen ended it I was sitting by the altar, thinking about love. During that period I often lapsed into drugged reveries in front of the altar, and love – its nature, whither?, and so forth – was often the subject of those reveries: oddly enough I still had something akin to a romantic attitude toward the whole business, though I perceived it now to be a moment of perfect possibility, of absolute sweetness and mutual clarity, that could never be sustained. I was in bad though not unusually bad shape, working behind most of an eight-ball of cocaine. My heart stuttered, my sinuses throbbed and whined, my joints ached, my lungs made sucking noises. Eventually I drifted off into a state just east of sleep, but once my eyes closed I saw the pages of *TV Guide* unscrolling on the backs of my lids, and when I began to be able to read the pro-gramme notes, the weird shit that was on, a primetime documentary on roach calling and robot sitcoms and a rerun of *The John Gacy Show*, and a call-in programme entitled *You And Your Police State*, I became interested, and that woke me up enough to want to do some more coke. I was groping around for my baggie when I spotted Kathleen standing a few feet away, butt-naked and grinning hugely, like a mean, toothy fish, with one hip cocked and her hands behind her head so as to show off her freckly little tits.

On second glance I realized it wasn't Kathleen after all. Kathleen, if I recalled correctly, had never been prone to billow like a sail in a light breeze, nor had there ever been, as was the case with the apparition, filmy stuff like angel hair trailing from her extremities. And I was certain that she did not have rips where her eyes and her pussy should have been, rips that opened onto flames and black gears turned by bone spindles. Otherwise the figure before me was her spitting image. Real or not, she was a lot more reality than I had been getting from Kathleen, and so when the figure said something I couldn't quite make out, I told her I loved her. 'I love you' was something I said often in those days, mostly when no one else was about, telling it to the walls, the light, responding to a disturbance in the air or a sudden longing or something I saw on TV that caused an emotional surge, even to noises that startled me, because there was so much unspent love inside me, I was like a man trying not to come, it only took a touch, a word, a dream, to bring it all out of me.

The woman-thing's grin got a slice wider and nastier, reminding me of the zoned expressions of the painted gods on the walls of the *botanica*, and that caused me to think she might be a visitation of some sort, one sent to punish me for my slipshod faith in the *orishas*. I was so tired and stoned, I felt more annoyance than fear, and I gave an inarticulate shout and flung out my arm at her in gesture of dismissal; but when I saw the same filmy, opaque stuff that frilled her fingers and elbows and sides trailing from my fingers, I was shocked from my stupor. At first I believed that the filmy stuff was an optical illusion. Tracers, I thought. Those afterimages of motion one sees when one is under the influence of a psychotropic drug and waves one's hand back and forth. But on examining my fingers I found that the stuff was palpable, slightly greasy and slick to the touch, like the unhealed skin beneath a scab. A feeling of horror washed over me. I pulled at one of the strands and felt a sharp pain where it connected with my hand. I shook the hand, hoping to rid myself of the fringe, which was — I realize — growing longer, thickening; but that did no good. My Swiss Army knife was lying on the arm of the sofa beside me, and I reached for it, intending to learn if the shit could be cut away; but as my hand closed about it, the fringe faded from view, like an icy rime melting, and when I looked up I found that the woman, or whatever she was — hallucination, fever, horrid dream — had vanished as well.

My heart was hammering, my breath labored. 'Fuck!' I said. 'What the fuck!' I got to my feet, thinking I should go to the *botanica* and consult with Beltran. But then I thought, No, un-unh, no way I want to deal with Beltran's smirks and insinuations about my manhood and snide comments on my cocaine habit. And that was all it had been, I decided. The coke firing a couple of weird synapses, the old CNS rendering a complaint, saying, Stop or else . . . Time to cut back. Order some food, get some sleep, take a walk in the morning, do some breathe-in, breathe-out kind of things. You'll be a better man for it.

The next day, to my surprise, I actually did as I had promised myself I would and went on a health kick. Orange juice, brisk walks, and greaseless food. And not a single line of cocaine. During the next three days I began to feel stronger than I had in months, strong enough mentally to field an eerie, distracted phone call from Kathleen and not let it depress me to the extent that I fell off the wagon. She told me, among other things, that she didn't know what she wanted anymore, that she wasn't happy, that she missed me; she seemed in essence to be saying I'm leaving, I'm staying, I think I've got a cold. I asked what her therapist had been saying, and she replied that the therapist hadn't said much of anything, because she — Kathleen — had been lying to her lately. I did my best to ignore what she said after that. After I hung up, refusing to slip into my usual post-call analysis-and-depression mode, I rode the subway into Manhattan and caught some Brazilian music at SOBs. I was beginning to feel a bit like my old self. But then on the morning of the fourth day, Kathleen called to tell me she had made her decision.

There was, I discovered, a kind of liberation in being dumped, a sense of relief, almost of exaltation, that came when the axe finally fell. As I listened to Kathleen explain herself, saying that she loved me more than she did Darryl, much more, but that love wasn't the only criteria you used in determining what was best for yourself, blithering on in some sort of New Age speak that she might have lifted from one of Darryl's witling books, *How To Achieve Denial And Self-Deception* . . . as I listened I wanted to say, What a crock! Rationalize things however you want, all you're doing is surrendering to fear, choosing the insipid, the secure, and the manipulable over a life of possibility. But that sense of relief, the sudden removal of pressure after all those long months, it was so overwhelming I could only sit there and gaze out my window at the new spring leaves on the branches, at the friated brick and tarred roofs of the buildings across the street. My face grew flushed, numb with heat; my chest ached; my heart seemed to have become huge and heavy, transformed into a chunk of cement. Nerves fluttered in my jaw, my arms. The poisons of grief and desperation began conjuring little sicknesses in every part of my body. Yet I made no response, remaining silent even after she had finished speaking, amazed by the buoyancy that accompanied these sensations, by the infirm lightness that had pervaded my limbs.

'Are you okay?' Kathleen asked, bewildered.

She must have expected a fight, an argument, certainly not silence. In picturing this moment, dreading it, I had expected much the same, but the fight had been drained out of me, and I felt at a remove from her, from everything.

'Michael?'

'I'm fine,' I said hoarsely. There was something in my throat, some obstruction warm as blood. The receiver was inordinately hot, thrumming against my hand.

After a pause Kathleen said, 'I'm sorry.'

The inadequacy of the phrase kindled a bitter amusement in me, but the thing was, the terribly sad, terribly desolating thing, she *was* sorry, truly sorry, for herself as well as him, because no one was getting what they wanted, not even Darryl, who would never have love from her, only a feeble loyalty informed by her lack of self-confidence.

'Listen,' I said, surfacing angrily from these thoughts, feeling the need to give anger a voice, to make a pronouncement; then I realized

that I had nothing to say. Something, a bird, a black one, landed with
a rustle among the leaves on the branch outside the window; I
watched it hop and preen.

'What is it?' Kathleen asked.

'Nothing.'

'You were going to say something.'

I started to deny it, but then I remembered our bargain. 'I'll make
some reservations,' I said. 'For next Friday. Not this weekend, but
the one after.'

There was another, longer pause. Finally she said, 'I can't.'

'That was the deal,' I said flatly.

'I know. But things are different now.'

'Yeah, some things. Not this.'

'It won't do you any good. I won't change my mind.'

'That's not the point!' I said, growing angry again. 'I've been
waiting out here for . . . Jesus! Nine fucking months! Hanging on by
my fucking fingernails, wandering around like a zombie. Now there's
this phone call saying, "Gee, I'm sorry, I can't make it." And . . .'

'I didn't ask you to wait that long!'

'The hell you didn't! You asked all right. And you knew I'd be
going crazy, because you were going crazy, too. We made love, we
wrote letters, we talked, we kept on planning a life together. You
weren't giving your marriage a real try, you were just hanging out
there, using the goddamn apartment!' I realized I'd gone too far, that I
had shifted the emphasis away from enlisting her emotions to
accusing her, and so had lost the advantage; but when she started to
object I talked through her. 'The only reason you're making this
decision is you're tired of not being able to make one. You're worn
out with all this. Hell, you admitted as much the other day. And I can
relate, you know. I'm worn out, too. I'm fucking exhausted.' I let out
a sharp breath. 'It doesn't matter. None of it matters anymore.
You've decided. I accept that. But I've lived all these months
believing I'd have one last time with you. Counting on it.' Here I
injected a note of sternness into my words, the slightest hint of
menace. 'I want what we agreed on.'

I imagined her sitting at her desk, toying with a pencil, downcast,
her eyes half-lidded, her lips pursed and petulant. Seeing her so
clearly made me subject once again to the power of her body, to the
ardour that could possess it, and I was filled with such a clean,
powerful longing, I did not think I could continue to manipulate her.
Indeed, I wondered if I had been manipulating her at all, if everything
I had said, everything we both had said, had not been part of a rote

litany, as inevitable in its process as every other element of the relationship had seemed.

'It'll hurt too much,' she said. 'Being with you again. It'll just make it hurt more.'

'Maybe in the short term. But it'll make us feel better about the way things ended.'

'I don't know,' she said tremulously.

'Christ, Kathleen! It's only a weekend.' I was disgusted by the wheedling tone that seeped into my voice.

'It's just I don't know if I can get away for a whole weekend. I've got . . . we've made plans.'

I'll bet, I said to myself. Now he thinks he's got her, ol' Darryl is probably making plans a mile a fucking minute. But maybe, I thought, his plans could work to my advantage. Under the circumstances, a weekend might be too long to spend with Kathleen, it might provide too much time for sadness and recrimination. If I could give her one night, a night without pleas or arguments, just love, maybe even a laugh or two . . . well, she wouldn't change her mind, not immediately, but when Darryl fucked up as inevitably he would, the memory of that night be the blade that finally cut the cord.

'One night, then,' I said. 'You can get away for that long. Just tell him you're going to visit your dad.'

'He'll want to come with me.'

'You can swing it. You've done it before.'

She made a noise – of frustration, I thought.

'That is important, Kathleen.'

'I'll try,' she said weakly.

I listened to the dial tone for a while after she had hung up. All the symptoms of lovesickness had returned with a vengeance: the dull, dead thickness in my head, the pressure in my chest of imminent tears; the heaviness in my limbs.

God, I was sick of feeling that way.

I considered calling friends, going to a bar, seeking sympathy in one way or another; but even then, even after hearing the sentence pronounced from her own lips, I could not give Kathleen up. And so, gathering myself, shaking off the effects of the phone call, I headed for the *botanica* to see what Senor Beltran could do for me.

5

My doctor has lately allowed me to look at the Autrey file, a voluminous folder crammed with police documents, the results of

medical exams, interviews, etc. Nowhere among them is there
evidence of anything that smacks of the paranormal, unless one
counts the various charms and occult items found in room 429 of the
Rahway Hyatt Regency, objects that he would characterize as
evidence of my pathology, nothing more. He hopes that confronted
by this massive compilation of bureaucratic rationality, I will begin
to question what he considers to be the delusional aspects of my
story. I will admit that he has raised a few doubts – given my mental
state, how can I maintain with absolute surety that my memories of
the last time Kathleen and I were together are accurate? Yet it will
take more than a few doubts to neutralize those memories. Delusional or not, they seem unassailable in their nightmarish particu-
larity, and now, now that I must face them once again, I find myself
hoping that they are accurate, for if they are then I may be able to
take comfort in knowing that I am not entirely to blame, that forces
beyond my control, those same forces I sensed close by throughout
the affair, were manipulating me for their own malefic purposes. I
have asked myself time and again how it could happen that two good
people could love one another and have it come to such a terrible
conclusion. And we *were* at heart good people. Despite everything I
have written about Kathleen, despite the truth of my words, she did
not intend any of the damage she did me, she was simply afraid,
insecure, imperfect; and for my own part, God knows I did not want
her to be hurt, even though I had sometimes behaved badly and had
bitter, vengeful thoughts. All we desired was the sweetness we
found together, and yet it was that sweetness, the distracting power
we conjured, that in the end worked to destroy us. I can almost
believe that love itself is a form of evil, an emotional plague visited
upon dreamers with too little life, whose telltale symptom is the
possession of one's will. It may be that Kathleen was right to be
afraid . . . Ah, to hell with it! There's no sense to the world, no
salvation to be found in it. Only fools pretend they understand.

Room 429 was a pleasant, spacious room, done in earth tones,
olives and browns and salmon, with blandly decorous furniture and
a clean smell; but as I sat there waiting for Kathleen, I began to
think of it as the sort of place where an accountant from Paramus or
East Orange might come to contemplate life's inequities, to thumb
through the snapshots in his wallet, gazing longest at one of an
overweight brunette with frosted hair inscribed, *George, I'll love
you forever, Carla*, to take out the Police Special he'd bought earlier
that day from an oily, chubby, beringed man driving a late model
Chrysler with a bumper sticker reading Kiss me, I'm Athenian, to

say a prayer he remembered from childhood, a little hedging of the bets, and then to splatter his brains across the photograph of Bridal Veil Falls mounted above the bed. The perfect place for unimportant tragedy. Vibrationless; reeking of vacancy. Waiting to be filled with someone's pain.

I had already partly filled it with mine before Kathleen arrived. The ceramic figures of Shango and Ogun lay together beneath the bed, and there were charms tucked everywhere: tiny sacks of herbs, amulets, a bottle of sacred rainwater collected from the hollow of a certain tree in Cuba, bloodied feathers, pieces of mirrors and more, all concealed in drawers, under chairs and pillows, stuck in the molding. The lesser charms of iced champagne, fruit, and cheese rested on the nightstand, along with some silverware and plates. Everything was in readiness. Only Kathleen was missing, and as the minutes leaked past, I grew anxious and began to wonder if she were going to stand me up. I paced about, switched on a bedside lamp, looked out the window at New Jersey's cement wilderness in the declining sun. I wondered if I should call her. Finally there came a knock at the door.

On entering, Kathleen went straight to the desk and set down her briefcase; then with her back to me, she shrugged off her raincoat and draped it over a chair. When she turned she flashed a nervous, afflicted smile that barely lasted long enough to notice. Seeing this, seeing how drawn her face was, I felt guilty for having pressured her. I knew I should tell her to leave – I didn't want to hurt her anymore, and this *was* hurting her, that much was obvious. I had it in mind to say this as I crossed the room to her, but I couldn't bring myself to speak, and for an awkward moment we stood at arm's length, just staring at one another. It was early evening, and a rainy grey light filtered through the drapes. Everything seemed dreary and exhausted, and I became aware again of my spiritual fatigue. My eyes filled. There was nothing we could do, I thought. No tactic, no clever fake could smooth over the rawness and regret we had brought into the room. But then she moved close and held me, her head resting against my chest. The way she felt, soft and pliant, her heartbeat rapid as a bird's, her scent – the flurry of impressions that arose from the embrace were an acid that washed the corrosion from my heart, and it was as if I were back at the beginning, feeling all the treasuring tenderness of new love. Then she lifted her head with a look of sweet expectancy, and I kissed her.

The kiss was tentative at first, exploring, but then tenderness turned to urgency, and we sank down onto the bed and soon were totally involved. If I could have managed a moment's distance, I would have understood that my plan had succeeded – the original feelings we had shared had somehow been renewed; our sexuality had become easy again, simple, a natural outgrowth of what we felt, expressive of a need for closeness rather than a mere mechanism to achieve orgasm. But I had no such distance. I was with her completely, lost in the turns of her body. Because we knew each other's needs so well, and there were no anxieties to overcome, no fears of inadequacy, it was better than it had been on the train to Montreal, and we made love for hours, saying almost nothing, just those phrases that served lovers as the stations of the breath. Perhaps it was simply an effect of the ruddy orange lamplight and the blurring of focus that attended the close proximity of our faces, but all the strain appeared to have emptied from Kathleen's features. She looked younger than she had when I met her, more girl than woman, with her freckles and her overbite. When she came her eyelids fluttered down so that the merest slivers of white showed beneath them.

Now and then the thought that this was the last time brushed against my brain like a cat rubbing against its owner's legs, but I refused to let it settle. I rejected the notion of loss, and lived in the moment for as long as possible. Eventually, however, there came an interlude in our lovemaking when we could no longer avoid that sad inevitability. I could see that recognition as a sudden clearing of the dazed softness that had pervaded her features, a sharpness in the eyes, as if she were studying me, memorizing the details of my face for some future nostalgia; and I'm certain that she could see a similar recognition in me. Yet even then we did not speak of it. More talk would have been pointless. I think we were both afraid that if we did speak it would ruin what little time we had left.

In a way I was happy then. I had proved something to myself, something that I had not realized I wanted to prove: that love could survive months of ill usage. And inspired by this to quit while I was ahead, I decided that I would make love to her one more time, just once, and then, before the light of morning could expose the illusion we had created, I would say a quick goodbye and send her away. I had forgotten my half-formed scheme, you see, my desperate and poorly conceived magical intent; I had forgotten charms and figurines, I had even forgotten the lineaments of obsession, and I was satisfied with what I had assured Kathleen would be the important satisfaction of that night, the understanding that while almost everything had been lost to us, we had formally acknowledged love, we had given it due respect, and in doing so had won lasting respect for all the good that had passed between us.

We were lying on our sides, facing one another, when I entered her, and I was amazed by how tight she felt after all those hours of making love; though she was still wet, it took a concerted effort to achieve full penetration. 'Careful,' she said as I worked my way in; she set her teeth in her lower lip, thrust with her hips, trying to seat me more deeply. Once I was inside her she gripped me so forcefully, I could barely move. In truth, I was so worn, so mentally enervated, I had no real urge to move, I was content just to have that closeness again. I held her hard against me for a very long time, delighting in the muzzy swirl of my thoughts, in the dissolute warmth of our bodies, a sweet confusion of flesh and spirit that seemed more extreme than ever, as if all our essential things were blurring, running together. A rush of emotion swept over me and I let my feelings out in words, telling her how much I loved her, that I was going to be all right, not to worry about me, this night had been the medicine I needed to cure the sickness that had been wasting me, and I could walk away now without recrimination or bitterness, I could truly accept things. If those words had been spoken to me, I would have thought them stupidly romantic, rife with faux nobility, but I meant every syllable, and Kathleen was affected by them – her eyes teared, and she made to lift her right hand.

Intending to touch my face, I think.

But her hand, resting on my hip, was moored there by strands of a yellowish white, opaque material that appeared to flow directly out of our flesh, our skins. Melted looking. Waxy and grossly organic in appearance, glistening, as if coated in saliva or some even less appealing fluid. Very much like the filmy stuff I imagined I had seen trailing from my own hand several days before.

The strands stretched with her movement, like unset glue, but only a little, and there was an excruciating pain in my hip, as if the skin were being pulled away from the flesh.

I cannot adequately describe what I felt then. My emotions ranged from denial to horror, running the scale of everything in between. It seemed impossible that this could be happening, and yet each time Kathleen tried to yank her hand free, I felt renewed pain. As, apparently, did she, for she cried out with each attempt. I grabbed her wrist, and the confusion and alarm in her face sharpened into terror. She screamed and tried to roll away from me; but she could not. Our hips and thighs were joined as well, the attaching strands so thick in places, stratified, like a mess of strapping tape and freshly applied mucilage, I could not make out the articulations of our limbs. My left hand and forearm were similarly joined to her waist and back, and there were thinner, frailer strands that had connected her breasts and my chest, but these had been snapped by her struggles.

Kathleen began to scream in earnest: raw screeches of animal fear. She thrashed and tossed her head about, causing us both more pain. My right hand, which had been resting on the pillow above her head, was free, and I used it to muffle her screams. Her eyes bulged, her spittle dampened my palm. I yelled at her, telling her to shut up and lie still, that was the only way we were going to get out of this, to go about it calmly. I, of course, was not calm in the least. Despite having a recognition that some portion of prayer or ritual must have proved effective, granting with insane precision my wish of being eternally bonded to Kathleen – and I am sure that this, along with my being accustomed to hallucination, to discomfort, was all that allowed me to maintain my equilibrium . . . despite having this much understanding of what was going on, my thoughts were in turmoil, and I flirted with hysteria. I pictured the figurines melting together beneath the bed, Oshun and Shango lapsing into a brownish black curdled mass, and I also pictured the lump of pulsing flesh we might become if we could not somehow break the spell and separate one from the other, and those images brought a tide of red darkness into my mind that threatened to drown the last vestiges of my rationality. A trickle of glee welled up from some spiritual bottom-land, and I thought how it was really kind of funny, even ludicrous, most certainly ironic, this surreal wedding of our flesh. But Kathleen's fear, less informed and thus more profound than my own, acted to shore me up, and after a few seconds I succeeded in regaining a measure of control.

I removed my hand from Kathleen's mouth and was horrified to see threads of filmy material, so faint as to be almost invisible, connecting her face and my palm; but these tore with only a mild stinging sensation, and seeing this gave me hope that the thicker strands could be broken.

Kathleen leaked a fuming noise, a sound that might have been made by a defective tea kettle, and burst into tears. 'What is . . . what's happening? Oh, God! What . . .' She gave a hiccuping sob, and I said, 'Just try to stay calm, all right? If we stay calm I think we'll be okay.' Her eyes rolled back, and I thought she might pass out; but then she tightened her lips, making a determined face, and nodded. But an instant later she began to shriek and flail about, and I was forced to restrain her again. Even after I had subdued her, after repeating my caution to remain calm, she shivered and twitched and begged me to tell her what this was, what had happened.

'I don't know, I don't know,' I said. 'Just hang on. Let me see what I can do.'

This was Beltran's doing, I thought. It had to be some fucking lie he had told, some voodoo trick. The son of a bitch was going to fucking die if I could get clear of this.

Of course I could not be sure of Beltran's guilt, but hating him acted to centre me, to give me new purpose. I examined the strands that linked Kathleen's right hand with my hip. 'Lift your hand,' I told her. 'Slowly. Lift it as high as you can.'

She complied, staring at the strands with a mixture of terror and revulsion; the gluey stuff stretched to the length of about four or five inches, at which point it began to cause pain:

Gingerly I pinched the thinnest of the strands between thumb and forefinger. It was slippery to the touch. Vile. There was pain, but it was bearable. I increased the pressure, twisting the slimy stuff. The pain intensified commensurately, but I made no headway in tearing the strand; I only managed to indent it with the tips of my fingers, and when I released the strand, the indentations smoothed over in a matter of seconds. My heart was racing, my hands were clammy, yet with half my mind I had achieved a modicum of clinical distance, and I was fascinated by the material. Skin reduced by several degrees toward the state of pure protoplasm, I assumed. A lot of fat in the substance – that would explain its yellowish cast. Pinching and twisting were obviously not going to work. A tool was needed. Something with a sharp edge.

It was then I remembered the cheese and fruit plate, and the silverware. Among the utensils provided there had been, I was certain, a paring knife.

'I have to twist myself around so I can reach the night table,' I said to Kathleen. 'I'll go slow. If you move with me, it won't hurt as much.'

'Why? What're you going to do?' Panic edged her voice.

'There's a knife on the table. I can't get to it without moving.' I wanted to hold her eyes but they kept darting side to side. 'I'm going to try cutting through it. I can't think of any other way. Except to call. If cutting doesn't work, we'll have to call for help.'

I thought she would object, but she only closed her eyes; she was very pale, and the freckles on her cheeks stood out sharply like a plague.

'Okay?' I said.

A nod.

'Okay, you've got to do this with me now. I'm going to turn my right shoulder toward the table, and you've got to slide in toward me and under me as I make the turn. You understand?'

Kathleen said something I couldn't make out, maybe it wasn't a word, maybe it was just another signal of helplessness, of abject fear, and I had to go along with her. I understood none of it. My mind kept trying to slip away and retreat into a place where no understanding was necessary. The horrid shit that bound us together was, I realized, beginning to smell, a faint reek of spoilage, and that brought me right to the edge of my limits. I asked Kathleen again if she understood.

'Yes,' she said. 'I . . . Yes.'

'It's probably going to hurt,' I said. 'You should be prepared for that.'

Another nod.

'All right, I'm going to count 1–2–3, Now. We'll start on Now. And we'll move very, very slowly. Ready?'

'Wait, wait.' She let out a shuddery breath; I could feel her trembling. 'Okay, I'm ready.'

There was indeed some pain, but that was not the most disturbing thing. I was still hard, gripped so tightly by the walls of her vagina and, I realized, by the gluey melding of our flesh, – our unnatural genital connection – I could not lose my erection; and as we negotiated the turn, my cock moved in her, taking advantage of whatever play it was allowed – the effect was like a sort of weird Kama Sutra muscle fuck, and the pleasure I experienced was so intense, it overrode the pain. My breath came quickly, the shallow respiration of someone close to orgasm, and even though she winced on a couple of occasions, so did Kathleen's. I fumbled at the table, straining to see over the edge, felt cold metal. A corkscrew. I pushed it aside with my fingers and touched the knife. After I had it in hand, I told Kathleen I was going to turn back to our original position. She made a sound of affirmation, but her eyes were squeezed shut, and a nerve was ticking in her jaw – I knew she was close to losing it. Again there was that incredibly intense genital pleasure. Against her will, I'm sure, Kathleen's body reacted, and as we finished the turn, she made a series of those choked, coughing gasps that always signalled the onset of an orgasm, and she arched into me, the fingers of her trapped right hand contorting, clawing at my hip. Tears started from her eyes, and after she had caught her breath, she said, 'God, it's like . . . down there, it's like that down there, too, isn't it?'

'Maybe,' I said. 'But we can still move a little. If we can get the rest clear, we should be able to . . .' I searched for the right words and found no reason for confidence. 'We'll be all right.'

When I made the first cut, slicing into one of the glutinous yellowish strands that bound her hand to my hip, the pain was severe. Kathleen let out a cry, bit her lip. The slice was neat, the edges sealed over rapidly. No blood, only a slight milky seepage. But it hurt like hell, and as I deepened the cut, even though I knew the pain was coming, it became harder and harder to bear. Kathleen whimpered, but managed not to cry out again, and I loved her for her courage – her pain threshhold, I knew, was not high.

It took me several minures, I'd estimate, to cut through that strand. After it was done the stuff began to shrivel, to lose its slick glaze and aura of vitality. It was dying, I realized. Just one strand out of many. But I had a moment of renewed hope.

'Look,' I said, nudging Kathleen's chin with my free hand. 'It's going to work. You see?'

She stared dully at the severed strand; a bubble of saliva formed at the corner of her mouth.

'Everything's going to be fine,' I told her. 'It'll take us a little while, but it's going to be fine.'

She displayed no reaction, continuing to stare at the severed strand with glassy bewilderment.

I did not know how much longer I could maintain a confident pose, especially in the face of Kathleen's despair; the prospect of cutting through dozens of strands, the realization of how great the pain would be, especially in the genital region, was not good to contemplate. Fear was simmering in me, and I wasn't sure how much more I could take before my control began to slip. It would be so easy to let go, to admit to the madness of the situation and drown in the chaos that beat at the corners of my mind like a thousand hot rustling wings. However, I repeated my optimistic prognosis to Kathleen and prepared to cut into a second strand.

As I sliced into it Kathleen came alert and seized my hand. 'Let me!' she said with what struck me as unnatural animation. 'I want to do it!'

'I've got it,' I said. 'Just keep still. It's . . .'

'No, I want to try. It might not hurt as much if I do it.'

I decided that I should let her give it a shot. Maybe if she occupied her mind with the cutting, it would diminish her pain.

'Okay,' I said, giving her the knife. 'But go slow. Don't saw at it. Use a slicing motion. You hear?'

She nodded rapidly, up and down, up and down, like a child excited to try out a new toy.

'Go ahead,' I told her, and gritted my teeth.

She did as I had instructed, making a small neat slice, but she did not react well, flinching, wincing. Her hand was shaking. 'Oh, no,' she said sadly, and I had the notion that she had been counting on something and had been let down.

'Keep going,' I said. 'You're doing fine.'

She made another, smaller slice, and said, 'Ah, God, no! It hurts!' Her chin quivered her eyes shifted about.

'You know it's going to hurt. Just take it easy.'

'I can't.' She gazed off above my head, as if responding to a voice only she could hear.

I had a sudden, brilliant apprehension of disaster. Fear spiked my manufactured poise like a red hot poker pushed through a mound of snow. 'I think we should call for help. This isn't going to work.'

'No, we can't, we can't call. Everyone . . . will . . . She trailed off.

'We have to call. We don't have any choice.'

'It hurts, Michael,' she said in a strangely uninflected voice, and then she stabbed me.

It is the things we do not know that rule us, and not the things we know; it is the things we are afraid of knowing that delimit our lives and hopes. I do not know if Kathleen understood that by killing me she would free herself – I had not even concluded this at the time. The stabbing was performed in such a casual manner, like a little girl trying to stab a solitary pea on her plate, it's hard to ascribe malice to the act. Easier to ascribe a loss of perspective, of balance – she may have thought she was doing something completely different. I cannot rule out malice; she was in pain, and she did not manage pain well. But the problem is not one I choose to dwell on. What I believe – and oddly enough I still cling to certain of my old beliefs – cannot survive further analysis of the question.

If it was an attempt to kill me, it was a pitiful one. The point of the blade glanced off my collarbone and deflected upward, nicking a tendon, and though it hurt, I was inured to pain and did not let it throw me. I caught at her wrist, squeezed it, forcing her to drop the knife. Ignoring the agony she must have felt, she threw herself at me, rolling on top of me, clawing and shrieking, spraying me with spittle, gone into panic. Her face worked, her eyes popped with terror. Each movement sent a burning sensation through the joined places of our flesh, but once again a despicable hot seepage of pleasure accompanied the pain, and as I wrestled with her, tossing her this way and that, doing my best to unseat her, the pleasure grew hotter and stronger, until in ungainly union we toppled off the side of the bed.

I landed half atop Kathleen and at first I could not get my bearings, my senses overloaded with contrary signals of pleasure and pain. I gasped for breath. My hips and groin and my left arm felt on fire. When I finally looked down at her, I knew at once that she was dead. Her head was jammed against the side of the night table, her neck broken; a jagged spear of bone protruded from the skin beneath the hinge of her jaw. There was so much blood. From the wound, from her mouth. Her eyes, still open, their lustre already glazed, stared up at me at an angle that, due to the extreme tilt of her head, was grotesquely coquettish. In reflex I pushed myself away, but I could not escape the embrace, and in making the effort, still lodged inside her, I came. A miniscule unburdening, a sprung leak that was all the more foul for its triviality.

That involuntary act of consummation in the body of my dead lover, that was the end of my reason. For an unguessable time I remained lying between her legs, bound to her, meeting her vacant stare, trying to read there some vital message, some remnant of the woman, the soul. My head filled with a humming sound, a heated throbbing pulse, as if my thoughts had been transformed into insects, and they in turn had ignited, become a hive of incendiary, crackling wings and crisped black bodies that continued to live despite the consuming fire. I began to hear Kathleen whispering to me, whispering the most intimate endearments, and it seemed that her eyes were semaphoring flashes of light, transmitting astral coordinates, informing me where she could be found if I were inclined to follow. This new horror shook me from my stupor, and once more I tried to free myself . . . and with a degree of success. The strands connecting us were, I saw, shrivelling, dying, and I was able to snap a couple of them; the attendant pain was not so great as before. I understood that if I waited, sooner or later they would all fall away.

But I could not wait.

Kathleen's voice kept after me, encouraging me to kiss her bloody lips, to fuck her again. I sensed a force marshalling itself behind those gone blue eyes. Before long, I realised, she would regain the ability to move, her head would wobble upright on the shattered neck, and her sticky mouth would spill the cupful of blood that had collected there, and her legs would lock behind my waist, and her hips would buck and bridge in clumsy zombie lust, and her clawed hands would tangle in my hair and pull me down to taste her crimson tongue, which would come flicking out with the alacrity of

a scorpion's tail, and we would go on with our tumbling fall in
unnatural congress, down through the floors of the hotel, down
through the earth itself, through rock and garbage fill and the graves
of New Jersey's wormy kings into the special hell reserved for lovers
who have sullied the principles that made them one, into the reeking
suety bath of their ultimate dissolution.

I spotted the knife lying on the floor beside Kathleen's elbow. The
blade was beaded with tiny yellow bubbles like globules of chicken
fat. I picked it up and, goaded on by Kathleen's whispers, I began
slashing wildly at the strands, at the dripping, gobbety ties that bind,
like someone clearing weeds. I was unmindful of the pain, unmindful too of where I sliced, and I nicked myself several times and gashed
Kathleen's waist and hips. At last I succeeded in freeing my arm and
partially freeing my hips; I pushed myself up onto both arms above
her, the missionary position allowing me access to the next area
where I would have to cut.

No, not cut.

Excavate.

A simple slice or slash would not serve me here.

I hesitated, unwilling as yet to commit this atrocity, and Kathleen
said, 'Please, Michael. Don't. I love you.'

I glanced up at her, my eyes skipping past the fresh blood on her
belly, past the defeated strands now melting into a noxious, bubbled
residue. There was a distinct gleam in her eye, and, if I were not
mistaken, the hint of a smile touching her lips.

Life in the old girl yet.

I placed the tip of the blade on her vulva. My knowledge of
anatomy was not strong, and I wanted to allow myself plenty of
room in order to avoid self-mutilation.

'Michael, please!'

The burning bees were swarming in my head again, and I felt a mad
hilarity rising in me like mercury in a glass stick on a hot, hot day. I
heard a faint music, some frenetic tune whose name I could not
recall played by a Disneyworld-type band, heavy on the tubas and
hooting clarinets, the kind of thing used to score those old cartoons
in which giant long-nosed rodents in suspenders and shitkicker
boots were chased by cow people with cleavers. Agitated, demented
music that caused my hand to tighten on the handle of the knife. I
probed with the blade, struck bone. Sliced downward through the
matted strands into the flesh at the side of Kathleen's labia. Blood
welled from the soft tissue as if squeezed from a sponge, and to my
great surprise and revulsion, she began making her special coughing

noise again. I'd never realised before how much it annoyed me, that noise. Why couldn't she just breath rapidly and then cry out like other women, instead of sounding like a cat spitting up a hairball?

I cut deeper, widening the gash I had made, continuing to explore with the blade, working as carefully as I could, until I felt a slight pressure on my cock and realized I must be close to the exterior of the vaginal wall. I experienced a mild professional glow. A nurse would be helpful, I thought. Someone to mop my brow and hand me my pearl-handled scalpel. Section, I'd say. Suture. Framistat. We'd exchange Hawkeye and Hot Lips patter to lighten things up. But all in all, the operation was going fairly well. The strands were shrivelling rapidly, falling away from my thighs and hips, as if I had located the source of the infection that had caused them to materialize. Kathleen's hips started to shudder, her gasping cough increased in frequency. Going over the top again. Who was I to begrudge her a little fun? I tried not to let her hoarse clamour disturb me, and I worked feverishly, wedging out a core from her flesh whose upper arc extended from the crease dividing her left thigh from the pudenda, across the upper reach of her labia majora, and then down. Each cut turned some delicate pink fold into raggedy crimson wreckage. Her internal structures were loosening, giving way, and I thought that within minutes, perhaps less, I would be able to withdraw. But the excess of blood slowed my progress. Time and again I had to mop it up with the sheet, which I had dragged off the bed; and even this stratagem was only marginally effective – it was impossible to see into the blackish red wells of the wound, to determine which of the bloody structures I observed was tendon, which gristle, and which merely tattered flesh. Kathleen responded eagerly to these gentler touches, however, heaving beneath me, and soon the first tremours of completion were shaking her hips and buttocks. Then, as I made a forceful coring motion with the knife, going in so deep that half my hand vanished into the wound, she spasmed, her breath vented in an erratic wheezing, and I was expelled, tumbling backward onto the floor, my groin draped in blood and flecks of gore and the putrescent, bubbled residue of the strands.

I rolled away and sat up, resting my back against the foot of the bed, not wanting to look at her. My emotions were amazingly controlled. It was a bit cool – I was starting to shiver – and I decided that I did not like being alone. But I felt pretty good, considering. I realized I would have to do something soon. Stand; shower – definitely a shower; call the police; flee, get a drink. Something.

There were so many possibilities for action, I could not choose among them. I stared at the olive drapes. The seam of night visible where they did not quite meet caught my eye. Staring at it made me no less cold, but eased my sense of solitude, and before long I felt myself growing slow and empty. I welcomed the feeling, and I stared fixedly at that black absence, focusing upon it with all my will. What was happening to my mind then was, I believe, like the flooding of a car engine: too much fuel, too much fierce sensation, causing a stoppage. Every now and then I felt a little lurch inside me, like one of those brief elevator drops one experiences just before falling asleep, and I would have a sense of wrongness. Otherwise I noticed nothing out of the ordinary, and I sat there, cooling, emptying, until I no longer recognized the clothes scattered across the floor or the briefcase on the desk or the appointments of the room, until I could not, if asked, have told the questioner how or why I had come to be there.

6

Lately I have only been pretending to take my drugs; I secrete the pills beneath my tongue, spit them out while pretending to cough, and then pulverize them into a pasty dust between my thumb and forefinger, all done surreptiously in order to avoid the notice of the surveillance camera. Yet it is not, as one might suspect, my memories of Kathleen that have caused me to seek refuge once again in madness. At least not them alone. I cannot deny that the images of that night in room 429 terrorize my dreams; but though I have not completely come to terms with my memories, though I remain depressed by the disquieting revelations that my writing has brought to light, I realize that the tragedy was no one's fault. Not Beltran's, not my own, certainly not Kathleen's. Fault was simply in the air. There was, I believe, no voodoo, no magic other than the unwieldly magic of existence. And the thing that has provoked my retreat is something far less sinister than the stuff of memory, or so it seems.

Fifteen months ago, not long after I finished writing the bulk of this memoir, a new day nurse came to work in my wing, a lovely brunette by the name of Diane Kinnear. As the weeks passed we developed a friendship, a friendship that recently has evolved into something more volatile. Her understanding and patient tenderness make the days of my confinement bearable; often she will call me at night, and I depend on those calls to see me through the black hours. Sometimes we talk about the future. Our future. That I have been mentally imperilled is of no consequence to her; she recognises that I have made great strides and has faith in my potential for a complete recovery. As does my ever-enthusiastic doctor. He tells me I may be ready for release in as little as six months.

Why then, you may ask, am I rejecting such a bright possibility?

I have detected in myself a distinct masochistic tendency, and I am concerned that because of it I may manufacture failure in my relationship with Diane and drift once again into a nightmare of obsession and loss. The idea of repeating myself endlessly, of engaging in bad love with Sisyphean obstinacy, is monumentally distressing. Yet if it was only this that troubled me, I might persevere in the process of recovery. Something else, something more subtle is the cornerstone of my terminal dismay. Simply stated, it is a disappointment with the world, a recognition that I no longer perceive value in those things that once appeared to offer a kind of salvation, a means of coping with the bitter realities that underscore our lives. Having seen love reduced to a stew of blood and meat and foulness, I have lost the virtues of a foolish heart, and now it occurs to me that the obsession of love lost may be the highest form of love, more rewarding in its intensity than the slack consolations and comfortable rewards of love won. That is too simple to be all the truth, but I will let it stand as a signal of the whole, gospel, and unadorned truth that sits at the bottom of my soul, a brooding monster that dictates its commandments in a language of disastrous noise. Like love, lucidity is not all it is cracked up to be.

It's raining now, a grey, driving rain that seems a form of dire interference, a chaos of streaks and smears that occludes the transmission of some universal pattern, and a heavier weather yet is beginning to lower about me. Indeed, it has been drawing closer and closer for several days. I am frequently visited by a din of voices, a tumult of colours, of tactile impressions. Odd fluttering things appear in mid-air and vanish when I try to see them clearly. My eyes deny the rightness of once-familiar shapes, and strange logics assail my brain. Even now the world is growing tenuous, malleable becoming a place whose only sense is the sense I contrive of it. Outside a motorcycle roars its mantra, Christ is a humming vibration, the walls make a drum for the rain. Birds with shattered glass eyes are plucking a rusty music from the barbed wires atop the asylum wall, and the shadows in my room bend toward me with the benedictive air of black saints. Everything is moving, shifting, aligning itself to the new conformation of my spirit. Gravity will be a dream, history a song, sex a white flower the size of heaven. The love

I feel at this moment is the delirious love of a martyr whose soul is a suicide, perfect, without direction and soon I will welcome the stupendous loss of feeling that not even the knives of light can pierce.